The Girl Who Wouldn't Die

MARNIE RICHES

avon.

AVON
A division of HarperCollins*Publishers*
The News Building
1 London Bridge Street
London SE1 9GF

www.harpercollins.co.uk

First published in Great Britain in ebook format by HarperCollins*Publishers* 2015
This paperback edition published by HarperCollins*Publishers* 2018

Copyright © Marnie Riches 2015

1

Marnie Riches asserts the moral right to
be identified as the author of this work

A catalogue record for this book
is available from the British Library

ISBN: 9780008271442

This novel is entirely a work of fiction.
The names, characters and incidents portrayed in it are
the work of the author's imagination. Any resemblance to
actual persons, living or dead, events or localities is
entirely coincidental.

Printed and bound in Great Britain by CPI Group (UK) Ltd, Croydon CR0 4YY

THE GIRL WHO WOULDN'T DIE

MARNIE RICHES grew up on a rough estate in Manchester, aptly within sight of the dreaming spires of Strangeways Prison. Able to speak five different languages, she gained a Master's degree in Modern & Medieval Dutch and German from Cambridge University. She has been a punk, a trainee rock star, a pretend artist, a property developer and professional fundraiser.

Marnie is the author of the bestselling George McKenzie series of eBook thrillers, the first of which, *The Girl Who Wouldn't Die*, won The Patricia Highsmith Award for Most Exotic Location in the Dead Good Reader Awards, 2015. In 2016, the series was shortlisted for The Tess Gerritsen Award for Best Series (Dead Good Reader Awards).

To Mum, who teaches me strength and perseverance.

PROLOGUE

Amsterdam, 20 December

Ratan Patil became aware of the noise before he had even opened his eyes. The drumming of shoes on hard ground. Was he in the middle of the flea-market on Waterlooplein? No, not a market-place. He could hear sporadic traffic as well as people scurrying past him with purpose; not browsing. Young voices. Laughter. Assailing him in a dizzying typhoon of sound.

Then sensation crept back into his body. He was stiff, cramped up like a foetus, freezing cold. His right hand throbbed as though it had been crushed under the weight of a mountain. Pain diced up the inside of his head in a violent frenzy. The intensity of it forced his eyes open.

It was dark, save for some light that found its way to him in thin perpendicular seams. He tried to stretch out his fingers to feel the space that contained him, but his hands were pinioned to his sides. He could make out his knees. He was kneeling and yet he could feel nothing below his aching hips. His mouth was held firmly shut, lips pushed together by something unforgiving on the outside, swollen tongue wedged up against his teeth by the dryness of the inside. But he was too tired to speak anyway.

Breathing in slowly through his nose, he could smell something musty, like old paper. He stretched his neck, hoping his nose would hit something solid within the strange prison. If he could just touch it, maybe he'd understand.

Cardboard? Yes, a large cardboard box.

Ratan's heartbeat sped adrenalin around his body until he was suddenly drowning in fear and confusion. The scream was trapped inside, unable to escape the duct tape across his mouth. Frustrated, realising his limitations, he forced himself to breathe deeply and let calm in.

He started to remember.

The party had been the best ever. He had finally spoken to Rani. And boy, was she beautiful up close. More beautiful than she had ever looked across the lecture theatre. They had shared a joint that the English girl had rolled with Californian grass. It had made him feel brave, and he had shared a kiss with Rani that had been languorous and full of promise.

That one evening felt like the start of everything he had longed for.

The biting pain inside his skull had come from the walk home. Weaving his rebellious body, heavy with hash, hope and Grolsch, along the inky waters of the Herengracht towards home was heavy work. His canalside slalom was punctuated only by vomiting once and taking a pee against the wall on a bridge.

When he was coshed over the head, Ratan had been completely taken by surprise. The shadow of his attacker was all that he had seen; a silhouette sprawled across the cobbled pavement, stretched and distorted with an arm raised in readiness for a second blow. The attacker held something long in his hand. A stick? A baseball bat? A hammer? Who knew? Ratan felt the weight of the weapon push his head forward at an awkward angle. His vision had pixelated to nothing, like a screensaver switching off.

Now, Ratan found himself kneeling and bound inside a cardboard box. He blinked in the semi-darkness, trying to fathom his fate. Then he felt buzzing against his belly, and a dim, phosphorescent light came on inside the box. A phone on vibrate?

But not his phone. His phone didn't make that noise. Then, in the fraction of his last bittersweet second, he remembered the rest:

Waking after the blow to his head, he'd known he'd been drugged. He'd expected the room to spin after so much beer and dope but here, everything had looked wrong. Blurred around the edges. He was lying on something hard and flat in a room with a strip light glaring at him from behind his attacker's head. The shadowy stranger bent over him, working carefully at arranging something on Ratan's chest. Furrows of concentration in the man's brow. Fastidious fingers working quickly but not poking or probing his flesh. Then the grinding sound of duct tape being unfurled and pressing down on his ribcage until Ratan moaned.

The assailant realised his victim was awake. A syringe full of liquid soon pumped sleep and forgetfulness back around Ratan's body.

And now, inside the cardboard box, a phone had vibrated once, vibrated twice. Its phosphorescent light was not the shimmer of hope at the end of a tunnel. It was a dim torch lighting the way to death; guiding his Jiva towards the path of his ancestors. Ratan had seen enough films to make an educated guess at what might have been strapped to his chest. It was too late for fear. He regretted not having taken Rani up on her offer of going back to hers for coffee. Now he would never—

Ratan's exploding body ripped a hole in the front of the Bushuis library on Kloveniersburgwal that was twenty feet high and seventeen feet and three inches across.

CHAPTER 1

Amsterdam, 20 December

'George! Wake up! It's me,' came a man's voice in the hallway.

Georgina McKenzie, called George by the select few she chose to count as friends, slept deeply on the lumpy old mattress on her bed. The insistent rapping on her door took more than a minute to register with her still drunk ears.

'George! Are you in there?'

She felt the morning trying to claim her from her stupor. She recognised the Groningen accent that wrapped itself thickly around her English name. Adrianus Karelse. Ad.

More knocking. 'Come to the door! I know you're in there. Come on. It's urgent!' Ad shouted.

Weak morning sunlight streamed through a chink in the blackout curtains, jabbing at George's left eye until it opened. She saw dust motes dancing in a shaft of light that illuminated her twenty square metres of crumbling splendour like a strong torch.

'Go away, Ad,' George said under her breath.

She hoisted herself to sitting position and looked around through sticky eyes. She was naked. There was a dark-haired man lying next to her. She yanked back the duvet and gave him a quick, appraising once over, shuddering with distaste at the sight of his anaemic pallor next to the latte warmth of her own skin. She groaned.

'Filip? Aw, not *Filip*, man,' she muttered under her breath. 'I'm never drinking again.'

'George!' Ad sounded agitated. His voice was squeezed tight. He knocked again.

'Coming,' George answered.

She swung her legs out of the bed, knocking over an empty Heineken bottle. It spilled flat, stale beer onto yesterday's underwear. The sight of the mess made her heartbeat accelerate.

Panic. What could she use to cover herself? She grabbed at a tea towel hanging off a straight-backed antique Dutch dining chair, shoved underneath a scratched Formica table for two. Covering as much of herself as she could, she undid the two locks on the door.

'At last,' came Ad's voice through the wood.

George opened the door five inches and shoved her face up to the gap, hiding her nakedness.

'What's wrong?' she asked. She squinted at her friend in the murk of the hallway. He was shaking like he had drunk too much coffee.

'There's been a massive explosion at the faculty library,' he said. 'Didn't you hear it?'

'What?'

'Bushuis library. I was on my way there. It's been wiped out.'

'What time is it?' George smacked her dry lips together and felt a draught on her back coming from the window. She wanted Ad to go away. She wanted her guest to get the hell out as well.

'Gone nine,' Ad said. 'Come on. You've got to see this. Let's go.'

Ad pushed the door open, taking George by surprise. He peered into her room and she knew then he had seen everything.

'Filip?' he said.

6

She could hear the ridicule in his voice. She flushed hot with embarrassment.

'Don't,' she said. 'Meet me downstairs in two.'

As she closed the door on Ad, she was sure she could see hurt in the intelligent brown eyes that hid behind his steel-framed glasses. She drew back the brocade curtains in sharp, angry movements, annoyed with herself for letting Ad see what she had done. Whom she had done. Why did he care so much anyway? He already had his blonde, Milkmaid childhood sweetheart back home. What was she called? Astrid or Margo or something like that. Screw him.

Feeling like her brain was packed with cotton wool, George peered out over the steep rooftops of Amsterdam's red light district. It had rained in the night, and now the roof tiles glittered in the morning sun.

She had the best view in the world; an exclusive view, hidden from those below. The judgemental. The respectable. The petty-minded. The paying punters who had eyes only for red-lit booths and the bongs in coffee shop windows.

Yes, it was a lovely morning. But then, on the horizon to her far right, George spotted a plume of black smoke. Thick and acrid, it curled up into the delicate blue of the morning sky like an angry fist. The explosion.

'My God!' she said. 'He's right. That's some fire.'

Wishing she had the time to scrub away the blunted memory of her conquest in a hot shower, she hastily sprayed deodorant over her body. She threw on freshly ironed jeans and a T-shirt, quietly chiding herself for putting clean clothes on a dirty body. She dragged her fingers roughly through her curly black hair.

'Lock up on the way out,' she said to a stirring Filip. 'Drop the keys in the coffee shop downstairs. Ask for Jan. Only give them to Jan, okay?'

'Are you leaving?' Filip asked, shielding his eyes from the glare of the day.

7

George answered him by closing the door behind her, relieved that she did not have to have the stilted 'let's just be friends' conversation over coffee made with almost sour milk.

Perhaps her imagination had been over-stimulated by the violent events that were unfolding just down the road. Or possibly it was just a paranoia hangover from the previous night's revelry. George was not entirely sure why, but as she undid the clanking, rusted U-lock that fastened her bike to the bike-rack, she felt inclined to look up.

She saw nothing but the unremarkable scene of dark, still water, the gnarled limbs of winter-bare trees, pointing to tempting shop windows that would later be crammed with sickly eye candy, dressed only in thongs and bras to satisfy the sweet, rotten tooth of the common, kerb-crawling Homo sapiens.

Flanked by Ad, George rattled on her old Dutch bike along the canals and through the slowly waking streets. Suddenly the awkward silence between them was punctured by the wail of sirens; the sound of screaming. Her heartbeat quickened. She felt the heat; smelled diesel.

'We've got to stay together, okay?' Ad said, looking back at her with watery eyes and a red, pinched nose. 'It's like hell on earth,' he said. 'You'll see.'

They rounded the corner of Bethanienstraat onto Kloveniersburgwal. Not yet cordoned off, the scene was spread before George like a poisoned feast.

Where the elegant period facade of the old library should have been was now a ragged, gaping mouth, belching fire and fume over the canal. Masonry and glass had been spat out into the street and into the oily water. Between the flashing lights of the emergency services, queuing like impatient customers along the narrow stretch of road, George glimpsed a blackened crater in the pavement the size of a bus. It looked as though demons had tried to swallow the place whole.

'Stand back! Move back!' Policemen shouted, waving away the crowd that had started to gather and gawp.

'Nightmare,' George said.

Two paramedics hurtled towards her, pushing an ambulance gurney with somebody strapped to it.

'Get out of the way!' one of them shouted at her.

Dumbfounded, she stepped up to the canal's edge to let the trolley through, hardly daring to look at its charred and screaming cargo.

The upper storey of the building exploded suddenly, hurling masonry and roof tiles into the sky. Screaming. Running. Horns honking.

'Get behind the fire truck,' Ad yelled, pulling her by her upper arm as brick rained down, bounced off the road and into the water.

She jumped over the fat fire hoses that snaked along the ground. Together, they squatted beside giant wheel arches of the red Brandweer fire service shelter.

'Jesus,' George said. 'What the fuck happened here?'

She peered out at the flaming building as it coughed up more and more of the injured on stretchers, some walking, clutching bloodied faces with lacerated hands.

Ad shook his head. His Adam's apple bobbed up and down. 'Gas pipe, maybe?'

George felt questions bubbling up inside her. She had been in Amsterdam for only five months but the library was an old friend to her now. A place where she could stroll through the halls of her mind in its book-clad gallery; a place where she could sit on the grand stone staircase and be reminded of Cambridge. The eastern wing of East India House – Bushuis library to the students – had stood on the canalside for over a hundred years and had never before, to George's knowledge, spontaneously combusted.

'Gas leak? I don't buy it,' she said.

Her eye was caught by pieces of A4 paper as they fluttered down from an office on the third floor. This solitary office had been left almost intact, as though somebody had just opened the doors of a doll's house to reveal what went on inside. George followed the paper's trajectory downwards until her gaze fell on a middle-aged man in a beige woollen coat with overstuffed shoulder pads that said 1990s Vroom & Dreesman: department store to the middle aged and woefully unimaginative. He looked grimly on the scene and spoke to a uniformed policeman. He made notes in a small pad.

'Come on,' she said, pulling Ad from their hiding place by his hand.

George steeled herself to walk towards the man, ignoring the flaming carnage.

A policeman barred her way.

'Get back behind the cordon, Miss!' he shouted.

'I want to speak to the detective,' she said, mustering as much authority in her voice as she could.

'This is not a sightseeing tour,' he said.

George did not hesitate even to look into the policeman's face. She lunged forward and tapped the man in the beige coat on the shoulder. He turned around. Dark eyebrows arched above large, steel-grey, hooded eyes. He had thick, straight white hair, and the sunken-cheekboned, strong-jawed face of a typical Dutchman, complete with a sharp, triangular nose. She did not know him but she knew his kind.

'What happened?' she asked.

'Get these kids out of here,' the man said to the uniformed officer.

'Please tell me,' George said.

She could see the man appraising her then with those piercing eyes. 'You're a detective, right?' she asked. 'I'm a student. Social and Behavioural Science. I was meeting people here.'

The uniform placed a heavy hand on her shoulder. 'Do you

want me to arrest you? Because you're going about it the right way, Missy,' he said.

'Please,' George asked the man in the beige coat. She gave him her big eyes. That usually worked on male tutors his age when her essays were late. 'They might be hurt.' She shrugged the uniform off.

Ad tried to pull her away. 'Come on, George. Let's go.'

The man cleared his throat and pulled something from his breast pocket. George caught a glimpse of a service pistol strapped close to his armpit. She also noticed he wore no wedding ring and had missed a patch on his neck when shaving.

'Did you see anything?' the man asked her, proffering a battered business card.

'No. I got here after … this.' She took the card and read it. It said, *Senior Inspector Paul van den Bergen, National Crime Squad.*

Van den Bergen simply said, 'Call me if you think of anything,' and turned away.

Ad pulled George back to the safety of the cordon and their bicycles. He took off his glasses and wiped his streaming eyes. Then he touched her on the chin gently.

'How did you know he was a detective?' he asked.

George looked at his soft, pale olive skin, streaked as it was with dirt. He was a wistful country boy in a bad, confused city. He could not have looked more different to Paul van den Bergen. She pulled away from his touch.

'A lucky guess,' she said.

He blinked hard at her and put his glasses back on. She knew he knew she was lying.

From his vantage point, high above street level, he could see her returning home. Waving up at the blonde prostitute neighbour. The shutter on his camera clicked as he caught her turning round, unwittingly peering in his direction. He was careful to back out of sight swiftly. It wouldn't do to rouse her suspicions at this

11

point. And yet he yearned to let her know he was there, thinking of her with both loathing and lust in his heart. Perhaps he could leave her a message … a sign.

He slipped on his jacket and hared down the uncarpeted staircase to catch a glimpse of her before she entered the building and was out of sight. Patting down his hair, he wondered briefly if she would find him appealing if she discovered his obsession with her. She was magnetic. Irresistible. He saw it in other men's hungry eyes too and that was the problem. They were his competitors. Each and every one of them. They had to be destroyed like the Indian; negated, scratched from life, absorbed into the hellfire. Now you see him. Now you don't. An angry red cloud of flesh made vapour.

How invincible he had felt when he had pressed the button and made the call. The effect of that small act was monumental. One minute the cardboard box was sitting there, innocently enough. The next … boom. A symbol of Amsterdam's colonial might had been razed to the ground. The inferno had filled him with joy. It was a curtain of smelted gold, reaching heavenward, casting a holy incense of cordite and human ashes to and fro along the canal. His heart had beat too fast, just how he liked it; adrenalin rinsing the disappointment and stinking mortality from his body.

Now he was observing his muse. His nemesis. He had plans for her.

CHAPTER 2

21 December

The laptop's monitor glared at George, daring her to begin writing her guest post for *Het Ogenblik – The Moment*. She dragged hard on her cigarette, praying it would somehow peel away the tension to reveal the inspired thoughts beneath.

'Coffee?' Jan asked, brandishing a glass percolator jug in her direction.

She hadn't realised he had been standing over her. The coffee at the bottom of his jug looked black and oily. It had been sitting there all morning.

'Go on,' George said.

Jan poured the jug's contents into the special mug that she insisted he keep behind the counter only for her. George sipped it and grimaced.

'You make shocking coffee,' she told him.

'Nobody comes to the Cracked Pot Coffee Shop for the coffee,' he said. He peered over her shoulder through smudged Trotsky glasses at the masthead for the blog. 'What are you writing about?' he asked.

'Nothing,' she said. 'That's the problem. I'm supposed to have done a blogpost about political unrest in the Middle East. I can't concentrate with everything that's going on.'

She punched 'De Volkskrant' into Google. The latest headline from the broadsheet stared at them.

'"Maastricht terror cell claims responsibility for suicide bomb",' she read.

'What about De Telegraaf?' Jan asked.

Her fingers sped over the keyboard until the monitor revealed: 'Jihad waged on Amsterdam. '

Scanning the text, there, within the third paragraph, she spied Senior Inspector van den Bergen's name. She tapped the screen.

'I saw this guy. He says the blast victim toll stands at twelve injured, two critically. One set of human remains has been found in amongst the wreckage.'

Jan tutted. 'Do they know who it is?' he asked.

'The dead body?' George read on, then shook her head. 'He doesn't say. Nobody saw anything suspicious. The cops are on the trail of a prime suspect.'

'"It's a miracle more weren't killed",' Jan read. 'Understatement of the bloody year. Hey, shall I roll you a joint?'

'At eleven am?' she said. 'Seriously? Is this so you can bump up my rent?'

Jan hooked his long, fuse wire hair behind his ear and wheezed with wry laughter. He turned to the murals painted in neon oranges, pinks, yellows and greens on the walls. Jimi Hendrix, a VW Camper van, Bob Marley, Jim Morrison and the peace sign. They were lit by a UV lamp that gave all the customers a Hollywood smile as a no-extra-cost bonus.

'I'm going to paint a new one in your honour,' he said. 'Our Georgina. An English hottie, smoking a joint and wearing nothing but hotpants and an afro. They'll come all the way from Brabant to buy my skunk and look at you.'

'Go and make some fresh coffee, you old pervert,' George said.

Jan was still laughing as he disappeared between the giant cannabis plants into the back office.

George frowned at the screen. She punched 'Amsterdam suicide bomb' into the search engines, draining the dregs of her coffee as she scanned the results: student discussion forums, more newspaper articles, some left-wing, some right-wing. She found scores of jihadist blogs listed, showing pictures of young men, holding replica guns with their heads wrapped in black fabric or Arabic shemagh scarves so that only their angry eyes were visible. The same name appeared on all of them, claiming responsibility for the Bushuis library explosion in bold type and large font.

'Abdul Youssuf al Badaar,' George said aloud. 'You don't look much.'

His photograph showed that he was an ordinary middle-aged Muslim man with the obligatory beard and mosque hat. He looked benign.

'Why in God's name would you organise a suicide bombing outside an almost empty student library on a Saturday morning?' she asked al Badaar's photograph.

She stared at the laptop screen for too long.

'I'm going to be late,' she said, glancing at her watch.

In a city full of architectural romance and finery, the faculty in Nieuwe Prinsengracht sat like an ungainly, stout Aunt by the canalside. Inside, Ad was alone at a cafeteria table for four.

'George!' Ad shouted. 'Over here!'

George could see the other students' heads bob up like curious meerkats as she approached. Joachim Guttentag said something to Klaus Biedermeier about her – she could tell – and started laughing too loudly. *Dumkopf bastards*, she thought. *Of all the Erasmus placements I could have picked, I had to get lumped in with those two German jerks.*

'Hasn't Fennemans started yet?' she asked.

Ad shook his head. 'There's a delay. He wants to see you,' he said. 'Urgently.'

George's heartbeat sped up. 'Me?'

'In his office.' Ad rubbed his shorn head and grinned. 'Don't

15

flirt with him now, will you? You know you're his favourite girl.'

George made a retching noise and made for the stairs, remembering how only last week she had been subjected to yet another of Fennemans' punishing bouts of public ridicule. He had whipped her term-end essay from the top of the pile with a flourish and held it in the air for all to see.

'Behold, class,' he had shouted, like a lesser Caligula, felling her in public for sport, with the glimmer of an erection in his depressingly tight trousers. 'This is what happens when you think too highly of yourself and show little regard for rules. I gave McKenzie here a FAIL. A big, fat FAIL. In red pen. See? And why?' The dramatic pause of a deluded despot, of course. 'Because this little lady here thinks she can hand in essays late.'

Eleven minutes late. But too late for him.

George climbed the stairs with deliberate sluggishness. Sighed resignedly when she reached the door that bore the sign, 'Dr Vim Fennemans, Head of Faculty'. Knocked twice and walked in.

Fennemans was sitting bolt upright behind his desk, a peculiar shade of grey. George realised why.

Senior Inspector Paul van den Bergen was wedged into an armchair just behind the open door. His long grey-trousered legs stuck out; George narrowly missed tripping over his brogue shoes in the small office. *Jesus, he must have size thirteen feet.*

'Ah, Little Miss McKenzie,' Fennemans said. He looked at his watch pointedly. 'So glad you could join us today.'

She watched van den Bergen closely to see what those sharp grey eyes told her. Did he see Fennemans for what he was?

Van den Bergen cleared his throat. He stood up and held out his hand to George. She shook it. Warm, dry palms. A firm grasp. He looked at her directly.

'Ms McKenzie,' he said. 'I saw you on the morning of the explosion. I gave you my card. Thanks for coming.'

Why had this man sought her out? How had he managed to

trace her after the most fleeting of exchanges in the midst of mayhem? George's racing mind was stalled by the sound of Fennemans scraping his chair on the linoleum floor.

'Sit down, girl!' Fennemans said.

He had put on his smart shiny jacket, George observed. He looked like he had had a blow-dry.

'Your hair's looking positively bouffant today, Dr Fennemans,' George said.

Fennemans thumbed the flaking skin on his earlobe. A smile formed a thin, translucent veneer over a thick layer of venom. 'Mr van den Bergen here thinks you may be able to help his investigation into the explosion. He thinks you—'

Van den Bergen leaned forward. 'Do you mind if I explain what I think, Dr Fennemans?' he asked.

He stared at Fennemans until the faculty head folded his hands over his belly in a gesture of temporary defeat.

'How can I help?' George asked. Excitement started to fizz in her empty stomach. She hoped van den Bergen couldn't detect the stale smell of marijuana clinging to her coat.

'You're top of your class,' van den Bergen stated. He pulled out a notebook. 'In your third year of a Social and Political Science degree at St John's College, Cambridge University, England,' he read. 'A prized exchange student on a scholarship. Outstanding results, excellent languages: English, Spanish, some Arabic – you know, I like your English accent when you speak Dutch – special knowledge of the politics of Muslim unrest in the Middle East and terrorist factions in the West. Your Cambridge supervisor says you have the finest analytical mind she's seen in years. Not a bad track record for someone who's only twenty.'

My Cambridge supervisor? George swallowed hard, desperate to know exactly how much he had found out about her in the space of two days. She tried to regulate her ragged breathing.

'Detective,' Fennemans said, standing up. He started to leaf through some periodicals stacked on a shelf. 'You may have read the highly regarded article *I* recently had published in *The Volkskrant Magazine* about tensions between Israel and Palestine. There's nothing McKenzie here can offer you that I, as Head—'

'I'm a senior inspector. Sit down, please.' Van den Bergen crossed his legs and flung an arm loosely over the side of his armchair, as though he were making himself feel right at home in Fennemans' space.

George did her best to hide a nervous smile.

Van den Bergen flipped over the page on his pad and fixed George with a steely gaze. 'You're a blogger,' he said.

'Yes. I'm just writing a guest post for *The Moment*.'

'A student rag,' Fennemans interrupted. His voice sounded strained. 'In my opinion, Inspector, you should know McKenzie lacks the experience and discipline to—'

Van den Bergen held a hand up to Fennemans. Leaned in towards George. She felt like Fennemans had been shut off behind soundproof glass.

'Listen, Ms McKenzie, I have to catch a Muslim cleric, allegedly operating a terrorist cell out of a mosque in Maastricht a.s.a.p.'

'Abdul Youssuf al Badaar,' George said. 'Yeah, I read the news.'

Van den Bergen nodded. 'Problem is, he's not a Dutch citizen, so we can't trace him easily. No tax or social security records connected to him. No address. No Europol or Interpol information. Nothing but a name, an online confession and a photo. And the fundamentalist websites where he's posted his claim to fame are all hosted in the Middle East, so there's a mountain of red tape for us to cut through to get the identities of web authors.' Van den Bergen stared down at his broad, square palms as though he were looking for clues there. He looked up and locked eyes with George. 'But personally, I'm wondering why a terrorist has targeted a student library in Amsterdam of all places. Does al Badaar have an inside contact or followers within the student population? Who was the suicide bomber?'

George absentmindedly reached for a cigarette and poked it

into her mouth. Fennemans clapped his hands together and pointed to a 'No Smoking' sign on the door.

'Are you *stupid*, McKenzie?' he shouted.

George clenched her fist until her knuckles were pale. She slowly took the cigarette out of her mouth, toying with the idea of lighting it as some small act of defiance. But no. Sally had expressly told her to keep out of trouble. To keep a low profile. And there was something about van den Bergen that intrigued her. She didn't want him to think her an idiot. Reluctantly, she put the cigarette away.

'So, where do I come in?' George asked.

'Maybe you could make your article for *The Moment* about the bombing,' van den Bergen said. 'See if you can reel al Badaar in with a provocative piece. *The Moment* has an impressive international readership, and these clerics and their disciples like mouthing off on the internet. If *you* get comments on your post, we can hopefully trace those. It's a long shot. But it's a shot worth taking.'

'What? You want me to spy? To be bait?' That fizz of anticipation in George's stomach had really started to bite now.

'Let's say you'd be our student intelligence source,' van den Bergen said, smiling. 'Obviously, we'll give you full protection if we think you're in any danger.'

The last thing George wanted was a babysitter with a police badge. She looked hard at van den Bergen. Today he hadn't missed a patch while shaving. He had the good, lightly tanned complexion of somebody who spent time in the outdoors. The expressive lines around his eyes and mouth said he was close to forty, but a head full of prematurely white hair made him look nearer fifty if you didn't look too carefully. Beneath the tailored raincoat that he wore, the slightly frayed collar of his shirt was open slightly. She could imagine the wiry musculature of a man who was still in good shape. She pouted as she made these mental notes.

'I'll do what I can,' she said, already imagining the dressing down she would get from Sally. 'Do you think he'll strike again?'

Van den Bergen stood up and stretched out his hand towards her. The conversation was at an end. He was already at the door.

'I hope not,' he said. 'But with the person or people behind this attack at large, who knows?'

Joachim Guttentag returned to his room that afternoon in good spirits. He had scored some whizz and coke from his usual man in the morning, knowing it would make him the most popular boy at the party.

Smuggling illegal drugs over the border into Germany was never a problem for Joachim. Apart from a change at Utrecht, the Nederlandse Spoorwegen train journey from Amsterdam to Cologne was short and completely unremarkable. By the time Joachim changed to a train bound for Heidelberg, the danger of discovery would be long gone.

He dialled Klaus' number on his mobile phone. After three rings Klaus picked up.

'Are you packed?' he asked his more popular friend.

'Nearly,' Klaus said. 'Are we good now?'

'Yes.'

'I'm sorry about what happened. I didn't mean to …' Klaus' voice was thick with contrition.

'Forget it. We'll work it out. Where are you? You sound like you're on a busy street.'

'Did you score?'

Joachim wondered why Klaus had ignored his question. There was definitely still unease between them after the argument. He could feel it. Perhaps the journey south would smooth things over. 'Yeah. Enough to last over Christmas, if need be. So, tonight at Maike's place in Utrecht?'

'Yes.'

'And then home by tomorrow lunchtime. A meal with my folks. See the boys in the evening.'

'Damn right. I've been sharpening my blade just for Gunter in Ghilbellinia, the fat bastard.' Klaus chuckled at the other end of the phone.

'The train leaves Amsterdam Central Station at 16.48,' Joachim said. 'I'll meet you at quarter past under the departures board, just to be on the safe side. Okay?'

The phone call ended. Joachim checked his reflection. He looked as well as could be expected for someone who would always be underwhelming. His mousy hair flopped onto his forehead as though it had given up. His skin had an unhealthy yellow tinge to it from too many late nights and cigarettes. He had still failed to put on weight despite eating an extra portion of frites with mayo every day. But his scars looked good. He fingered the one that ran from his left eyebrow to his jawline. It was the deepest. He had packed it to make sure it wouldn't heal without leaving a good deep *schmiss* – a scar. It was the one that made girls want to find out more about this mysterious German stranger. Duellers nowadays were supposed to be discreet about their fraternity exploits; their obsession with sharp swords; their ostentatious wearing of the sash and cap. But if it made him more interesting to women …

Joachim picked up his list from the neat, dust-free desk in his uncluttered room.

'Cola and snacks,' he said, flicking his finger at the paper.

He collected his wallet from his desk and shoved his feet hastily into his trainers. He had just enough time to run to the Albert Heijn on the corner before he left. Kiosks in the train station were so much more expensive and Joachim was a careful sort. Klaus was right. Why should he put his father's money in the pockets of the Blacks and Arabs?

As he slammed his door shut, he realised he had left his jacket on the end of the bed. It didn't matter, though. He would be back within ten minutes, tops.

It was an ordinary beginning to what would almost certainly

be an ordinary journey home at the end of the semester except that, under the bright lights of his local Albert Heijn supermarket, Joachim felt like he was being watched.

As he gathered his shopping and entered the alley that led back home, he just had time to register a stinging sensation in his neck before everything went black.

CHAPTER 3

South East London

Ella Williams-May stared intently at the flickering old TV set, willing the night to pass without incident. A dark-haired actress was bouncing up and down on naked actor, Richard Gere's lap. *Officer and a Gentleman.* The movie was so old that the quality of the picture would have been fuzzy even on a top of the range HDTV. But her mother liked Richard Gere and late-night pre-Christmas television was all about the repeats.

'Turn it up,' her mother said. 'I can't hear it.'

Ella tutted and turned the volume up a fraction.

'More,' her mother said.

'But we won't be able to hear if they come,' she said.

'Like I'm bothered tonight?' her mother said. 'I should be out partying, not babysitting you. It's nearly Christmas, anyway. Can't see anything happening tonight.'

Her mother dragged hard on her cigarette and exhaled through her nostrils. Ella thought she looked like a dragon when she did that. Letitia the dragon. With her shining long claws painted in rainbow colours; studded with diamanté; always fake.

Letitia the dragon took a swig from her glass of vodka and orange, rose from her sagging armchair and snatched the remote control from Ella.

'Louder, I said,' she barked. 'Who's the bloody parent in this house?'

Ella said nothing. Ella knew they should keep it low. Ella knew there could still be trouble.

Richard Gere's friend had just hanged himself when trouble started.

Low voices out back. Dark shapes moving beyond the fence. Then, a broken bottle on the back path. Smash. Footsteps running away quickly. Whistles.

Ella grabbed her hockey stick.

'Kill the lights,' Letitia shouted, her cigarette twitching between her shaky fingers.

Loud knocking at the front door, then …

'Don't go,' Ella said. 'It'll be—'

Letitia slid silently into the kitchen at the front. Ella followed, keeping low; creeping stealthily. She raised her head above the windowsill but Letitia was already standing tall, flailing her arms around, shouting.

'Those bastards set fire to my house!'

Ella rushed to the front door ahead of Letitia. The door was open now, flames bubbling up the council's standard-issue red paint, quickly extinguished with a pot full of liquid flung by Letitia. Letitia always had something fun in the pot standing by the door, ready to throw when the occasion demanded. Now the door reeked of petrol and piss. Glass on the floor out front. And, by the gate, an intact Coke bottle with a singed rag stuffed in the neck that had failed to ignite properly.

'Petrol bomb! They petrol bombed us!' Ella said, transfixed by the tableau before her.

She ran inside, heart thudding. She picked up the phone.

'Don't call the police!' Letitia shouted. 'Are you mad? Think I wanna be labelled as a grass?'

Ella ignored her and dialled 999. She held the receiver to her ear and squatted in the lounge where the flickering screen of the

TV was the only source of light. Richard Gere was smiling now. Talking without sound. Lips moving. Carefree. Smart in his uniform. In the seconds she waited to be connected, she heard their voices again at the back. She could see them through the net curtains, moving below the streetlight.

'Which service do you require, please?' the woman at the other end asked.

'Police. Quick. They're here,' Ella said.

The gate clicked as they crept into the garden. Right up the back path; brazen now. Ella could see their hooded silhouettes as they skulked by the door. She fired the details of her name and address at the woman on the phone.

'Come quickly!' she shouted.

Too late. Ella screamed.

It takes more than one go to smash an entire window in with a crowbar. The crowbar doesn't do a clean job and glass is much harder to break than people think. Danny and his boy smacked the window hard, twice, and left only small shards stuck to the white UPVC frames. They had had a lot of practice lately.

Oh Danny Boy, Oh Danny Boy, the sirens are calling, Ella thought.

Their trainer-clad feet pounded away, accompanied by laughter and whistles. Down through the twists and turns of the alleys they would run, like rats hastening to the sewers. Always knowing where to go to ground. Ella knew this much.

Letitia was standing by the back door, staring down at the wreckage on the carpet.

'How can they do this? Nearly Christmas, man. Look at the fucking mess. And now the cops are coming. I told you not to bloody ring them.'

Ella stared at the glass strewn at her feet. She looked around at the dismal living room. Sagging three piece suite, peppered with cigarette burns and food stains. Scratched coffee table. Old stereo, a relic from the early nineties. Drunken, balding Christmas tree, perched in the corner like a sad, old glittery tart at a crap party. There was nothing left to steal. There was nothing left to break. She shut her eyes and swallowed hard. She thought about her just-in-case hammer under her pillow. Then she kicked the despair aside.

'I'll help,' Ella said, grabbing a dustpan and brush from the cupboard under the sink.

The wail of sirens heralded the approaching police but something caught Ella's eye. She looked up from sweeping the glass, wondering what the bright light in the back was. The tree. The tree, the only attractive growing thing in Ella's garden, was a prunus kanzan – standard council issue that bore racemes of pink candyfloss blossom in May. There was something different about it now.

Ella edged closer so that the icy wind whipped through the empty window frame and made her ironed hair slap up and down on her shoulders.

In the small garden, the tree looked like a bright Christmas message from the Ku Klux Klan. Fire licked along its slender branches. A flaming cherry tree, blooming unnaturally early. Ella spied the dark figure standing behind the fence, admiring his handiwork. One of Danny's boys.

Oh Danny Boy, Oh Danny Boy, I hate you so.

Twelve sleepless hours later and Letitia was holding a black bin liner open.

'Stuff that shit in the bag. Come on! Quickly,' she said, staring at Ella.

Ella put the handbags into the bin liner one at a time.

'Grab a pile, for Christ's sake. We ain't got all day.'

Ella looked up, checking that they weren't being watched.

The factory where her mother worked was cavernous. Cardboard box high-rises stretched up to the double-height ceiling, looking like an oversized 3D model of the housing estates in Deptford. Each box was stuffed full of flashy Taiwanese hand-bags.

'There's no one there. I checked,' Letitia said.

'Are you sure?' Ella's heart was pounding. She scanned the walls for CCTV cameras.

''Course I'm fucking sure.' Letitia started to grab handbags herself and piled them in fast. 'Everyone wants one of these,' she cooed. 'That is some proper bling. Fiver a pop. Easy money, man.' One of her false nails flipped off and flew across the floor. 'Bollocks! My Christmas nails. That's your fault.' She treated Ella to a withering glance.

Cold fear roiled around Ella's insides, making her wince. A storm was coming. Letitia had broken a special occasion nail. She knew she needed to do something; say something fast if she was to head off her mother's emotional hurricane.

'You just hold the bag, Mum. I'll work faster, yeah?'

As she stuffed the handbags into the bin liner, her breath came short. She had to get done. Had to get out before they got copped. First Danny's boys, now this. She hated this life. Last thing she wanted was a criminal record for the sake of PVC ghetto crap adorned with zips and diamanté. Letitia didn't see it that way.

'Hello!' A man's voice. Cheery but questioning.

Letitia looked up. 'Out the back with the bags,' she said.

'Who the hell?' Ella said.

'Now!'

Ella knew the drill. She grabbed both bin liners and flung each one out through the opening that gave way to the loading bay below.

As she did so, she could see Letitia coming out of the back room. Wheeling the mop bucket before her now. Swinging her ample arse from side to side the way the older men like. Singing softly.

'Oh, morning, Fred,' she called.

27

'Letitia. You nearly gave me a heart attack. Didn't expect to see you until after New Year, love.'

'Making up time, you know. I got an hospital appointment early next week. Can't afford to be short on money.'

'I've got a flask. Would you like a nice cup of tea?'

'No. I'm finishing up. Them toilets was a disgrace after the Christmas party …', tutting, '… but they're clean now. See you on the second anyway.'

Ella could hear that old Fred had bought it. She swallowed hard, looking at the drop into the loading bay. It was a good eight or nine feet. Ten even. She knew her knees would jar even if she bent them.

'Just grit your teeth.' She jumped to the concrete below and bit her tongue as her legs screamed in complaint. She grabbed the bin liners. They were fat and unwieldy. The booty inside weighed like dead bodies. She prayed they wouldn't split.

When Ella reached the rendezvous point around the corner, she dumped the bin liners on the ground. Her arms would ache for a week. The icy chill bit into her face and hands but the sweat poured down her back and under her breasts on the inside of her anorak. She took a packet of Marlboro Lights out of her pocket and tapped a cigarette on the side of the pack. Flick flick. She tried to get the weak flame of her disposable lighter to stay for long enough to light up but it was no match for the gusting December wind.

'I am some Olympic-sized idiot,' she said, finally getting the cigarette to light. She inhaled deeply and felt lightheaded from the nicotine rush. Fatigue pressed down on her fifteen-year-old body like super-strong gravity. Pulling her down, down, down.

Letitia appeared from around the corner, grinning like she had just won the lottery.

'Good girl,' she said, looking at the bin liners.

'Did he suspect?' Ella asked.

'No way. Let's get these bags home. Check out our haul.'

Ella picked one of the bin liners up and started to walk towards the bus stop.

'Oi!' Letitia shouted. 'Get back here and take the other one. I ain't gonna lose another nail.'

Ella stopped in her tracks. *Bitch, bitch, bitch, you're a bitch all day long.* She quickly weighed up the odds. Start a thing in the street and attract attention to bags full of hooky gear? No. She was smarter than that.

Ella listened to the hiss of the kettle while she watched Letitia in the reflection of the cooker splashback. Bags were scattered all around. Counting. Five, ten, fifteen, twenty …

'I reckon there's a couple of hundred quid's worth here. Maybe more,' Letitia said. 'I am so going dancing on New Year's Eve.'

Going out. Leaving Ella alone. *Oh, Danny Boy …*

'Can I stay at Aunty Sharon's?' Ella asked.

Letitia sat up. 'Who's going to look after the fucking house?' She looked indignant. Hurt even.

Ella felt anger seething beneath the surface – raw, negative energy. 'If they come back and you're out, how the hell am I going to cope on my own?' she asked.

Letitia was on her feet now, gesticulating wildly, horrible words rattling out of her mouth like carriages on a runaway train.

'I ain't asking you much, you ungrateful little cow. I've got to flog these down the pub. How else am I supposed to put food on the table? Cleaning? You think that pays enough? You thought of getting a bit of cash in hand yourself instead of keeping on at me with this bullshit about school and scholarships?'

Ella turned her back on Letitia. She squeezed the tea bags out of the cup and opened the fridge.

'We're out of milk,' she said, sighing.

Letitia fell silent. And as though her bitter words had never been spoken, she reached into the back pocket of her jeans. 'I got two quid here. Get a pint of semi-skimmed at the shop and some chocolate for yourself.' She smiled at Ella.

Mad cow.

Ella walked quickly through the back streets. She scanned the streets for Them. Daylight didn't guarantee anything. There was an older guy up ahead dressed in expensive designer gear. He was being taken for a walk by a Doberman and a Staffordshire bull terrier. Instinctively, Ella folded her arms and quickened her pace. Don't make eye contact. Keep away from the dogs.

As she neared the man, she allowed herself quick scrutiny of his face. Nobody she knew but almost certainly a dealer. Gold teeth. Diamond studded watch. Patterns shaved into his hair. The dogs started to bark and rear up on their stubby hind legs.

'Get down!' the man shouted. He looked her up and down. He winked. 'Don't worry, love. They're harmless.'

Shying away from the trio, Ella broke into a run. The shop was near. The shutters were down over the window. A cock and balls spray-painted on them. But the open sign hung in the shatterproof glass of the door. Through bulletproof Perspex, she exchanged cash for milk and a Mars bar.

Voices outside. She peered nervously over to the seating area. Tonya and Jez: two of Danny's 'boys'.

'There she is,' she heard the girl say.

'Oi, sweetheart!' the boy shouted to her.

Ella looked round. Jez held a flaming branch in his hand. He threw it towards her like the devil's javelin. It landed a few feet away, still burning. 'See you later, gorgeous!'

Ella sprinted back to the house. Her hands shook as she fumbled with the key in the lock. She flung the boarded door wide and slammed it shut. Lock. Bolts. Safe. For now.

In the lounge she heard a man's voice. Older by the sounds. She walked through to the kitchen, still shaking and put down the milk.

30

'Miss Williams-May, Letitia, can I call you that? We've been watching you for weeks. We've got it all on camera.'

Another voice spoke. Younger this time. 'You're going down, love.'

Then the first one again. 'Unless …'

There was muffled, clandestine conversation between the three that smacked of tacit agreement.

Ella walked into the lounge. Two large men in plain clothes sat on the sagging sofa. She could tell instantly that they were some kind of police. You just knew, didn't you? They seemed to fill the room, and her mother seemed to have shrunk.

Letitia looked over at Ella. Tears were standing in her eyes. She wiped them away hastily and lit a cigarette.

'Ella, make these nice detectives a cuppa, love,' she said. 'They need a favour from you.'

CHAPTER 4

Amsterdam, 23 December

He had watched her leave.

The skeleton keys in his possession made light work of the locks. Inside her bedsit, her well-scrubbed lair, he took his time. Touching her things. Licking her toothbrush. Smelling her clothes. Holding her satin knickers like a glove while he pleasured himself onto her pillowcase, imagining her still lying on the bed.

Finally, he left her a souvenir from his visit. A symbol of his potency and poetry. A courtship ritual signifying that he was coming closer to the time when he would take her. He placed a match in the middle of the floor. From the door, there was no way she could miss it.

'So he wants you to spy? Like a cyber special agent?' Ad asked, flushed and wide-eyed behind his glasses.

'Sort of,' George said, pushing through the drizzle and hoping it wouldn't put her cigarette out. This cycle back to town after the second lot of end of semester exams was beginning to feel like an interrogation.

'Are you going to do it? Sounds dangerous to me.'

'How's it dangerous?'

'Luring bloody terrorists to your door.'

'It's just online, Ad. They can't find me.'

'Don't be so sure. These Al Qaeda type guys aren't stupid. Your name will be all over that blog.'

George fell silent. Even if Amsterdam was full of overseas kids, dipping their toes in louche Dutch waters, finding an Englishwoman amongst the students wouldn't be that hard. She'd told van den Bergen yes. She'd been lured by the thrill of being needed. How had she been so stupid? *Daft tart.*

They were past Roeterseiland now, back in the centre where Christmas trees stood in every shop window, festooned with tinsel and fairy lights. Closer to home, the narrow old buildings leaned inwards as though they were trying to get a better look at one another. On the canal, a glass-roofed barge full of tourists chuntered past. George could hear the monotone of the guide speaking over the PA. She felt certain they would be freezing their tits off.

Ad broke the silence.

'How come you're not going home for Christmas?' he asked.

'My folks are dead,' George said.

Out of the corner of her eye, she could see the look of surprise on Ad's face. He opened and closed his mouth. 'I'm so … sorry. You never told me,' he said.

George swallowed hard. She reminded herself that she was under no obligation to tell him anything. It had only been one kiss and he'd regretted it afterwards. He had the Milkmaid.

'You never asked,' she said.

George locked her bike against the railings and looked up. Inneke's curtain was closed. Katja was standing topless at the adjacent first-floor window. Her red light was on, giving her a slightly demonic glow. George waved at her. Katja grinned back, pushed her boobs together and pouted in Ad's direction. She pulled a strap of her thong up and down on her tanned hip. George shared a silent guffaw with her Polish neighbour as she took in Ad's crimson-faced look of horror.

'She's only winding you up,' she said. 'Come on up.'

Inneke's departing punter pushed past them on the stairs as George led the way to the top.

'Can't you get a different room?' Ad asked. 'It's not right, living here.'

'What's not right about it?' George asked as she pushed her key into her door. 'It's a decent size, it's dirt cheap and it's central.'

'But strange men, coming and going at all hours. Your neighbours …'

'Are brilliant,' George said.

She walked inside. That morning, she had cracked open the bleach; expunging the nasty taste of a heavy weekend by scrubbing at non-existent dirt with a toothbrush. The tight deadline for *The Moment* had driven her to the launderette with her dirty clothes and soiled bedding. Now her room was tidy. It smelled strongly of lemons.

So, when she caught sight of an unstruck match in the middle of her dark grey carpet, she frowned. It had not been there before. Definitely not. She picked it up and examined it. Large-sized cook's match. Pink head.

'What's that?' Ad asked.

'Nothing,' she said. She scanned the room quickly and thoroughly. The locks hadn't been forced. Nothing had been stolen. Maybe Filip had dropped it in the bed and it had fallen from the duvet cover. Maybe.

And yet, hadn't she looked at her carpet before she had closed her door, congratulating herself on finally getting a stubborn wine stain out? Had there been more oversized matches in the overflowing ashtray? *Check the trash later.* She pushed the mystery aside and shut it inside her paranoia box.

'You bring me the money, you lump of shit!' the girl shouted down the phone.

34

Her voice was hard and sour. She sounded older. Two years older now, he could hear how experience and too many cigarettes had stripped the alluring freshness from her voice.

'I know you can get it, Fennemans. I know all about your seedy social life and the scumbags you hang out with. I want it in that fucking left luggage locker at two pm.'

'That's a ridiculous demand. I can't get it that quickly,' Fennemans said, almost choking on his words.

'I'll call the police. I'll get off this phone right now and call—'

'Okay. Okay! But make it three.'

'Two thirty.'

'Fine.'

After his morning constitutional, Fennemans had opened his front door to find post on the mat. He had bent to gather up the mixture of brown and white envelopes. Some junk mail. Bills mostly. But what was this? A personal letter. Handwritten on good stationery. No postmark. He had presumed it had been hand-delivered.

Dear Dr Bastard,

If you don't give me €10,000, I am going to tell the police about what you made me do. Call me immediately to arrange a meet.

Jannek

A sweat had broken out on his top lip. He re-read the words. €10,000? That kind of money wasn't easily come by. What he did have spare, he spent on his … hobbies.

He had fixed himself a double gin and tonic to steady his nerves. Downed it in three gulps. Felt the alcohol spark warmth in his stomach. But it still hadn't taken the edge off his anxiety. This was unexpected. The matter of Janneke had been dropped as it had been with Rosa Bianco; silence supported by those he could rely on within the university. Blind eyes duly turned. He had started to feel untouchable. And now this …

'Bitch!' Fennemans shouted at the wall. 'I'm going to nail you to the wall. Nobody crosses Vim Fennemans and gets away with it.'

His fine mind had whirred into action. Reluctantly, he had pulled his mobile phone from his coat pocket and made the call to the only person he knew who would have that amount of cash knocking about at short notice. A person who would not take kindly to him forfeiting the repayment.

With his soul remortgaged yet again to the devil and the loan agreed, Fennemans had remembered how Janneke was in her freshman year. A slip of a thing in hotpants with bare legs and pumps, looking all of fifteen despite being a voting adult. She'd come to him for advice on accommodation. Worried that she had moved in with hard-drug users who had stolen her stereo to pay for their next hit.

It had been so easy.

'Oh, poor Janneke. Don't think twice about it.' There, there. A friendly pat on the shapely knee. 'I'm looking for a tenant. The girl I had before has dropped out of college unexpectedly. Why! I'd charge you much lower rent than you're paying now and I'm hardly ever at home. You'll have the run of the place.'

At first, he had engineered chance collisions as she came out of the bathroom wearing only a towel.

'Ha! Silly me. I should have known you were in there.' The thrill of planning his seduction was almost as satisfying as the act itself.

Then, making sure she saw him naked. By accident, of course.

'Oh, I didn't realise you were home. I didn't mean to embarrass you.'

He could see her blanch and he liked it. She would struggle and that would make it even more worthwhile.

Then, moving in for the kill, as he had done on previous occasions. Pouring too much wine at dinner. Seeing her giddy, her

36

guard down. Licking his lips as he spied her Lolita's chest, the buds of a late bloomer, just sprouting. Detonating the bomb in good time.

'Janneke, we need to talk seriously for one moment about the end of term tests. You know, the external examiner has told me that she might have to fail you.'

The shock and sorrow in her eyes. But he had already worn her down throughout the first term and a half by marking her artificially low. Making her believe that she was nothing without him. Homeless, penniless, mentorless.

'Terrible, isn't it? But you know, *I* could persuade her to look more favourably on your work.'

The hand on the knee, moving up her firm thigh to her lovely cotton panties. The look of realisation crawling across her pretty face.

'Do you wax?' he had asked.

By that stage, he'd had enough waiting. She was his until the end of the academic year. Who the hell would take her word against his anyway?

Now Fennemans checked his watch. When the designated time came, let her come and count it. He would emerge from the hiding place. The boot would be on the other foot. Feeling for his pocket knife, he rehearsed in his head how he would hurt her. Hold the blade to her kidney. Threaten to report *her* for blackmail and extortion. Get the money back so he could make the same-day repayment that was a condition of the loan. Get even. Slate clean. A brilliant and foolproof plan.

George wiped over the keyboard on her laptop and switched it on. It clicked and whirred into action, greeting her with a merry tinkle. She flung herself into her straight-backed chair.

'I don't like you doing this,' Ad said, perching on the edge of the threadbare chaise longue. He pushed some woollen wadding back in where it had spilled out like fat from a whale carcass.

George looked round and sighed heavily. 'Look, I'm going to do it. You can either ignore me and leave … or help. Which is it going to be?'

She opened her Hotmail and stopped listening to Ad's lecture about cyber safety. In her inbox was an unread message from Sally. Her mouth went dry. *It's been weeks.* She opened it.

From: Sally.Wright@cam.ac.uk   11.35
To: George_McKenzie@hotmail.com
Subject: Your mother

Hello George,
I hope you're enjoying the sights and smells of Amsterdam!

Two things: First, I've had a letter from your mother asking you to make contact with her as a matter of urgency. I know how you feel about this but I'm just letting you know that I have a number for her if you change your mind.

Secondly, I've had a Dutch detective asking questions about you. His name is Paul van den Bergen. He said he was looking to enlist a student to help him on a case. Under the circumstances, you should decline.

As always, when you respond, please ensure your email connection is secure – https://

Best wishes
Sally

Dr Sally Wright, Senior Tutor
St John's College, Cambridge Tel … 01223 775 6574
Dept. of Criminology Tel … 01223 773 8023

Her mother. George briefly allowed herself to drown in the pain. Count backwards. Five, four, three … Then she fought the flood-waters back, salvaging poise from the heartbreak like reclaimed land. She deleted the message from Sally and turned to Ad.

'Well?' she asked. 'Are you my partner in part-time espionage?'

Ad groaned and stretched. His sweater lifted up as he did so and George caught a glimpse of his navel hair. Milkmaid's territory.

'Okay,' he relented. 'If it makes you happy.'

Van den Bergen was walking in long strides down Damrak to Central Station, with his junior detective, Elvis, trotting at his side.

'So, nobody living opposite saw anything. All those people. It's a joke,' Elvis said.

'Do you think curtains are a good Christmas present for someone who's just moved in with her boyfriend?' van den Bergen asked, wishing Elvis wouldn't swing his leather-jacket-clad arms in such an idiotic manner when he walked.

'Did you keep the receipt?'

Van den Bergen's hip clicked rhythmically as he loped towards the departures board. He grunted. Same shit, different year. An afterthought of a gift that Tamara never wanted. A rejection that his ex-wife would gloat over until next year. Those were the joys of fatherhood now. But he had more important things on his mind.

'The bombing is tied to the Social and Behavioural Sciences faculty,' he said, peering up at the flickering, changing destinations.

'Weren't you there with Vim Fennemans the other day, boss? Didn't you recruit one of his students as an informant?'

'Platform Ten. Fast train to Maastricht.' Van den Bergen started stalking briskly towards the platform. 'Even if this mosque terror cell checks out, we need to start looking into the university people that regularly frequented or were involved with Bushuis library,' he shouted over his shoulder at Elvis, still clutching Tamara's ugly curtains in their anonymous Hema bag.

When he barrelled into a middle-aged man with a paunch, he was at first annoyed and then surprised.

'Fennemans!' he said, noting that Fennemans quickly slipped something shiny into his pocket and was looking furtively over at a woman in a purple bobble hat. 'What a coincidence. Funny how you keep cropping up!'

With Ad gone, George thundered down to the back yard. Darkness had fallen now. She wedged the door open so she could see under the light cast by the bare bulb in the corridor. Fifteen minutes and a handful of ash, cigarette butts, coffee grouts, snotty tissues, one used condom, one portion of rotting take-out jerk chicken, an entire ball of hair and a bout of dry-heaving later, she returned to her room with the only spent match she could find amongst her detritus. Filip had definitely used it. She remembered him lighting his cigarette with it afterwards.

She washed her hands thoroughly in scalding hot water, dried them on her wash-worn Margate tea towel and held the charred match up against the one she had found on the carpet. The one from the carpet was a full inch longer and twice as thick.

'Someone's been in my room,' she told her reflection in the window.

She wedged one of the straight-backed chairs under the door knob, like she'd seen people do in films. Turned every light on. Went into the kitchenette and grabbed a bottle of cheap red wine by the neck, holding it like a weapon. Pulled every door open fast. Large store cupboards. Wardrobe. Empty. Behind the sofa. Nothing.

'You're just imagining it,' she said aloud, swigging hard at the cheap wine. She held one fist against her head and clenched her eyes tight shut. 'Filip must have dropped it out of his pocket.'

Fully clothed, she grabbed the laptop and clambered into bed. There was her half-written blogpost. At last, the words gushed through the tips of her fingers onto the worn, shiny keys of the laptop. It was a congratulatory piece; she was devil's advocate now, heralding the Bushuis library bombing as a political triumph against the West. She invited al Badaar himself to leave a comment; to sow the fertile political seedbed of the university's undergraduate population with doubt.

Pressing the publish button, she knew she would never be asked to write for *The Moment* again. *Now, let's wait and see …*

CHAPTER 5

Amsterdam, 24 December

It was fiendishly early. With such a lot on his mind, he hadn't slept a wink. Dawn had not yet broken, but he could put off preparations no longer. Today was the day.

He looked down at Joachim's unconscious body, lying on the slab. Running a finger along his forearm up to the cannula that stuck out like an angry surgical thorn, he marvelled that Joachim was so sinewy. His skin was almost the colour of the urine that had gathered in a catheter bag attached to his penis. He flicked the warm, heavy bag. It needed to be changed. Last one.

It was time to unhook him now. He pulled out the needle, which had carried saline solution and sedative into Joachim's body since the snatch. Checked the clock on the wall. He had precisely two hours to get his houseguest prepped and in situ before the sedative wore off. That was okay. The box was already assembled.

Padding to the kitchen, he made himself a coffee. His secret workshop was cold. He needed his fingers to be warm and nimble. Attaching plastic explosive to a man's body and rigging the wiring was a fiddly job.

He returned to the workshop and began assembling the things he needed from his shelving units. A roll of thin,14-gauge

42

electrical wire, wire cutters, gaffer tape, disposable mobile phone and the other intricate components that a home-made bomb required. Everything was brightly lit by the harsh overhead strip lighting. Freezing concrete beneath his sock-clad feet. Cold air on his skin. Hot coffee in his stomach. His senses were in overdrive now. When his probing gaze fell upon his bolt croppers, that was when he started to get really excited.

He took Joachim's index finger and wrapped a plastic tie tightly around the base as a tourniquet.

'Think of it as signing my guest book,' he said to the sleeping Joachim.

When the bone in Joachim's finger cracked under the pressure of the bolt croppers' blades being squeezed together, he thought it sounded just like the walnuts his mother liked to crack open in front of the television during winter. Seeing the severed finger that ended abruptly with a red fleshy cross section marbled with yellow fat, skin, muscle and a nub of bone nestled within … he held it up to the light to get a really good look … that made him think of the strings of raw sausages in the butcher's shop window from when he was a child. He liked sausages, though his father would never allow him to have them in his presence.

As he opened the deep freeze and put Joachim's finger into a vacant hole in the test-tube holder, he chuckled to himself. Funny how even the strangest of things could spark off wistful childhood memories.

In the morning, George awoke with a hangover that measured eight point nine on the Richter scale. There were fifty-four comments on her post already. Angry comments. Wishing her dead. Telling her to get back to England with the other stinking foreigners. But there, amongst the vitriol, was exactly what she had hoped for.

Allah is great. We are unified against the immorality and greed of the West. The Maastricht Brothers in Islam will continue to

43

tear down the walls of your universities until Christianity's unholy teachings are expunged and only the word of Allah is left. Abdul Youssuf al Badaar.

George sucked on her cigarette, staring at the statement until the words looked jumbled on the screen.

She pulled her mobile phone out from under her duvet and punched van den Bergen's number into it. After three rings he answered.

'What?' he barked.

'Have you read my blog?'

There was a brief pause the other end. 'Yes.'

'So? Did I do well?' George smiled and kicked the duvet off.

'Great. Thanks. Look, I'm busy with forensics. I'll be in touch.'

The phone went dead.

'He put the phone down on me. The cheek of it!' George stared at the mouthpiece of her mobile.

George stood under a hot shower, watching the tiny beads of water clinging to the glass like glittering strings of binary code. Van den Bergen's rejection and the prospect of spending another Christmas accompanied only by a bottle of wine and a large bar of chocolate held her spirits down. And Ad would be tucked up with the Milkmaid by now.

'Goddammit. I hate Christmas!' she shouted at the mildewed shower tray sealant.

When she returned to her room, she flung her heavy wash bag onto the bed, accidentally knocking her pillow off. Groaning, she picked up the pillow and noticed a greyish stain on the burgundy fabric.

'That's odd. This was clean on after Filip,' she said, frowning.

She scratched at the stain and gave it a tentative sniff. Dried though it was, the smell of semen was still instantly recognisable.

En route to his destination, he had a little extra job to do.

From his vantage point, parked right outside, he could see the jaunty fairy lights twinkling on a Christmas tree within. An advent candle shone on the windowsill. Merry Christmas, cheating bitch.

He looked back at Joachim's box. No sound. No movement. He had five minutes. That was all he needed.

Wearing black overalls and with blue plastic overshoes stuffed into his pocket, he opened the glove compartment to the van and pulled out the hunting knife and clipboard.

His tread on the block paving was so light that nothing heralded his approach. Pulling on his overshoes. Rapping on the door's flimsy woodwork with a sure fist. Clipboard in hand. ID at the ready.

When the door was opened, her eyes flicked absently over the ID card in his hand.

'There's a possible gas leak?' she asked.

Still, she had not looked at him properly. She seemed distracted. Her scrutiny finally turned to his face. She balked.

He left her no time to react further or speak. Pushed her inside, spun her round and dragged her along the hall into the house with a strong arm around her neck. Knife at the throat.

'Make a sound and I'll puncture your carotid artery. I want the money. Take me immediately to the money. Don't try anything heroic. I want all of it. If you try to fight, I'll kill you. Understand?'

She nodded. He held her tightly to him in this tango of terror. Then he noticed from the sudden warm feeling against his leg that she had urinated. Stupid cow.

The tip of his blade had pushed its way into her throat enough for a bead of blood to have appeared.

'Count it,' he said as she waved the wad at him. He didn't look at her face. Only at the money.

'Please don't kill me,' she said in a whimpering, simpering girl voice.

Ordinarily, of course, he loved being begged by a woman but he didn't have time for that sort of nonsense today.

'What did I say about making a sound?' he asked.

With the envelope full of money in his top pocket and his overshoes stuffed back into his overalls, he was back in the van and pulling out of the drive before the girl had bled to death.

Van den Bergen took off his glasses, rubbed his tired eyes and stared blankly at the screen. Cardboard shreds. Clear evidence of plastic explosive and a mobile phone detonator having been used. Several molars containing fillings that weren't from Europe. And a body part.

He started to chew on his Biro thoughtfully. De Koninck, the forensic pathologist, might eventually be able to track the dental work down to a specific country. Shreds of card intermingled with the human remains meant nothing to him though. Not yet, anyway.

In his peripheral vision, he could see Chief Inspector Olaf Kamphuis pulling on his coat and waving to one of the secretaries. He started to lumber over towards him. Van den Bergen could not stifle a groan.

'I'm leaving,' Kamphuis said, chins wobbling. 'I'll be back tomorrow evening to see how things are going.' He ran a finger around his shirt collar and gave van den Bergen's feet a venomous stare. 'Am I going to have the pleasure of firing you for incompetence, Paul? Remember, I have the full weight of the Minister of the Interior and Kingdom Relations behind me. It would be quite a Christmas present.'

Van den Bergen gnashed his molars together and considered a response. Kamphuis did love his games.

'I think the payout for constructive dismissal is quite hefty these days, isn't it? That's a very generous Christmas present you have in mind, Olaf. Too kind. Don't choke on the ginger biscuits, now, will you?'

Kamphuis laughed wryly. 'Very good, Paul. Touché, you big, lanky arsehole. See you tomorrow.'

With Elvis out for burgers and IT Marie gone for the evening, van den Bergen found himself alone in the office. Alone, baffled yet again by his job and utterly hacked off. His phone rang. It was his counterpart in Utrecht, Teun van der Putte.

'Yes,' he snapped.

'Paul? Get your ass over here immediately. There's been another bomb.'

'Jesus. I wonder where that is,' Ad said.

George felt his heavy breath on her hand. He smelled of deodorant and warm skin. When his knock came at her door, she had been poised to hit this unexpected visitor, thinking it might be her ejaculating intruder. The Stalker. She turned the words over in her mind, sampling how they felt, buckling under their ominous weight. But it had just been Ad, abandoning his early train back into the fluffy, baby pink arms of the Milkmaid. He had come bearing yuletide pity and a gift in a small, carefully wrapped package.

Happiness burned inside her with the white hot brilliance of magnesium held over a flame. Ad had a gift for her. He had delayed his return to Groningen. For her. She untied the blue ribbon and peeled back the expensive paper with trembling fingers.

'*Tea bags?*'

George had not been able to contain the look of horror. She knew it had usurped the delighted smile and planted a flag of bitter indignation on her face. What had she been thinking anyway? Jewellery and perfume were things a man bought his girlfriend. The Milkmaid got those. She got fucking tea bags.

Ad had looked instantly wounded. 'Sorry, I thought ...'

Forcing her teeth to show in an encouraging fashion, she had hugged him quickly and assembled the words of gratitude in the right order before speaking them. 'That's the perfect present for me! Very sweet.'

He looked relieved. 'You're always out of tea.' His face flushed. 'Listen, can I check the train times?'

George had nodded and passed him the laptop. It was then that they had seen the headline on *de Volkskrant*'s home page.

'Second suicide blast hits Utrecht. Live footage.'

Now, she focussed her attention on the YouTube video, posted only moments after the explosion. The amateur cameraman was talking fast as he shot the bedlam. He sounded frightened; exhilarated.

Springweg, Utrecht.

As soon as he gave the location, George scrutinised what she could see of the building behind the flames in the early evening twilight. What kind of a place was it? Was it another library? It was too far away from the camera phone for her to see any detail but she was curious.

'It looks central. Let's see,' she said.

She punched up Google Streetview and found the building when it had still been whole – crisp in the daylight and discreet. Hebrew writing was just visible on the portico above the door but otherwise there were no discernible religious markings on the facade. No Star of David. But with its high-pitched roof and adjacent tower, it was unmistakeably a place of worship.

'This is it,' she said to Ad, tapping a fingernail on the screen.

'A synagogue,' he said. 'These bastards are making a statement.'

George frowned. She made a rasping noise as she sucked her teeth. 'This isn't connected to the university, though. There's no logic to any of it.'

Van den Bergen drove well in excess of 100mph to bridge the distance between Amsterdam and Utrecht. His tired body was suffused with adrenalin and a grim euphoria of sorts.

Emergency vehicles with their strobing lights beckoned him towards the mayhem.

Teun van der Putte was standing at the scene, backlit by the blaze.

'Paul. Good,' he said, slapping van den Bergen on the upper arm. He proceeded to fill van den Bergen in on what had happened, wincing visibly every time a sheet of glass from a nearby house blew out onto the street.

'Any witnesses?' van den Bergen asked. The heat was over-whelming. A thick slick of sweat had already started to cling to his body.

Teun looked over at ambulances already swallowing up casu-alties and at the fire trucks that lined the street – motherships, connected by hoses to their battling fire crew. He blinked hard and wiped his sooty glasses on his shirt. 'Not a fucking thing, would you believe it?'

Van den Bergen nodded sagely. 'Same in Amsterdam.' He watched as evacuees trod gingerly over the glass that littered the pavement. Grimaced and wept as they looked up at the flames and their ruined apartments. 'How many dead or injured?'

'There's a few neighbours with lacerations from their windows blowing in. But there didn't seem to be anyone walking on the street when the bomb went off.' Teun shouted over the hiss of the hoses.

'Christmas Eve. Everyone's either in with family or out drinking,' van den Bergen said, watching a weeping man as he was ushered to the place of safety beyond the police cordon. Beneath the blanket that covered the man's shoulders, van den Bergen saw that he clutched a little girl of about four to his chest. Her forehead was covered in blood.

'It's impossible to know how many were inside the wreckage

until the fire's out,' Teun said. 'But we did find a bit of what we think is the suicide bomber. As soon as we arrived. It had been blown right out of range of the fire.'

'A bit?'

'A big bit.'

CHAPTER 6

25 December

As George applied her lipstick, she wondered if Ad had lingered well into the evening, delaying his journey home because of her. More likely because of the Utrecht bomb, she decided.

Wearing her usual tight-fitting jeans, a T-shirt that smelled strongly of washing liquid and thick Primark cardigan that had started to bobble under the arms, she had made no attempt to look festive beyond the slick of colour on her full lips. Like Jan and Katja, her makeshift Christmas family, would give a shit!

She shrugged at her reflection in the mirror. Then she picked up the framed photograph that she had got an elderly American tourist to take of her and Ad back in October. They had been standing beneath the impressive arched portico of the Rijksmuseum, which Ad had offered to show her around. She was grinning like a fool at the camera. Ad's arm was draped around her shoulder. He smiled uncertainly, as though he had been caught with his fingers in the proverbial cookie jar.

'Merry Christmas, Ad,' she said.

She blew a kiss at the photograph, pulled on her Puffa jacket and left for Jan's in good time. As she undid the locks on her bike, she looked around and missed the pair of eyes that were fixed intently on her.

'Merry Christmas, darling,' Katja said, showering George in sticky pink kisses.

George immediately wiped her cheek with the back of her hand like a horrified child expunging the kisses of a hairy-chinned great aunt.

Katja seemed unaware of the tacit rejection. She took off the tinsel that was hanging around her waist like a belt and wrapped it around Jan's neck. 'I love Christmas. Such a shame it's not snowing. The one thing I really miss about Polish Christmases is the snow.'

Katja gazed towards the window wearing an almost wistful expression. She pulled her bright red hair back in a ponytail and quickly turned her attention to Jan's food preparation. 'But what the hell is that you're cooking, darling? It looks like a dish of festive turds.'

Katja peered over Jan's shoulder and into the large crock pot that he was stirring. George sidled up on his left and saw that he did in fact seem to be preparing stewed turds.

'Is this some vegetarian crap?' George asked, wrinkling her nose.

Jan banged the spoon on the side of the crock pot and looked at her with a raised eyebrow through his steamed-up Trotsky glasses. His roll-up cigarette hung artfully out of the corner of his mouth.

'It's sausage surprise,' he said in an exasperated tone.

'But I thought you were a veggie,' George said.

'Vegan.'

'Vegan?' shrieked Katja. 'That's a crime against nature, you hippy.'

George could see a hurt expression on Jan's face. He pushed his glasses up to his forehead, revealing large, puffy eyebags beneath red-rimmed, small blue eyes. He spoke with his cigarette still in his mouth.

'I'm cooking pork sausages just for you, you judgemental Polish tart. I knew you wouldn't understand the finer philosophical points of veganism.'

George felt frivolity wash over her as she watched her landlord threaten Katja with a drippy spoon. He was wearing a batik kaftan today with his stick-thin hairy ankles clearly on view. The fact that he was cooking in bare feet made George feel slightly itchy. The fact that the kitchen floor was strewn with lentils, what appeared to be Rice Krispies and garlic peelings made her positively twitchy. But Jan in his own natural habitat full of ethnic handicrafts, burnt-down candle stubs and second-hand pock-marked furniture was still a comical sight.

'How can a vegan cook meat in his own pots, Jan? Let alone eat it,' George said.

Jan was still stirring conscientiously. 'I'm a practising hypocrite. Now go and fetch me my packet of Drum from the sideboard.'

As George returned to the cooker with Jan's pouch full of tobacco, she noticed the inch of ash from Jan's cigarette fall into the stew. For a split second, he looked blankly at the ash, sitting on top of the sauce. Before she could comment, he sniffed and stirred it in.

George opened a bottle of strong Duvel for herself. The only way she was going to survive the food hygiene non-standards of Jan's Christmas dinner would be to down as much beer as possible. She reasoned that the alcohol would kill off any germs in her stomach.

When George's phone pinged with a text from van den Bergen, Katja was busy explaining how a woman could still breastfeed if silicone implants were inserted through the nipple. Jan was assembling pudding. George was busy chasing the last of the surprisingly tasty sausages around her plate, more than half way on her journey towards being medicinally drunk.

'What do you want, Senior Inspector?' George asked her phone's display.

What do you know about this girl?

Van den Bergen had sent an accompanying attachment, which was a photo of a blonde woman. George did indeed recognise her face. She was a drop-out politics student in the year above. George had met her once briefly in a bar where some of the other students hung out. Joachim and Klaus had been all over her like a rash. The evening was memorable because the woman had thrown a glass of beer all over Joachim but had left with Klaus.

She texted van den Bergen back.

She's called Janneke something or other.
She's one of Fennemans' old students. Why?

The answer came back as George was enjoying her pudding of hash-cakes and ice cream.

She has been murdered.

'Cheers,' Fennemans said to his mother.

They clinked glasses together. He watched as the elegant matriarch of the family sniffed the contents of her champagne flute.

'Asti spumante?' his sister asked, staring at the rising bubbles. 'At Christmas?'

'It's prosecco. And a good one at that,' Fennemans said.

His mother swept her carefully coiffed white hair to the side, sipped the sparkling wine cautiously and swallowed in what appeared to be a reluctant manner. 'Oh, Vim. I wish you'd let me open the Laurent Perrier. The Italians are far better left to their chiantis and barolos. Did you buy this at the supermarket?'

His mother turned to his sister. 'Vim has never had much of a nose for wine, has he? Not like us, darling. You get your palate from me.' She patted his sister's manicured hand. The two of them exchanged self-satisfied smiles.

Fennemans had been feeling celebratory when he had arrived. That feeling had long since evaporated. With every bite of his foie gras on toast, he wanted to tell them both to drop dead. Drop dead, drop dead, drop dead.

Every Christmas, the enmity surged inside him like a noxious, mushrooming cloud. Mother would be condescending and would take his sister's side in some ill-informed debate about politics, made tedious by the fact that his mother and sister were intensely conservative and ignorant of anything that happened outside of the Netherlands. His sister would belittle him at the dining table and then spend the evening boasting about how well her legal practice was doing and how successful her Swiss paediatric consultant husband was (he would be there, of course, if it weren't for the fact that he was saving precious little lives on Christmas Day).

'I said, when are you going to get yourself a woman, Vim?' his mother asked.

Her beautifully made-up eyes peered at him over her Bulgari spectacles. Fennemans realised she had been waiting for an answer for more than thirty seconds. He had been too lost in a labyrinth of his own hostility to hear her.

His sister snorted and collected up the empty starter plates. 'Vim get a woman? Come on, Mum!' She turned to him with an unpleasant smile. It was as though he had never grown beyond the age of ten, with Sofie, the favoured twin; older by fourteen minutes, preferred by a country mile and indulged without temperance once his father, the erstwhile arbitrator, had been taken by his dicky ticker that Mother had fed to bursting point with butter and cream and fatty pork. 'Who'd have him with his cheese feet and boring jazz collection?'

'Okay. That's it. I'm going,' he said, rising from his chair quickly.

Last year, he had contemplated doing this but this year, he was really doing it. He was walking away.

'Sit down, Vim. I've made venison,' his mother said.

He slammed the door behind him. That felt good. He crunched down the gravel drive. That felt better. Got into the car, drove around the corner out of sight and parked up. He pressed the buttons on his mobile phone.

'It's Fennemans,' he said. 'Look, you've got your money now. We're straight, aren't we?'

'I suppose so.'

'Well, can I see the girls this evening? I need to unwind.'

'I'm away on business.'

Fennemans looked out of the windscreen at the sprawling, well-tended houses and gardens that suffocated him on all sides. 'Please. I'm your best customer, aren't I? You said it yourself. Can't you make a call?'

There was a pause and some laboured breathing at the other end of the phone. 'Six o'clock at the house. Bring cash and give it to Aunty Fadilla.'

Fennemans hung up, gripped his steering wheel and allowed himself to exhale slowly through pursed lips. He reached over to the glove box and took out the packet of cigarettes that he kept there as an emergency. One wouldn't hurt. He took out the box of matches and lit up, enjoying the nicotine rush as it slapped him about the head. Smiling to himself, he tossed the match out of the car window.

'Of course you can come in,' Janneke's mother said to van den Bergen, holding the door wide.

Though the rims of her eyes were bloodshot, van den Bergen could see the likeness between the mother and the photo of the dead daughter that had been stapled to the case notes, accidentally left in his in-tray by the Christmas admin temp.

She wrung her hands. 'They've only just let me come back and clear up. I was at my sister's when I heard. I don't really want to be …' Her words tailed off and headed down a blind alley.

Van den Bergen smelled death and grief in the air. It made his hip ache.

'I'm very sorry for your loss, Mrs Polman.'

He looked around the tidy house and felt empty on the woman's behalf when he saw the Christmas tree with its fairy lights turned off. There was a large dark stain on the wood floor.

'Would you like a coffee?'

'No thanks. Can I see Janneke's room please?'

'But the police have already been.' She looked helplessly towards the stairs. 'I suppose you're just doing your job. You'll find him, right?'

Van den Bergen watched as Janneke's mother's chin dimpled up and her eyes filled with glassy tears.

'I'll be in the kitchen,' she said.

In the dusty silence of the dead girl's room, he looked around at her things and tried to get a feel for who the girl had been. Who did she know that wanted her dead? Why would somebody want to cut her throat? And what the hell was he doing here, snooping into another detective's case when he should have been concentrating on al Badaar?

Quietly, at the back of his mind, van den Bergen acknowledged that she had been a Social and Behavioural Science student. Like Joachim Guttentag, who had just been reported missing by his parents. Both belonging to the same faculty that had been targeted by a suicide bomber. He made a mental note to get Elvis and Marie to look into Guttentag's disappearance if he still hadn't showed by the New Year.

He looked through her books. There were no academic texts. Nothing to indicate that she had been a studious girl. There was no makeup. No posters of bands on the walls. No photographs of boyfriends. The room had an impersonal feel to it and yet he could tell from the slept-in bedding and the drawers full of clothes that this was indeed her main abode. He decided that she had stripped from it any trace of femininity or her previous life as a student. Why? What had happened to Janneke Polman?

'I brought you a coffee anyway,' her mother said.

Van den Bergen jumped and turned around to see the weary woman standing against the architrave of the door. He smiled at her. 'Thanks,' he said. The coffee was black. He hated black coffee but he drank it anyway and steeled himself not to pull a face. 'It's good coffee. Listen, Mrs Polman.'

'Call me Lydia.'

'Lydia. Why did Janneke drop out of college?'

Lydia pushed a stray lock of hair behind her ear. 'She was struggling with her studies. Weird really. She'd done so well in her first two years. Then suddenly, she starts doing really badly in class. Had trouble with her accommodation too.'

'Didn't she live here with you?'

'We're too far out here, really. She wanted to be in the centre, near all her friends. Wanted to be independent, you know. They fly the nest and you never expect to get them back.'

Lydia sighed and wiped a stray tear with shaking, work-worn fingers.

'I thought she'd do okay when she moved in with Dr Fennemans.'

Van den Bergen cocked his head to the side and held up his enormous hand. 'Wait. What did you say?'

Lydia was still wringing her hands, except this time, van den Bergen noticed that she was toying with something purple and woollen. A purple bobble hat that he had last seen in Central Station.

'You?' George said, trying not to let the alarm show in her face. Despite the calming effects of the beer flowing through her veins, her heart was thumping hard against her ribcage. 'What do you want?'

58

She had only just got to the communal door and put her key in the lock. The whole of the red light district was almost empty of punters, neighbours and passersby. Now that the early evening darkness and cold had cloaked everything in semi-silence and shadow, the canal was a black, stagnant blood vessel bisecting a dead street. So, the tap on her shoulder was wholly unexpected. Inexplicably, here was Fennemans, standing two feet away from her, smiling like a creepy fucking idiot beneath the streetlight. His nose seemed more bulbous than usual. Though his bouffant hair had lost some of its va va voom, she noted. And the shaft of yellow light from above revealed the dusting of dandruff on the collar of his overcoat. He smelled of rotten meat and cheese beneath an old fashioned fug of what George recognised as Paco Rabanne.

'I was passing this way,' he said, still smiling. 'You Brits make a big deal out of Christmas Day, don't you? So, I just wanted to wish you a Merry Christmas.'

George took her key out of the lock and stood perfectly still. She stared at him, willing him to go away.

'Can I come up for a drink?' he asked.

George's mind was racing. This was wrong in so many ways. Fennemans hated her. She hated him. This was her personal space. Her turf. He was encroaching.

'How do you know where I live?' she asked, taking a step towards to him so that the gap between them had closed uncomfortably. She was mindful of her body language. Careful to thrust her shoulders forwards and make herself look as threatening and large as possible. This arsehole was not to get any wrong messages. Happily, he took a step backwards.

'I'm your tutor. I just …' The childish smile had started to fall from his face.

'Don't come to my home,' George said. She felt bolstered by the 8.5 percent alcohol content in not one, but six Duvel beers. Ordinarily, she knew she would have skirted around the issue and tried to politely brush Fennemans off. But now …

'This is inappropriate. You're not welcome here. It's my space. Do you understand, Dr Fennemans?'

George stood her ground, balled fists on hips. His expression changed. The smile was suddenly replaced by something else. George couldn't tell if it was weary resignation or annoyance. It was difficult to assess under the streetlight. But all the while she stood there, willing him to walk away without a confrontation, she was seized and held captive by a paralysing anxiety that she didn't want him to know about. Then, with silence hanging opaquely between them, Fennemans dug one of his gloved hands into the pocket of his overcoat as though he was reaching for something.

CHAPTER 7

2 January

When Ad opened the door to his Museum Quarter apartment in Sluitstraat, George pushed passed him.

'Do you know Fennemans showed up at my place over Christmas? Offered me a half-smoked packet of cigarettes as a peace offering. I told him to fuck right off. Got any of that nice Leerdammer?' she asked.

'Oh, Happy New Year to you too,' Ad said, clearly bemused.

George's brain was whirring today, processing all the information that had come her way in the last week. Al Badaar's still-untraceable comments. *The Moment* being denounced as a pro-terror virtual rag, thanks to her blogpost. The Jewish community in Utrecht, publicly decrying the local police's inability to arrest a perpetrator. She felt like she was riding the rollercoaster right up to the top. It was a good feeling.

She heard Ad close the door behind her. Casting a glance around the anonymous-looking boys' living room, her gaze rested momentarily on a card which sat coyly on a bookshelf by the flatscreen TV. It had Santa Claus on the front, blushing and receiving a heart from Rudolph the red-nosed reindeer. It said, 'Happy Christmas, Boyfriend' in green, shiny lettering. Her rollercoaster became stuck half way up and she didn't like the look of the drop to the ground.

George tried to marshal her thoughts. An empty food cupboard and hunger to see her friend had driven her here. *Ask him about a sandwich. Ad always has food. Focus.*

Ad reached out to take her coat.

'Coffee?' he asked.

'Is that card from your girlfriend?' she heard herself say before she could claw the words back. *Damn.*

Ad frowned incredulously as his flatmate, Jasper, shuffled out of his room. Jasper, normally so preppy and clean-cut, was wearing pyjamas and scratching himself. His blond mop of hair was dishevelled. He sported a day's worth of stubble.

'Happy New Year, guys,' he said in English with a thick Dutch accent. He picked up the disgusting Santa card and waved it at her. 'Mine,' he said. He winked at Ad.

'You came back yesterday?' Ad asked him.

'Never went home. I've been at Marianne's until last night. House-sitting while she's working round the clock on the bombings. The stuff she's been telling me would give you bloody nightmares.'

'Aren't you supposed to be at lectures?'

'Med students don't start 'til tomorrow. Anyway, I've got man-flu. It's going round.'

'What do you mean you don't believe in sudden flu?' Klaus said to the detective.

He watched the ratty little man with a quiff and leather jacket looking around his apartment. Joachim had been reported missing, and now the police had eyes for everything. Especially this fool. And the girl. Where had she gone? She said she needed to use the toilet but she had been five minutes and counting. Even women didn't take that long to pee. He hoped she wasn't snooping around his medicine cabinet. And fuck it if he hadn't left his bedroom door ajar.

'I mean, you two had arranged to travel to Heidelberg together,' the detective said. 'Via Utrecht. That's what Guttentag's mother told our colleagues in the Baden-Württemberg police.'

'Yes, I've already answered their questions. At length.'

'Imagine how Joachim's parents feel. You're supposed to be his friend, aren't you?'

Klaus rolled his eyes and strode over to his Gaggia coffee machine. 'I'm not going to grace that with a response.' He started to grind some beans and then fixed himself an espresso. He didn't bother to offer one to quiff boy in his ill-fitting Elvis get-up.

'We've checked his phone records,' the detective said. 'You called him only an hour or so before you were due to meet, didn't you? You were possibly the last person to speak to Joachim before he disappeared. What did you say to him?'

Klaus wracked his brains for the right thing to say. What would get this idiot to leave him in peace so that he could unpack and get on with the new term? He had some nice pralines in his case that would go well with the coffee. If it was an invited visitor that was sprawled all over his elegant leather sofa, Klaus would have been only too happy to share them. But he had no intention of getting them out in front of this nagging toe rag. And where was that girl?

'Look, I was feeling ill. It came down suddenly. You know how flu is. One minute you're shivering a bit, the next you're on your back. I went out for paracetamol. Ask the shop owner on the corner. He'll corroborate what I'm telling you. And then I was in for the rest of the night with the stereo on. The walls are thin here. Ask my neighbour. I bet he heard my every cough and fart.'

The detective looked at him with suspicious eyes like black marbles. 'Woah! We're a bit defensive, aren't we? Nobody's accusing you of anything, Klaus.'

Just as Klaus began to feel sweat bead under his arms, the girl finally emerged from the bathroom. She had bad skin that clashed with her red hair, Klaus noted. But she had an excellent figure. She was a three out of ten head with a seven-and-a-half body. Maybe even an eight. He would probably fuck her if he had met her somewhere dark, like a nightclub and if he had had enough to drink.

She hooked the red hair behind her ear to reveal small pearl earrings, which Klaus liked.

'We're very, very busy with the investigation into the bombing, as you can imagine,' she said, perching on a chrome kitchen barstool. 'But obviously, Joachim is a student of the department connected to the Bushuis attack and we can't afford to ignore an exchange student going missing over the holiday period. We need your help, Klaus. Where could Joachim be? What other friends might he be visiting?'

She was looking at him with inquisitive eyes. He tried to select a label for the particular shade of blue that her irises were.

'Look,' he said. 'I'm as stumped as you are. I cried off sick. That's the last I heard of him. I can't think where he could be. I hope you find the poor guy soon. He owes me a round of drinks and thirty euros.'

As the detectives stood to leave, Klaus was quick to show them out, deftly pushing the door to his bedroom shut en route.

Breakfast *à trois* felt distinctly awkward to George. Together, they sat at the kitchen table in silence. Ad stared at the screen of his laptop, intently reading the responses to George's blogpost. Jasper sat playing with his balls through his pyjama bottoms and slurping his coffee loudly.

'Do you have to do that?' she asked him.

Jasper shrugged, stretched out his legs and farted loudly. He laughed heartily at himself. George wished he would go back into his room or go out. Men like Jasper were deliberately provocative. Looking for a reaction. She knew she was an easy target for a wind-up.

64

Ad looked up from the laptop. 'You're a pig, Jas. You're making the milk in my coffee curdle.'

'What is all this anyway?' he asked.

George told him about her blogpost and al Badaar's response.

Jasper gave a low whistle. 'You shouldn't be running the gauntlet with such a psycho,' he said, slamming his coffee cup down onto the table. He didn't use a coaster.

George's eyes locked on the cup like a heat-seeking missile. 'Use a bloody coaster, Jasper!' she said. 'Anyway, this matters. Some lunatic is out there, co-ordinating a bunch of suicide bombers. We're all in danger.'

Jasper stood up suddenly. George wondered if he was going to poke fun at her in some way but instead, he left the kitchen. Moments later, he reappeared, clutching a piece of paper.

'Look,' he said, placing the paper on the table.

It was a computer print-out of a photo. The colour photo was of a severed foot.

'What's that?' Ad asked, grimacing and putting his half-eaten sandwich on his plate.

George snatched up the print-out. The foot was large and veined. The toenails were neatly trimmed. The owner was clearly brown-skinned. There was an ornate tattoo around the ankle that looked like a pattern drawn by a henna artist.

'It's gone viral among the med students this morning,' Jasper boasted.

'Whose foot is this?' George asked.

Jasper flung himself back onto his chair and rocked backwards. 'It's a photo of the only intact body part recovered from the Bushuis library bombing. They call the tattoo an anatomic variation. Somebody somewhere did that tattoo or has seen that tattoo. The police wanted to keep the foot under wraps until they had identified the bomber. But apparently some old detective pissed off *someone* in the forensics team. So *someone* leaked it and it's doing the rounds on email.'

George's heart started to beat wildly. 'How much do you know about what forensics have found out?' she asked. Jasper had a propensity to show off. She looked into his bright blue eyes and wondered how well her bullshit detector was working after such a late night, surfing the web for mad Mujahidin, self-defence tactics and celebrity stalkers.

Jasper shrugged. 'Apparently the human remains had to be scooped up into bags. Apart from some teeth and this foot. They've not found a DNA match on the national criminal database but they've narrowed it down to an Asian man.'

'No surprise there if it's fundamentalist Muslims,' Ad said. 'That tattoo looks familiar though. Maybe it's common.'

'I think they're going to try to place the fillings in a couple of the molars. Pinpoint the country where they were originally put in the bomber's mouth. They can tell the bomber's age from the teeth and ossification of the bones in the foot. They can start to build a bit of a profile from there.'

Yes, he was showing off now. George could tell. But it didn't have the feel of bullshit.

'How do you know all this, Jasper?' George asked, sniffing hard.

Ad chuckled and pushed Jasper in the elbow. 'He's shagging none other than Doctor Marianne de Koninck, head honcho on the forensics team!' he said. 'Sender of terrible Santa cards, lonely divorcee and—'

'She's in great shape for an older woman,' Jasper said, grinning at Ad.

'So, have they found anything else interesting?' George asked. She wanted to press hard for information. She could feel the burn of curiosity inside. She needed facts like a fix. She realised, suddenly, this was more for her than just idle interest or the novelty and flattery of being needed as an informant by the police.

Jasper picked up the cafetiere of coffee and poured himself a fresh cup. 'Only thing I know is they found shreds of cardboard at the scene,' he said. 'Nobody can work out why. They thought maybe it was debris from the offices but Marianne was working in Utrecht and apparently it's the same score there. Cardboard. Weird eh?'

George looked at Ad's furrowed brow as he listened to his flatmate. *Cardboard. A placard? A box? Detritus from the bomb site?*

'Did they find any human remains there? In Utrecht?' she asked. She didn't think for a moment that Jasper would know any more at such an early stage.

'A head,' he said.

Ad spurted his mouthful of coffee all over his plate. George snatched up some kitchen roll and started to dab at the coffee-splashed tabletop with it. She stared at Jasper, open-mouthed. Dumbfounded.

'They've found an almost unscathed head,' Jasper said as though it was the most ordinary observation in the world. 'Must have been blown clean off like the foot in Bushuis. Blunt trauma. But everything else was incinerated or just blown to smithereens by the blast and fire.'

George winced and put her kitchen roll down. She tried to imagine the force that was strong enough to rip a man's head from his body.

Jasper leaned forward. His face was bright pink with what she presumed was excitement. His breath smelled of coffee and sore throat. Clearly, there was more …

'And get this,' he said. 'The Utrecht bomber was white.'

CHAPTER 8

3 January

'A dead white bomber changes everything,' George said. 'I want to get in touch with Marianne de Koninck. Ask her about the head … Do you think Jasper will give me her number?'

'I think you should bow out gracefully from this thing,' Ad said. 'Van den Bergen's been using you. Let him choose somebody else to spy for him.'

It had been Ad's idea to cycle down to *de hortus* – the botanical gardens. He thought she was looking overwrought. Thought the change of scenery would do her good. His treat. Now they stood side by side in the butterfly greenhouse. George breathed in deeply, wondering if this was the sort of private place where he might cross the line and kiss her again. She stared at a giant blue butterfly sitting on a glossy fat leaf of a breadfruit tree. It flapped its shimmering wings and she entertained the notion that the tiny disturbances it created in the humid air were somehow responsible for the chaotic whirl of thoughts and emotions that churned inside her; in equal parts intrigued by violent death; consumed by desire for Ad; in fear of her stalker.

Ad kicked at the ground. 'You're not listening, are you?'

George looked at him. Imagined his delicate-featured head detached from his shoulders. She pushed the ugly thought away.

'Come on. I'll buy you cake at the orangery,' Ad said.

Arm in arm, they brushed past the oversized leaves of a Chilean giant rhubarb, stretched out towards them in supplication like a beggar's hands. Past the man who had been standing in the plant's shadow, observing them for the last fifteen minutes. As George followed Ad back outside from the warm and tropical damp into the cold January air, in the furthest reaches of her peripheral vision, she thought she saw someone staring straight at her. She turned around quickly. There was nobody there.

In the orangery's airy café, George pushed a large piece of chocolate fudge cake around on her plate. Ad was chatting away about the first essay assignment of the year for Fennemans. But George wasn't listening. She was transfixed by one of the full-height windows. It reflected what was going on behind her, and in the glass, she thought she saw someone familiar. Was it Filip? She dropped her fork onto her plate with a clatter and turned around. Nobody there.

'You're acting really strangely, you know,' Ad said.

I'm smoking too much weed, George decided. *I'm getting a paranoid head on. That's all.*

'I had a late night,' she said. 'You know. Research.'

'Come over to Ratan's with me. I promised Rani I'd drop by. She's been driving me nuts, asking where he is. Has he been to football? Did he change his mind after the party? Like I'd know! Nobody's heard from him since before Christmas.'

Ad's mobile phone suddenly pinged. He picked it up and frowned at the screen. Then he smiled.

'Anything interesting?' George asked.

'It's Astrid. She's coming down this weekend.' He tapped away at his keypad with his thumb. He was smiling but George could see his demeanour was stiff. Maybe he felt on show; exposed with a cynical audience watching and judging his every move.

George delved into her coat pocket and pulled out a ten-euro note.

'Look,' she said. 'It's all I've got. I'm going. Thanks for this. I'll see you later. I've got Cambridge stuff to do.'

Ad looked up at her with eyes that seemed to betray both relief and disappointment. Or maybe he just looked up at her and felt nothing. George couldn't tell.

'It was my treat,' he said. 'I don't want your money. One friend to another. You needed a break.'

He held the bank note up to her. *One friend to another.* George swung her bag onto her shoulder and walked away, leaving Ad clutching her money. When he didn't run after her, she felt like somebody had put a hand inside her chest and squeezed her heart hard.

'Hey, honey,' Katja shouted as George entered the coffee shop. 'Come and join us.'

Katja and Jan were sitting together at a table by the till. Katja was wearing her pre-shift clothes: jeans and a pink, baggy sweater. They were drinking coffee. Jan was smoking the largest joint she had ever seen. It looked like a Cuban cigar.

'What's up with you, little Georgina?' Jan asked in English. 'You look like somebody took a piss in your *vla*.'

George threw her bag onto the floor and shrugged. 'You wouldn't believe me if I told you,' she said. She looked at Katja's backstreet Botox trout pout and forced herself to smile. 'Have either of you seen anyone hanging around my flat?' she asked.

Jan dragged hard on his spliff. 'You mean the spotty boy?'

'Ah, Mr Lover Man from before Christmas,' Katja nodded, knowingly.

George groaned and grabbed the joint from Jan. When she was satisfied that the tip was still dry and spit-free, she inhaled the pungent smoke and felt instantly as though somebody had pushed down hard on her head.

'His name's Filip,' she said. 'He's not that spotty.'

'Honey, you can do so much better,' Katja said. 'And I thought you had it going on with the other one. The pretty boy with glasses.'

George looked at her short fingernails. She looked anywhere but at Katja. Katja leaned forward and held her gently by the chin. George reluctantly met her neighbour's ice-blue eyes.

'There's nothing going on between me and Ad,' George said. 'He's a friend. The other one was just … just a booty call.'

Katja let her chin go and clapped her hands. 'If you're going to have such low standards, darling, you should sell it. Men would pay through the nose for a piece of that perfect round ass. You can sublet my room when I'm off shift.'

'No thanks,' George said, feeling the corners of her mouth jerk upwards into a smile. 'But cheers for the offer.'

'Any time, honey.' Katja drained the contents of her coffee cup and wrapped a piece of her blood-red hair around her index finger. 'Any time. It's just supply and demand.'

James Brown suddenly shrieked inside George's pocket, making her jump. She held her phone to her ear. It was Ad.

'Can you come over to Ratan's?' he said. 'I need your help.'

He needed her. Trying to make nice after *de hortus*? A mischievous glimmer of glee sparked within her, lighting up the dark places.

'Why?' she asked. 'I'm busy.'

'The landlady hasn't seen him either but she won't let me in his room. He could be ill in there or dead or anything, I suppose.'

'You think *I* can charm the landlady?' she asked.

There was a pause. 'The landlady's Black,' Ad said.

George sucked her teeth. This wasn't quite the show of contrition she was hoping for but it was something. 'He's just off Herengracht, isn't he? Hartenstraat. I'll see you in about ten. Wait outside.'

'Had you received any threats prior to the bombing?' van den Bergen asked Fennemans.

Fennemans sat behind his desk, running his fingers along the wooden tabletop. Van den Bergen felt like the academic had cultivated the wide-eyed, questioning appearance of a bewildered child. He had not worn that face when he had given George McKenzie a hard time and called her 'Little Miss'.

'None whatsoever, Detective,' Fennemans said.

'It's Inspector.'

'*So* sorry. As I've already told you, I can only assume that the Bushuis bombing is unrelated to the faculty. That the terrorists just selected a university building at random.'

'And do you have any connections to Utrecht synagogue?'

'None whatsoever.'

Van den Bergen surreptitiously looked around Fennemans' office. He noticed the books bearing his name, prominently displayed on a shelf. He noticed that there were no family photographs on the desk. But there was a framed photograph on the wall of Fennemans standing outside the temple carved into the rockface in Petra.

Van den Bergen pointed to the photo. 'I see you've travelled in the Middle East.'

Fennemans tutted. 'Of course. I'm a senior lecturer specialising in the politics of the Middle East. Jordan is one of my favourite places. The snorkelling there is simply superb.' He laced thick fingers together over a yellow silk shirt. 'Have you been?'

'No.' Van den Bergen sniffed and wondered whether now was the time to say what he knew would result in a shit-storm of almighty proportions blowing up around him. He thumbed his stubble and tapped his teeth with his Biro. 'You taught Janneke Polman, didn't you?'

Van den Bergen watched Fennemans' reactions carefully. He sat perfectly still. He didn't flinch. He continued to smile inanely with those ridiculous child's teeth that he had. But van den Bergen noticed the pupils in Fennemans' eyes shrink suddenly to the size of pinheads. At the same time, almost spontaneously, a sheen of sweat appeared on his upper lip and forehead.

'Why, yes. I seem to remember she was one of my students. She dropped out, though. Mental ill health. Poor girl.' Fennemans' voice was even and calm. Polite interest. Nothing more. 'I hope she's not involved in the bombings in some way.'

'She's dead. Murdered.'

The small teeth disappeared and gave way to a gasp and raised eyebrows. His pupils dilated now. 'Oh, no. What a pity. Such a waste. When was this?'

'Christmas Eve. Around lunchtime.' Van den Bergen was stabbed in the chest by stomach acid. He was careful not to show his discomfort in front of Fennemans. 'Tell me, Dr Fennemans. What were you doing on Christmas Eve around lunchtime?'

'What are you insinuating?' Fennemans gripped the edge of the desk and stood up. 'I had lunch with a friend and then travelled down to my mother's for Christmas.'

'I'd like the name and telephone number of your friend, please. An address too. And your mother's contact details.' Van den Bergen started to scribble on his notepad but noticed Fennemans getting redder in the face. He paused and peered up at a very agitated-looking man.

'Are you harassing me, Inspector?'

'Just trying to eliminate people from our enquiries. That's all. Especially in light of the Rosa Bianco case.'

Fennemans walked briskly to the door and opened it. He was twitching visibly now. 'That case was thrown out,' he said, spitting slightly as he spoke. 'It was a miscarriage of justice that it ever reached court. I was the real victim there. She almost had my reputation in tatters. I had a breakdown!'

Van den Bergen remained in his seat and bounced his right foot across his left knee. Rosa Bianco. A sweet girl with the delicacy and innocence in her face that her name promised. Tamara's roommate in her first year at university.

73

'Was that before or after you raped her and beat her to a pulp?'

'*Goodbye*, Inspector,' Fennemans said.

The statuesque landlady opened the door for George and glowered at Ad.

'He's late on his rent. Not like him. Ratan's normally a good kid,' she said in heavily accented Antillean Dutch. 'You sure you're not police?'

George gave the woman her best smile. All teeth. 'I swear. Just worried friends,' she said. 'Thanks. We won't touch anything.'

George advanced inside the dark room. Ad skulked behind her, shoulders hunched. She saw that the landlady still stood on the threshold, watching with meaty arms folded over her floral viscose-clad bosom. 'I promise,' George said.

The woman nodded and left.

Ad drew back the curtains and coughed as the dust was disrupted on the heavy mustard velvet. George held her hand up to her eyes. The sudden warm sunlight felt like an invasion in the cold room. She shuddered.

'I don't like snooping around someone's space, you know,' she said.

Ad stood over a desk underneath the window. He leafed through some papers and picked up a book. George approached and squinted at the red, black and white cover. The edges were curling upwards from frequent use.

'*The Gun and the Olive Branch*. I've got that,' she said. 'Israeli–Arab conflict. Pro-Palestine.' She was close to Ad now. She could smell the sandalwood scent of his aftershave.

She took a step back and looked around. A coffee mug stood on the bookshelf. She peered inside. Mould grew in round, green blotches on the surface of the half-drunk contents. But the room was generally clean. Ratan's bed was made. Clothes were hung in an orderly manner on an industrial clothes rack. No cup rings anywhere. No marks of him being a slob. *So why the mould?*

74

George lifted the cup to her nose and sniffed. Coffee with milk.

'He's not been here since before Christmas judging by this cup. At least not for a good few days. And he must have last been here after dark,' she said.

'Because the curtains were shut?' Ad suggested.

'Right. He never kept his date with Rani. My guess is he hasn't come back since the party.'

George walked over to a cork pinboard that was screwed to the wall. Three eight-by-ten-inch photographs were stuck to it with drawing pins. Ratan with Mum and Dad outside a house painted white. The paint was peeling. The sun was bright. It looked like a suburb of somewhere far away. Mumbai. Ratan with other young Indian men his age in a room, drinking Royal Challenge beer. University friends maybe. Ratan on a tropical beach with two girls who looked Thai. Gawky. Wearing shorts. Bare feet. Bare ankles.

George felt as though everything had ground to a halt inside her body. Her mouth prickled cold with realisation.

'Ad. Come and look at this.'

Ad drew near and studied the photograph she was pointing to with a slightly trembling finger.

'What am I looking at?' he asked, shaking his head.

'You remember you said you recognised that tattoo from Jasper's photograph? The one of the bomber's foot?'

Ad's face suddenly seemed to drain of all colour. 'Oh, Jesus,' he said.

CHAPTER 9

Later

'The Executive Board of the university wants a head on a platter,' Kamphuis said. He rubbed his naked lady statue and rocked back on his chair. 'I'm going to give them yours, Paul.'

Van den Bergen sat in the too-low visitor's chair in front of Kamphuis' desk and felt a stabbing, grinding sensation in his hip. With a surreptitious glance at his watch, he worked out that he had about an hour before the last lot of painkillers wore off. Then he would be in trouble.

'So tell me. Why are you harassing Fennemans?'

Van den Bergen sighed. 'Questioning. Not harassing. Janneke Polman was a lodger of Fennemans and overnight went from top-drawer student to dropout. I bumped into Fennemans at Central Station when me and Dirk were heading off to Maastricht to interview the imam.'

Kamphuis set the metal balls clicking on his retro desk-toy. But he was still staring at van den Bergen with obvious contempt. 'And? Central Station hasn't got a bloody restraining order on a university academic, you dick.'

Van den Bergen was careful not to let Kamphuis see his irritation. *You are stone. An obstinate lump of stone. You are impenetrable and unmoving.* 'But Polman was there,' he said. 'I

76

remembered this purple bobble hat. It was so distinctive. And then her mother has the same one in her hands when I visited …'

Van den Bergen went quiet. He felt his eye begin to tic and hastily put his glasses on in a bid to conceal it.

'*You went to the girl's house?*' Kamphuis shouted. 'It's Nieuwman's case! You're a senior inspector, you cretin. As such, *you* are tasked with responsibility for solving the biggest terrorism mystery Amsterdam has ever seen. And here you are, jerking around with a bog standard homicide of some dropout kid who was probably hocked up to a loan shark or dealer.' Kamphuis rubbed his face. 'Why? Why do you always get knee deep in everybody else's shit, Paul?'

'Rosa Bianco,' he said simply.

Kamphuis threw his arms in the air, revealing sweat stains that had turned the fabric of his red shirt a dark ruby colour, seeping outwards in a ring like life's blood from a mortal wound. Van den Bergen was reminded of the tragic dark stain on the floor in Janneke's parental home.

'Fennemans was acquitted,' Kamphuis said through gritted teeth. 'And I've got enough to worry about without having his heavyweight, fat-fee-charging legal representation, not to mention the public prosecutor coming down on my head all because Dr Vim spent an unnecessary ten weeks in pre-trial detention. And now,' he was violently poking himself in the chest, '*my* senior inspector is persecuting him on the basis of circumstantial evidence. Nice, Paul. Really nice.'

'He's got to be a prime suspect in Polman's murder.'

Kamphuis tapped his finger on the desktop. Rata tat tat. 'Where's the ringleader for my suicide bombings? Where's al Badaar?'

Van den Bergen groaned softly. 'I'm going to pick up a prescription in a minute. The pharmacist is a Muslim woman in a headscarf. Shall I bring her in? Will you be happy then?'

Kamphuis pulled a sandwich out of his desk drawer and started eating noisily. 'Just get me a Muslim fundamentalist so I can kiss the minister's arse without the shitty aftertaste.'

'I've got to see him now!' George shouted over the counter at the uniformed officer.

He looked at her with cool detachment. Remote and getting further away like an ice floe at low tide. George sat heavily on her mounting agitation. 'I know he's here,' she said, injecting politesse into her stricken voice. 'They said he was in a meeting. But please, I need to speak to him urgently.'

The policeman eyed George up and down like some security scanner at Schiphol airport: checking for anomalies, bullshit and bombs. She noted that he didn't subject Ad to the same sharp-eyed scrutiny.

'Tell me what it's about,' he finally said.

When van den Bergen appeared in the Prinsengracht foyer, he ushered George and Ad quickly to a private room. George had been storing up a verbal storm to unleash on him after he had put the phone down on her. But now, seeing him harried, worn down, haggard, with demons on his shoulders, the storm dissipated and left her with only dead calm.

She tossed the photograph of Ratan standing on the Thai beach onto the table. Van den Bergen picked it up. He put on reading glasses that hung around his neck on a cord and squinted down his nose at the photograph. His eyebrows bunched above questioning, bloodshot eyes.

'What …?' he asked

'Your so-called bomber,' George said. 'Look at the tattoo on his ankle.'

Ad cleared his throat as if to remind van den Bergen that he was in the room too. 'Ratan Patil. He's my … our friend from uni. We were all at a party together the night before the bombing of Bushuis library. He's been missing ever since.'

Van den Bergen rubbed the grey, early afternoon stubble on his chin. He frowned at George over the glasses.

'How do you know about the tattoo?' he asked her.

'This guy—' George began.

Ad put his arm in front of George. 'There's a forensics photo gone viral among the med students. A friend showed it to us the other day. By chance, we—'

'We asked Ratan's landlady if we could take a look in his room to check he hadn't collapsed or anything,' George interjected. 'I spotted that photo on his pinboard.'

Van den Bergen breathed in deeply. He pursed his lips and looked again at the photograph of the smiling Ratan: knobbly knees, ears sticking out, clearly delighted by his Thai female companions.

'Do you think he was radicalised at college?' he asked.

George mentally tutted and rolled her eyes. 'This guy's a Hindu,' she said. 'Ratan *Patil*. Not Muslim.' She could feel a scathing comment brewing. She tried to bite it back but it was too hard. 'Is it just that they all look the same to you?' she said.

Van den Bergen thumped the table so hard that George jumped. Ad cleared his throat.

'She didn't mean—' Ad said.

'Listen, you two …' van den Bergen said.

He leaned in closely. George could see the open pores on his nose and smell oranges on his breath.

'… I have something tantamount to a signed confession from the leader of a fundamentalist Islamic terror cell,' he said. 'My bosses want this case solved yesterday and—'

'Ratan was not Muslim!' George shouted. 'Ratan was a beer-swilling Hindu from Mumbai. And we've heard your second victim in Utrecht—'

'George, don't!' Ad said.

'—was white!'

Van den Bergen straightened up abruptly and breathed in

sharply. 'How do you know about that? Where are you getting your information from?'

'It doesn't matter,' George said. 'We're getting it. Okay? And I can see from your reaction that it's good. So unless your al Badaar is secretly radicalising infidels in their sleep, I'd say you're hunting the wrong man.'

Van den Bergen sat in silence. He looked at George and then at Ad. He shook his head and ran his large hand through his thatch of platinum hair. He smiled.

'Cagney and bloody Lacey. I've got Cagney and bloody Lacey on the case.' He turned to Ad. 'Which one are you? The blonde or the brunette?'

Ad opened and closed his mouth. He was almost grey. George could see that Ad wasn't used to police attention. She wanted to take his hand and squeeze it but her thoughts were stalled by van den Bergen standing.

'Come with me, you two. I need you to do something for me, and it's not pleasant.'

It was cold in there, close to where they kept the bodies. The floors were tiled and the light was harsh. George's breath came quick as she and Ad followed van den Bergen down the aseptic corridors of the Forensics Institute.

'The national forensics centre is in The Hague,' van den Bergen said, 'but we wanted to get an analysis from the Utrecht site here in Amsterdam. In case there were commonalities between Utrecht and the first bombing.' Then he stopped suddenly at a set of double doors and turned round. His expression was grim. 'Wait here.'

George fiddled with the buttons on her flimsy jacket, wishing she had worn a jumper that morning. And yet, despite the cold which made her nose tingle at the tip, she knew her armpits would be ringed with sweat. She could feel the moisture running down past her bra onto the waistband of her jeans. Adrenalin.

She looked at Ad. His grey pallor betrayed fear, or was it that he was going to throw up?

'Have you ever seen a dead body before?' she asked, tugging his sleeve gently.

He pushed his steel-framed glasses up his nose and smiled weakly at her.

'Not unless you count my dog, Bart,' he said. 'You?'

She shook her head. Suspected what van den Bergen was about to show them. She shivered at the thought.

The double doors flapped open. Van den Bergen emerged.

'Follow me,' he said. 'We're ready.'

George fell into step with Ad behind the inspector. Had she bitten off more than she could chew? Ad took her hand. It felt warm and comforting. She felt like they were children venturing together into a dark forest full of ill intent and misadventure.

They entered a cluttered lab, where serious-looking people busied themselves over tiny test-tubes, pipettes and microscopes. Their heads were covered by white mop caps, they wore surgical masks over their mouths, white coats over their clothes.

Van den Bergen led them to a windowless office where a woman was already seated. She was dressed in green scrubs. Her caramel-coloured hair was cut short into the nape of her long neck, which suited her sharp features. Though she was relatively youthful-looking, she exuded cold authority which betrayed her age. George calculated that she was probably about forty years old.

'These are the kids for the ID,' van den Bergen said simply.

The woman rose and held her hand out to greet George first and then Ad. George was sure she could see a flicker of recognition pass between Ad and the woman.

'I'm Dr Marianne de Koninck,' she said. 'I'm the head of forensic pathology team.'

Van den Bergen pulled two bent wood chairs out for George and Ad. He indicated that they should sit.

81

'Dr de Koninck here has just come up from the autopsy on the only deceased victim from the Utrecht blast,' he said. 'We believe it's the bomber.'

George sniffed and took a deep breath. The contents of the office were unremarkable: filing cabinets, a light box for viewing x-rays, desk, lamp, chairs. She realised that they weren't going to be shown a cadaver after all. She exhaled heavily with relief.

'Dr de Koninck. If you will,' van den Bergen said.

The pathologist took some large photographs out of a brown envelope. She laid them on the table. George looked down at them and gasped. The photographs showed only a head, covered at the neck with green gauze. It was not apparent that the head had been decapitated but from what Jasper had said, she knew that only the head had been found severed and intact.

George gulped down bile and a late breakfast of stale pain au chocolat. She clutched her hand to her chest. 'Joachim.'

Ad coughed.

'Bin?' was all he said.

Van den Bergen whipped a wastepaper basket out of nowhere just in time for Ad to vomit into it. George wrinkled her nose as the acidic smell stung in her nostrils. She rubbed Ad's back, pulling some tissues out of her jeans pocket. The pathologist walked to the water cooler in the corner of the room and came back to the desk, proffering a plastic cup to Ad.

'Okay?' she asked. 'Drink. And don't worry. You're not the first.'

Ad nodded, clinging to the bin with white knuckles.

George rubbed the knees of her jeans, counting: one, two, three on the left. One, two, three on the right. *Keep it together*, she told herself. *Oh, God. I hate the smell of sick.*

The pathologist sat down, seemingly unmoved by Ad's outburst. 'The inspector tells me you two have just identified the first bomber as a student.'

George nodded.

'So, you know this one too, then,' the pathologist said, looking down at the nightmarish images.

George nodded. 'You bet. We both do,' she said, nodding towards Ad. 'This is Joachim Guttentag. German exchange student. From Heidelberg. Total ...' George wanted to say what she really thought of the arrogant, racist jerk. But then she looked at the mournful photo of a lifeless boy. The derision died in her throat. 'He's, er, was, I mean, a bit of a ... er, not wildly popular. Him and his pal, Klaus, are into ritualistic duelling and all that old fraternity, funny handshake crap.'

Ad breathed out deeply beside her. His voice sounded wobbly and unsure. 'He's on our politics course. Was. He was going home for Christmas.' He blew his nose loudly. 'He told me about his plans when I asked him to come for a coffee with the others at the end of term. Him and Klaus were getting the train down south. They were going to some meet with his frat buddies in Heidelberg before going home to their families.'

George sucked her teeth. 'Poor Joachim. My God.'

She forced herself to look at the images. Joachim's eyes were unfocussed, bloodshot and dull, his complexion too yellow to belong to the living. George could see a band of dark purple bruising just below the jawline, before the green gauze concealed what did or did not lie beneath. This was a photograph of a shell. Grief suddenly washed over her and threatened to overcome her.

'What happened to him?' she asked.

The pathologist spoke quickly, with an air of brisk efficiency and complete detachment.

'It's an interesting case. There's evidence of subconjunctival haemorrhage, as you can see from the bloodshot eyes, and the indented fracture to the skull and extra-dural haemorrhage, which you can't see in the photo, make it clear there was blunt trauma ante-mortem.'

'What do you mean?' George asked.

'The deceased was hit with something like a hammer before

83

death but not killed by the blow.' She pointed out the bruising beneath the jaw with the tip of a Biro. 'The contusions you see around the jawline indicate strangulation or hanging. There's some peculiar scarring on the cheeks on both sides and then a large, deep scar down the left side of the face, here. But they're old wounds. I was wondering if it could be self-harm, although subjects suffering from depression normally cut their arms. But now you've told me he's a dueller, it makes sense that they're the ritual scars from mensur fencing. We were going to check dental records but what the inspector needs is a quick ID and it looks like you've given it to him.'

George put one hand on Ad's shaking arm and shuffled in her seat. 'So he was beaten and tortured before he blew himself up. Is that what you're saying?'

The pathologist nodded. 'This doesn't look like straightforward terrorism, if there is such a thing. Nobody has ever seen a suicide bomber look like this before, even where we've been able to retrieve large sections of the body that haven't suffered blast injuries or flash burns.'

'And this guy is white,' George said.

The pathologist nodded. 'Yes. Exactly.'

'It's possible he was a convert,' van den Bergen said. He had perched on the edge of the pathologist's desk and now shifted his position with a grunt. He took off his glasses and started to polish the lenses with the cuff of his shirt.

'Jesus! He ain't no Muslim convert,' George said softly, reflectively. 'This guy was right-wing. Fascist.'

'Aha,' van den Bergen said simply.

George wondered if there was sarcasm in his response.

Van den Bergen exchanged satisfied glances with the pathologist. He stood up, unfolding his tall frame until he towered over the room like a king. He smiled at George. His face suddenly looked softer, as though the force of gravity now bore down on him just a little less than it had before.

'Thank you, Miss McKenzie. Mr Karelse,' he said. 'You've been a great help.'

The smell of Ad's vomit and the photographs suddenly made George feel trapped in the room. She wanted to leave. But as she grabbed the handle to the door, the nagging feeling that van den Bergen hadn't made the same intellectual leap that she had stayed her hand. She turned to the inspector.

'You know what this means, don't you?' she said. 'You're not looking for a bunch of Mujahidin.'

'What do you mean?' van den Bergen asked.

'An Indian Hindu and a right-wing white man? Probably Lutheran. Both exchange students. One clearly tortured or beaten before the explosion. Forced into whatever he did. Untraceable declarations that Maastricht Muslim fundamentalists did it? And one of the bombings was outside a synagogue.'

'What's your point?'

George looked to the pathologist for a reaction but found none. She looked back to van den Bergen's hungry eyes.

'Have you thought this could be the work of neo-Nazis trying to make Muslims look bad?' she said. 'Maybe Joachim was going to blow the whistle on something he was privy to. Instead, he got popped himself. Just saying ...'

He followed the boy down the street with phantom-light steps, calculating how he might best take this one. This was just part of his reconnaissance, but preparation was always key, he found. He liked to observe how they moved first; to gauge their strength and agility. It would influence everything from his choice of weapon to the time of day he would make his move.

This one would not present a challenge. In fact, none of them would really. They were all physically inferior and psychologically unprepared.

As he made his way to the faculty on Nieuwe Prinsengracht, thinking about his craftsman's tools and revelling in being the hunter hiding deliciously in plain view, he noticed that she was not there. He felt a mixture of frustration and panic kindle inside him. Here the rest of them were. Chatting about their Christmases. Scandalised by the Utrecht bomb. Bemoaning their academic responsibilities or nagging parents or how stony broke they were. But no sign of her.

As people greeted him lethargically, wishing him a Happy New Year – a sentiment which was almost certainly not backed up by genuine interest and certainly not affection – he quickly switched from planning his next abduction to wondering how he could hurt her for standing him up.

CHAPTER 10

4 January

'So, tell me. What were Joachim's religious leanings?' van den Bergen asked the red-faced German boy in the visitor's chair. The harder the tone he used, the brighter the boy's ears became. Other than that, van den Bergen could see he was like an impenetrable Black Forest fortress.

'He was Lutheran. Of course. Like every good white German should be.'

Van den Bergen shifted in the borrowed desk chair of Vim Fennemans, grimacing at the pervasive smell of unwashed feet. It was ironic that he should have requisitioned this office for the interviews, given that Fennemans and the university's board were now making noises about suing him personally for harassment and slander. Kamphuis was only half-heartedly trying to intervene. At this rate, he could lose his job, his flat and his allotment. Screwed on a grand scale. But panic over that would have to wait.

He leaned forward to try to assert physical dominance over the boy. Biedermeier was, after all, big in that meaty, almost American, way.

'Come on! Joachim was the perpetrator in a suicide bombing. A group of Muslim fundamentalists are claiming it as a planned triumph in a religious war on Europe. Think, Klaus! Who could

Joachim have become pally with without your knowledge? What were his links to Ratan Patil?'

The boy shrugged and looked blankly out of the window. 'I told your detectives when they rudely descended on my pad, I don't know a thing. This tragedy has come as a terrible shock. My personal loss is enormous.'

Van den Bergen scribbled in his pad that the boy's response sounded flat and rehearsed. Biedermeier was completely lacking in the sniffling symptoms of grief. Come to think of it …

'Your flu seems to have cleared up,' he said.

'What?'

'You told my detectives that you had been suffering from flu.'

Van den Bergen wondered what his gut was telling him, when Biedermeier started to chuckle almost silently.

'I have a strong German constitution,' he said.

Perhaps his gut was merely telling him he was due another antacid. Biedermeier's body language was utterly unfathomable. And yet, van den Bergen felt certain that this boy's story was more complex than being a case of, 'It could just as easily have been me, if only fate hadn't intervened to save my Aryan hide with man-flu.' Van den Bergen didn't believe in fate.

There was a knock at the door.

Van den Bergen looked at his watch. 'Enter!'

When the door opened and he saw the figure silhouetted by the harsh, corridor strip light, he felt a stabbing pain in his chest.

'Excuse me. Excuse me. Sorry, can I get through?'

There was a flurry of politesse within earshot and George looked up to see Ad, making his way to her, along the line in the lecture theatre. He was wearing her favourite navy cable-knit jumper and reefer jacket. She imagined him a Dutch sailor on shore leave. Exotic in her mind's eye.

'Howdy, partner,' Ad said to George, dropping his pens from his unzipped bag. He bent double to pick them off the ground, banging his head on the desk's underside on the way back up. Not so exotic.

'Howdy,' George said, feeling her spirits lift slightly. She mimed blowing the smoke from her finger pistol and put it in her imaginary holster.

Throat clearing and a cough over the PA system. Fennemans. George caught sight of him down the front, preparing to hold court in his too-tight jacket over his too-large gut.

'When you're ready, Mr Karelse,' Fennemans yelled into the whistling microphone. 'The whole of Year Three has been waiting for your arrival. Perhaps we can begin now.'

George could see the flush of hot embarrassment creeping into Ad's hairline as the girl next to her willingly, gladly, moved to let Ad sit down.

Fennemans embarked on his monotonous adventures into the politics surrounding the first Gulf War. The lecture theatre fell almost silent but for his voice. Only pens scratching away on pads could be heard.

When Ad started to write in her notebook, George was only dimly aware of it. He clicked his fingers and delivered her from her studious reverie. She looked down and read what he had written. His hand was easy to read, neat, straightforward, uncomplicated.

Biedermeier is sitting over there.

She looked at Ad and furrowed her brow. She mouthed, 'Where?' He pointed to the far side of the lecture theatre.

She peered over the heads of the other students, strained her neck to scan the tiers full of conscientious scribblers. Then she spotted him. Dark blond cropped hair. Florid, sow-like neck. The smart casual clothes covering the bulky, honed body that screamed upper-middle-class jock. His type looked the same in mainland Europe as they did at Cambridge.

She started to write on her pad, enjoying the intimacy it created between her and Ad. Her writing was tight and hard to read but she knew Ad would decipher it.

Why's he not locked up?

Ad shrugged. More writing.

V. d. Bergen has questioned him about Joachim. Everyone's being pulled into Fennemans' office to be interviewed this morning.

George frowned.

And?

Remko told me Klaus cried off going to Heidelberg at the last minute.

George narrowed her eyes and looked over at Klaus. Had it been an *et tu, Brute* moment for Joachim and his lost head? Was poor, sweet, legless Ratan's only crime the crime of being brown?

Ratan had stood up to Klaus at the start of the year. It was in the cafeteria at Bushuis. Klaus had started pestering Rani about being Sri Lankan. Why wasn't she wearing a headscarf like the other good little Muslim girls? How come countries like Sri Lanka, which had been colonial outposts in grand, European empires, had done nothing but tear themselves apart with civil war since the white man gave them back to the natives? Weren't they, like children, incapable of ruling themselves?

Rani had blanched. Tears stood in her eyes. Then Ratan had stood on his tiptoes and fought her corner, publicly reviling Klaus and branding him indelibly as an ignorant bully.

Had that been the start? Had Klaus delivered Ratan and

Joachim as incendiary mouthpieces for a rhetoric that Hitler had started and Biedermeier's pals wanted to finish?

A rustle of whispers sparked up among the students around her. George blotted out the peripheral white noise. But Fennemans had started to walk and talk with his roving mic headset. Madonna with a paunch and a small dick heading straight for her. Ad nudged her but it was too late.

'This is a whole heap of shit,' van den Bergen said to Elvis. He rubbed his face and sipped sourly at his coffee. He started to flick his Biro against his front teeth in a way he knew annoyed everyone but which was somehow useful for marshalling his thoughts. 'Okay. We've got an academic pervert who has potentially murdered a student, strutting round like some fucking bantam cock, parading his *legal* immunity. And we've got a really bloody strange right-wing German kid—'

'Possibly the most likely prime suspect yet,' Elvis interjected. 'I'm hearing from the other students that Biedermeier and Joachim had a falling out before Christmas. There's your motive.'

'Yes. Young Klaus arose from his timely deathbed better than Jesus or The Terminator put together. Now he's parading his amazing *flu-busting* immunity around the same department.' He grabbed at his stomach, although really it was his head that hurt. 'What do you think?'

Elvis sat in the corner chair, behind the door. He swung his thin right leg over his left knee and fingered his sleek, dark sideburns. 'Did you see Fennemans' face when he showed up in the middle of Biedermeier's interview? Pretending he'd forgotten something for his lecture. If looks could kill … He's out to crucify you, boss. Sorry.'

Van den Bergen could see a cruel glimmer of schadenfreude behind Elvis' eyes. He shook his head. 'I know. But what bothers me more is there seemed to be some kind of connection between Fennemans and Biedermeier.'

There was a knock on the door. Elvis opened it and told the girl who was next to wait in the corridor.

''Course there's a connection, boss. Biedermeier is Fennemans' student,' he said when the door was firmly closed to prying ears.

Van den Bergen stretched out until his hip cracked. 'No. I mean there's something complicit between them. For a fraction of a second there, I could see ... Shit. I just don't know. And in the meantime, we're wading through taking alibis and statements from hundreds of kids and staff in this building alone. What if there's another bomb because we were just too slow with the paperwork?'

He thumped the desk. 'Bollocks!'

'Give me that, McKenzie,' Fennemans said. He held his hand out for the pad to be passed along the line.

George looked up at him. He was looking more teddy boy than Barry Manilow today. *Down with the kids. Giant anus.*

'It's just notes,' she said, putting her arm across the writing.

'Pass it.'

Think before you speak. Don't rise to it. Think.

'Why? So you can read it out to everyone and take the piss? This ain't nursery school. I don't have to give you nothing.'

As soon as George had said the words, she regretted it. *Stupid, stupid, stupid!* The words had trotted out on prickly, hairy legs.

Fennemans looked at her with a face that rippled merrily with smug satisfaction.

'Get out of my class, McKenzie,' he said. 'Now!' He pointed to the door emphatically.

George sucked her teeth and started to pack her belongings into her rucksack. Excitement blistered up on everybody's faces. Heads turning round. Softly spoken exchanges. Shocked at the English girl.

Ad stood abruptly and hastily packed his notepad and pen into his bag too. George paused momentarily to watch him.

'Hey!' she whispered. 'You don't need to—'

'Come on,' he said.

The students sitting between George and the end of the row all stood to let her and Ad pass. All eyes were on them. George felt emboldened by Ad's support. Proud. And at the same time, utterly annoyed at herself.

As she reached Fennemans, he folded his arms and treated her to a mean smile that turned the corners of his thin-lipped mouth downwards.

'If I don't have you thrown off this course, at the very least I'm going to have you excluded from lectures, Little Miss,' he said. 'I'm going to put you under my personal, beady-eyed supervision. You won't be able to shirk so easily then, will you?'

Don't play into his hands, George counselled herself.

She felt Ad place a reassuring hand on her shoulder and she bit back the words. *Fuck you, Fennemans. You bouffant ponce.*

'Sit down, Karelse!' Fennemans barked at Ad.

'No,' came Ad's response.

George felt lightheaded. Adrenalin picked her up like a rabid dog and shook her body around. She couldn't remember anybody in her twenty years fighting her corner before. Certainly not in front of a room full of her peers, aching to see a gladiatorial show-down.

As she left the lecture theatre, George caught a glimpse of Klaus. He turned his scarred face towards her. His eyes locked with hers for a shred of a second. She felt fear blossoming in her stomach like bindweed. Her confrontation with Fennemans was instantly shelved. Breathing more quickly now, she pushed the doors to the lecture theatre open and broke the connection with Klaus.

George marched straight to Fennemans' office, with Ad following at a brisk pace.

'What are you doing?' Ad asked. 'I thought we could go for a coffee.'

George said nothing. She kept walking until she was there. She could hear van den Bergen's rich, tired voice beyond the door. She didn't knock.

Van den Bergen was sitting behind Fennemans' desk with legs outstretched. Collar open, outdated, double-breasted suit. The beginnings of a white goatee today, which she liked. A butch-looking girl with shorn hair, whom George didn't know personally but recognised from the odd lecture, was sitting in one of the institutional imitation leather armchairs by the door. A man, roughly in his thirties wearing a leather jacket and jeans, sat and took notes in a pad. A detective probably. One of van den Bergen's flock, George decided.

'Didn't you see the sign?' the younger detective asked. 'Do not disturb.'

Van den Bergen leaned back in the chair and folded his arms behind his head.

'Detectives Cagney and Lacey. Good morning. You know, you're interrupting official police business?' he said.

George spied the mirth behind his grey eyes. The butch student shuffled forward on her seat, uncomfortable.

'Can I go now?' she asked. 'I've told you everything I know.'

Van den Bergen nodded and thanked her. When she had left, the small room still felt too full with the four of them. George could smell Fennemans' sweaty feet and dog biscuits. She hated that smell of ridicule. She rolled her eyes and sucked her teeth in a quiet, reflex rebellion. Sat down on the chair with Ad perched on the arm.

'Do you want me to take notes?' the younger detective asked van den Bergen.

George had seen him at the police station, around the Bushuis bomb site but she had never spoken to him. She didn't like the way he looked her up and down with miserly black eyes that were too close together. Stupid quiff haircut. He put her in mind of a young, thin Fennemans.

Van den Bergen laced his fingers over his lap and pressed his thumbs together, smiling like an indulgent teacher.

'No, Elvis. Let's hear what my two young friends have to say that's so urgent,' he said.

George sat on the edge of her seat.

'Klaus Biedermeier,' she said.

'Yes?' van den Bergen asked, raising his eyebrows.

'You haven't arrested him.'

'Why do you think we would want to arrest him?' Elvis said.

Van den Bergen held up his hand. 'Let Georgina speak,' he said.

'He's got to be your prime suspect. Hasn't he?' George said, hotly.

Van den Bergen stroked the fledgling goatee on his chin. 'He doesn't look much like a Muslim cleric.'

'Oh, come on!' George said. 'He could have rigged that bullshit on the web.'

Van den Bergen leaned forward. 'Leave the detecting to the detectives, Georgina. We can't charge Biedermeier with anything. His alibis check out. There's not a shred of hard evidence to link him to Joachim's or Ratan's death. If we made convictions based only on hunches, the Netherlands police would be no better than a gang of gossiping pensioners, would it? I'm not in the business of witch-hunting.'

George thought it odd that the bequiffed detective snorted. But she was more preoccupied by the embarrassment that had sneaked up on her like an unwelcome visitor. She flushed hot.

The shame of making a scene twice in the space of thirty minutes drove George from the office quicker than a wet sneeze on a packed tube train carriage.

'Coffee, then?' Ad asked as they trudged out into the cold comfort of the winter sunshine.

George nodded.

'Don't worry about Fennemans,' he said.

She shook her head, suddenly, unexpectedly feeling tears pool in her eyes. She looked away so that Ad would not see. Undid the lock on her bike in silence, trying to digest the curdling, indigestible knot of regret, fear and curiosity.

'Have you got any Charlie on you?' Klaus asked Fennemans.

He gripped Fennemans' arm and then let go, realising that, if anyone came into the men's toilets at that moment, it would look strange.

'Don't even speak to me, unless we're in class and it has to do with your studies,' Fennemans said. He spoke with all the venom of a cornered cobra. 'Certainly not while the police are here.'

'But the guy's not in his room.'

Klaus had had a difficult morning. Returning to the wholly abnormal 'normality' of the new term without Joachim was hitting him harder than he had anticipated. In fact, it was unexpected. He felt cold and clammy. He definitely needed a pick-me-up and wasn't prepared to wait.

Fennemans stood at the urinal. Klaus could see he was trying to piss but had dried up with an audience.

'Get out, Klaus.'

Klaus felt panic surge through him. 'I've got to score.'

'Not my problem. Goddammit! I can't pee with you watching.' Fennemans hastily zipped his trousers and washed his hands.

'Will I see you at the club?' Klaus asked, feeling somehow that Fennemans' scorn felt almost like his father's.

'Just keep your mouth shut, Biedermeier.'

When they sat together, coddled in the UV glow and heavy, leafy stink of Jan's coffee shop, George turned to look at Ad. She pushed away the desperate ache; the longing to be held by somebody that gave a hoot. She dredged her soul for the discipline that she knew was buried there, beneath the frustration. She found it, pulled it to the surface and cleaned it off. And then she turned her attention to the task in hand, like always.

'We're all exposed,' she said. 'I think everyone on that course is a target.'

Ad nodded. Thoughtful brown eyes framed by the bows of his strong, dark eyebrows.

'What was that thing with Filip before Christmas?' he asked.

'Nothing. Listen. We need to find out more about Klaus if the cops are just going to sit on their hands.'

'What do you mean?' Ad put his arm along the length of the backrest behind her.

'How about you cosy up to Klaus? See what he and his Nazi friends get up to.'

Ad threw his head back and laughed. 'You're funny!' he said. Then he stopped laughing. 'You're not serious?'

George placed her Cambridge mug on the table carefully. She aligned the handle perfectly at ninety degrees to the side of the coaster. She pulled a cigarette from her packet and tapped it on the side. She flicked her lighter into life and dragged hard. Exhaled the plumes of blue smoke. Locked onto Ad's eyes.

'Deadly fucking serious,' she said.

CHAPTER 11

South East London

Sitting by the window in the language lab, Ella stared blankly down at the hockey pitch below. Girls with blue legs, wearing short skirts, scrabbled around after the ball like bantam hens. Jerky movements, twisting this way, now that. Jolly bloody hockey sticks.

'Williams-May!' Bradbury shouted. '*Ecoutez et repetez!*'

Ella heard Bradbury but was too tired to answer. She turned around to face the teacher. White, dumpy, middle aged, secure in the knowledge that she would have a satisfyingly solid pension from an unsatisfactory, stolid life.

'What?' Ella asked.

Tittering from her schoolmates. Nudging each other. Waiting to see how Bradbury would react.

'What?' Bradbury said, rounding on Ella, all floaty viscose and righteous indignation. 'Did you just "what" me? You need to make more effort than this, young lady, if you want to do well.' She bore down on Ella with well-meaning and bad coffee breath. 'And that doesn't just go for your studies.'

The bell rang shrilly throughout the school, cutting Ella free from the noose of the school's surrogate umbilical cord. Ella lost no time in gathering up her things and brushing past Bradbury on the way out.

As she headed to the bus stop, navigating her way through the Mercedes, BMWs and Audis that flanked the school, parked self-ishly, crookedly, awkwardly by stay-at-home mothers that cared only for transferring darling Tamsin, Olivia, Arabella and Labia to their next structured activity in air-conditioned, four-wheel-driven luxury, Ella thought about her task.

'You get pally with Danny's slippery little bastards,' the older detective had said. 'You feed us information that can lead to a conviction further up the food chain. We turn a blind eye to your mother's itchy fingers. Simple.'

That had been the deal. Detective Gordon Thomson – more gargoyle than man, with his too-high colour and bulbous purple boozer's nose – had thrown Letitia a lifeline. But to reap the happy handbag harvest, Ella was designated sacrificial lamb to appease the gods.

She sat on Hades' bus as it flowed against the course of the Styx, taking her from the suburban paradise of Dulwich back to her concrete hell on earth. *How am I going to get with those lunatics?* she thought. *Nearly a fortnight now and still nothing. What did I ever do that's so bad?*

The Victorian grey brick houses moved closer together and grew smaller and dirtier. More kids got on the bus. Ella clutched her bobbled black wool coat over her blazer, hiding the private school badge. Shouting black boys and white boys who wanted to be black boys from tougher schools, full of crisps and patties and attitude, bounced around the top deck. Taunting her. Taunting each other. Boastful and free now. Hastening home to change their clothes, trading one uniform for another. Some becoming Buffalo child soldiers, fighting for easy money in the tower blocks.

Ella tried to make herself small. She grasped her rucksack and held it close to her chest. The bus stopped. Heavy feet thundered up the stairs and there, in a bright pink Juicy Couture velour tracksuit, was her opening. Tonya. One of Danny's girls. When

Tonya swung herself into the seat diagonally opposite Ella, she seemed only to register the boys' wolf whistles.

'She got some cushion for the pushing, man. I'd like a go on that,' one of the boys said.

Tonya was all hands held high and head swaying from side to side now. Earrings jangling against her beautiful, hard little face.

'Yeah, and you look like your cushion's already being pushed by your mates, fat boy.'

Ella's sharp ears picked out some murmuring amongst the boys. *Danny's girl. Danny's girl. Leave well alone, mate. Don't know what you messing with, innit?*

When it was almost time to alight, Ella knew she had her chance.

'Love your tracksuit,' she said to Tonya as the bus slowed. 'Where's it from?'

Tonya looked her up and down. Her sneer was so pointed that Ella felt she had been scratched from head to toe.

'I know you. You is freak girl from down the way,' she said.

'Ella. My name's Ella.' Her heart threatened to jump up into her throat but Ella forced it back down.

Silence. The doors to the bus hissed open. It was her last opportunity to make a connection. *Damn you, Letitia. You owe me big time for this.*

Ella pulled a crushed packet of cigarettes out of the side pocket of her rucksack. *Quickly now. Quickly before she walks away.*

'Want a cig?' she said to the back of Tonya's bouncy, tongued extensions. Her voice trembled. She prayed it would stop.

Tonya turned round, hand on hip. With the swift hands of an experienced snatcher, she swiped the packet from Ella's grip and offered Ella one of her own cigarettes.

'*You* want a cig?' she asked Ella, grinning.

Ella grinned back.

'Sad cow,' Tonya said, grin gone. She threw the cigarettes on

100

the floor and stamped on them with her Nike hi-top-clad foot. 'Let's see what you got in your fucking bag then.'

Ella had a split second to decide how to play it. Run, or a face-off too far from the relative safety of home? Maybe only hangdog persistence was left.

'Look, I was only trying to be friendly, yeah?' Ella said. She steadfastly held onto her rucksack. If her textbooks were stolen, Letitia wouldn't replace them for the school. The school wouldn't understand about a run-in with a Tonya.

Tonya raised her hand to slap Ella but stopped short. 'Why you wanna be friendly with me all of a sudden?' she asked, frowning. 'You like it when we smash your windows in, do you? Is you one of them perverts that like being treated like shit? A machoist?'

'It's masochist.'

'Yeah, whatever, weird girl.'

Ella conceded silently that Tonya was not a total idiot. She was right to question her sudden friendly advances. What answer could she give? *Think, for Christ's sake. You might not get her on her own again.*

'I'm sick of being inside looking out. You look like you get all the fun. Maybe I want some,' she said.

Tonya twirled her hair around her index finger. 'You think a skank like you can muscle in on my scene? You fancy me or something? Or maybe you fancy Danny. Yeah, I bet that's it. All the girls want him but see, he's mine.'

Ella could feel frustration starting to heat her blood. She was so sick of being in the middle of everyone else's games when all she wanted was to go to school and quietly learn her way out of the ghetto. She quickly wracked her brain for stratagems to connect with Tonya but her memory served up only the basic child psychology that she had seen Letitia using on her boyfriends. *Maybe it will do the trick.*

'Fuck you, Tonya Perkins,' Ella said. 'I thought you were

different. A bit cleverer than the others. But you ain't that different. So fuck you.'

She walked away, counting … She'd got to four when she heard Tonya's voice.

'Oi! Wait up, weird girl,' Tonya shouted.

I'm in.

Ella began by doing what she knew best. What Letitia had trained her to do all her life. She became a mirror, offering Tonya the reflection of herself that she most wanted to see.

Yeah, you is well pretty. Yeah, you is so witty and clever, man, that you could piss all over them stand-up comedians and them University Challenge *dicks. Yeah, you so have the finest arse in all of South East London. I'm telling you, Danny really loves you, girl. No doubt, you is so going to be blinged-up and looking like a rich woman when Danny pulls off a big job.*

Scratch the surface, and Ella recognised Tonya as the crude, dumb sadist that she always guessed she would be. And yet …

Her persistence had got her to the gates. But entry to Danny's crew comes with a price tag, of course. Ella had started with the small stuff. Lookout while Tonya and Big Michelle did over an old lady for her pension. Tonya and Big Michelle had smacked that old bitch up good, leaving her weeping on the stairs of the flats. Ella had applauded, dying quietly inside, cursing Letitia. Then came slashing a grass' tyres. At least there had been no look of bitter disappointment or fear to contend with. Then, a bit of graffiti on the shop shutters. Easy peasy lemon squeezy. Finally, she became responsible for cutting, weighing and bagging up lumps of hash.

'You getting the knack for this, spod girl. You been wasting your time with all them boring books,' Tonya had pronounced and Big Michelle agreed.

'She got a well innocent-looking face, innit?' Big Michelle

102

pointed out, big arms flapping. 'We gonna get away with blue murder 'cos ain't nobody gonna suspect her mug.'

Cackling laughter. Clickety clack heels through the alleys some nights. Thighs on show. Nikes the rest of the time. Good for making a quick getaway. Ella started to like the adrenalin buzz. But the silent remorse afterwards was suffocating.

When Danny's boy, Jez, had first summoned her to be vetted by the king himself, she could see that Danny had eyes bigger than his belly. Nodding, smiling, touching her hair, checking her shape.

Disappointment and shame threatened to overcome her when she saw him. She had wanted him to be a monster. But Danny was all that. Built like a swimmer. He had the soft, dark eyes of a more sensitive soul with curling lashes. A mixed ancestry had given him high cheekbones, a strong jawline and a straight, narrow nose. Mocha chocalata yaya. Even in his uniform of G-Star Raw and Superdry, Ella wondered if there was a deeper finesse to Danny.

'I hear you doing all right as the new girl in the crew,' he said, gold tooth glinting in the Ikea lamplight of his absent mother's living room. 'If I'd known you was such a honey, I'd have got Jez and the boys to lay off yous. You wanna suck my dick?'

Finesse? Was I fucking mental?

'No thanks.'

'You a lesbian?'

'Why? 'Cos I won't suck your dick?'

Ella's heart pounded. She felt like somebody had clamped her head in a vice and was squeezing hard. On the one hand, his advances felt like violence. Danny already had his tough cut of stewing steak but now he wanted to carve off his pound of sirloin too. Ella's flesh hadn't been on the menu when she'd agreed to take on Detective Gordon the Gargoyle's 'mission'. She had algebra to do.

On the other hand, she didn't want to betray her real intentions to Danny. Last thing she needed was to be tailed by that weirdo, Jez; her meet with the Gargoyle discovered and reported back. Vengeance would come to Letitia's door in the form of another Molotov cocktail. A flaming apocalypse of a drink that even a rum'n'Coke chaser wouldn't douse. Also, it had been one year, two months and fifteen days since Ella had dumped her first boyfriend. Danny was fine. She was no virgin and she knew the score … She felt a spasm of anticipation.

Then, feeling both used and elated afterwards:

'I thought me and you were friends!' Tonya protested. 'And now you been fucking my fella behind my back, innit, you skank!'

Danny was conciliatory. 'Hey, hey. I got enough love for both of yous, yeah?' He grabbed his crotch. 'No need to get feisty. I got something special lined up. An important job. I need both of you in my inner circle. Know what I mean?'

Not really, arsehole. Ella nodded, curiosity sated for now.

But her need overcame her scepticism. She had started to feel Stockholm-syndrome-sexy. Letitia's baby was sweet sixteen now and only a shadow of that mother lingered. So, Ella saw the invitation to join Danny and his girl as a warm bonus in her new life of subterfuge and pretence. Teenage kicks. And maybe it had been a happy compromise for Tonya too. Ella could tell that she didn't trust Danny not to walk off with her into the urban sunset.

Now the three of them shuffled around on the creaking Argos divan. Danny's bed, so Danny led. Two years' worth of dust on the MFI bedroom furniture. High five. For real. She didn't tell the Gargoyle about these bits.

'What is he planning?' the Gargoyle asked, staring straight ahead in the Ford, exhaling cigarette smoke off to the side, where it hit the window and left a blueish-yellow patina.

Ella looked at the Gargoyle's whisky drinker's nose. It confirmed her suspicion that life chasing Dannys was stressful. She carefully noted his frayed collar and the grime on the cuffs of his overcoat.

'I don't know,' she said. 'He said it was something big.'

The Gargoyle fixed her with soft, bloodshot eyes. 'Be careful,' he said. 'Are you being careful?'

Ella nodded. 'I'm right in there. They haven't got a clue. They trust me.'

The Gargoyle patted her hand. It was a fatherly pat but her eyes still flicked to his crotch. Just to check.

'When the time comes, will you let us mic you up?'

Ella lifted her eyes and stared blankly out of the windscreen. It was leafy here. Near school and away from the sharp scrutiny of Jez, who moved around the estate like an insomniac puma in the undergrowth. Danny's twenty-four-seven sentry. But this was not his territory, *thank God.*

'Look, this is very difficult for me. I don't want to lose my …' She searched for the words. She'd read them in a book. She wanted the Gargoyle to understand. '… my moral compass. I think that's the phrase, isn't it?'

The Gargoyle nodded slowly and lit another cigarette. 'You'll get counselling when you've finished. I know it's hard. We'll look after you.'

She could feel tears rolling hot down her cheeks now. She was drowning in guilt. The shame of enjoying the excitement and low-rent glamour. She was Danny's cheap teen porno-queen. Just like Tonya.

'All I want to do is get some …' The words jostled for space in the back of her throat before they came out. '… space. I need silence and … and … calm and … clean. I want to study and just be left to …' She flapped her hand in front of her face. Ella was an expert in holding it together but, today, the seams were all coming apart. She shook her head violently. 'I'm just really struggling to …'

'Cope?'

'No.'

'Sleep?'

'No.' The Gargoyle wouldn't let her get a word in edgeways. *Shut up!* 'I'm struggling to do my schoolwork.' There. It was out.

'Schoolwork? Is that all?' He started to chuckle quietly.

She looked at him dumbfounded. *Bastard!* He just didn't understand. 'Is that all? I've got my GCSE mocks next week. I'm in the middle of revising. That's *everything.*'

She stiffened. At that moment, she realised the Gargoyle couldn't throw her the buoy she needed to keep her afloat. She would have to save herself. *An iron discipline and a backbone of steel. That's what I have and that's all I need.*

'Do you want to duck out?' the Gargoyle asked, offering her a blue packet of Kleenex. 'I know we're asking a lot. But it's—'

'No,' Ella said. 'This is about more than saving my mother's arse. I'll see this through because it's the right thing to do.'

'Good girl.'

CHAPTER 12

Amsterdam, 10 January

From: George McKenzie
To: Sally Wright 11.28
Subject: Stuff going down

Hiya Sally,

Thanks for your emails.

Things have gone a bit weird here with the attacks in
Amsterdam and Utrecht. But I'm okay. Paul van den Bergen
just wanted some insight into political stuff. I've just left
it at that, don't worry.

Just thought I'd give you the heads up: I've got into a spot
of bother with Dr Fennemans. It's nothing big, but I have
to sit his lectures out until the start of next term and go
for one-to-ones with him instead. A fate worse than death.
The guy's a misogynist idiot.

Everything else is fine.

George

PS: Did my mother say what she wanted to speak to me so urgently about?

George stared at the email. Her finger hovered over the mouse button. Part of her didn't want to begin a dialogue about being in hot water with Fennemans. Riling Sally would risk killing the Cambridge goose and its golden eggs. But it made sense to warn the senior tutor of the fracas up front, before Fennemans had chance to malign her.

George read what she had written again. And again. She dusted the screen and her keyboard.

'Just send it!' she shouted, finally forcing her finger to override her ambivalent brain.

Next, she listened again to the angry message left on her mobile phone two days into the new term by the PhD student who was the editor of *The Moment* blog. She could hear the fury in his normally passive voice.

'George. It's Bert de Vries. I'm not going to take your post down, because *The Moment* believes in freedom of speech, but I'll tell you now, it's eloquent but it sucks. I'm really *really* annoyed at you. We've put a disclaimer on the blog. I don't want trouble with the bloody police over pro-terror writing. Call me. I want an explanation.'

George growled and threw her phone onto her bed. She lay on her chaise longue, staring at the cracks in her ornate ceiling. Melancholy threatened but she pushed it aside.

'I'm doing the right thing. Bert's opinion doesn't count,' she told the ceiling. Sat up abruptly. 'And Fennemans ... well, he can just fuck off.'

Briefly she wondered about her mother. The unanswered demand for attention had been trying to force its way out of the confines of her paranoia box since Sally had mentioned her making contact. George kept steadfastly pushing it back inside. *There's no room for her bullshit now. Screw her.*

George stood and looked out of her window. Her stomach growled but she knew she had only two tangerines in the food cupboard. She checked her hair and carefully ringed her eyes with black eyeliner. She threw on her winter boots and her sheepskin coat. Ad would have food. Then she remembered it was Saturday. Ad would have the Milkmaid in tow.

Trying and failing to quell the burgeoning tide of jealousy that was rising within her, George clattered down the stairs. It was dry outside. Her breath steamed as the mid-January air bit into her chest. There, in the red light district with its narrow alleys and lascivious back streets, she felt suddenly bricked in; suffocated.

She resolved to cheer herself up with some flowers. Pulling on her hood and dragging hard on her cigarette, she pushed past Japanese tourists, families out shopping with small kids and coach parties full of Americans being led by umbrella-toting guides to the wide banks of the Singel canal. The flower market was in full swing. Amongst the hyacinth smells and cupcake colours, George's heartbeat started to slow.

She bought a bunch of bright yellow tulips and a packet of syrup waffles. She wandered aimlessly among the crowds in silence, snaffling down the sweet, late breakfast she didn't even like. Drinking in the hotchpotch of houseboats, four- and five-storey houses and Dutch faces, she tried to evoke the delight and wonder she had felt when she had first set eyes on that place. It had reminded her of the pots of pansies and petunias her mother helped her to grow as a child. The time before, when she was small and things were good. One day, she would have her own garden where she could grow delicate, beautiful things.

Peering ahead, George's gaze fell on a young couple holding hands. They looked like a clipping out of a wedding magazine. Picture perfect, sta-pressed, spray-starched. The lavender-scented love of the blonde and long-limbed. Ad and Astrid, tiptoeing through the tulips. Seeing them was ripping a Band-Aid off an already angry wound. She turned abruptly, with the intention of heading back towards the Cracked Pot Coffee Shop.

But then she spotted something in her peripheral vision that made her pulse quicken. Short-term memories started snapping into place. It was the third time since beginning her stroll up Singel that somebody had bobbed into the shadows when she had turned around quickly. Too tall and broad to be a woman.

Decision time. Fight or flight?

George realised she was one of a dwindling number of foreign students. Feeble prey for an unseen predator. She quickened her pace. Hastened towards familiar turf and friendly faces. Was she still being followed? She turned around surreptitiously. Her pursuer had definitely slipped inside a flower stall again. Only about five metres behind her now.

By the time she reached the fringes of the red light district, she was almost running. She had to check herself, slow up, appear unruffled and in control. But as she reached the entrance to the Cracked Pot Coffee Shop, her instincts screamed at her that somebody was standing right behind her.

She stopped short and turned around quickly, keys wedged between each finger on her right hand in a makeshift knuckle-duster. She was ready. Heart drumming inside her chest.

Ad sat in the café in silence. He studied Astrid's face as she ate her ham and cheese sandwich. Her manners were impeccable. She took small bites and dropped no crumbs. She didn't forget herself and start to speak with her mouth full, churning her food around like clothes in a washing machine on spin. Unlike George. She wore a miniskirt with leggings underneath that emphasised her gazelle-like legs. Her straight blonde hair was tied using a leather hair barrette. It pushed its way out of its bondage to form a perfect bouncy fan. Effortlessly elegant. Unlike George. Her skin was blushingly clear. Her blue eyes were shiny. She was, to all intents and purposes, a real Dutch beauty. Unlike George. And yet, Ad mused, Astrid was too perfect, like a well-groomed Afghan hound at a dog show. He felt instantly guilty for thinking such a thing.

'So, my parents and your parents had dinner last weekend round ours,' she said, stopping between mouthfuls. 'It was *so* funny because your mum and my mum ... can you guess?'

'No.'

'They had worn the same skirt!' She started to laugh.

Ad observed that it was a delighted titter. Even if the observation had merited it, there was no lecherous guffaw, no hiccoughing, no silent heaving. No smutty anecdote to follow.

'Fancy that,' Astrid said.

Ad smiled and tried to imagine his blousy mother wearing something as equally floral and polyester as his future mother-in-law. Had they electrocuted each other with static when they embraced? The mental image crumbled as he noticed Astrid leaning towards him, expecting a response.

'Fancy,' he said. 'How's work?'

Astrid pushed her plate away with the second half of her sandwich untouched. 'This new girl has started. The manager has put me in charge. I'm showing her the ropes on laces, water-proofing spray and colour restorer. It's the till next week. I've got to explain how the store room is ordered.'

Ad nodded sagely and kept nodding as Astrid expanded on how the credit card of local councillor, André de Vos, had been refused when he tried to buy loafers, and how Mrs Kooper had bought her son the wrong-sized shoes for school, despite the advice she was given. After ten minutes of uninterrupted foot-wear-based reporting with very little drawing of breath, Astrid paused and cocked her head on the side inquisitively.

'Are you listening, darling?' she asked.

Ad had, however, been thinking not of Mrs Kooper but of

Klaus Biedermeier, who had just walked into the café, presumably fresh from the flower market as he was clutching a large bunch of roses wrapped in green paper.

Klaus strode confidently over to a group of well-dressed, loud students. Ad recognised them as mainly law students. They were all members of *het corps* – the conservative student fraternity, comprised predominantly of the sons and daughters of solicitors, judges, surgeons and politicians. Right-wing old money. *Jasper was right when he said the toffs hang out here*, he thought. *Now, how am I going to play this?*

Klaus gave his bouquet with a flourish to a very blonde girl wearing pearls, who blushed, said something and caused great jollity among the group. Ad strained to hear their conversation above Astrid's gossip about Lies Oostendorp's wedding dress choice.

'We thought you weren't coming,' one of the men said in English laced with a Rotterdam accent. He was big. He looked like he rowed or lifted weights or just ate too much *stamppot*.

Klaus pulled out a chair loudly enough to make the other diners turn around. He straddled it in a manner that said he owned the space and tucked his hands behind his round, blond head. When he spoke, all Ad heard was Klaus saying – also in English but with a clipped German accent – 'market' and 'most beautiful girl, ha ha ha'. He proceeded to turn his back to Ad and hold court with his cronies. Ad could no longer hear what was being said, much to his chagrin. His ears zoned back into Astrid's excited chatter.

'... enjoyed it so much at church on Sunday,' Astrid said. She frowned and waved her hand in front of Ad's face. 'Are you listening to me at all?'

Ad looked into her questioning eyes and stroked her cheek. 'Yes, love. Every word.' A plan started to take shape, quickly sharpened by the oxygen that his pounding heart was speeding to his brain. He reached out for Astrid's hand. 'Hey, come with me. I want you to meet someone,' he said.

'Oh, you're not going to introduce me to one of your intellectual nerdy pals, are you?' she said. 'Not another of those foreign students. They all reek of garlic and I can't understand a single word of what they say.'

'You might like this one,' Ad said, pulling Astrid towards his target and wondering if Herr Biedermeier would sniff out his subterfuge, even with a perfect Aryan girlfriend on the arm.

The journey across the café was tough. His common sense told him to sit back down and mind his own business, keep Astrid away from a possible killer. But in a disobedient corner of his mind lurked the insistent voice of George. *Cosy up to Klaus. See what he and his Nazi friends get up to.* He thought about Ratan's severed foot and decided that the small risk to Astrid of just saying hello to a suspect was worth it. After all, he could protect her. Couldn't he?

Ad could feel his cheeks burning hot as he approached the large gathering that now seemed to be hanging on Klaus' every word. One by one, the well-heeled law and accountancy students all looked up at Ad until, finally, Klaus himself turned around. He was smiling. It made his white scars, like hairline fractures over his cheekbones, change shape. They etched a new, relaxed pattern on his face. When Klaus spotted Ad, however, his smile faltered. The scars settled into their usual map of haughty condescension.

'Well, if it isn't Karelse, our little lefty freedom fighter.' As he said this, Klaus looked Astrid up and down with the sharp-eyed scrutiny of a hungry cheetah sizing up a meal. 'And who is this?'

Ad made the introductions. He felt sure he detected in Klaus a hint of admiration ... or was it jealousy? Astrid was a very beautiful girl. Nobody ever failed to be wooed by her dazzling smile or the winning, soft tones of her voice. Everybody loved Astrid. Mostly.

Klaus, suddenly the German gentleman, pulled out his chair

and offered it to Astrid. He picked a pink gerbera from the little glass vase on the table and gave it to her. 'Fräulein,' he said with a flourish. He clicked his fingers at a waiter. 'What will you have to drink?'

Astrid's face turned quickly crimson, in contrast to the blonde girl holding Klaus' roses, whose face was turning quickly green, presumably at the Prussian prince's treatment of the interloper.

Ad placed a protective hand on his girlfriend's shoulder. 'We're not stopping for a drink just now,' he told Klaus. 'But I wanted to come over and pass on my condolences about Joachim.'

The students at the table all looked down at their laps. Klaus seemed to remember his grief. Ad tried to make a mental note of every physical change as he responded to mention of Joachim's death. His eyes seemed to darken. His shoulders drooped slightly. His lips narrowed to a line. Was this grief or was he merely a great actor?

'Yes,' Klaus said. 'Thank you. It's difficult for me to put my sorrow into words right now.'

Ad couldn't work out if the stilted, formal ring to Klaus' words was a symptom of there being no substance to his grief or just a symptom of being a German, speaking English haltingly. But the show of emotion seemed too pat on the heels of his exhibition of chivalry and jollity.

Klaus thumbed his chin, as if considering something. Then he said, 'The police won't release Joachim's remains. It's screwed up. Joachim wasn't a terrorist. And no way was he secretly rubbing shoulders with a bunch of towel-heads. So we're having a memorial service for him. If you want to come ...'

Ad nodded, looked at his watch and motioned to Astrid that it was time for them to leave. 'I'd like that very much,' he said.

'But don't bother bringing the English loudmouth. I notice you've not been with her the last week.'

Ad stifled a smile. George's expulsion from class offered itself as a fortuitous and vital piece in the new jigsaw, which depicted

114

Ad as a fledgling right-winger and Klaus as his potential new guru. It seemed too easy.

'We've fallen out,' he said.

'Over that disgraceful, pro-Muslamic blogpost that everybody's talking about?' Klaus asked.

His sharp blue eyes seemed to be searching for the truth in Ad. But Ad knew he was not a natural liar. He hoped that Klaus wouldn't see that his hands were shaking slightly.

'Yes. I suppose so. I realised she wasn't …' He didn't know how to finish the sentence. Surrounded by all those preppy law students whose soft, cashmere exteriors almost certainly concealed hearts already compacted into stone, he felt like he needed to leave. Quickly. Before Astrid contradicted him.

Klaus nodded. He'd clearly said enough. 'Good. Good. Interesting,' Klaus said as he looked at Astrid and smiled. 'I'll be in touch.'

Ad was not entirely sure he could rely on his legs to carry him out of the café but when he got outside, he felt triumphant and kissed Astrid, silently thanking her for her unwitting bravura performance.

'You never told me you had such *charming* friends,' Astrid said. 'I like the look of them much better.' She linked him and put her head on his shoulder. 'You've got to be careful who you hang out with while there are terrorists on the loose. And to be honest, I never did like that English girl. I'm glad you've ditched her as a friend.'

'Yes, my love,' Ad said, wishing he could go straight round to the Cracked Pot Coffee Shop.

Remko Visser came out of The English Bookshop on Lauriergracht, whistling. It was a cold, late Saturday afternoon. The light was already failing fast and streetlamps were popping into life to augment a dwindling sun, wreathed in thick cloud as it was. Rain fell steadily, making the lenses in Remko's glasses steam up. But he felt good. He had just picked up *Memoirs of a*

Revolutionist by Peter Kropotkin. It was in English but he'd had it recommended to him by George. He'd been waiting for it to come into the shop for a while.

He thought about going round to his parents' house to cadge dinner but then he realised they were going to an *Aufruf* at the synagogue for somebody's engagement after the Saturday service. They were probably still lingering with their cronies, pronouncing loudly about the bride-to-be and possibly fighting over the last bit of pickled herring or fish ball.

Maybe a kebab on the way home, then. Yes, a nice falafel. With garlic sauce and extra chilli.

He made his way towards the Herengracht and started to amble along it, drinking in the smell of diesel as a motorboat chugged by. The jolly tinkle of bicycle bells made him think fondly that spring was not too far away now. It was still getting dark early but, hell, optimism cost nothing, did it?

This feeling of well-being was amplified when a beautiful blonde girl wearing a bright pink duffle coat walked towards him. Her ponytail danced high on her head. She had bow-shaped lips and slim ankles, although he couldn't tell if she was flat-chested or well bosomed underneath the coat. He smiled at her as she passed, but she didn't see him.

When he reached the Hartenstraat bridge, he felt a sudden pang in his chest. Ratan. He remembered Ratan on the night of the party, grinning like a lotto winner, covered in Rani's lipstick. Only three weeks ago and now the world was on its head. Joachim was dead too. He hated Joachim. Klaus was okay. At least he was a bit charismatic. He had the sense to keep his mouth shut when Joachim had been sounding off about Jews and blacks. But Remko knew the pair of them were both arrogant pricks, really. Still, Joachim didn't deserve to die. He felt interminably sorry for the sallow-faced, gangling dork. Nobody in the faculty believed he and Ratan had been suicide bombers for a fundamentalist Muslim cause.

Suddenly, the canal looked bare and desolate. The trees were still without their leaves. He realised that spring was still a long way off. Remko shivered and pulled the zip of his anorak up to his chin.

He continued to walk, hood on now and head bent against the wind that drove the rain into his face. Presently, he felt curiously self-conscious. He looked at the reflections in the windows of the shops and houses but saw nothing out of the ordinary; nothing apart from a Remko-shaped man walking with his hood up, carrying a bookstore bag in heavy rain. He glanced behind him, intuiting a malign presence. Definitely nobody there. He picked up his pace. Home was not far now.

When he felt something heavy sting the back of his head and sank to the ground like a large stone hitting the bottom of the canal, the only two things that he was aware of were, firstly, that it was odd to be hit on the head in Oudespiegelstraat, even if it was a small alleyway, and secondly, that his attacker was both strong and nimble to be capable of dragging him inside—

Remko Visser passed out and did not wake up until agony and the strange smell of burning petrol, flesh and plastic roused him. By then, it was too late.

CHAPTER 13

Later

Fennemans arranged the hothoused tulips in a charming blue glass globe vase that he had picked up from a junk shop. The tulips were yellow. He liked the colour scheme.

'Very Swedish,' he said.

Saturdays were often empty and lonely for Fennemans, but the memory of his meeting with Saskia, and the news that the university's costly legal machine was already cranking up on his behalf had filled him with the same warm, happy feeling that he often got from standing in a shaft of strong sunlight on a radiant, crisp winter morning.

'You know we all care so much about you, Vim,' she had said.

The skin on the hand with which she had patted his arm was loose and wrinkled now – covered in freckles and the start of liver spots. Those blue eyes that had once looked so sharp, almost crystalline, were now ringed with white; the skin above and beneath them was as baggy as hell.

'You're such a good friend after all these years,' he had said, tucking a stray lock of her coarse, grey hair behind her ear. His eyes travelled down to the spare tyre that now represented the span of her hips, where once her bones had jutted out, framing a flat, taut stomach. The clinging fine-knit sweater she was wearing for their meeting only accentuated the unsightly spread.

She blushed. 'It wouldn't do to lose our best scholar to a pack of lies, now, would it?' she said. 'Poor Vim. So vulnerable. So easy to malign.'

'I know, Saskia,' he said, shaking his head and putting his hand on her knee. 'We sensitive ones are always easy prey for predators like van den Bergen and, in my case, grasping little girls looking for attention.'

He leaned forward and kissed her gently on the cheek. He felt the heat from her skin. As far as he was aware, within the university at least, only he had ever been able to thaw Professor Saskia Meyer's arctic exterior.

'I'll make sure no expense is spared on any legal work that needs to be undertaken,' she said. 'And the Executive Board will stand behind me in upholding your reputation, my sweet.' She caressed the inside of his thigh, smiled wryly and opened the door for him to leave.

Another chaste kiss on the forehead was all he had needed to seal that deal.

'Adieu, darling Saskia,' he had said, putting his hand dramatically over his heart.

As he had turned to leave, he shuddered to think the two of them had spent all those sweaty afternoons engaged in clandestine fucking in her bohemian old apartment. It was a long time ago now. Perhaps it had been the thrill of having an affair with his supervisor that had made it possible for him to get it up for her.

'Thinking of you, Vim!' she had shouted after him, blowing a kiss.

As he put the blue vase onto his kitchen windowsill in the dusk half-light, he realised quite how sweet the relief was. He really was invincible. And now, the banging from below reminded him that he had matters to attend to. Not such an empty Saturday after all.

Poised to fight, when George had turned around, there was nothing out of the ordinary to see. A gaggle of giggling teenaged girls, some lost tourists, a dog without a collar sniffing its pee on a lamp post and a limping man, making his way past the slick-haired tout, Hans, into the live sex show next door. Nothing. Her only attacker had been her own sneering terror.

George marched upstairs with her bunch of tulips. She had squeezed them so hard that some of the stems were beyond hope. She slammed her door behind her and double-locked it. She wedged a chair beneath the knob and drew the curtains. Then came the cleaning. She scrubbed her already clean kitchenette. All day long.

Now her dry fingers stank of bleach, as she dragged hard on her spliff. Jan sat next to her in a booth downstairs, nodding sagely at nothing in particular while his number one hippy helper looked after the cash register. Outside, angry rain lashed in torrents against the shop-front window.

'I was hoping the inspector guy would have called me,' she said, passing the spliff to Jan. 'I've ruined my reputation for him. Trying to help, you know? Everything's gone to shit. My head's a mess.'

Jan took off his steamy glasses and cleaned them on the edge of his batik T. 'The pigs use you up and spit you out.'

George was just about to tell Jan what she thought about Paul van den Bergen when Inneke and Katja walked in, both wearing civvies. Tight jeans. Hooded tops. Anoraks over the arm. They were barely wet.

Jan looked up. 'Ladies! Ladies! Is this not peak time for businesswomen such as yourselves?'

Katja pointed to the lashing rain. 'Business is slack as a pensioner's fanny.'

'We made an executive decision,' Inneke said. 'Half an hour's downtime with you and early home.'

Inneke and Katja slumped into the booth, either side of George

120

and Jan. George could smell sex and coconut oil on Inneke. She wondered if she showered before she kissed her kids good morning.

Katja looked over at George and flashed her with a trout pout smile. 'You okay? You look like you spent a penny and lost a dollar.'

'It's lost a pound, found a penny,' George said, feeling sourness push her internal pH value down to pure acid. 'I've had a weird day.'

'You got any beer in this place, Jan?' Inneke asked.

Jan summoned hippy helper to bring over the emergency Heineken.

For an hour, the four of them shared their woes. Jan's arthritis and maintenance payments to his ex. Inneke's wrangles with the kids' school and payments from her ex. Katja's lopsided nipples and unsavoury client demands. Finally, George told her neighbours about her possible stalker and the matches.

'Part of me thought it was the guy who stayed over,' she said. 'I've not returned his calls. But maybe it's someone far worse … Maybe doing that blogpost has attracted the wrong sort of attention.'

'Sounds to me like this bomb thing has got you paranoid, honey,' Katja said. 'Looking for danger where there is none.'

Inneke straightened up in her seat, coddling her can of Heineken. 'No, Kat. She's right to be suspicious,' she said.

George looked at her with the overly analytical eyes of the very stoned. 'What do you mean?'

Inneke sniffed conspiratorially. 'I mean, Amsterdam's a funky place these days. All sorts of shit going down all the time. Weirdoes and wackos having a pop at the girls. Girls coming in from odd destinations.'

'Oh?' George said, inclining her body forward.

Katja seemed to cotton on. She was all nail extensions now, flapping her hands like a drag queen drying his varnish. 'Yes!

Inneke's right. Back in November, Saeng, the Thai girl who rents space above Fag Butt's Gay Porn, had a nutcase.'

'What happened?' George asked, relighting the spliff and considering Katja through a purple cloud of smoke.

'Oh, it was terrible,' Inneke said.

'This trick gets the hump when she says no to him,' Katja continued. 'He brings out a hip flask. Pours vodka down Saeng's gullet. Sets it alight. She goes up like a torch.'

'Jesus,' Jan said.

'She'll not work again,' Katja said, shaking her head solemnly. 'Think she's in some kind of rehab for burns victims now. Skin grafts and all that shit.'

George grimaced. 'Poor girl. Did they get the lunatic?'

Inneke shook her head. 'No. Nobody could remember him coming or going. Saeng wouldn't give a description.'

'Why the fuck not?' George asked, wiping imaginary dust off the ring-pull of the beer can.

Katja flicked ash that was hanging precipitously from the spliff in the direction of the chunky terracotta ashtray, missed and dropped a shower of black smutty flakes all over the table. George mused that it looked like a lesser Pompeii. She steeled herself to refrain from asking hippy helper for a cloth.

'Well,' Katja said, leaning in, passing a wet-tipped spliff on to Jan, 'the guy threatened he'd find her if she blabbed. I heard she's going back to Thailand. She's outstayed her fortnight's holiday visa by five years anyway.'

'No,' said Inneke, 'she's going to London.'

'Would she get into the UK?' George asked, eyeing the spliff's wet tip nervously as Jan dragged deeply and passed it to her.

'A couple of English guys fake Dutch papers for girls if they've got the right money. Get them over on an EU visa.'

George nodded and looked at the spliff in her hand. To smoke, or not to smoke? Her choice was heavily laden with responsibility and import. Not to smoke. George knew that the tip would feel cold and damp between her lips from another person's spit.

'Inneke?' She passed it on. Kissing was one thing but cold, second-hand spit was another thing entirely.

Inneke coughed as she inhaled the hot smoke. 'That's the other thing,' she said. 'You talk about Saeng getting hold of a dodgy visa. Well, these bombings … We've noticed girls coming in from the Middle East in the past year. Really young too.'

'Unusual,' Jan said, proffering his pouch of tobacco to George, who began to roll a fresh joint. 'Muslim girls? A long way from home here. Spiritually, I mean.'

George spread the damp, fragrant tobacco along her runway of paper – a blank foil for the green chunks of Californian grass that would light the way for take-off. Up, up and away. 'Why do you say "these bombings" and then mention Middle Eastern girls?' she asked Inneke. 'Middle Eastern from where?'

Inneke sipped her beer and glanced at her watch. 'Well, you know. The bombers are meant to be Al Qaeda, aren't they? And these girls … I've heard they're from Taliban land.'

'Afghanistan?' George asked.

Inneke nodded. 'Yeah. That sort of place. A few of us have tried making conversation with them on the street. In the summer. You know, when it's hot and we hang out.'

'And?'

'Well, they don't speak. They're drugged. That's pretty obvious. They have an older woman as chaperone. Indonesian Tom says rent's paid by some intermediary guy that nobody ever sees. Speaks Dutch on the phone with an accent. I've heard rumours that those English dudes provide them with paperwork. A month at most and they're gone. The girls down the way say they're going to the UK.'

'Mules maybe?' asked George. Her brain had started to effervesce with the logistics of such a conspiracy. She liked the poetry of it and at the same time hated the politics of it. Eastern girls coming west. Trading a prison of the mind for a prison of the flesh, carrying dope like a platter of poisoned dates; a sickly sweet offering of Eastern hospitality. Then, selling their virtuous Muslim souls for asylum in infidel London.

'Yes. Mules,' Katja said. 'Definitely. Then who knows? If they can't get paperwork, maybe stowaways on board—'

'Ships that pass the Hook of Holland in the night,' George muttered. 'So you think the bombing is some kind of Talibanesque retribution on the Netherlands, allowing itself to be used as a conduit for Afghan prostitutes and drugs?'

'Why wouldn't it be?' Katja asked.

'Because I have a theory that it's right-wingers,' George said.

'A slur campaign?' Jan said.

'Precisely. Or a red herring. Pin the tail on the Muslim donkey. Maybe. Might be a neo-Nazi response to girls from the Middle East passing through. Dunno.'

'Are you going to tell Captain Pig, the detective, about your neo-Nazi thoughts?' Jan asked.

'Let's just say I'm looking into it,' George said, trying to blow a smoke ring and failing. She thought wistfully of Ad. 'I have a man on the job.'

CHAPTER 14

12 January

'You okay?' van den Bergen asked. 'Don't puke in the car. It's just been valeted.'

George was slumped in the passenger seat of Paul van den Bergen's car, irritated by the way the slip mats weren't properly aligned. She had spent the rest of her weekend holed up in her room, using cooking wine as a panacea to acute anxiety and loneliness. She knew that asking to meet van den Bergen was attention-seeking behaviour, but she didn't care. She wanted to feel needed and safe.

'Posh wheels,' George said.

Van den Bergen gave a hollow laugh. 'Perk of the job. Anyway, they had no option. It's the only thing I can fit my legs into.'

Just the rumble of his voice felt like a hammer hitting her repeatedly at the base of her skull.

'It's very ... there's a strong smell of leather in here. I don't like ...'

She pressed the electric window button in the door panel of his gleaming black Mercedes E Class. The window slid down obediently, allowing the biting wind to whip the Monday morning smells of canal water, piss from a nearby public urinal and the weekend's abandoned kebab garbage into the German precision-engineered haven. She had walked all the way over to Westermarkt for the meet. It didn't smell any different on this side of town, she noted. *Should I mention the stalker?* she wondered. *No. I don't need a father. I can deal with it myself.*

'So tell me,' she said, fixing her attention on the side of his head. He had nice-shaped ears. 'Any leads?'

Van den Bergen thumbed his goatee. George noted that he still had a strong jawline for a man of his age. No signs of jowling. She liked that too. He smelled of sport deodorant and was dressed casually for a change in jeans, which made his long legs look even longer, and a black polo shirt. It made him appear younger and less formidable in the absence of padded shoulders.

'Not a one,' he said. 'My boss insists I bag him a cleric. We've pulled in a couple of copycat fundamentalist bloggers. One was a kid with mental health issues. The other ... well, it was just a dead end.'

He smacked the dash three times. 'Fuck it!' he said. 'The real perpetrator is running rings round us. I don't know how he's doing it. We thought we'd be able to trace the comment on your blogpost but we couldn't. I can't believe this bastard has IT Marie stumped!'

George sighed heavily, wishing she could light a cigarette. She looked up at the fabric ceiling of the car and shut her eyes tight. 'My instincts tell me ... I've got this hunch about right-wingers. I really think you should arrest—'

Van den Bergen glared at her, irritated. 'Leave the investigation to me, okay? I'm only filling you in as a courtesy.'

'Thought I was your student eyes and ears,' George said, holding back the urge to poke him hard in the chest. 'You'd still be trying to ID those body parts if it wasn't for me.'

George could just feel acerbic words trying to burn their way out of her mouth when van den Bergen's mobile phone rang. He pulled it out of his breast pocket. There was a brief and clipped exchange with someone who was clearly a superior.

'Yes, I'm not far from there. Straight away. Of course.' He rang off and looked at George with narrowed eyes. 'I've got to go.'

'Homicide?'

'You can get out now.'

His implied rejection felt like a stinging slap.

'No,' she said, wondering how he would react.

He leaned over her and opened the car door for her in that impressive way that older men with long arms do.

'Please yourself,' she said, not wanting him to see how much it smarted.

Ad walked with purpose and determination towards Amsterdam's Central Station. It was a dry morning but freezing cold. The biting wind howled up the main thoroughfare of Damrak. He clutched Astrid's hand, guiding her past the neon plastic smorgasbord of shop signs.

It was 6.12am. Astrid's Intercity train to Groningen departed Amsterdam Central at 6.26am precisely. With a change at Hilversum, she would be back in Groningen by 8.52am, allowing her to be in work by 9.30am on the dot. It had been the same routine for almost three years and Ad had made sure that Astrid had never missed the train.

He readjusted her heavy, pink weekend rucksack on his shoulder and momentarily let go of her hand to wipe sleep from his left eye. Astrid snatched his hand back and squeezed it hard.

'I'm going to miss you, honey bunny,' she said.

He felt her trying to manoeuvre him round so that she could catch his eye but Ad could only think of the twelve minutes she had before the train doors shut irrevocably for departure.

'Yes,' he said. 'Come on, we're late.'

He lengthened his stride and pulled her sharply to the left to dodge the second number 5 tram of the day, travelling from Central Station to A'veen Binnenhof. The palatial facade of the station with its red brick and neo-Renaissance spires was just beyond Prins Hendrikkade now. He pulled Astrid over the bridge. The dark green water was filled with queues of empty glass-topped cruise barges, waiting to choke the day's eager tourists with diesel fumes. He checked his watch again. 'Faster,' he said.

Standing on the platform, Ad slowed his breathing to calm his beating heart.

'Made it,' he said.

He put the rucksack on the ground between them and held her hands. She was pink-cheeked and out of breath.

'I've had a lovely weekend,' he said. 'Thank your mother for the cake.'

Astrid smiled at him with white teeth that were perfect, like small, evenly sized pearls. 'Are you coming home in a fortnight? It's Dad's fiftieth. He's having a party.'

Ad swallowed and looked at the clock. 'You'd better get on. They're going to close the doors.'

He leaned forward for a kiss. Astrid had always been a proficient kisser. In the beginning, they kissed with sweet-sixteen gusto. Sore lips, saliva and hard tongues. He had taken this to be passion, especially when she had let him fondle her boob under her jumper. As the years progressed, she had refined her kissing technique to be deft and clean. Tongue moved in, locked with his. Tongue moved out. Done. Still, he felt a visceral wrench as she boarded the train. Her jaunty hair arrangement bounced in its clip as though it was waving goodbye.

'I'll call you and let you know when I've got a free weekend,' he said.

She leaned over the threshold and kissed his cheek. 'Let me know how you get on with Klaus, darling. He seems great. You should definitely go to that memorial for your friend.'

Ad felt a jolt of realisation as she treated him to another pearly smile. She really was a Dutch beauty, like one of his mother's scentless baby-pink cultivar roses in bud.

She straightened up and groaned as she picked up her rucksack with both hands, although Ad knew it was not too heavy for a girl who was five foot nine and about ten and a half stone. Astrid thought it was unfeminine to lift heavy things when there was a man around.

'Have fun at work,' he said. 'I love you.'

'I love you too, honey bunny.'

As the train pulled away, Ad felt a void in the pit of his being that could only be filled by one thing.

When George rounded the corner between Keizergracht and Leliegracht, she spotted van den Bergen's car and then the inspector himself. Harried, frowning, chatting confidentially with another police officer. He was gingerly handling what looked to be a wallet with latex-gloved hands. Uniforms were cordoning off the area around an unprepossessing-looking large refuse bin. A young uniformed officer vomited on the ground, while a police-woman rubbed his back sympathetically.

'What's in the bin?' George muttered. She breathed in sharply.

George felt the bin drawing her like a magnet to its macabre contents. She knew instinctively it would be something unpleasant. She thought of chicken carcasses from the dinners her mother had made when she was a child. Things in bins that were once alive were never put there in good shape.

Van den Bergen spotted her and scowled. 'Go home,' he mouthed.

She watched him as he peered in the bin, balked and said something to his colleague. His colleague spoke into a walkie talkie. Suddenly three uniforms approached George, the only early morning spectator so far, apart from the curtain-twitching neighbours.

'This is a crime scene, Miss. Please back up to Keizergracht,' one said.

'I want to talk to van den Bergen,' she said.

'No,' the officer said.

Just as she was about to turn and leave, she heard heavy footsteps and felt a large, strong hand grip her shoulder.

'Wait,' van den Bergen said.

She spun around to meet him, heart suddenly picking up to a thunderous hundred and sixty beats per minute. He looked regretful, almost wistful.

'I need to tell you a name and see if you recognise it,' he said.

'What?' she asked, hearing the waver in her own voice.

'There was a wallet in the bin. Undamaged, so put there after … no money missing. Might not be the victim's but—'

'Tell me!'

'Remko Visser,' van den Bergen said.

'Oh, God.' George's face went instantly cold and numb.

'George—' van den Bergen began.

'Let me see him,' she said, shaking.

'No. There's not much … Forensics will ID him.'

'I have to see.' She turned back towards the bin and pushed past van den Bergen. He reached out and grasped air as she broke into a sprint.

With van den Bergen on her heels, George glanced up at the surrounding apartments. It was such a public place.

She steeled herself to peer over the rim just as she felt van den Bergen grab at her coat. All she caught was a snatched glimpse of blackened remains and an overpowering toxic stench on the air.

'Get back!' van den Bergen shouted through gritted teeth. He yanked her away from the bin, almost dragging her to the ground. 'I'll put you under arrest if you ever try to contaminate my crime scene again!'

George opened and closed her mouth but nothing came out. Her knees felt like jelly. Remko. Was he rammed in there like an over-roasted suckling pig at Trinity May-Week Ball? Maybe it was a mistake. Maybe it wasn't him after all.

'Nice try!' van den Bergen growled as he frog-marched her

back towards his car. George could feel his hot breath against her ear. 'Aren't photographs gruesome enough for you? You have to see the real thing?'

He paused momentarily by a group of uniforms, still clutching the back of George's sheepskin coat in an iron grip. The uniforms turned towards him deferentially.

'Get forensics here! Get a fucking tent round that bin. *Now!* And police that bloody cordon. I can't have every Tom, Dick and Harry trying to get a look at what's inside.'

The uniforms dispersed like a group of scalded children caught chalking rude graffiti on the playground tarmac.

'Get in the car!' van den Bergen demanded as he pressed his fob to deactivate the car's alarm.

George's breath came short. She felt nauseous but she did as she was told. She glanced back over to where some uniformed officers were now busy trying to erect a forensics gazebo around the bin. Others had begun knocking on doors of neighbours, notepads in hand. A grey-faced old woman sat sobbing on her doorstep. Perhaps she had made the foul discovery.

George was certain van den Bergen was going to bawl her out. She sat and waited.

'What are your thoughts? Initial first impressions?' he asked, calm as stagnant water and just as opaque.

George frowned. 'What? Aren't you going to give me an ear-bashing?' She quickly processed a theory. 'If it's Remko … He's Jewish. Anti-semitism could be a possible motive,' she said.

Van den Bergen nodded. 'But that might not be Remko and this is not a suicide bombing.' He stared straight into her eyes. Suddenly George felt like a bicycle being stripped down to its composite parts. 'The wallet may have been tossed in the bin by a mugger,' he continued. 'Remko might be in bed at home, sleeping off a hangover. My officers are trying to get hold of him now.'

George reached for a cigarette and jammed it into her mouth without asking. Lit up. Inhaled. 'But what if it is him?' she asked.

'This is an arson incident or probably the victim died by some other means and the perp set fire to the evidence. The other two are bombings. Organised. Terrorism.'

'This isn't about suicide bombers!' George said, the exasperation coming through in her voice. 'I've been telling you all along. Ratan and Joachim are victims, not perpetrators.'

'So if this *is* Remko, how do you know there's a connection between him and the other two?'

George wanted to give van den Bergen the 'are you totally stupid?' look but then she realised he wasn't and she shouldn't. He was not Fennemans.

'They're all politics students,' she said. 'That's the common denominator.'

'But Ratan and Joachim were exchange students. Remko's not. What's the motive then?'

George pictured Klaus Biedermeier and imagined why he would target those three men in particular. 'Ratan was Indian. Remko's a Jew. If it's a neo-Nazi doing this, then Joachim just got in the way. But the personal connection's still there to Biedermeier. Klaus gets sudden flu and stands Joachim up. Too convenient.'

Van den Bergen opened a window in the car and cleared his throat. 'But again, the other two were explosions.'

'And this is burning.' George polished the gear stick with the woolly cuff of her coat as she thought. 'Maybe it is just about fire.'

'A ritual?'

'Cleansing, maybe.'

'So what would you do next, Cagney?'

'Why are you interested in what I think?' George asked. 'You told me to leave the investigating to you. You're the experienced detective.'

'What would *you* do next?'

She looked up into van den Bergen's ageing, handsome face and saw sparkling curiosity in those grey eyes.

'I'd forget about al Badaar for now.'

'If Visser was Jewish, that fits with the bombing of a synagogue and the death of two other infidels. It could still be Islami—'

'You asked me what *I'd* do, remember? I'd go back through homicide records here and in southern Germany. I'd look for connections with the far right and Klaus Biedermeier. The guy's a first-class anus. I'd go to Heidelberg and have a chat with his pals. See what he gets up to on his home turf.'

'And?'

'I'd look for a link in the murders to arson or possibly biblical rituals. Fascism is supposed to be faithless, but some of those neo-Nazis justify their hatred by alluding to the Lutheran bible. I mean, what do these Heidelberg frat boys get up to? All that hocus pocus funny handshake crap. Maybe it's got its roots in some kind of religious lunacy or playing with fire instead of swords.'

George shrugged. Van den Bergen nodded slowly.

'Write another blogpost,' he said to her. 'Do something provocative about ethnic cleansing.'

'No! Why? The editor of *The Moment* has black-balled me now anyway, thanks to you.' She folded her arms and sucked her teeth. Being branded as politically 'off' smarted.

'I want to see what comes back. I'll have our guys monitoring responses at our end. I think our man is hiding in the student community. I agree with you there. But we need to draw him out. Maybe you could post comments on other current affairs blogs. Ones that get a lot of hits.'

George sighed. 'I'll think about it.'

Van den Bergen leaned over and opened the car door. 'Forensics have just arrived. I'll be in touch.'

George looked at him askance. 'Is that it? Class dismissed?'

'Go home, George. Lock your doors and do your internet thing. Ask around about Biedermeier. Discreetly, you know. The other kids on the course.'

'But I got thrown out of lectures. I've got to have one-on-ones with Fennemans.'

'Do what you can and watch yourself around Fennemans. I'm not supposed to say anything but I'm pretty sure he's ...' He chewed on his bottom lip as if debating whether to tell George exactly what he thought Fennemans was. 'Just be on your guard, okay?'

Ad put on a pot for one of strong Douwe Egberts, clipped out the savings coupon from the new packet and filed it into his coupon tin. When the coffee was brewed, he assembled a milky *koffie verkeerd* in a glass. George liked it that way, although she preferred to call it a latte.

She had not been home when he had swung by on the way back from the station. He had been hoping she would at least return his calls. When his phone did ring, it made him jump. He didn't recognise the number.

'Hello,' he said.

'Hey, Ad! Klaus.'

Ad fought to keep the surprise out of his voice. 'Hi, Klaus. How are you?'

He dropped his teaspoon onto his saucer with a clatter. Willing his senses to sharpen, he took a swig from his coffee.

'Good,' Klaus said. 'I know you're at the lecture later but it's hard to talk when everyone's there. I wanted to fill you in on Joachim's informal memorial thing.'

Klaus spoke on the phone with warmth in his voice that Ad had hitherto not heard. Was he seeing the side of Klaus that so many of the other students found charming and charismatic, but which he had only interpreted as arrogance and idiocy? He felt suspicion poke him in the back of the neck. Klaus hated him because he hung out with George. The friendly overtures had to be off-key.

'Yes,' Ad said, grabbing a pen and pad from the kitchen drawer with his free hand. 'Go on.'

'It's going to be in Heidelberg. Is travelling a problem for you?'

Ad searched for mockery in Klaus' voice but there was none. He thought about the cost of a return train journey to southern Germany. Apart from rent, he only had three hundred euros left in his account to last him the term. *Ouch.* Maybe Jasper knew of some pharmaceutical company trials he could earn money from by being a guinea pig.

'No. Fine. I've not been to Heidelberg since I was a kid.'

'I'll show you around.' Klaus' intonation was so flat that the offer sounded more of a command than a suggestion. 'We can get the same train.'

'Oh, great. I'd like that. I'd like that very much.' *What the hell am I agreeing to?*

Ad thought about backing out from George's hare-brained scheme, but then the image of Ratan's severed foot and Joachim's lifeless head prodded his conscience. He stayed on the line.

'Right,' Klaus said, breathing out, almost as though he was relieved. 'We'll go Friday night, if that's okay with you. My frat buddies can put you up in their house. You'll like it. It's very comfortable. The train departs Amsterdam at 16.41. There's a change at Cologne. We'd get in just before midnight but that's not going to be a problem, is it?'

'No.'

'I can meet you under the departures board in Central Station.'

Ad nodded. 'Yes. I'll meet you at about quarter past, just to be on the safe side.'

In his head, a voice screamed, *This is exactly what happened with Joachim! He's going to blow you up and say he had flu. Or maybe he'll get one of his cronies to do it. You're an imbecile, Karelse!*

'And Ad ...'

'Yes?'

'I'm really glad ... I really appreciate ...'

'It's okay.'

135

'It seems I got you all wrong.'

Ad wondered how he could bolster Klaus' belief in him; make his facade more solid and convincing. 'Yes, well,' was all he could manage.

When he rang off, his hands shook violently. He redialled George's number. Straight to voicemail.

'Damn! Where the hell are you when I need you?' he shouted into the phone.

CHAPTER 15

Later

George returned to her room. Before doing anything else, she carefully scanned the carpet for matches. Then she wedged the dining chair under the door. Next, she picked up an unopened bottle of wine by the neck and looked behind or under all large furniture. Finally, she flung open all the cupboard doors. Clear.

She washed her hands in very hot water twice, being careful to rub each soapy hand three times before rinsing. She started to polish the leaves of her gardenia while the kettle boiled. Tears were trapped inside her, as though today her emotional roller-coaster had stuck half way up.

Was it Remko? Was it Remko? What if it was?

She drove the memory of the bin from her mind. Knew she couldn't afford to be sucked into a downwards trajectory. After all, she had her one-on-one rendezvous with Fennemans at 1.30pm.

The kettle clicked. George picked up the jar of coffee only to discover that there was less than half a teaspoon of granules left. She put it into her cup anyway and had the concoction black, as there was no milk in the fridge. She switched on her stereo and cranked Dizzie Rascal up to number seven. She booted up her laptop. Checked Hotmail. There was one message in her inbox. It was from Sally Wright.

'Oh, here we go,' George said. 'What the hell do you want?'

From: Sally.Wright@cam.ac.uk 10.02
To: George_McKenzie@hotmail.com
Subject: Your mother again

Hello George

Sorry to nag but I've had your mother on the phone five times in the last couple of days. She says she has urgent news to tell you and desperately wants you to make contact. The number she's using at the moment is 07777 417321 although she changes that every three weeks and you only have one week from tomorrow left on that one. I've tried telling her that you're out of the country but perhaps it is something worth listening to???

I read your blogpost for 'The Moment' and was surprised and a little shocked by it. I trust you will tell me your thinking behind it when next we meet.

Any follow-up with the detective? I hope not.

Stay safe and all best wishes

Sally

Dr Sally Wright, Senior Tutor
St John's College, Cambridge Tel ... 01223 775 6574
Dept. of Criminology Tel ... 01223 773 8023

'Leave me alone!' George shouted at the screen.

She slammed the lid of the laptop shut. She plugged her dead phone into her charger. Three messages from Ad pinged at her in greeting. She was surprised by a sudden lump in her throat.

'Pull it together, George! For God's sake.'

Ad's voice rang clear on the recording. He sounded happy at first. Had she got the text? Did she want to meet for a late breakfast? In the following message, he sounded jittery. Klaus had been in touch. Ad had made arrangements to go to Heidelberg with him on Friday. The third message sounded like Ad trying too hard to speak in a calm, measured way. She had heard that voice before when he had written essays using her notes and prayed that Fennemans wouldn't discover the corner-cutting.

'Hey, George. Let's meet for a coffee after Fennemans. And why is your phone going straight to voicemail? I hope you're okay.'

George smiled wistfully. She started to dial his number but remembered he was in the middle of a lecture. She, on the other hand, had to finish off her essay for Fennemans.

Sitting at her little Formica dining table, facing the wall, she started to read through what she had written about Saddam Hussein and the legality of the American invasion of Iraq. As she trawled through her notes, poised to write the ending, the image of the body in the bin popped into her head. It made her drop her Biro.

'Damn!'

Her concentration levels were like a one-bar connection to the internet, sputtering and cutting out roughly every thirty seconds. She wrote four sentences. Then she texted van den Bergen.

Let me know when you ID the bin man.

She wrote six sentences. Arranged her pens and pencils into parallel lines. Stood up, rubbed her numb bottom and strode over to the window. Peered into the rooms that were also on the top floor in the houses on the opposite side of the canal. It had been a while since she had done that. Normally, she preferred to admire the tiled rooftops.

When she had moved into Jan's attic, she had been careful to analyse what she could about her neighbours opposite by looking in through the windows. The narrow canal which divided the street below meant that the windows were a good distance away, so she used the zoom on her camera. It wasn't perfect but it sufficed. From this, she extrapolated that those rooms that technically faced onto her own contained: cardboard boxes stacked about ten high and a bare bulb; what looked to be some kind of artist's atelier; and, finally, what George reasoned had to be a prostitute's room, since the brown and orange 1970s curtains were almost always shut.

Feeling her curiosity suddenly piqued, George dug out her camera and used the zoom to look once again into the neighbours' windows. The atelier still looked like an atelier. Full of large, half-done canvasses. Today, a man in a boiler suit with what seemed to be a very large 1970s Burt Reynolds moustache was painting something rubbish with vigour. The prostitute's room still had the curtains closed. The box room was still full of boxes but George noticed that there was something reflecting the light in the window itself.

'Now, what's going on here?' she said. She tried to zoom in further but the camera was already doing its best.

Was it a dream-catcher? Was it an optical illusion? Just somebody's light reflecting from a window on her side of the canal? No, too far away. Then, frowning, she realised what it was.

'I'll swear blind that's a camera lens,' she said. 'Or maybe a telescope. Shit!'

Was it angled towards her room? It certainly looked that way. She felt fluttering in her chest. Dizzy. Shaking her head in disbelief.

'How long has that been there?'

She looked back and forth from the lens to her window, narrowing her eyes and cursing. The angle was right. She was certain of it. And the gabled windows to her right and left – the attic rooms of the adjacent houses – were too far away to be the subject of interest for the unidentified Peeping Tom.

'Somebody's been spying on me!'

Feeling a mixture of indignant outrage, panic and curiosity, she threw on a baggy purple mohair cardigan and marched down to the small bridge that led to the opposite side of her street. She was still wearing her slippers. But here in the red light district, where sex shops competed with audience participation sex theatres, the kerb-crawlers and Monday morning passersby paid her no heed.

'I'm going to fucking nail this bastard right now!' she promised herself.

As she pushed open the glazed door to the building that provided such an excellent vantage point for her dedicated stalker, her dedicated stalker opened the cardboard box containing his new CCTV equipment, ran a finger over the small but perfectly formed hi-res unit and started to dismantle the old camera tripod set-up that sat in the window. He knew she was only downstairs now. His gaze landed on the lump hammer that sat on the only chair in the room, along with his phone and keys.

He crept down the stairs and watched the conversation unfold through the glass door which stood ajar:

'Who rents the store room upstairs?' she demanded of the behemoth of a shop assistant who stood in the sex shop, stacking the shelves with red rubber cocks. These were sandwiched between rubber fists and Jack Rabbit brand vibrators in gaudy pinks and purples. The assistant was easily seven feet tall and around the twenty-stone mark.

Looking her up and down, the assistant shrugged. 'You police? You don't look like police.'

'Do police wear slippers?'

The assistant nodded and pointed at her with a rubber cock. 'Why you wanna know?'

'I live opposite at the Cracked Pot,' she said. 'I just need to find out who's renting your store room. They overlook me.'

The assistant scratched his giant head with the cock. 'I don't know about the upstairs tenants. I'm just a dildo-peddling sales monkey. The boss isn't in. Come back later this evening. About seven.'

She gave him a quick smile. 'Nice cock.'

Should he walk in now and lure her upstairs? His breathing quickened at the thought. A chance meeting on the stairs. Oh, how nice! Fancy that. What a strange coincidence. Yes, come upstairs and inspect the room, by all means.

The lump hammer sat heavy in his trouser pocket; the handle protruding to allow for snap decisions. She turned in his direction.

'For Christ's sake, Paul, you're already up to your neck in it over haranguing Fennemans. Do you really want to rattle a German politician's cage now?'

Normally, Kamphuis saved a short-tempered bark for van den Bergen, reminding him vaguely of an overweight pit bull terrier that had had steak wafted under its snout, only to have it taken away. Today, he noted that his boss' voice was more begging than barking.

'Look, Olaf, it's not my fault if there's a neon sign flashing above Biedermeier's head, saying, "fishy as hell."' He cleared his throat and contemplated whether he was chesty today or not. He had been peeing a lot lately and had had back ache. Maybe his kidneys were failing.

'His father's a duke! A CDU backbencher. Come on, van den Bergen! And you told me the boy's alibis are—'

'He's a messed-up frat boy!' van den Bergen shouted. He

142

thought about the clips he had seen on YouTube of young men, dressed like some perverted amalgam of the Marquis de Sade and a medieval knight. Hacking chunks out of each other. Boasting for the camera that they were part of something noble, ancient and brave. 'Everyone's saying he has fascist proclivities. I'm going to speak to my opposite number in Baden-Württemberg and pull the kid's file. Him and Fennemans are the only—'

'Nearly a thousand people connected to that faculty either as students or employees! And you have to pick the two trickiest bastards to point the finger at. What the hell happened to al Badaar? He was such a lovely, simple hate figure.'

Kamphuis hoisted himself out of his expensive desk chair and paced to the window. Van den Bergen thought he looked haggard and grey. He wondered if the drinks sessions he boasted of in expensive brasseries with the commissioner and the cabinet spin doctor from the Ministry of the Interior and Kingdom Relations were so relaxing and enjoyable nowadays. Almost a month and the case was still unsolved. No, perhaps Kamphuis was not immune to stress after all. His ample, obsequious arse was on the line too.

Van den Bergen started to bounce his right foot over his left knee.

'Stop doing that! You know it irritates me,' Kamphuis snapped.

Van den Bergen continued to bounce his foot. 'You're blinding yourself to the facts, Olaf. Let me do the investigating. It's what I'm good at. I don't mind being unpopular. You do. Just let me do my job.'

Despite the personal cost of crippling stomach ache and tension in his shoulders, Van den Bergen had appealed to whatever better nature Kamphuis possessed.

Kamphuis sighed heavily in response. He continued to stare out of the window in silence.

'Just keep Fennemans off my back,' van den Bergen said, making his way to the door. 'Oh, and IT Marie asked if you can stop flirting with her when she's on earlies? It breaks her out in hives.'

Before Kamphuis could come back with an incensed response, van den Bergen hurried back to his desk. Poking the buttons with excited, determined fingers, he placed the call to the Baden-Württemberg State Police HQ and waited an agonising two hours for Inspector Dieter Mann to come back to him. When the phone eventually rang, he was so charged with coffee and anticipation that he shook.

'Well?' he asked.

Van den Bergen pictured a scene that matched the lightness in Mann's voice: the German inspector (probably well-liked and better paid than him), seated comfortably at his quality oak desk (with a real leather desk chair that was actually adjustable), enjoying cheesecake and coffee (that his team had brought him willingly, without spitting in it first).

'I hope the Dutch like lurid, scary stories as much as the Germans, Paul, because I'm just about to email you one over that the Brothers Grimm would be proud of.'

'You're late!' Fennemans barked at her.

'I know. I'm sorry. I've got stuff going on,' George said, flinging her bag to the floor and pulling out her essay.

Fennemans stroked his paunch and smirked. 'I'm not interested in your personal traumas. Don't come to my supervision late again.'

George looked at his bouffant hair and willed it to flop or part in the middle – something which might puncture the overblown, overstuffed wanker and let a little of his air out. The hair stayed put. She kept her cool. The telescope and the bin man had damped down her red mist. Thankfully.

'Read out your essay and we'll discuss it,' he said, waving his hand with a circular motion like a king greeting his minions.

'When can I start going to lectures again?'

'Read!'

As George read what she had written, the optimist in her felt hopeful that Fennemans would be impressed. Despite the tumult amongst the students generally and the nightmarish half-life she had been leading since identifying Ratan and Joachim, she had managed to read long extracts from over ten academic texts on the subject matter. Tracking them down without the Bushuis library collection at her disposal had not been easy, but George was nothing if not resourceful. She had bought the necessary texts at the VU academic bookshop in De Boelelaan and had photocopied the sections in the faculty, being careful not to open the books so wide as to crease up the spines. Then she had returned the books to the shop along with her receipts and got a refund. George thought that, under the circumstances, that displayed ingenuity and commitment.

Fennemans groaned. 'Is this confrontational style of argument what they teach you at Cambridge? Because I'm afraid it doesn't cut the mustard with me or the syllabus here.'

George looked at him, dumbfounded. The optimist inside her quickly keeled over and died.

He rubbed his blobby nose and gave her a nasty smile. When he moved his hand away from his face, her eye followed it and rested on a bottle on a low cabinet behind him. Gin. Was he drunk at 1.45pm? She looked back at his face. He was staring at her cleavage, which was barely on show.

'You're going to have to try harder than this, Little Missy.'

George dug as deep as she possibly could to mine the last seam of patience at the very core of her being.

'I'm sorry you feel that way. I gave that essay my best shot, Dr Fennemans,' she said. 'I researched—'

'You lack self-discipline. You clearly haven't read the texts on the reading list. You've gone off syllabus. Do you think you can make up your own degree course, my dear? Do you think special allowances are made for you? Is that what Cambridge produces?

Slackers who think they're entitled to it all without putting the effort in. Without having natural intelligence. Your attitude stinks and frankly, Little Miss McKenzie, I think you're lazy.'

Jesus! What is this?! George knew that Fennemans was one of those petty-minded, insecure men who felt threatened by intelligent, assertive women. From digging around on the internet and eavesdropping on gossip, she had ascertained that Fennemans had climbed through the ranks of the university's hierarchy quicker than his age and experience would normally dictate; a sycophantic Robin who had snatched Batman's cloak and mask undeservingly and by nefarious means. *So, shaky self-esteem is at the root of this bullying? That don't make it right, arsehole.*

When her mobile phone pinged in her bag, George ignored his sarcastic comments and read the text despite Fennemans' obvious exasperation. She had hoped it was from Ad, but it was, in fact, from van den Bergen.

```
Come and see me for chat. Get cab to
allotments at Sloterdijkermeer. I'll reim-
burse. Call me when you get there.
```

Fennemans' irritating voice buzzed on like a September wasp, drunk on its own potency and venom.

Without saying a word or explaining where she was going, George put her essay carefully into her bag, put on her coat, rose from her chair and left Fennemans on his own in the office. It wasn't until she unlocked her bicycle outside that she realised she was still wearing her slippers.

Klaus took his sword out of its case and examined it.

'Beautiful,' he said.

He pressed the pad of his finger gently against the cold, hard tip. It was a little blunt but still sharp enough to take a man's finger clean off. It had been too long since he had last used it in

146

a duel. He placed the sword ceremoniously on his Danish teak coffee table, careful not to make a dint with the heavy hilt on the table's oiled finish.

'Now, where did I put it?' he said. He went over to the kitchen area in his apartment and rummaged through the nick-nacks drawer for his whetstone. It was a matter of pride to Klaus that he kept all of his knives sharpened. Using a whetstone made him feel like a real craftsman.

Flinging himself onto his leather sofa, he started to sharpen the last twelve inches of the sword. The repetitive action relaxed him, and for the first time, he was able to chew over for a prolonged period the imminent memorial service for Joachim.

'I will be gracious. I will shake his family's hands. I will look them in the eye. I will not say anything stupid,' he told himself.

Klaus knew his own shortcomings. He was an excellent orator. The ability to charm strangers was always instantly available to him on demand, like ordering room service in a fine hotel. But he was not a truly emotional person, unlike every other gushing idiot in his family, who hugged and wept and declared true love, as though they were auditioning for a part in ZDF's B-Movie of the Week. That was one effect that he could not conjure at will. The more he was expected to show emotion, the more anxious he became until, suddenly, he found he could not focus on people's faces but had to look at their chests or feet instead. Once upon a time, his mother had suggested he was tested for borderline autism but Klaus remembered overhearing his father saying, 'Klaus is just a spoiled, wilful little shit. He'll grow out of it.'

'Fuck you very much, Papi,' Klaus said, thrusting his newly sharpened sword into the gut of his imaginary father.

Klaus' phone rang, shattering the illusion. Staring at his phone display, he didn't recognise the number. When he answered, it was some second-year law student he had met at a party before Christmas. Walter something or other. Desperate for a walk on the wild side.

'You told me you knew where I could score some quality gear and a little whore,' Walter said.

Klaus swallowed hard. 'Did I give you this number?'

'Yes.'

He must have been out of his head at that party. 'I'm busy right now, I'm afraid.'

'Come on, mate. You promised. You said you knew a club where the girls were really special.' Walter's voice was infused with sickly pleading.

The irresponsibility of passing the club's details on to yet another student with a flapping mouth was buried by the joy at bestowing hedonistic largesse upon a new member of the Biedermeier fanbase. Klaus gave him the number of Aunty Fadilla.

'Have fun!' he said to a now jubilant Walter.

His dealings at the club required no grand shows of affection. Thankfully.

'Don't worry, Klaus. Joachim's memorial service will be fine.' He looked at his reflection in his laptop lid. 'Just go through the motions.'

Klaus rearranged his lips and teeth into a satisfactory grin. But still, nagging at the back of his mind was the ultimatum from the Lusatian at the National Democratic Party of Germany head-quarters. He had taken a pile of cash and he was expected to deliver something special for the cause. Springing from his sofa, he swung his sword around and lopped the top six inches cleanly from his parlour palm. He would deliver Ad, of course.

CHAPTER 16

Later still

'Know anything about gardening?' van den Bergen asked George.

George nodded. 'I was plant monitor at school when I was ten. I grow things on my windowsill from seed. Does that count?'

Van den Bergen's knees cracked as he lowered himself onto a foam kneeling pad, resting on top of some mosaic paving that looked newly laid. He was wearing baggy old denim dungarees with a dirty grey sweatshirt underneath. On his feet, he wore the largest pair of wellington boots George had ever seen.

'Not really,' he said. 'But you can still pitch in. Pass me the box of tubers.' He nodded towards a cardboard box sitting just inside what George could only describe as a self-contained summer-house. Thrashing rock music blared out from a battered-looking portable stereo, sitting on top of a wooden orange box just inside the door.

'What the hell is that angry crap?' George asked.

'"Territorial Pissings",' he said, smiling.

'What?'

'Nirvana. Makes me feel energised. I'll turn it off if you like.'

She looked around at the dense evergreen backdrop to the allotments. The air smelled of damp earth and wet pine trees. A rash of daffodils and early tulips had flared up almost everywhere.

George now realised why van den Bergen's fingernails had been grubby when he had been interviewing students in Fennemans' office after the Utrecht bombing. They had been ingrained with good, honest, clean dirt from the ground. George didn't mind that dirt.

'Aren't you meant to be solving a spate of terror attacks and a murder?' she asked.

'Even senior inspectors take time out.'

'Is this your special place, then?' George carried a box of what looked like assorted testicles covered in dust over to van den Bergen and placed them on the paving in front of him.

Van den Bergen teased a tower of large, black plastic pots apart and delved into a rubber trug full of compost. He put a handful of the crumbly black matter into the pot.

'Yes,' he said. 'I come here to think.' He wiped his face with a muddy hand and smeared two brown stripes across his cheek. 'And to get away from things.'

'Let me guess. You like plants better than people,' George said, squatting beside the detective.

Van den Bergen chuckled and placed a fistful of tubers on top of the compost. 'Infinitely more so.' He pushed a black pot towards George. 'Here, you do some and I'll share my flask of coffee with you.'

George felt a burning itch to wipe van den Bergen's muddy face. Instead, she knelt down on a roll of horticultural fleece that van den Bergen passed to her.

'Why did you ask me here?'

Van den Bergen cleared his throat. 'When I got back to file my report at the station, I pulled what I could find on Biedermeier.'

George stopped what she was doing momentarily, stared at van den Bergen, trying to second guess what he would say. 'Oh?'

'You're very persuasive, Georgina. I think the technical term is nagging.'

'And?'

'Biedermeier sort of has a criminal record back in his home-town.'

George put her pot carefully onto the paving. 'Sort of? Go on.'

'Grievous bodily harm on an old Turkish guy. High jinks gone wrong after a heavy drinking session when Biedermeier's final term of senior school was over. The old guy makes his way home from visiting his daughter and her family, gets some racial abuse from a couple of the lads in the group. Next thing, Biedermeier smashes a heavy bottle of white beer over the guy's head.'

George knew from van den Bergen's crinkled-up eyes that he was studying her face for a reaction. Was he quietly irritated that he had not checked up on Klaus before a twenty-year-old girl had pointed the finger of suspicion towards him? No, van den Bergen wasn't competitive like Fennemans. He bore none of the sickly, cloying stink of the insecure.

She kneeled up, being careful not to grin or show any kind of 'told you so' smugness.

'Anything else?' she asked.

'Class A drugs. Cocaine. In Biedermeier's first year at univer-sity.'

'No!'

'Yes.' Van den Bergen treated her to a smile. 'Biedermeier and Joachim belong to the duelling fraternity but duelling fraternities, aside from being a little odd and archaic, aren't full of violent criminals and potential terrorists. No, those two idiots flirted out of school with a group of genuine, grown-up and reasonably well-organised fascists. Skinheads, heavy metal-heads, wearing big boots and military surplus. Lots of swastika tattoos. Lots of aggressive-looking piercings. You know the stereotype, right? It's a stereotype for a reason. Anyway, the local German police knew all about the alliance as they had been watching these thugs for a while.'

'Had Klaus and Joachim actually signed up to—'

'They were just buying drugs from one of the gang members. Deals out of a heavy metal pub. The Graf, Klaus' father, got wind of his son's unsavoury extra-curricular activities. He's a well-connected man. Asked the police to step in and nick Klaus with a couple of grams on him.'

'Tough love?'

'Precisely. But Big Daddy gets his legal representation to squash the charges. His sole aim was to put the frighteners on his errant son.'

George smoothed compost over the top of her tubers and patted the surface perfectly flat. 'And what happened with the GBH charge?'

'Thrown out. The judge decided the evidence was circumstantial because it was dark, and now the old man wasn't sure about the ID. The arresting officer hears from an informant that Big Daddy has paid the victim to change his testimony. So, the old Turkish guy lost his hearing in one ear thanks to the blow, but Biedermeier senior has a lot of clout and a lot of money. Now, technically—'

'Technically, Klaus hasn't really got a criminal record, then,' she said. 'He beat the system.'

'But he's still guilty as hell. It's on file. The boy's bad news. Tell me, is it the latest fashion to wear carpet slippers outside? I've got a daughter just a bit older than you but I haven't seen her about town in her slippers.'

'*You've* got a grown-up daughter?' George could see hurt momentarily flicker over van den Bergen's eyes. He said nothing. *Back to the slippers.* 'A footwear oversight. So what are you going to do about Klaus?'

Van den Bergen stood up with a slight groan, knees and hip cracking. She felt the muscles in her neck contract as she looked up at him. They were almost too close to one another. He took a step backwards in his enormous boots and disappeared inside the summerhouse.

'Well?' George said. She pulled her mobile phone out of her pocket and glanced at the screen. Nothing from Ad.

Van den Bergen emerged from the threshold carrying two fold-down chairs and a large, old-fashioned, tartan Thermos. He shoved the flask into George's hands and set the chairs up. Gestured to George that she should sit and then carefully unscrewed the lids of the Thermos to reveal steam that curled upwards like a fragrant, ghostly snake being charmed from its two-ply glass basket.

'Watch yourself. It's hot.' He handed George the smaller cup full of black coffee and poured one for himself into the larger cup.

George felt frustrated by his silence as he sat and sipped his drink, staring into nothingness.

Presently, van den Bergen sniffed. 'I can't see it being *just* Klaus. A lone wolf? A serial killer?' Van den Bergen sampled the words on his tongue. 'Never heard of a serial killer that blew people up. As far as I know, human bombs are strictly terrorist group activity. Organised.'

George looked at van den Bergen's ears in thought. They were almost perfect.

Focus, you dozy cow. Two pieces of jigsaw puzzle on opposite sides of her imaginary games table moved towards each other and clicked together.

'Cardboard at the scene of both bombings, wasn't there?' she asked. 'Perfect crime for a serial killer. Stuff your victim in a box and leave them outside the target. Boom. Maximum impact. No evidence left.'

Van den Bergen nodded slowly. 'It's an interesting theory, Detective Cagney. But our Klaus hasn't even got a car. Who could carry a body in a box without a car? That sounds like the work of more than one person. And there would be witnesses. Plus, most serial killers hunt on their own or in one consistent ethnic group, which isn't the case in this situation. No, I'm still liking the organised terrorism angle with Biedermeier in the picture somehow. My idiot boss still likes al Badaar and his Maastricht brothers. He doesn't give a shit about stomping all over the Muslim community's sensibilities. He just wants congratulatory headlines. All we can do is keep an eye on Biedermeier from a distance and rely on informants to report back if he gets up to something obviously suspicious.'

'Like what?'

'Like threats. Publicly made. Boasting about stuff connected to the bombing. Anything like that.'

Threats. George thought briefly of the matches on her carpet, the semen stain, the sense that she was being followed and the lens staring into her room. Was that a threat from a homicidal psychopath or some neo-Nazi headcase that didn't like her kind?

George's lips prickled cold. She drained the coffee to counter the strange sensation.

'You okay?' van den Bergen asked. 'You look like you've got the weight of the world on your shoulders.'

'I'm fine,' she said, deciding to keep the problem to herself until she was sure it wasn't her overly fertile imagination.

George stood up and stretched. She leaned over and rubbed the dirt off van den Bergen's cheek carefully, gently. *Yes, I'll try fighting my own corner first, but van den Bergen will protect me if I mess up.* She was possessed by a sudden urge to kiss him and lingered a little too long. She moved closer into his personal space, close enough to feel his warm breath on her chin. She parted her lips. *What am I doing?* Her cheeks glowed hot. Van den Bergen looked at her with surprised eyes.

'George!' he said. His voice sounded strangled. He was still sitting but he arched backwards to put distance between them.

The spell was broken and George stood up. 'Sorry. I felt dizzy after kneeling or something. Lost my balance,' she said.

The inspector looked at her with an air of suspicion but his expression quickly returned to normal. He rummaged in the front pocket of his dungarees and pulled out twenty euros. He held them out.

'Get a taxi back into town. Keep the receipt and the change. I'll get them from you when I next see you.'

George stooped down to pick up her bag. As she was about to step out of van den Bergen's allotment, back onto the path that led towards the exit, she turned back. Van den Bergen had already returned to his dahlias.

'Why are you involving me in all this?' she asked him. 'Confiding in me, like I'm one of you lot?'

He looked up and smiled. 'You may think I'm an old fart but I have good instincts. My old fart's instincts tell me you are ...' He seemed to search for the words as he studied the tuber in his giant hand. 'You understand people from here.' He clutched at his belly through the yoke of his dungarees. 'You're a natural. That's what my old fart's instincts tell me.'

George grinned reluctantly.

'Just keep your eyes peeled but stay out of mischief,' he said. *Like hell, I will.*

'Ow!' the giant cried, lips splayed against the unyielding surface so that he spoke like a man with toothache. 'That hurts, you loony bitch.'

Back in the sex shop, George yanked the giant's head to the side and pushed her face right into his so that she could smell his eggy breath. 'There was a camera pointed at my room this morning. Now it's gone. Who is renting that room?'

Just as suddenly as George's brain had succumbed to red mist, normality seemed to strongarm its way back into the room. George realised that the giant had just the sort of ears she didn't like. They had black tufts of hair growing from the ear-holes and long, red, fleshy lobes. They felt greasy. George hated greasy ears. Feeling disgusted, she let the giant go.

He sat up and rubbed his ears. 'Mad cow,' he said.

He reached under the counter. George snatched up a jumbo-sized blue dildo, wondering if the giant was going to pull out a weapon. When he didn't, she set the dildo back on its shelf, next to the gimp masks, as though she had just been browsing. A crawling feeling of deep stupidity started to infest George as she realised what a risible situation she was in; engaging in a stand-off with a man twice her size, threatening him with a range of sex toys and the prospect of ear injury.

The giant had in fact pulled out a blue, canvas-backed ledger – the kind that book keepers use. He opened it and leafed through several pages. His lips moved as he silently read the book's contents to himself.

'University.'

George took a step back, puzzled. She frowned. 'I don't understand.'

'The university rents that space.'

'You've been telling every horny little fucker in town about the set-up I've got,' his thoroughly indigestible associate said.

'No. Absolutely not. I've been utterly discreet,' Fennemans said, as he scrutinised this man – his accuser, his out-of-hours social secretary.

His associate jangled a bin lid of a gold and diamond watch that was unutterably crass. And who did he think he was impressing in those ridiculous low-hanging jeans?

'If you're so tight-lipped, why've I got another fucking kid on the phone to Aunty Fadilla, asking for a go with the girls?' This asinine oik's aggression visibly rippled off him, like heatwaves over a desert dirt track. 'By invitation only, Fennemans! It's not playgroup for your students.'

Fennemans didn't like dealing with him face to face and certainly not in his own home. Making arrangements over the phone or liaising with him over a coffee at the faculty was one thing. But this very physical confrontation on his own turf … it dampened Fennemans' spirits. He had been looking forward to an early night. Being challenged in this way simply did not make for the right ambience.

'Before you point the finger at me,' Fennemans said, 'you should give Biedermeier a grilling. I don't know what a young lad like him is doing in a place like that anyway.'

'He needs discreet too. He's got a thing for girls that wouldn't cut the mustard in the circles he moves in.' He prodded Fennemans in the shoulder. 'Unlike you, he's got the money.'

Fennemans felt like he was being poked with a sharp stick. '*I've* got the money,' he said defensively. 'You got back everything you were owed, didn't you? Within twenty-four hours! My tab's clear.'

The man lit a cigarette, tossed his match into an ashtray that was really only intended for display and exhaled acrid, blue-brown smoke into Fennemans' face.

'You'd better have a fucking big pile of cash for Aunty Fadilla when you next come over, then. It's new girls. Fresh in. You'll have a nice time.'

The man slapped his shoulder and grinned at him in a way that made Fennemans itch.

'W-What happened to the other girls?' Fennemans wondered if the anxiety strangling his own voice was obvious.

'What I do with the girls isn't your business. Saying that though, one's done a runner. The one who always wears her hair in pigtails. If you see her, give us a shout.'

Fennemans nodded in a staccato manner. 'Yes.'

'Just make sure you come and fill your boots before they get too manhandled.' He started to laugh, as though he had made an excellent joke.

'I don't think I'll come round for a while,' Fennemans said. 'I need to keep a bit of a low profile.'

The man stubbed out his stinking cigarette. 'Suit yourself. You'll be back. An old dog like you.'

Fennemans was relieved that the banging downstairs had started up after his rancid little associate had left.

The persistent knocking was so loud that Ad's heart sped up. As he walked down the hall, armed only with a wooden spoon, he visualised himself as one of the three little pigs, waiting with knees like jelly for the wolf to huff and puff his door down. He glanced through the spy hole, breathed a sigh of relief and opened up.

'You're early,' he said.

'Someone from the university is stalking me,' George said. 'I'd put my money on Klaus.'

Ad was sure she had been crying. Puffy eyes and a constant sniff were a dead giveaway. She pushed past him and went into the living room, which was mercifully free of housemates. The smell of Indian curry wafted in from the kitchen. He heard her stomach growl loudly.

'When did you last eat?' he asked.

'Rice Krispies at breakfast.'

He wanted to put his arms around her but he sensed she was prickly and agitated.

'I've made something traditionally British for you!' Ad said, grinning. He was wearing a striped butcher's apron.

George flung herself onto his sofa, rubbed her face with her hands and groaned.

'Did you hear what I said? Klaus is stalking me.'

'What do you mean?' Ad took off his striped apron so that she could see he was wearing a smart blue shirt and a pair of Diesel jeans underneath. He had never worn such trendy jeans before but they had been reduced by seventy-five percent and he was fairly sure they were the sort of thing George would like. He had been careful to hide them from Astrid.

When he caught George looking at him suspiciously, he felt himself blush. She had noticed. She was definitely going to say something about the jeans.

'Somebody's been putting things in my room. A Peeping Tom,' she said.

Maybe she hadn't noticed his clothes at all.

Ad listened in horrified silence as George related a sinister tale of being followed, observed like a lab rat and subjected to trespass. She blinked continually like a blind man desperately trying to see the way forward. Waiting for his reaction.

He had to sound reliable and knowledgeable. 'Can't you get Jan to put extra locks on your doors?' he asked. 'Tell van den Bergen!'

George shook her head. 'I don't want to tell anyone else. I'm not a baby. I've got my pride.'

Ad took hold of George's hands and looked at her palms. He liked the way the creases in the skin looked like a map of somewhere interesting. He wanted to protect her.

'Stay at mine,' he said. 'Especially while I'm in Heidelberg. Stay here.'

'No. You're the one at risk. You're going away with the prime suspect! I mean—'

'Please. I can't go to Germany worrying that somebody's trying to … Even if Klaus is with me, where I can keep an eye on him, he might … he's probably got an accomplice.'

He hoped she could see the pleading in his eyes. His body was pulsating as she drew fractionally closer. The air was still between them. He hardly dared to breathe. He noticed everything. Her eyelashes. The warm tone of her skin. The heavy floral smell of her perfume. Closer now. Then:

'Oh, and Remko's possibly been murdered,' she said.

Ad backed away, breaking the current of electric desire that connected them.

'Jesus,' he said. He stood up, snatching up his wooden spoon. 'The rice is burning.'

His heartbeat started to slow as he entered into the kitchen, fighting back the cloud of steam.

159

As he scraped the slightly singed basmati rice from the bottom of his pan, George then told him all about the man found burnt to a crisp in a refuse bin, with Remko's wallet providing the only funereal trimming in an otherwise spartan plastic tomb.

'So, you're probably spending the weekend with the faculty's very own serial killer,' she told him, wearing a smile that was devoid of all mirth.

CHAPTER 17

South East London

'I need some money,' Letitia said, fingers drumming on the sticky top of the fridge, hip thrust to the side in indignation. She held her free hand out, all nails.

Ella sucked her teeth. 'I ain't got no money,' she said.

'Lying little cow. I know you getting big backhanders off Danny. You selling his stash now. And since when did you talk like some sassy two-bit drug pusher? That school of yours squashed the street out of you years ago.'

Ella clutched her bag tight to the side of her body. She wasn't letting Letitia get anywhere near her hard-earned cash. She knew she would only spend it on vodka and cigarettes and an expensive trip to the hairdressers. Ella was saving it for something better. She had opened an account that only she knew about. In the money she deposited there were enshrined all her hopes and dreams. It was for university.

'It's all right for you,' Letitia said. She straightened up and flicked her hair extensions over her shoulder. 'Running with the pack now like that bastard never made our lives a misery.'

'Oh, spare me the guilt-trip,' Ella said. 'You decided to stay round here. The Head offered to pull strings for a better place in a better area when I started at that school. Why didn't you take it?'

Letitia opened and closed her mouth. Ella knew she was thinking up a barbed response or some bullshit to throw back in Ella's face.

'No way was I moving to some stuck-up boring shithole full of wanky, curtain-twitching bastards. You got to be amongst your own.'

'Bollocks! It's because you were too busy wallowing in the crap. It's all you know! And it's you that got me into this lie.'

'You got *me* nicked, remember?' Letitia's voice was shrill. Her eyes were flashing with anger.

But Ella felt bolstered by her subterfuge. She knew being one of Danny's girls was only temporary and there were elements of her new life that made her stomach turn. The violence. Being part of that. Making other people's lives a misery. It brought her down; pushed her into black corners where she felt as though all the happiness in the world had been sucked into a vacuum beyond reach. It was a price she had to pay though. She had to keep up the front. Eyes on the long game. But at least now, her world didn't just revolve around this house, that mother, those threadbare, broke-ass circumstances.

'No, I don't remember!' she shouted. 'You were the one flogging bent handbags. You ruined your little fiddle all on your ownsome, *Let-it-ia*.' Head wobbling from side to side like she'd seen Tonya do to Jez when he was being a dick.

'Show some respect!'

'I haven't got a shred of respect for you. You pimped out your own kid so you could avoid getting your collar felt.'

'I would have done time.' Letitia spoke through gritted teeth. She started to edge towards Ella, aggressive and puffed up like an angry adder.

Ella fleetingly wondered if Letitia was going to slap her. She hadn't been slapped by her mother in a long while. For that, at least, she was thankful.

'It was your first offence,' Ella said. 'You would have just got a fine or a bit of community service at worst. Anyway, thanks to me, everyone's off our backs now. Police and Danny's lot.'

Letitia lunged for Ella's handbag. 'Give it me, you cheeky little tart!' she snapped.

Ella swung the bag out of her mother's reach, but Letitia swiped at it with determined talons, scratching Ella's skin deeply as she did so. Rummaging through the contents like a rabid dog snaffling through meat scraps, she pulled out a wad of notes.

'Jackpot!' She was smiling now, rubbing the twenties between her fingers.

'What you going to do with it? Buy meat? Make us a nice dinner for once?'

Letitia laughed out loud and stuffed the money into her jeans pocket. 'Meat? You fucking joking? I got a date with Primark now, you dopey bitch. Think of it as tax. Mum tax.' Letitia grabbed Ella by the neck and kissed her on the cheek. 'Ta, darlin.'

Later, after Ella had done her shift with Tonya and Big Michelle selling dope, Special K and Miaow Miaow to the kids in the tower blocks, who were hoping for weekend respite from reality, Ella found herself sitting alone on the swings in the local park.

Danny, who had become more concerned with buying weight of anything he could get his hands on than with the childish smashing of windows for fun, was off 'on business'. Ella had excused herself from going drinking with Tonya and Big Michelle. The novelty of sensory overload was wearing thin after eight months. She wanted to think things through in silence. Chew over her plans and take stock of where her involvement with Danny and the others was taking her.

It was a bitter night. She clutched her Puffa jacket close to her body and watched the smoke of her breath in the moonlight.

I don't want to go back. I can't face another row. I'm being torn apart from all sides.

She looked up at the moon's purifying glow and felt like she wanted to tell it her secrets.

I've got to get out of this, moon. Give the police what they need and get out of all of it. Danny, Letitia. The lot. The Gargoyle said he would make that happen. I can do this. I can see it through. I'm strong. I got my GCSE grades. I've just got to keep it going a bit longer and get my A levels. I can't fuck up. I won't fuck up. I'm going to make this happen, moon. I swear to you. I'm getting out of here.

'All right, Ella?' a nasal voice said from the opposite side of the small park.

Ella's breathing came fast and short. She peered into the shadows to see who the voice belonged to but she already knew.

'Jez! I thought you was with Danny.'

'Nah. I had to sort out some scamming junkie grass but I'm finished now.'

As Jez stepped out of the shadows and into the moonlight, Ella shuddered. She didn't want to think about what sorting out a scamming junkie grass entailed. Actually, she did.

'What did you do?'

'Gave him a little poke in the eye with a hot iron. I thought it would make a cool popping sound but it didn't. Wasn't as good as I'd hoped.'

Ella's stomach churned. She was a police informant. What would Jez do to her if he knew about the Gargoyle and their cosy little meets in his car?

'Can I sit with you?' Jez asked.

No! Go away, you freak. Ella nodded. 'Yeah. Sure.' Smiling weakly. Showing just enough enthusiasm.

He chose the swing next to her and sat down. He pulled a packet of cigarettes out of his Puffa jacket pocket and offered her one, which she accepted. Then he produced a Zippo lighter from his jeans pocket. He clicked the lid open, flipped the wheel. The lighter became a beacon of flame in the night.

'You always overfill it!' she said. 'How do you not burn your-self?'

Jez laughed. His face was illuminated as he lit his cigarette and hers. He was not unattractive but there was a cruelty and absence of conscience behind his deep-set, black eyes. Worse than Danny even. Danny gave the orders but Jez executed them with vigour and almost evangelistic joy. He was a sadist. Everybody could see it. Ella, especially.

'I do burn myself,' he said. 'All the time.'

'So why overfill it?'

'Like you need to ask?' He extinguished the lighter and reig-nited the six-inch torch of yellow fire. He waved it in front of her face.

Ella could feel the heat and leaned back on the swing.

'It's beautiful,' he said. 'And I like the pain. It gives me back control; order out of chaos.'

Without hesitation or need for a second opinion, Ella diag-nosed Jez as deranged. *God, get me out of here fast.* 'I never had you down as some philosophical geez, Jez.'

'Yeah well. Lots you don't know about me. Lots I don't know about you, innit?'

Ella figured, he was just like any other boy. He liked the sound of his own voice. She would let him speak for five minutes, make her excuses and go.

'Go on then, Jez. Tell me about how you come to be tangled up in our little gang. You got five minutes and then I gotta get back, yeah?'

Jez smiled at Ella and started to swing gently. The metallic creak and clang of the swing as it moved back and forth made Ella's teeth jar.

'I wasn't always from round here,' he said. 'I lived round the way. Fucking Millwall territory, man!'

'You like from some family full of skinhead nutters?'

Jez ran the flame of his lighter up and down the steel chain of the swing and then snapped the Zippo shut. 'My mum's side of the family are proper BNP, English Defence League and all that shit. But my dad ... My granddad went mental when Mum got up the duff with me.'

'How come?'

'My dad's a Saudi.'

George looked at his black hair and black eyes. Foiled by the pale, slightly freckled skin of a Celt. She had never had him down as mixed race.

'Bringing up an Arab's kid in white Bermondsey, man. Imagine.'

'Jesus,' Ella said, nodding. 'Must have been tough. Was your mum and dad married?'

''Course not. Dad was already married with a proper family near Marble Arch. Respectable councillor or some shit. Had a big electricals business too. Came round at the weekends and taught me a bit of Arabic and the Qur'an when Granddad was out at a footy match. I think the word for it is clandestine.'

Ella looked at Jez with a degree of surprise. It had not occurred to her that he had the intellectual capacity to learn English properly, let alone Arabic. She hooked her arms around the swings and looked at his bow-shaped lips, as he sucked on his cigarette. Hidden depths.

'So why did yous move here, then? Was it to get away from—'

'Dad's proper family found out about Mum and me when I was about nine or ten. Went fucking ape. I'm getting earache off Granddad about blacks and Pakis and how I'm not one of 'em, so that's okay. And I'm getting big time rejection off my dad suddenly, who don't want to know his love child no more.'

'Did your mum just want to start fresh?'

Jez looked at her with intense black eyes and laughed. 'No, man! I set the fucking house on fire.' He laughed heartily and threw his head back so he was looking right at the full moon.

A werewolf of a boy. A feral, half-human mistake made from bits of skin with an incomplete heart. Or perhaps this was just

166

a superficial veneer of his own making, concealing the hurt beneath.

'That was the best, yeah? I'd been messing around with fire and stuff anyway. And I get this idea when Dad's round and him and Mum are screaming at each other and that … you gonna love this … if I set fire to the house, it's gonna make everything all right. Dad will rescue us and show he cares and everything will get back to normal.'

'And what happened?'

'It worked. He ran upstairs and rescued me, just like I planned. So that means he loves me, don't it?'

'But you moved.'

'Yeah, well the house burned to the ground, didn't it? Council shifted us here.'

'And your dad?'

'Fire investigator worked out I started the fire, didn't he? So Dad says I'm a fucking head case and that's the last we seen of the bastard.'

Ella succumbed to the sudden wave of sympathy that washed over her. She reached out to pat his hand. But then, the momentary lowering of her defences betrayed her.

'Will you go out with me?' Jez asked. 'We could go see a film.' Jez obviously thought that in telling her his story, he had broken through an unspoken barrier.

'I'm one of Danny's girls,' she said. At that moment, she wished more than anything that Danny was there to put a territorial arm around her. To save her from having to salvage a happy ending to this squeamish proposition from a boy who delighted in cruelty.

Jez stood and put his face right up to hers. She could feel his breath on her nose. '*Well, fuck you!*' he growled, rattling the chains of her swing violently.

Terror thumped Ella in the gut so hard, she felt like she had been wounded by a sawn-off shotgun. She gripped the swing, forcing herself to stay utterly cool and unruffled on the surface.

She breathed hard through her nostrils, keeping her lips tightly shut. Was he going to hit her? No.

Jez took two steps backwards and started to point and laugh at her. 'Got you!'

At that point, Ella prayed for the big job to be on, just so it could all be over.

CHAPTER 18

Amsterdam, 16 January

At ten past four, Ad stood beneath the departures board with a thumping heart. His tinnitus ears registered their protest at the abstract chatter of animated voices, the hurried clacking of heels and the tooth-jangling squeak of trainers on a hard floor. Tourists and weekend travellers lugged heavy bags to their onward destinations like reluctant old turtles carrying oversized shells. It wasn't quite time for rush-hour mayhem but Amsterdam Central Station was busy enough to heighten Ad's anxiety.

He felt lightheaded – a feeling only worsened by the Diet Coke that he was drinking. He kept visualising the cook's knife in his bag that George had insisted he conceal there. If he was stopped by the police, he would have some explaining to do.

Klaus appeared at precisely the right time. He carried a large, leather-trimmed weekend bag and a long rectangular hard case that looked like it might contain a snooker cue. He wore stone-coloured chinos. Beneath an unbuttoned brown overcoat, which had the expensive sheen of cashmere and pin-stitching on the edges of the collar, Klaus wore a crisp white shirt with a pale blue silk tie and a navy wool blazer with brass buttons. Only his brown moccasins looked a little well-worn, but Ad could see they were leather-soled and probably hand-lasted, judging by the rest of his attire. Klaus looked like a count's son. His face was flushed pink. This gave his very blond hair the appearance of being slightly green-tinged.

'Hello, Ad. We're on time.' Klaus clasped Ad's hand into a formal handshake which revealed a Longines watch and the cufflinks of an older man.

'What's in the case?' Ad asked.

'My sword,' Klaus said.

Ad dropped the bottle of Coke on the floor as his trembling fingers refused to play ball. The contents exploded into coffee-coloured foam and covered the toes of Ad's best shoes. He followed Klaus to the platform, already feeling at a disadvantage.

'So, was Joachim your best friend then?' he asked Klaus once the train had pulled away from Amsterdam. It started to rock and roll through the ugly grey outskirts of Amstel, picking up speed as it shot out into the flat green quilt of the surrounding countryside.

Klaus rubbed his scarred cheek. His blue eyes wandered to the scenery, as though he were consulting the fields and wind turbines for a response. 'No. But we were bound together by our experiences here and because we are, I mean, *were* both members of the same duelling fraternity.' Klaus turned to focus on Ad. He put his hands behind his head and looked down his straight nose at him. 'What happened with you and the English girl?'

Underneath the table, Ad gripped his knees. 'We were never really that friendly. She hung out with me for the first term and I enjoyed practising my English sometimes. Then we had a big argument. I think she was jealous of my girlfriend, so we're not speaking now. We don't really see eye to eye.'

Klaus yawned, showing a mouth full of strong-looking teeth. 'They are culturally too different from us. And I'm not surprised she was jealous of your girlfriend. Astrid is a rare beauty.'

Although he knew that eulogising about the blonde-haired, blue-eyed Astrid might curry favour with Klaus, Ad was keen to divert the conversation away from her now. He felt as if using her as leverage to find out more about this potentially dangerous man was an abuse of her trust in him. It was bad enough that he was falling out of—

What would George do? She would turn the tables on Klaus. 'Do *you* have anyone special?'

Klaus laughed. 'I'm too busy at the moment. I'm committed to a political cause, actually. And to my studies.'

'What kind of cause?'

'I'm involved in the National Democratic Party of Germany.'

Ad already knew what kind of party the NDP was but prompted Klaus to explain it to him anyway. He kept the demeanour of someone politely interested.

'It's an alternative to the CDU,' Klaus said, 'with … er … an emphasis on preserving Germany's traditions and a German's right to first dibs on employment.'

'Preserving traditions?'

'More cultural identity really.'

'Whose cultural identity?' Ad could feel himself interrogating Klaus. He didn't want to put him on edge. He wanted to tease information out of him.

Klaus smiled an easy smile. 'Why, true Germans of course,' he said. Then his expression became serious and he lowered his voice. 'And I'm telling you this because I've met your girlfriend and I think I understand you a bit better now.' He winked at Ad.

Ad squashed the urge to bark with laughter. *This guy is an upper-class simpleton. He's made sweeping assumptions from a five-minute encounter with a blonde girl.* 'Is this a family thing then? Your political leanings, I mean.'

Chuckling and another glance out of the window. 'You must be joking. My father's a major backer of the CDU. I got interested in the NDP just to piss him off! I'm the prodigal son.'

Klaus hoisted his weekend bag from the seat next to him onto the table and pulled out a packet of crisps. He offered one to Ad, who accepted and silently berated himself for breaking bread with a fascist. He had to remind himself that George had sanctioned this weekend. Then, feeling like he didn't want to be obligated to Klaus for anything, Ad took out from an Albert Heijn bag the pile of ham sandwiches he had made at home for the journey and carefully wrapped in foil. He reluctantly offered one to Klaus, which Klaus accepted with a facial expression that betrayed he would have preferred something more expensive and sealed in plastic. Ad was convinced that Klaus probably didn't even know what a savings coupon looked like.

'Are all your friends involved in this nationalist politics thing?'

'No, not in the slightest. Well, one or two are. We're not exactly popular.'

'Is it because you're Holocaust deniers?' Ad immediately berated himself for bating Klaus. The last thing he wanted was for him to clam up.

Klaus shook his head. 'Ad, Ad, Ad,' he said through a mouthful of ready salted. 'Our party's motto is, "Think about it but never show it". No, when I said we're not popular, I mean the party only has five hundred members in the whole of Baden-Württemberg.'

'Why support a lost cause then?'

'It's not lost!'

There was an edge to Klaus' voice that Ad was not entirely comfortable with. He thought briefly about the knife in his rucksack, safely wrapped and useless above him on the luggage rack. He prayed he wouldn't need to use it during the weekend.

'In Mecklenburg-Western Pomerania and Saxony, the NDP actually has seats in state parliament.' Klaus said. 'But enough about boring old politics. This weekend is about remembering Joachim and the injustice that's been done to his good name because of Muslamist militants boasting about something they didn't even do.'

'Yes, poor old Joachim.'

'And I'm going to show you around some of my favourite haunts. Maybe you'll even get to see a duel. That's a real treat.'

Ad looked out at the acres of polytunnels, laid across the Dutch fields like silvery, fat worms in the steel-grey twilight.

What a treat.

'Come on in, Paul. I'm almost finished here,' Marianne de Koninck said.

Van den Bergen had been perched silently against the door frame, watching the attractive forensic pathologist dissecting, weighing and evaluating the minutiae of this man's life right up until the moment he was killed.

'Don't be squeamish,' she said, snapping off her latex gloves and heading for the sink.

He pulled a face as he looked down at the eviscerated corpse on the slab. The bin man's blackened ribs had been sawn apart to reveal the now heartless, semi-cooked contents.

'I'll just finish making these notes,' the pathologist said, turning away to speak monotonously into a Dictaphone. After a while, she clicked the recording equipment off. 'Right, done,' she said brightly, as though she had just finished her weekly shop at the supermarket.

Van den Bergen eyed up her lithe runner's form underneath the ugly overalls. 'The human body is so beautiful,' he said. 'Right up to the point where it's mutilated. We're all stinking and horrible on the inside.'

The pathologist laughed. 'You're such a cynic!'

Van den Bergen put his hand in his trouser pocket and prodded his aching hip. 'This job and a bullet in the hip made a cynic out of me a long, long time ago. And this place … how the hell do you work here? It's freezing and depressing. I prefer a pissy holding cell to this.' He wafted a hand around to indicate the austere tiles and the glare of the overhead lights. 'Don't you get nightmares?'

The pathologist grabbed his arm. 'I'll make you a coffee.'

173

Van den Bergen relished the warmth of the contact but pulled his arm away. 'I haven't got long. Just give me the low-down.'

In the presence of the corpse, the pathologist told van den Bergen how it had come to be on her slab.

'It's Remko Visser, all right. Dental records match. He suffered trauma to the head. The skull was indented by something with a square edge – I'm guessing a lump hammer or something of that ilk. It caused a bleed on the brain but that didn't kill him.'

Van den Bergen breathed in deeply and closed his eyes. He dreaded the return visit to the Visser family, wondering with ever-diminishing hope where their only son was; barely clinging on to sanity, as fate swept away all they held dear on a rip tide of grief and loss. 'Go on.'

'His index finger is missing with a plastic tourniquet still attached at the stump.'

'The kind you find in hardware stores?'

'It had melted, but yes, I would guess so.'

The pathologist left Remko Visser's body without a backwards glance and started to head down the glum, chilly corridor.

'He was definitely still living when he was set on fire,' the pathologist said. 'Petrol in his lungs.'

Van den Bergen was possessed by a sudden urge to go round to Tamara's flat, hug her and blow raspberries on her cheeks like he had when she was little. He slid his hand into his pocket and fingered his mobile phone.

'Do you think Visser felt anything?' he asked, silently praying that the boy had been out cold.

Marianne de Koninck unlocked her office and held the door open for van den Bergen. 'He felt everything,' she said. 'Arms raised defensively; the classic pugilistic stance of someone meeting their end in an inferno. Melted plastic under the fingernails where he'd scratched at the inside of the bin. There's absolutely no doubt that he was fully conscious when he was burning.'

Heidelberg's main train station is reputed to be the architectural jewel in Deutsche Bahn's crown. Opened in 1955, it is an elegant building full of windows and space, both reflecting modernity without being brutalist and carrying from the past a whiff of art deco as well as the unfortunate whiff of piss.

When Ad and Klaus arrived, it was midnight. Ad yawned and steadied himself against the pitch and roll of the sleep-deprived. He followed Klaus through the station without speaking, only dimly aware of the sgraffito of the sun god, Helios, above the clock on the wall of the main hall. He was not concerned with architecture or the station's seedy ambience but rather that he needed to urinate badly.

They headed out towards the taxi rank. The starless sky was overcast. A light drizzle started to descend. Ad buttoned up his reefer jacket and put up the collar against the January cold.

'Old town,' Klaus told the cab driver of an ageing BMW.

The cab driver eyed Klaus' scars and sniffed.

'You want to put those bags in the boot?' he asked with a rolling Swabian accent.

'No thanks,' Ad said.

Klaus ignored the driver entirely and had already got into the cab, putting his weekend bag and sword case on his knees.

'I'm dropping my friend here near the Corps Rhenania on Hauptstrasse,' he said. 'Take us to the junction with Friesenberg. We'll walk it from there.'

Ad saw the cab driver sizing him up in the rearview mirror. He wondered how the man was judging him. Did he think he was one of Klaus' number? An entitled, arrogant bigot with a frat membership for life?

He looked away from the cab driver's searching eyes and watched the inky blackness of the River Neckar speed by to his left. On the opposite shore, the pitch dark was punctuated by a braille strip of lights, dusting the banks with their homely glitter as they blazed in the windows of grand old houses. To the right,

175

beyond Klaus' bulk, were the silhouettes of steep-roofed historic buildings. By day, Ad remembered the buildings were like beautiful courtiers wearing elaborate costumes. But they skulked silently by the river now; shy and retiring in their widow's midnight black.

Presently the taxi stopped and Klaus handed over a ten-euro note. Ad immediately pulled out his wallet, stuffing a five into Klaus' free hand.

'What's this?' Klaus asked.

'Haven't you heard of going Dutch?' Ad said. 'We like to pay our way.'

Klaus pushed the five back at Ad, trumping his gesture of generosity. 'I don't need it. Come on. We're wasting time.'

They marched slightly uphill, along a tree-lined street with only a couple of grand villas on either side. High above the street to the left, Ad saw the crumbling castle, floodlit and magnificent among the trees. The blackened windows in the facade peeped like watchful eyes through the icy mist in which the castle was partially wreathed. He felt like he was being observed by a host of sinister spectres.

'Come on,' Klaus said with excitement audible in his voice. He pushed against a tall wrought iron gate and led Ad inside a garden surrounded by high walls.

'Where's this?' Ad asked.

'Corps student accommodation.'

'Jesus.' Ad looked up at the three-storey villa. Its pale render glowed in the streetlight. Most of the tall, shuttered windows were lit from within. Through a ground-level window, he glimpsed a heavy wooden chandelier hanging from a high ceiling. On the dark, wood-panelled wall he spied several mounted stags' heads complete with colossal antlers.

'Membership has its benefits,' Klaus said.

Klaus knocked on the door with the large brass knocker. Voices inside sounded jubilant. Footsteps. Then the door was opened by

176

a small, dark-haired man whom Ad judged to be in his second year at the university. Not quite haggard enough to be a third-year student. Too much stubble for a fresher.

'It's Biedermeier, guys!' the small man shouted to the house's occupants within.

Inside, there was much embracing, clapping of backs and greetings given in German by raucous, well-spoken voices. Ad stood by an open guestbook on a table by the door. He glanced at the names that were written there. Each was signed with a flourish in one column and then printed in another. All names were ended with two numbers. 54:32. 47:23. 15:21. Klaus took the pen and signed his name, ending it with 47:33. What did it mean? He frowned.

'Who's this then?' one of the men asked.

Klaus laid claim to Ad by flinging a cashmere-clad arm around his shoulder. 'This, my friends, is a Dutchman.'

Ad smiled weakly and stuck out his hand, prepared to shake with the housemates like a gentleman, but they all jeered and started to crack jokes.

'Hey, guys, what do Dutch kids get for Christmas? Coupons!'

'Hey, hey! Why did Ikea stop opening stores in the Netherlands? They couldn't afford to keep restocking the free pencils any more!'

'I've got one! How do you tell a Dutchman from a Belgian? Burn a five-euro note and see which one sweats the most.'

Ad swallowed hard. He was outnumbered. Resentful that he didn't dare fire back at them an entertaining anti-German joke that his father had taught him when he was twelve. 'Ha ha. Yes, very funny. Hello, I'm Ad Karelse.' He tried to make himself heard above the laughter.

Despite the ridicule, one by one, the frat boys all grabbed his hand and shook it. He was ushered into a communal lounge and pushed into a deep old leather sofa. The decor was wood-panelled old German gentleman's club. The air smelled of wood polish and dust beneath a fug of Marlboro cigarette smoke. There was a faded Persian rug on the floor. On the walls were the stags' heads he had spied from outside together with mounted foxes and even a moose. The sad, glassy-eyed taxidermy was interspersed here and there with old oil paintings of young men wearing fraternity caps and sashes over military-looking dark uniforms. Next to one such portrait hung a curling A1 poster of a naked blonde with enormous silicone breasts and a red thong.

'Drink! Bring the Dutchman drink!'

'*Feuerzangenbowle!*' Klaus bellowed.

'You bet,' said the small man who had opened the door. '*Krambambuli! Krambambuli!*'

Ad's mastery of German was not as strong as his command of English. He wondered what the bloody hell a fire thingy bowl was. What kind of a battle cry was *Krambambuli*? Perhaps they were going to burn him alive.

Klaus punched the air, set his sword case on the table and clicked the locks open.

Ad's pulse quickened.

'Ha ha. Are you going to run me through with your sword and then roast me?' Ad asked.

Klaus smiled sardonically and pointed the tip of his sword at Ad's heart. 'Like a sacrificial Dutch lamb.'

CHAPTER 19

17 January

Rattling along the old streets on her boneshaker of a bike towards the well-heeled Old South district, George wondered if she still had the knack of breaking and entering. Going to Klaus' apartment had been an impulsive decision. But she was sick of feeling impotent and alone in Ad's bedroom with only the lingering scent of him on his bedsheets for company. Now she giggled in the dark; savouring the early morning adrenalin pick-me-up. *Just like old times.*

Klaus' Daddy Dearest was definitely picking up the tab for his son's Vondelstraat address. The street was lined with BMWs and Mercedes, parked too close together beneath winter-bare trees like upmarket sardines in a tin. The spire of a church at the end of the street pointed up towards the pink haze of the city's night sky, which may or may not have contained a watchful, vengeful Calvinist God.

George breathed in. The air was clean here. No whiff of rancid kebab meat, burgers, pot, piss or trash.

Being careful to hang back in the shadows, she spied the communal entrance to the old house that had been divided up into exclusive flats. Illuminated by the glow of the Victorian-style lamp posts, she could see a buzzer entry system.

'Don't tell me I've made this trip for nothing,' she muttered. Her watch showed it was almost 2am. 'But at least it's Friday night. Maybe I'll catch someone coming home from a club.'

George smoked her way through three cigarettes and, at 2.34am, her patience was rewarded by two young women click-clacking down the street towards her. The sequinned, miniskirted good-time girls laughed like their lives depended on it and shouted out the contents of their drunken heads for all to hear. Somebody leaned out of a third-storey window. Threatened to call the police. Blowing raspberries at their disgruntled neighbour, the women staggered to the front door of Klaus' house on vertiginous platform heels.

Now's my chance.

George crossed the road. Made like she was just walking down the street on the way somewhere. Hood up. Hands in pockets.

The women unlocked the communal door. Giggling. 'Did you see that guy? He definitely wanted to score with you.'

George was within three feet of the door as the women pushed it open and clattered inside. She prayed they would not look back to see why the heavy security door had not clanged shut behind them. She wedged her foot in the gap. George rejoiced silently that she had worn her heavy boots.

When the women's chatter had been swallowed by a closed door somewhere on the first floor, George nimbly climbed the stairs to the second floor. Clean, grand and brightly lit, the communal area looked like an upmarket hotel with an ornate mirror on the landing hanging above a half-moon table. She caught her reflection. Even without her hood up, she would stand out as an intruder. How many shabbily dressed women would be skulking around an apartment block like this? *No time for second thoughts. Shelve it.*

Klaus' door loomed before her. Flat number 5. Yale-style lock and old two lever mortise. From her pocket, she pulled out her keys. Her steady fingers immediately found her two prized skeleton keys and she silently prayed that Klaus' apartment would have no alarm system. The locks clicked. Good. She pushed the door open only to hear the musical tinkling of an alarm on its thirty-second countdown.

'Just my luck!' she said through gritted teeth.

Panic grabbed hold of George and threatened to throttle her. 'Keypad? Keypad?'

She pushed the door closed, moved quickly down the hallway and spied a keypad on the wall just out of sight of the door. Lifted the flap. Yes, she recognised the type. Four digits and a tick to unset. But which four? She didn't know Klaus' date of birth. Her phone pinged loudly with a text. *Not now!* But reflexively she grabbed at it. Stared at the display. Beeping, reminding her the time was almost up. Dropped it through trembling jelly fingers.

Come on. Come on.

'Lift your top up so I can skewer you properly,' Klaus said, grinning at Ad.

Ad's eyes widened behind his glasses. He had instinctively folded his arms and crossed his legs. Reluctantly he revealed his midriff.

The sword that Klaus held was about three feet long, maybe longer, with a basket over the hilt bearing corps colours in dark blue, white and red stripes. The blade had been sharpened on both sides. Now, it stuck in the skin just below Ad's heart. Ad nervously bit the inside of his cheek. The others didn't seem disquieted by the sight of this … public execution.

Ad's bladder was suddenly pushing to empty itself in fear. Another few seconds and the floor would rush up at him, knocking him out cold.

Klaus started laughing merrily like an evil Santa.

'Jesus! Why the fuck are you laughing?' Ad asked in a strangled voice.

Suddenly a large steel stockpot was produced by a lanky man

181

with strawberry-blond hair. He hung it over a small fire in an old, open brick fireplace at the end of the lounge, which Ad had hitherto not noticed. Into the stockpot, the man poured three bottles of red wine. He tossed in some orange peel and a bundle of spices.

'*Krambambuli!*' Klaus swung the blade away from Ad, marched over to the fireplace and balanced the blade of his sword over the pot. Onto it, one of his comrades placed a white cone.

'Oh, it's bloody *glühwein!*' Ad said, breathing out a sigh of relief. 'You bastards!'

He dared to shuffle over to the fireplace to get a better look.

'What's that white thing?' he asked Klaus.

'It's a sugar cone. We soak it in rum. Pass me the bottle, Carsten,' Klaus said to the strawberry blond.

Carsten pushed a bottle of Bacardi into Klaus' hand and Klaus carefully poured the rum onto the sugar cone in a steady stream until it was soaked. He produced a box of matches, lit one and set fire to the cone which burst into blue flames. The cone began to caramelise and bubble brown. The smell was delicious. Ad thought briefly that if he was going to be beheaded or have his throat slit in his sleep, it wouldn't hurt to try a little of the punch.

'We'll drink a toast to Joachim,' Klaus said solemnly, as he ladled the concoction into punch glasses.

Ad clasped the hot glass between his chilly fingertips. The lenses in his glasses steamed over, so he took them off and put them into the breast pocket of his shirt. The florid fraternity faces were suddenly a blur, but though he could see nothing in detail, he could sense sombre sobriety momentarily settling on the men's shoulders.

Klaus cleared his throat. 'To Joachim. A fine German man, whose only crime was being in the wrong place at the wrong time.'

Ad squinted in the firelight, trying to see Klaus' face. *Damned*

182

crappy eyesight. He pulled out his glasses and pushed them back up his nose. The steaminess had dissipated. Tears stood in Klaus' eyes. *Crocodile tears just for show?*

Klaus spoke in a wavering voice now, full of emotion. 'Our brother's honour is being called into question but we know what kind of a man he was. He will be avenged.'

'*Prost!*'

Vengeance? What kind of vengeance? Grievous bodily harm vengeance or common garden homicide?

Ad started to drink his punch. The strong alcohol stung his nostrils and burned the back of his throat. He felt his body start to thaw.

Gradually the mood lifted amongst the frat boys. After half an hour, Ad finally managed to pee. He locked himself into the toilet, urinated for almost a full minute and then texted George.

```
Got here OK. Missing u. Nothing 2 report.
Klaus signs name with 47:33 at end. Weird.
Are u safe?
```

There was no response. He assumed she had gone to bed.

After an hour and a half of drinking, Ad was completely blotto. He had lost his glasses. He sprawled across the sofa, watching the others' childish antics with blurred vision, and listening to typical bawdy lads' jokes through ears that no longer made sense of much. The ten percent still-sober part of his brain prayed silently that he would wake in the morning, still alive. He knew he was at the mercy of these alcoholic buffoons. But as the room spun around uncontrollably, the ninety percent inebriated part of Ad's brain pondered the recipe for *Krambambuli*. George would love it.

The very last thing Ad registered before losing consciousness was the blurred vision of Klaus lumbering towards him, carrying a hunting knife.

'Bitch. Come on!' George yelled, fumbling with the phone. 'A text from Ad!'

She tried to open the text and brought up the internet instead. Useless fingers. Fat fingers in woollen gloves. Crap burglar. But still the alarm's countdown tinkled on. Inbox. Open. Ten seconds now. Nine. OCD brain had to know what it said.

```
Klaus signs name with 47:33 at end.
```

Six. Five. How about punching in 4733? She entered the numbers on the keypad. Fuck. Still tinkling.

Tick.

Two beeps signified the end of the countdown. No alarms and no unwelcome surprises. George almost wept with relief. She shook from head to toe but galvanised herself to lock the front door. She kicked her shoes off.

'Breathe. Just breathe.'

Adrenalin pushed her from one room to another; first pulling the blinds, then daring to switch on lights to have a good look. It was a small but expensive apartment, furnished with modern Danish teak pieces. Fitted kitchen in black gloss. Looked like it had hardly been used. Small square living room with tall windows, mercifully overlooked by a hotel, so unlikely a nosey neighbour was watching. Leather sofa. Ultra-modern and uncomfortable-looking dining set with a round oak table and four chairs that were moulded to fit the curve. Abstract art on the wall.

'This guy has no personality,' George told herself. 'There's nothing about this place that says anything about its owner. Apart from money.'

She ran her gloved finger over the top of the large HDTV. No dust. He had to have a cleaner. Or maybe he shared the same hygiene obsession that she did. George snorted. She didn't want to have anything in common with Klaus.

'Let's see what your bedroom says about you.'

George switched on the light. The bedroom faced onto a small courtyard garden at the back. There was a double bed squeezed up against the window, a nightstand and one wardrobe, all in the same modern style as the living room. Over the bed was a giant framed poster of the metal band, Rammstein. George grimaced. On the opposite wall was a poster of what George assumed was another metal band called Stahlgewitter. It was a classical painting of an angel carrying a sword with the name *Auftrag Deutsches Reich* emblazoned across the bottom. *Stahlgewitter* was written in gothic script. She wasn't sure what *Auftrag* meant but she decided that *Deutsches Reich* was probably some kind of neo-Nazi reference to the Third Reich. She wrinkled her nose at the poster.

'There must be something else here.'

George looked around. She opened the drawer of the nightstand. One packet of condoms, unopened. A pair of nail scissors. A packet of Ritalin without a pharmacist's label.

'Privately prescribed and doled out for ADHD?' George wondered. 'Or coke replacement? Which is it, big boy?'

She spied a vanity mirror with traces of white powder under the rim.

'Ho ho ho. Still being naughty, are we?'

The shiny cover of a pornographic magazine caught her eye.

'*Big n Black*,' George read aloud. 'Oh really, Klaus? Is this your guilty pleasure, Mr *Deutsches Reich*? Nice chunky-assed sisters with big hooters for a five-knuckle shuffle on your Aryan Bockwurst?'

She shuddered and put the magazine back in its drawer.

Next, the wardrobe. She flung the doors wide. Klaus liked his clothes. Expensive suits hung inside along with scores of polo shirts in different colours, five pairs of chinos and three pairs of jeans. It was all very Tommy Hilfiger or Ralph Lauren. Expensive pastels. Fresh smelling.

She was just about to close the doors when she spotted something. She parted the clothes. The back of the wardrobe was decorated with photographs of Ratan, Joachim, Remko … in fact most people from the class. Certainly, most people in her circle of friends, including Ad. *And me. Where did he get that photo from?* It was her matriculation photograph from her first term at St John's. Interspersed among the class photos were clippings from the newspaper articles, covering the bombings and the investigation.

'Oh, come on! How can he not be involved?' George said. She took out her phone and photographed the collage. But then she realised that she couldn't possibly show it to anyone other than Ad, as she would be implicating herself in breaking and entering. 'How can I convince van den Bergen to get a warrant and search this place? Bollocks.'

George put everything in the wardrobe back as she'd found it. She then went systematically back through the flat, opening every drawer she could find. She photographed the exact layout of the contents with her phone, rifled through what was there, looking for anything that might be incriminating and then put each item back in the exact position it had held in the photo she had taken. Finally, she went back into the bedroom and looked beneath the bed. There was a laptop on the carpet.

'Bingo.'

Ad tried to open his eyes. His left eye was gummed shut with something. There was a dull ache above it on his brow bone. His right eye spied a fuzzy living room, lit by a solitary standard lamp. It was still dark outside, but the timorous chirrup of the odd bird and the thrum of car engines on the main road told him dawn was probably close. He could smell stale cigarettes, alcohol and sweaty feet. Snoring rumbled close by and kitchen noises clanged further away.

Gingerly, he tapped his left eye. That felt fine. The eyelids just seemed to be stuck together. He prodded his eyebrow. Sharp pain lanced through a dull, throbbing hangover headache. He could feel crust, as though he had a wound that had started to scab up overnight. He looked at his fingertips. They were smudged with dark red.

'Blood?'

Then he remembered Klaus holding a hunting knife. Or had he imagined it?

'Where are my glasses?'

He rolled off the sofa and started to grope around the floor. All he could see was the blurred, busy pattern on a red Persian rug, lit by a still-flickering tea light in a glass jar. After some searching, he came across his glasses under a coffee table. *Thank God they're not broken.* He put them on and realised that Klaus had been sleeping next to him on the floor. He lay on his side with the hunting knife by his hand.

Ad grabbed Klaus by the shoulders and flipped him over onto his back. His bleary blue eyes shot open. He looked at Ad quizzically, breathing heavily through his mouth. Ad quickly straddled his chest, pinning him to the ground, snatched up the knife and held the tip of it near his throat.

'What are you doing?' Klaus asked. 'You're hurting me.' His breath stank like a distillery.

'Why is my eye covered in blood? What did you do to me?' Ad's voice was hoarse and cracked.

Klaus, seemingly unafraid of the knife at his throat, threw Ad off him with ease and sat up. He looked at Ad and started to laugh. Ad knelt beside him, still holding the knife like an idle threat.

'I'm sorry,' Klaus said, pointing at Ad's forehead.

Ad stood up, spied the mirror over the fireplace and walked over to it on shaky legs. He slammed the knife onto the mantelpiece, looked into the mirror and scowled.

'Jesus. What the hell have you done, you idiot?' He touched the stinging skin above his eye carefully. He could see a superficial cut on the brow bone, which had bled heavily into his eye

187

during the night. It looked like someone had tried to gouge his eye out. But the most obvious problem was that he was now missing an eyebrow. He spat onto the cuff of his shirt and wiped the dried blood away. The skin underneath was livid and shiny.

Klaus hovered behind Ad, grinning. 'Sorry, mate,' he said. 'It seemed very funny at the time. Think of it like a bit of an initiation ceremony into the circle.'

'You shaved my bloody eyebrow off with a hunting knife? You're completely mad.'

'We were all very drunk. *Krambambuli*.' Klaus seemed to think this was an adequate explanation for Ad's missing eyebrow.

Ad stared at the bulbous-headed German and felt anger expand within him like a black hole, threatening to consume everything in the room. *I'm going to punch him. I can be an alpha male. This is it.* But innate aggression was not Ad's strong suit. *You naval-gazing, spineless prick, Karelse. Just hit him. Take out his jaw with a well-placed right hook, for God's sake.* He clenched his fist. Caught sight of himself in the mirror. *I look like some knuckle-trailing cave man.* His resolve wavered momentarily. That was enough to make the black hole collapse in on itself, taking the anger with it and leaving only a dim nebula of frustration and disappointment in its stead. He forced a smile.

'Very funny. You got me,' he said, punching Klaus gently on the arm, feeling his metaphorical balls shrinking up inside his body and cursing himself for it.

Klaus clapped him on the back. Glanced at his watch. 'Come on. Might as well get showered. We've got a big day.'

Checking her watch, which now said 5am, George took out the laptop and booted it up. There was no login to speak of, so no password was necessary. First, she checked the internet browser's history. She brought up the National Democratic Party of Germany's website.

'Far-right rubbish.'

Other than that, Klaus seemed mainly to have been visiting porn sites, heavy metal band websites and, interestingly, her article on *The Moment*'s blog. She checked to see if Klaus had a Blogger or WordPress login name, wondering if he had acted as a spoof al Badaar or one of the trolls who had flamed her for her article. But Klaus' laptop had not remembered any login details, so she deduced that he probably wasn't registered. He had clearly only been a passive spectator as the al Badaar fiasco had unfolded.

George knew Klaus' email address. He had been copied in on a round robin sent by Fennemans at the start of the term. Fennemans was too stupid to Bcc everyone and had listed everyone's email address in the Cc header instead. She was desperate to log into Facebook under his name but knew any of his insomniac friends would see instantly that he was online if she did so.

She did, however, open his Hotmail, which had the password saved. She glanced down the subject header but found nothing interesting. Then she searched for emails from Joachim. Most from the last week of Joachim's life were banal comments about lectures or their arrangements to visit family and friends from the fraternity in Heidelberg. But then, George came upon a thread that made her hold her breath long enough to feel dizzy.

The thread was dated three weeks before Joachim's death and two weeks before Ratan's.

From: JoachimG@yahoo.com 18.32
To: k_biedermeier@hotmail.com
Subject:

You've gone too far this time. I'm ratting you out and you'd better get over it. You know you're in the wrong.

From: Klaus Biedermeier (mailto: k_biedermeier@hotmail.com) 16.23
To: Joachim Guttentag

Subject: Re:

But you're jeopardising all my plans. Everything I've been working towards for months.

From: JoachimG@yahoo.com 16.07
To: k_biedermeier@hotmail.com
aSubject: Re: Re:

I accept your apology but I'm still going to say something about your crazy, hare-brained scheme. You're going too far.

From: Klaus Biedermeier (mailto: k_biedermeier@hotmail.com) 15.49
To: Joachim Guttentag
Subject: Re: Re: Re:

I'm sorry about before. I hope we can still be friends and that you understand what I'm trying to do. It's for the greater good.

Klaus 47:33 88

'Got you, you bastard!' George said.

CHAPTER 20

Heidelberg, later

Had Ad not had a stinking hangover, he would have thought the red stone colonnades that stretched upwards to support the vast vaulted ceilings in the Church of the Holy Spirit were nothing short of stunning. He would have thought it was rather like being inside a dinosaur's ribcage. But as he sat on a hard wooden seat, breathing in the over-perfumed smell of strangers in their Sunday best, nausea threatened to make even more of an idiot out of him than his missing eyebrow. The stained glass windows were too colourful. The giant church organ that ground out hymn after hymn was deafening. He was bathed in cold sweat.

Several students read aloud depressing extracts from Schiller and other *Sturm und Drang* classics. An overweight soprano sang Brünnhilde's solo from Act 3 of Wagner's *Götterdämmerung*. Not a single mention was made of the fact that Joachim had actually been identified as the perpetrator behind the Utrecht synagogue bombing, whether that had been his intention or not. Ad thought the entire service was like some mawkish ode to erudite Joachim's German perfection. But he still felt sorry for the hapless young man who had died so violent a death.

Why had Klaus not taken the podium to eulogise about his dearly departed friend? Sitting to his left, Klaus looked stiff and

191

formal in his fraternity uniform, holding his cap on his knee. Ad had expected him to be amongst the other frat boys who were all seated in the second and third rows behind Joachim's weeping family. But instead, Klaus had chosen to sit next to Ad as though he too were an outsider. He fidgeted with his sash, picking imaginary specks of fluff from his trousers. Ad was not so hungover that he didn't notice this behaviour and think it odd.

Outside, when the service was finished, Ad was swept away from Klaus on a tide of mourners into the middle of the congregation. He found himself making small talk with a mousy-looking girl from Klaus and Joachim's class. At first, the girl batted her eyelashes at him and ran a hand coquettishly through her hair. She introduced herself as Moni, short for Monika. But when Ad said he had come with Klaus, her behaviour abruptly changed like cold draught suddenly whipping through a warm house.

'You're friends with him?' It was more of a sneer than a question.

'Not friends. I'm sort of representing my faculty.'

'Which is where again?'

'Amsterdam.'

Moni short for Monika snorted. 'Oh yeah. I remember now. You're Dutch, then,' she said.

Ad could see from her wandering eyes that she was already seeking out other people for conversation. *Be direct. Be analytical. Be like George.* 'So, were you expecting Klaus to say something about Joachim?' he asked her.

Moni short for Monika clutched at her pink leather handbag as though Ad were about to steal it. She was now looking steadfastly at his missing eyebrow. 'Not really. Klaus and Joachim were in the same frat house but they weren't especially close. Not until they went on the exchange year. Then Joachim starts trying to be like Klaus. Starts spouting the same NDP rubbish when he comes back for the weekend.'

'Oh? Wasn't he into that before?'

192

'I think Joachim's family is pretty conservative. So, I don't know. Maybe. But they wouldn't have wanted Klaus to speak today.'

Ad fingered his shiny bald eyebrow. 'Why not?'

Moni short for Monika glanced over her shoulder as though she was about to impart a great secret. 'Klaus might seem popular but most people think he's a prize arsehole. Nobody apart from the über-toffs really like him and not just because of his political views.'

'What do you mean?'

She stared at Ad in silence for longer than was comfortable. She seemed to be judging him; assessing whether he would betray a confidence and go running back to Klaus.

'Honestly, I'm not his friend,' Ad said.

Moni short for Monika chewed her lip and nodded. 'They're all scared of him. Biedermeier's trouble.'

Ad narrowed his eyes. He felt like she had more to say. Perhaps he wouldn't get this chance again. 'What kind of trouble?'

'The *wrong crowd* kind of trouble.' She winked conspiratorially. 'The other frat boys aren't all cut from the same cloth as him, you know. But there's always a rotten apple in the barrel and Biedermeier's it.' She wiggled her index finger round at her temple. 'He's …' she seemed to be selecting the correct words from a range of possible insults '… off balance.'

'Where are we going?' Ad asked.

As the gathering dispersed, Klaus had latched back onto Ad, steering him along beautiful cobbled alleyways with pastel-coloured buildings on either side. It was picture-postcard perfect but Ad was sweating freely with trepidation beneath his only suit.

'You'll see,' Klaus said.

Ad could hear boyish exhilaration in his voice and remembered what the mousy Moni had said. Off balance. A euphemism for completely mentally unstable.

Up ahead, a group of five or six frat boys, also in pseudo-military uniform, were clearly making for the same destination. Klaus started to chatter animatedly, as though Ad was an old friend and, perhaps more worryingly, as though he'd had amphetamines with his breakfast potatoes and egg.

'I'm looking forward to this. I know you're going to love it,' he said, clapping Ad on the shoulder.

'Love what?' Ad looked at Klaus.

'You're going to watch me duel.'

'What?'

'A couple of boys have come over from the corps in Freiburg. It's all set up.'

Ad felt dread erupt in his stomach, sending crippling frost up his gullet. He winced, barely able to force words of protest out of his mouth. 'I don't really want to watch a duel,' he said.

'Yes you do,' Klaus said. 'You can tell all those pussies in Amsterdam what real men do to prove their honour. At a proper university.'

Twenty minutes later, Ad stood in a sports hall breathing too deeply through his nose. His head was still exploding from the hangover. He silently prayed that he wouldn't vomit over his best shoes in the middle of Klaus' duel. It was a surreal feeling, being stuck in a room full of strange men his own age, who had elected to slice each other's faces up in the name of building character. Ad did not like blood. Especially other people's. The memory of the pathologist's wastepaper bin popped into his head. He remembered how it had smelled of scented tissues and pencil sharpenings before he had vomited into it. He swallowed down a lump of unruly bile.

'Bring it on,' Klaus said to the onlookers as he strutted into the room wearing a chainmail hauberk over a leather apron. A high leather collar peeped out of the top of the ensemble. On his face, he wore steel goggles to which was attached a broad metal nose guard. His right arm was covered with a padded leather arm guard. His left hand was hidden behind his back. He wielded

194

his sword with his right hand, slashing the air with a whipping noise that Ad had only ever heard in samurai or Quentin Tarantino movies.

'He looks like an alien,' Ad said under his breath. 'What the hell …?'

Another man, shorter than Klaus by at least five inches, walked to the centre of the room. He was wearing the same medieval-style regalia and bug-like goggles. Ad supposed this was one of the Freiburg frat members. The smaller man mounted a platform, which made him equal to Klaus in height.

There was a sense of eager expectation amongst the men in the room. Ad could see it in the way they fidgeted and spoke too quickly, too loudly. But what was this? An older man stood at the sidelines with a medi-pack and a suturing kit at the ready. Was he a doctor? Ad felt dizzy and had to steady himself against the wall.

To the right of Klaus and his short opponent stood other frat members. He recognised Klaus' partner as Carsten, participant in the Feuerzangenbowle debacle.

Is Carsten there in case Klaus dies or something? Are they going to stab each other? Yes. They're going to bloody stab each other. They're only a few feet apart. He's going to ritually slaughter the short bloke and I'm going to die. Oh my God. And yet, they're all smiling and nodding.

The excitement in the air was almost palpable, but though he could feel it, Ad did not understand it even in the slightest.

With swords crossed high above their heads, the duelling began. The clash of metal made Ad's fillings throb in his mouth. Klaus sliced downwards at an angle. The short man blocked it, and chopped back at Klaus. Neither man seemed to move or dodge the other's downwards lunges. Klaus' razor-sharp sword slid into his opponent's cheek. The man barely flinched.

'Christ!' Ad said, loud enough to attract angry stares from the others.

He slumped against the wall, increasingly lightheaded as he watched the short man bleed freely down his face. Then Klaus took a hit. More blood. No baulking or reaction whatsoever from the crowd. *These people are all mad.*

Ad felt vomit rise quickly, ruthlessly in his throat. He sprinted to the toilet just in time to avoid defiling his shoes.

Some time later, he was still leaning over the toilet bowl, spitting into the water, when he heard Klaus' voice on the other side of the cubicle.

'Are you okay?' Klaus asked.

'No.'

'It's over now. You can come out. I won. I've got a new number. I'm 52:35 now.'

Ad blew his nose loudly on some toilet roll, flushed the toilet and unlocked the cubicle door.

'Bloody hell. You look terrible,' he said, cursorily glancing at the red, weeping cuts on Klaus' face.

Klaus raised his hand to touch the wounds. 'They've been stitched.' He spoke in a clipped, mealy-mouthed way, as though he could no longer move his facial muscles freely.

'Do they hurt?'

'Of course they fucking hurt. We don't use anaesthetic.' There was more than a hint of pride in his voice.

'You're an animal.'

Klaus laughed with a stiff, expressionless face. But his eyes were positively brimming with joy. 'Come on. Let's go and drink beer. A lot of beer. I've got some friends I want you to meet.'

Ad groaned. He felt like Klaus had reached inside his battered body and punched him in the heart. He had never been so homesick in his life. But at 8pm it was too late to go back to Amsterdam. Ad was stranded in Heidelberg with a psychopath and all his dysfunctional friends.

'What's with the number?' Ad asked, washing his face in the men's room sink.

He forced himself to look properly at Klaus in the mirror. Klaus looked like he had been carved up for Sunday lunch and sewn back together again.

'The number of my *schmissen* – my cuts. I've now given fifty-two and received thirty-five. We all sign our names with our numbers. I was at 47:33 for a long time because I've been away but now I've got a more impressive number. I'm no longer the fresh faced Fox now. I'm a fully fledged Bursch. It's a mark of my achievements.'

'You think slicing each other's faces up is an achievement?'

Ad made a mental note that Klaus seemed impervious to fear, other people's sensitivities and pain. It was like someone had switched off his humanity. At that moment it occurred to Ad that Klaus did indeed have the ideal predisposition to be a murderer. And yet, there was a side to him that seemed lonely and vulnerable; desperate for acceptance.

Klaus held open the toilet door. 'You Dutchmen have no breeding, do you? But that's all right because I've got another educational surprise up my sleeve.'

Inside a heavy metal pub on the other side of town, atonal death metal blasted from large wall-mounted speakers in every corner of the pub with screaming, snarling vocals that could have been recorded by the Devil himself. The sticky floor shook with the unrelenting thud of the music's frenzied base drum. The walls were black. The clientele stank of patchouli and sweat. Almost everyone there was tattooed, full of piercings, with shaven heads or short Mohicans.

Klaus and Carsten looked like flamboyant stuffed parrots on a supermarket shelf full of bald battery chickens. But several of the men at the bar greeted Klaus with obvious warmth and familiarity.

'Hey, fellas! It's the Graf. All right, Graf?' one of the men said in a thick Swabian dialect.

They engaged in a complicated handshake with Klaus, nodded at Carsten, looked suspiciously at Ad.

Ad noticed that two of the men had badly executed blue-grey swastika tattoos on their necks. Like almost everyone else in the room, the three men wore washed out heavy metal T-shirts and drainpipe jeans or long combat shorts. One, with a bad blond Mohican and a strange ring embedded in his earlobe that made his ears look distended like an Amazonian tribesman's, wore a beat-up biker's leather jacket. He had a tattoo of a skull and 'SS' in gothic script on the side of his shaven head. These men were clearly in their late twenties or early thirties. Their pot bellies and prematurely lined faces betrayed a decade of heavy drinking and smoking.

'What's up then, Klaus?' the Mohican said. He gesticulated at Klaus' face with his beer glass. 'You been fighting again?'

Klaus laughed. He shifted from one foot to another; jittery, animated. 'You know me. Keeping up traditions. Now I'm looking for a bit of R&R.' He winked at the Mohican and put a wad of notes on the bar.

'You want the usual?'

Klaus nodded. 'Yes.'

The Mohican counted the money out of Ad's line of sight. He stuffed the wad in his inside pocket and gestured to one of his skinhead friends with a nod of his head. The skinhead walked over to a man sitting in a corner on the other side of the pub. Ad struggled to get a good look at the man through the clusters of drinkers gathered around tables in the pub. A girl stood up at the wrong moment and obscured his view.

Klaus seemed to be following the skinhead's progress. The skinhead started to make his way back and nodded to Klaus. Both men moved towards the toilet and disappeared behind the door. Carsten followed two minutes later, leaving Ad standing at the bar with the Mohican. The numb feeling Ad had experienced after the duel was quickly stripped away and replaced by blind panic.

'Who are you?' the Mohican said, eyeing Ad's suit up and down.

'Friend of Klaus.'

The Mohican nodded and smiled, revealing four gold incisors in the front of his otherwise rotten smile. 'Any friend of Klaus is a friend of ours, isn't that right, Friedrich?'

Friedrich, the second skinhead, grinned at Ad and punched him hard in the shoulder. 'You're a bit dark, though. You sure you're not a Jew boy? You've got a funny accent.'

Ad swallowed hard and pushed his glasses up his nose. 'I'm Dutch. My mother's family were French. Olive skin, see.'

The Mohican seemed to be weighing up this information. He frowned and looked into his stein of beer. 'The French are okay. Some good boys down there. Especially in the South of France. Got to keep on top of all those Muslim bastards. But the Dutch. Bunch of nigger-loving fucking hippies …' He looked back up at Ad with hard blue eyes. 'Are you a nigger-loving fucking hippy?' He grabbed Ad roughly by his shirt collar and pulled a scabbed fist back, ready to strike.

Ad closed his eyes tightly.

'Only joking, pal!' the Mohican said, putting Ad down. He brushed the front of his suit carefully with the same hand he had been about to punch him with. 'You're all right if you're Klaus' mate,' he pronounced. 'Now drink.'

The Mohican ordered Ad a stein of strong lager, and Ad, more frightened at that point than at any other time during the weekend, was obliged to drink. He wondered in merciful silence if these men were behind the bombings. Was Klaus just some upper-class current account to them? This is what Moni had meant by the wrong company. *I've got to get the hell out of here.*

Klaus emerged from the toilet looking waxy and talking too fast. He rubbed Ad's cropped hair. 'Fancy a couple of lines?' he asked.

Ad looked at him blankly and then made the narcotic

connection. 'Er, no thanks. I have painful sinuses. I'll stick to beer.'

While forcing himself to make small talk about music with the skinhead, Ad strained to eavesdrop on a conversation between Klaus, Carsten and the Mohican above the death metal din. He picked up on Joachim's name and mention of the NDP but that was all he could make out.

Ad's phone buzzed in his pocket. He repaired to the toilet, holding the door open for a man with a limp. The man's face was so badly disfigured that Ad was felt compelled to look away. *What a crazy place.*

Inside a cubicle, he read the text. It was from George.

```
Van den Bergen confirmed Remko's dead. Get
evidence if u can. Come home 1st thing.
```

Ad was uncomfortably hot in his suit, but that was just the beer, not panic or grief. He felt bolstered by alcohol; gripped by determination. This weekend would not be a waste of time.

He willed himself to urinate, flushed, splashed his face with water and went back into the fug of the pub. He threw himself into raucous chatter, pretended to get blind drunk and pulled out his best politically incorrect jokes, much to the delight of the others. He clasped Klaus, Carsten, the Mohican and the two skinheads to his chest and took pictures of himself with them using his cell phone. Over the course of two hours, Ad made sure that he took chummy photos that encompassed everyone in the room from different angles.

By 3am, a fight had broken out between four skinheads. One was bottled in the head. Another sliced his best friend's finger off with a pen knife. The floor was wet with blood and beer. But the Mohican still stood, propping the bar and watching in amusement.

Ad had just made the silent decision to leave when someone

planted a punch on one of the skinheads, sending him reeling into the barstool next to Ad. *That's it. I'm off. I don't care if I have to sleep in the doorway of the train station until the first train leaves.*

Ad sidestepped the mayhem and put on his jacket but the Mohican seemed to anticipate his departure. He gripped Ad's shoulder with fingers of iron.

'Where do you think you're going, Jew boy?'

CHAPTER 21

Stena Hollandica ferry, North Sea

A nun's habit and wimple are hot garments to wear, particularly in the lounge of an overheated ferry. But the layers of heavy cloth were not the only reason for Ella fanning her face with a fast-food menu. Underneath her vestments, her pulse thumped furiously as though it was counting down the seconds to the grand finale, the showdown, the shootout.

'I'm dying in here,' she said to Tonya, rolling her eyes. She shoved a finger underneath her wimple and had a good scratch. 'I don't know how those poor cows wear these.'

Serviette in hand, Tonya lifted up her habit, showing thick black stockings, wrinkled at the ankle. She surreptitiously shoved her hand under the black cloth and up to her chest. She looked around cautiously and started to rub her midriff with the serviette. 'My tits are pouring with sweat 'cos of the plastic. It's fucking minging.'

'Oi. Stop swearing,' Ella said, feeling a rictus grin set hard on her clammy face. 'Nuns ain't supposed to swear.'

An elderly woman in a lilac fleece and polyester elasticated trousers passed close by to them and nodded. 'Sisters,' she said, smiling.

Tonya sucked her teeth at the woman. The woman gave Tonya a confused look, smile faltering now.

Ella was forced to kick Tonya under the table. 'You're carrying weight under this shit and so am I,' she said. 'If we're rumbled, we're gonna get nicked. Now stop acting like you're cussing in Catford and be nice, yeah?'

Tonya tutted. 'Where's Big Michelle at? She's been gone forever.'

Ella pointed at the toilet door on the other side of the lounge. At that moment, Big Michelle wobbled out, pulling up tights through the habit's thick fabric. She made the sign of the cross at Ella and started to laugh raucously.

Inside, Ella felt stretched tight like an over-wound clock. Any minute now, and the whole thing would be blown apart. She wiped her mouth repeatedly with a hot hand until her grin disappeared; perused the menu in morose silence, taking care not to touch the microphone and small recording device strapped to her torso along with the bags of ecstasy. It was not going as she and the Gargoyle had hoped.

The Gargoyle. She thought about him; pictured him the last time they had met before this final Sister Act.

'Are you sure you're up to this?' the Gargoyle had asked her.

'Ready as I'll ever be,' she said, gripping the car's passenger seat as though it was going to save her from what was to come.

The Gargoyle had smiled sympathetically at her. His whisky drinker's nose was even more veined than before. He was red in the face and breathless. He looked old.

'You okay?' Ella had asked, offering him a piece of gum.

The Gargoyle nodded. 'It's giving up smoking. Bloody stressful after forty years. I'm not sure I've got the moral fibre. But the old ticker, you know ...' He had patted his chest and given a hollow chuckle. 'This is a young man's profession.'

'So, can we run through the plans again?' Ella had asked, polishing his dashboard with her sleeve.

The Gargoyle had taken out his pad and read his notes back to her.

'You're sailing to the Hook of Holland on the *Stena Hollandica* with Danny, Jez, Tonya and Big Michelle. You're wearing a microphone. The mic will record up to one hundred and four hours of material but it's saved onto a memory stick which will be on your person. You give that to us when you finish. Now, you've got six and a half hours there and back on the ferry to talk. Make sure you get Danny to sing like a bird about his networks, the nutter Jez and all the heavy stuff he does on Danny's say so, the lot. The Dutch police are aware of the situation. They'll be watching.'

'They won't jump the gun, will they?' Ella had asked, feeling her fingers go cold with nerves.

'No. Don't worry about them. My opposite number there is a man who really knows his onions. He's after the Dutch supplier but he's playing the long game. There'll be no jumping the gun.' The Gargoyle had closed his eyes as though he was trying to marshal his interrupted thoughts. 'So, you get to Amsterdam. Danny makes the connect.'

'He won't see the mic, will he?'

'No. Just don't let him grope you and make sure you change into whatever fancy dress he's got planned in a toilet. Now, stop butting in and listen.'

Ella breathed in too deeply and felt lightheaded. She looked at the Gargoyle's shirt collar and spied a line of grey grime inside. She knew he was divorced. Men never looked after themselves properly once they'd got used to a woman doing everything. That was his excuse. But the grime still made her cringe slightly. Lately, things like that had been really bothering her. She had been washing her hands. A lot.

'You divvy up the gear and bring it back on the ferry as planned,' he said. 'If you have any doubts at all, dump the mic behind the counter in the Riva Bar. Got it? We've got someone there. Last thing we want is you blowing your cover.'

'He's going to find the mic, I just know it.' Ella could hear in her voice the judder of her heart against the inside of her chest.

The Gargoyle patted her hand. It was a fatherly pat. It felt reassuring. 'Stop worrying. You'll be fine.' He inclined his head towards her, frowning. 'Look, you're sure you can do this? I mean, it's been a long time now. You haven't got … attached, have you?'

Ella shook her head but in the private space of her thoughts, she nodded, just slightly. *It had been the best time of her life, gift-wrapped in shit.* 'Don't worry about me,' she told the Gargoyle. 'This isn't just about saving my mother's arse any more.'

The Gargoyle nodded, smiling in a kindly way. 'You're a clever young woman. And a sticker too. I admire you for that, Ella. And I'm personally grateful for everything you've sacrificed. I can't begin to imagine how horrible it must have been.'

Ella walled the violent memories, the dirty feelings and the guilt up inside her head. *This was always about me and the Gargoyle and doing the right thing in the end.*

'I knew what I was getting into,' she said. 'You mustn't feel bad. You've been okay. Just make sure you deliver your side of the bargain and I'll deliver mine.'

The Gargoyle smiled. His relief was almost tangible. She knew he was a man of principles. An old-fashioned straight cop. 'Good,' he said, patting her hand again. 'And I want you to know, if you want, there's a future for you in the police. You could be an undercover detective any day of the week.'

Respect. The Gargoyle was the first person ever to show her respect, and she liked that. Better than a hit from a bong. Better than a line of coke. It was as though the clouds had parted and the sun had shone through warm and bright, just for her. The feeling quelled some of her fear.

'Cheers,' she said simply. 'Go on. Plans.'

'Right. You all get nabbed by our fellas. We bang you up like the others. Don't want to blow your cover, do we? Not yet. But I'll be there at the port. I'll get you out, of course, and then we've got all the evidence. We sort it out from there. Simple.'

'And then, new life, here I come?' Ella had said. It was the fourth time she had asked the Gargoyle this since she got in the car.

'Yes. New life, here you come. After you've testified, obviously.'

It had all seemed so simple in the car, talking in confidence with the Gargoyle. And it had all gone according to plan – up to a point.

Danny, Jez, Tonya, Big Michelle and Ella had boarded the *Hollandica* wearing respectable business suits, carrying accountants' briefcases full of nothing much and small weekend suitcases containing wads of notes wrapped up in towels.

They whiled away the journey there talking about the deal; gossiping about Danny's contact.

'He's called Stijn, man. And it's pronounced like stain!' Danny said.

Jez spat beer all over the floor of the bar. 'No way.'

'Way. How can people take him fucking seriously with a name like that? His nickname's the Rotterdam Silencer. I wish I had a nickname like that. These Dutch are off the hook. But they're good for the gear and no messing around. And they're opening doors to new business. This, my friends, is just the beginning.' He rubbed his hands together and grinned a handsome, professionally whitened grin.

Ella could see genuine enthusiasm in Danny's eyes. The thrill of the chase. A challenge. He was visualising piles of cash and a Bentley, she knew. Over the last twelve months, he had risen from council estate nail in everyone's tyre to serious contender. No wonder the Gargoyle was so keen to put a stop to him. Danny was a man with a plan.

The Hook of Holland was windy and drab. But Amsterdam ...

When Ella emerged from Amsterdam Central Station, she fell immediately in love. Exhilarated by the mix of romance and history and beauty and sleaze, she imagined herself an enraptured, drown-proof Ophelia, drifting willingly down the canals in diaphanous flowing dress with tulips entangled in her hair.

'This is well smart, man. I am so coming back here one time,' she told Tonya, keeping the Ophelia reference locked inside her secret box of better quality thoughts.

Tonya looked at her askance. 'But it's full of fucking foreigners. These is weirdo Europeans, innit? They is well naff. It's like twenty years behind the times here.'

'But you can still get burgers, man,' Big Michelle said. 'And smoke dope in public!'

The meet was in a warehouse on a faceless business park, some miles out of town. But even on the tram, until the old part of town gave way to the inevitable modern ugliness of urban sprawl, Ella soaked up every last visual detail she could and savoured the flavour of somewhere new.

Tall, thin buildings with facades that were topped with rooflines like step pyramid peaks or clock faces. Houses listing inwards, outwards, to the side, sometimes propped but always buckling in improbable ways, threatening to dive into the canals. It was green. Tree-lined streets and small parks. Like London but so much nicer. She smiled at passersby through the windows of the tram. They looked well-heeled, carefree, clean. Exotic to her tired eyes.

Exchange of goods was easy. Inside the empty factory, which looked like it was ordinarily used for labelling and packaging up deodorants, judging by the workstations and conveyor belts full of lidless, half-assembled products, Danny handed over the money to Stijn. He was a middle-aged man who looked like an insurance broker. Smart, pale grey, double-breasted suit. Very shiny shoes. Conservative blue tie and white shirt combo. Nothing too flashy. He was flanked by two younger men in casual clothes who could have been bank tellers on their day off. Stijn handed over bags and bags of pills. Ella and the other girls were shown to the toilets and given outfits to put on.

'Fucking nuns?' Tonya shouted.

Stijn threw her a roll of surgical tape. 'Strap the bags close to your body. Under your tits, where they'll be easily covered. Around your waist. Take your makeup off.'

With a dry mouth and a frenzied heartbeat, Ella had fumbled around in the toilet with dithering fingers. Her aluminium microphone was the size of a matchstick. Its single battery and flash stick took up little space. The equipment was taped just below her breasts, where the bags of pills were also supposed to be concealed. *Don't damage the mic. Don't let anyone see. Once you're on the ferry, you're home and dry.*

The three emerged in full habit and wimple, complete with heavy swinging rosary at the waist.

'You look gorgeous, girls,' Danny said. Laughter all round. Witty Danny. Low-rent charmer.

But something was wrong with this picture. 'Hang on,' Ella said, frowning. 'Why aren't you and Jez dressed up?'

'I ain't putting on no dog collar, man!' Jez said.

Danny folded his arms, played with his earlobe. 'Me and Jez are making our own way back. Got some other things to discuss, yeah? We'll meet you back home. You'll be fine.'

'Home?' Tonya said, hand on hip. 'We're going to fucking Harwich. How we gonna get home from there without yous? What if we get nicked?'

'You won't get nicked. You don't need me to hold your hand to catch a train, do you, girl?' Danny held Tonya's face in his hands and looked into her eyes. Danny the manipulator and his subtle art of persuasion. What Jez achieved with a crowbar or baseball bat, Danny achieved with the right words, the right tone, a reassuring look from those seemingly sensitive eyes.

Tonya looked at the floor at the same time that Ella's hopes and expectations hit the floor. *No Danny. No Jez. And this mic isn't feeding into a laptop. I've no way of telling the Gargoyle. Shit. This thing could go belly up.*

'Just keep cool, right?' Tonya said to Ella and Big Michelle as they walked towards passport control. 'And try to hide your nails. Nuns don't wear extensions.'

Ella had already tripped up over her habit twice. She was hot and sticky. Wiping her face on her sleeve, she wondered if the recording equipment was sweatproof.

'Eyes front,' Big Michelle said. 'Don't make no fucking eye contact.'

Please let it be over with. Ella clutched her falsified passport in a shaking hand. *Sister Aquinata, Sister of Mercy, Hail Mary, full of grace, Deus ex machina be mine.*

Customs officials, police, passport control, immigration officers, snuffling German shepherds, all seemed to swoop at once. Ella was cuffed, read her rights, taken away. But during the elaborately staged Euripidean drama, she didn't spy her Heracles, the Gargoyle. *Where the hell are you, Gordon? This is the bit where you swing in on a crane and carry me off to safety.*

CHAPTER 22

Amsterdam, 18 January

George scrubbed briskly at the gas rings from her cooker with wire wool. The water in the sink was scaldingly hot. The corrosive, soapy scouring pad nibbled away at her fingers, but she didn't care because she felt she deserved it. It was 11am. She had not slept.

Never before had she managed to trash her room with such abandon in such a short space of time. But on returning to her own place, she had received the news from van den Bergen that the bin man had been identified as Remko. She felt certain she had sent Ad reeling into the arms of a murderer.

Now, three hours and forty minutes into her cleaning penance, remaking that which she had unmade in a bid to snuff out her anguish and anaesthetise her grief, she felt idiotic and weak. And though Jan would probably not charge her for the smashed lamp and the broken vacuum cleaner, she would still feel obliged to replace them. She made a mental note to herself never to vacuum cigarette butts or broken glass again.

She said a silent prayer for Ad's safety.

'Jesus. Why hasn't he got his phone switched on?' she asked the gardenia on her windowsill.

George flung the iron gas rings into the sink, splashing her top with hot, pink soap scum. She thumped the draining board in frustration, dried her hands on her tea towel and retreated to her living area. She punched Ad's number into her phone. It went straight to voicemail.

'Balls. Let's try van den Bergen,' she muttered. She called van den Bergen's number for the fifth time. This time, it rang.

'Van den Bergen. Speak.' His voice was gruff. Burdened.

'At last. It's me. We need to talk. I want to hear what the pathologist said and I've got some ideas ...' George's tired mind tried to assess her options at high speed. Should she tell him about Klaus' apartment? Should she speak to him before Ad had had chance to debrief her? Should she tell van den Bergen about her stalker?

But George had no input. Her option was selected for her.

'Listen, I've not got time for your thoughts right now. I'm busy solving four murders.'

'*Four* murders? I thought you said—'

'One of the critically injured victims of Bushuis died in the night. A librarian. Fifty-four-year-old mother of two. Oh, and I've asked my German counterpart to bring Biedermeier in for questioning again. I'll call you.' The line went dead. Van den Bergen had gone.

George clutched the phone to her chest and marched to the window. She opened the heavy curtains, flung the window open and growled aloud at the rooftops.

'For God's sake. This is killing me!' she shouted.

Suddenly she heard footsteps stomping up the uncarpeted stairs to her landing. Shuffling outside her door. Someone knocked three times. Impatient knocking. Jan didn't open up until one on a Sunday. Inneke and Katja wouldn't be in work until around two. She was not expecting anybody at that time.

George grabbed her broom which had been propped against the wall. She carefully turned the mortise key and released the

Yale with her left hand, while gripping the broom handle in the right.

As the Heidelberg police descended on the frat house where Klaus was staying, Klaus strolled along the Philosopher's Walk, high in the hills above the town. The air was sharp. Clear as a bell. His hangover had gone now and he had every intention of climbing to the café at the summit which served most excellent hot chocolate and cake.

He was wearing borrowed technical outdoor clothes and sturdy hiking boots. But even in Carsten's thick red fleece and heavy parka, Klaus felt the cold shroud of winter still clinging to the hillside.

Further down, closer to the sparkling Neckar, the pathways were full of strolling families, walking off their rich lunches. But now, climbing steeper and steeper, weaving among the trees, Klaus had not passed a single soul for over twenty minutes. It was a pure, poetic kind of solitude. Solitude that he found most acceptable.

Yes, it had been an enjoyable weekend. He reflected that, despite the need for his hasty departure, Ad had been a game individual for whom he had a new measure of respect. Perhaps the Dutch weren't so bad after all.

The trees rising up towards the summit carried an inch-thick layer of virgin-white hoar on their branches. The dry brown leaves that carpeted the ground beneath were frosted with glittering ice. He observed that they looked like the topping on a sparkling Streuselkuchen. Klaus loved the Philosopher's Walk; loved revelling in the thought that he was treading paths worn smooth in the hillside, generation after generation, by owners of the finest German academic minds. This idea appealed to Klaus' love of continuity. He liked to fantasise that he was a big political thinker, if nothing else.

He came out of the forest into a clearing which held a stone amphitheatre built during Hitler's reign. Klaus breathed in deeply and smiled at his surroundings. To him, it was a perfect fusion of what man had fashioned and what nature had provided.

For a few minutes, he sat in the weak sunshine and let the warmth bathe the healing cuts on his face.

When he heard a twig snap some way off, he looked around to see what Sunday adventurers were heading his way. He prepared to greet them with a nod and perhaps even a formal, 'Good day'. Nobody came. Then a twig snapped closer by. Was it a deer? Probably.

George flung the door wide and pounced, treating her visitor to a face full of bristles.

'Ad!' George shrieked, dropping the broom.

'Ow.' Ad rubbed his jaw. 'Nice to see you too.'

She pulled him inside and flung her arms around him. 'Oh, my God! You're safe. Thank Christ.' She ushered him to the sofa. 'Sit! Sit! I'll make you a … hot water?'

Ad gave her a lopsided smile. At that point, she looked at him properly for the first time. He was wearing a suit that looked as though it had been in a fight with the jaws of a refuse truck. The side of his face was bruised. He sported a fat lip. His eyebrow was cut up and missing … well, his eyebrow. He stank of lager and stale cigarettes.

'What the hell happened to you?' she asked.

When they had exchanged stories, George made Ad take a hot shower. She gave him one of her T-shirts and a pair of navy jogging bottoms to wear. The jogging bottoms were six inches too short on him but at least he smelled and looked better. She let him use her toothbrush. She had never let anybody use her toothbrush before.

They sat together in silence while Ad sipped his hot water. George was the first to break the silence.

'I wasn't expecting you back so early,' she said.

Ad looked at her and shook his head. 'I couldn't wait to get out of there. I've never been punched before, let alone been roped into a bar brawl. It's a miracle I got to the train station alive. Thankfully they run all night to Cologne. I made the first connection back to Amsterdam.'

George rubbed his arm tenderly. 'I should never have suggested you go.'

He winced and took her hand. 'It's okay. It was my idea too. We got what we wanted. Look …' He took his phone out of his jacket breast pocket and brought up the series of photographs he had taken. The images were small on the phone's diminutive screen.

'Send them to my email. Let's get them up on the laptop,' George said.

The photos popped into her inbox one after the other. 'What are these of?' George studied the crowd in the heavy metal pub through narrowed eyes. 'Bloody hell!' She shook her head slowly in disbelief. 'Ad, these guys are rough. Look at that one with the SS tattoo!'

'I know. I just thought, if I get photos, maybe they'll be of some use to van den Bergen.' Ad started to point out the characters he had come across and related what he knew about them. 'They all treated Klaus like a king.'

'And how was Klaus?'

'Lapping it up. Revelling in it. And nobody touched him during the fight in the bar. He just stood on the sidelines and watched.'

George told Ad about her discoveries in Klaus' apartment, while she flicked from one photo to the next. 'You can smell this lot just by looking at them.'

Ad pointed to a photograph of a dark corner of the pub. He and Friedrich, the skinhead, were posing in the foreground. 'See this guy in the background with the disfigured face?' Ad asked. 'I've worked out that he was the one doling out the coke to everyone. The skinhead took money from the Mohican, wandered over here. This guy's sitting all on his own, nursing a beer. I think Klaus maybe knew him too. He nodded at him but they never spoke.'

George ran her finger over the smooth screen of the laptop and looked at the photo. The man was blurred but she could still see that he was scarred. Badly scarred. But she had the strange sensation of a memory tapping at her brain, asking to be let out. 'I recognise this guy,' she said. 'I can't think where from, but I recognise him. At least I think so.'

'He walked with a limp.'

George could feel Ad staring at the side of her face. She was distracted from the photograph, unable to place the disfigured dealer immediately. She turned to Ad. Her eyes locked with his. 'You're a genius,' she said. 'Taking these photos ...'

'The murderer could be in that bar,' he said.

George frowned. 'But Klaus is the murderer.'

Ad stroked her cheek. She could feel the heat of his fingers on her skin and felt her heartbeat start to pick up pace.

'I think he's maybe involved,' Ad said, stroking her eyebrow. 'But ...' He leaned in towards her. 'I was so desperate to talk to you.'

George reached up and touched the sensitive swelling on his bottom lip. 'I could have lost you.'

'You didn't.'

Ad started to kiss her on the mouth gently. George put her arms on his shoulders and responded, feeling need sear through her tired body, burning all the panic and frustration away. She felt his tongue against hers, felt his stubble burn the skin around her lips. His hair was soft and smelled of her shower gel. Warm skin beneath the borrowed T-shirt. If she could have been wired up to the Dutch national grid at that moment, she could have powered the whole of the Netherlands with her sexual energy.

He pushed her steadily down onto the chaise longue. She let the laptop slide from her knees to the floor; felt his weight on her, felt his hands exploring her skin beneath her top. He kissed her more urgently now. Hands moving down. Massaging the hot, glistening bud of her arousal. Bodies fusing.

'Oh, I've waited for this,' he said.

Then her phone rang.

'Shit,' she said.

'Ignore it.'

She wrapped her legs around his back. But the phone persisted. It was lying on top of the bedside cabinet, in George's eye-line. She knew she shouldn't look. She knew she should let it go to voicemail.

'Ignore it,' Ad gasped, eyes tight shut and a look of rapture on his face.

She looked at the display and squinted. 'It's van den Bergen.'

'What? Come on, George!'

'I've got to—'

The same impulse that made George scrub the toilet in a certain sequence; that need to order and categorise made her unable to continue. The phone was ringing, so Ad had to stop. The two things were simply mutually exclusive.

George pushed at Ad's shoulders and he withdrew.

'Fuck!' he shouted.

Heart and groin pounding, she lunged for the phone and answered it.

Minutes later, she hung up on van den Bergen. Ad's ardour had visibly waned. She summoned the most apologetic face she could muster.

'What did he say, then?' Ad asked, gently pushing her away.

'Klaus is going to be brought back to the Netherlands for questioning. The German police are apparently raiding the frat house where you were staying right now. Van den Bergen's just waiting on a warrant to search his apartment in Vondelstraat. He wants you to meet up with him at the station later. Tell him what you saw and overheard. Downside is, I can't say a single word

216

about his laptop or the crazy stuff in his wardrobe. I'll just have to leave it all for van den Bergen to find for himself.'

Ad propped himself on his elbow. George could see that the glorious lust in his eyes had fizzled. *Why can't we go back ten minutes and do it all differently? I'd turn my phone off this time. Shit.*

'I'm not sure,' Ad said quietly.

George looked at him and frowned. 'Not sure about what?'

Ad put his arms behind his head and stared up at George's ceiling. 'I had eight hours of travelling to really chew this over. Klaus. You know, he's a dick but I don't think he's a murderer.'

George sat bolt upright and hid her nakedness with a cushion. 'What? But he's already got a record for GBH. He's violent and coked off his head most of the time. He's linked to all three victims.'

Ad shuffled onto his side so he was facing her now. He stretched out his arm to caress her shoulder but, this time, George was the one to push him away.

'He's stalking me!' she said.

'Is he though? This weekend, I learned a few things about Klaus,' Ad said. 'He's a shocking fascist and an extraordinary turd. But he's generous to a fault. Paid for everything despite my protests. He's lonely as hell because he's unpopular as hell. Screwed-up little rich kid.'

'Oh, diddums. Poor baby.'

'Wait, George. Let me finish. He's childish. I thought he was allowing me to see his weird world so he could … I don't know … ensnare me or something. Do me in. But he was just showing off like a little boy. Trying to curry favour. Belong to something where he's accepted. Now, these thugs in the bar …'

The fact that Ad was defending Klaus irritated George like a tick that had got under her skin. She was torn. She needed him. But on the other hand, his support of Klaus felt like a betrayal. Something snapped inside her.

'Look, what is this shit?' She glared at him, openly hostile now.

'What do you mean?'

'You and me. Here. Now. Are you going to fuck me or what?'

Ad opened and closed his mouth. He seemed to avoid looking directly into her eyes. 'I … er … the moment's passed right now. I told you not to answer the phone.'

'Oh, so it's my fault.'

'Well, yes. And the other thing is Astrid.'

George shot off the chaise, and stood bolt upright. She instinctively shoved her right hand on her naked hip and started to waggle her head from side to side, left hand raised, eloquently helping to spell out her displeasure.

'Oh, so the Milkmaid's in bed with us now, is she?'

Ad pulled his knees into his chest and curled himself up into a ball. 'If me and you are going to be lovers, I owe it to her to break up with her first.'

George felt red mist blowing out of her ears like a child's cartoon character. 'It's a bit late for that, Ad. You should have thought of your gentlemanly principles *earlier*.'

You're sabotaging it, goddammit. Shut your trap. Take a step back. You're going to screw it all up for yourself. But George's unbridled temper thundered away. She gathered his clothes into a bundle and opened the door. She tossed the bundle onto the landing and held the door open for Ad.

'Get out,' she said.

Ad's eyes darkened, emanating almost tangible hurt and naked fury. George the romantic hadn't thought Ad had much anger in him. George the cynic was not surprised at all. *Ah, now we see it. Not just a sensitive flower. Passive aggressive arsehole. Festering away on the sly. Typical. Just what I don't need.*

'Come back when you've grown a pair, Ad. I need a real man.'

Klaus sensed that somebody was approaching from his right. He peered ahead into the trees but spied nothing. He heard the tinkle of metal as something fell behind him onto the stony ground. A hard, small object landed heavily and squarely in the hood of his parka.

He turned around and spied a man lumbering off awkwardly towards the trees on his left. A stumbling man.

'Hey!' Klaus shouted. He could not see the man's face but he recognised his gait from somewhere.

Klaus rummaged in the hood of the parka; grasped the thing that had been tossed into it by the stranger. It was a hand grenade, the kind of Second World War relic found in army surplus stores. Klaus wondered if it was still live. Then he noticed the pin was missing.

CHAPTER 23

Remand Wing, Women's Prison, UK

'Where the hell is Gordon Thomson?' Ella asked the anorexically thin psychologist, who was sitting opposite her in a dismal day room with screwed-down tables and chairs.

She could see the woman was only in her late twenties. She guessed she was a recently qualified quacktitioner, tasked with observing and labelling the off-cuts of society that were stuffed all day long into seven foot by ten foot cells like dysfunctional lab rats. 'Detective Gordon Thomson. I had a deal with him. Where is he?'

Under the psychologist's trousers, she wore pink heart socks; one sock pulled much higher than the other. This bothered Ella. But Ella was now beyond being capable of cool, objective judgement. She decided that because the woman was not answering her question and because she wore terrible, uneven socks, she was a loser.

The psychologist smiled at Ella and scribbled something into her pad.

'So tell me, Ella. How would you describe your homelife? Do you get on with your mother?'

Ella thumped the table. 'Listen, Dr Whateveryournameis. I was an informant in a drugs bust. I had been working with

Detective Thomson for over a year to gather evidence for the case against Daniel Spencer, Jeremy Saddiq, Tonya Perkins and Michelle Ogumbe. I wore a wire to a drugs pick-up in Amsterdam. I was supposed to be put into a safe house awaiting their trial. And now I've been in here for a month waiting for a trial date! On remand, like a common fucking criminal.'

The psychologist nodded and began to write in her pad. She took a dainty sip from a cardboard cup of coffee and continued. She said nothing.

'Well?' Ella shouted.

She squinted at the psychologist's pad and tried to read the notes upside down. It took her a moment to decipher the scribbled handwriting.

'Delusional? Possibly suffering oppositional defiant disorder? You cheeky bitch!'

Ella stood up and regretted the chair being bolted to the floor. She understood perfectly why the other inmates liked to throw furniture around whenever the opportunity presented itself.

'Sit down, please, Ella.' The psychologist spoke with a calm, almost impassive tone.

Ella threw herself heavily back onto the chair and played with the ribbed hem of her too-tight, standard-issue tracksuit top. She wore no bra because they had provided her with no bra. 'Why was I refused bail even?'

The psychologist smiled sweetly. 'Speak to your legal representative.'

'He's trekking in the fucking Andes for charity. I can't get hold of him.'

'Well, that's not my area. Now, do you ever feel like you want to hurt yourself, Ella? Do you get sad or angry?'

'What?'

'It's common for girls withdrawing from alcohol or substance misuse to have negative feelings …'

'You think I'm a user? And a suicide risk? A cutter?' Ella sucked

221

her teeth, knew she was throwing a surly teen pose but couldn't help herself. 'I'm not a bloody addict! I'm an in-for-mant! Now where's Gordon?' She folded her arms and stared at the avidly scribbling psychologist until their eyes met. 'Well?'

The psychologist flicked through the pages of her pad and skimmed what appeared to be an earlier entry from Ella's induction week. 'Detective Thomson's had a heart attack. He collapsed the morning that you were arrested. He's in intensive care.' Her tone was flat, devoid of any sympathy or even feigned surprise.

Panic. Ella was gripped by panic now, although it made sense. That's why she hadn't heard from him.

'He must have left instructions about me,' Ella said, trying to be as non-threatening as possible. She realised she had to play up to the quack. Let her see she was educated and sane. Try to find common ground and stop cussing her out like a mouthy ghetto bad ass.

'Look, Ella, I know this must be frustrating for you. You think Detective Thomson had cleared the way for your release.'

'I don't think it.'

'Unfortunately, CID haven't found any paperwork to back your claims up. And Detective Thomson is not well enough to be contacted right now.'

Damn, damn, damn. You've hung me out to dry, Gordon the Gargoyle.

'But the recording equipment I was wearing?'

'I'm not the person to speak to really. Like I said, you should speak to your solicitor. Have him liaise with the police. I'm here to assess your well-being. Now, how would you describe your sexual orientation?'

Ella said nothing. She clenched her hands into tight little fists, stood in silence and walked to the door. The psychologist made no attempt to encourage her to sit back down. Willing herself to keep a lid on her simmering frustration, Ella banged on the glass until one of the screws appeared and showed her back to her cell.

Her cell was a dreary, godforsaken place. The only window was barred – of course. One solitary, small pane opened to let in fresh air; the tantalising, heartbreaking whiff of freedom.

When she had first arrived, after she had endured the indignity of sitting on BOSS – the grey plastic Body Orifice Security Scanner – to see if she had wedged anything useful, dangerous or narcotic up her hoopla, she had been greeted with a risible welcome pack of toothpaste, shampoo, soap, sweets and orange squash. Now her little juvie luxuries, shopped for by Her Majesty at her leisure, were gone. All she was left with were walls full of smelly brown stains where the other inmates had spat on the drab paint in an attempt to stick up posters of their favourite pin-ups and bands or photographs of the children they weren't allowed to see regularly. Shop-soiled, unmade bedding and a toilet without a seat. That was Ella's cold comfort now.

At five thirty sharp, she was let out of her cell. Happy hour and a half. A chance to have a fight with one of the other lovely ladies. Or play cards. Perhaps she would peruse the erudite pages of the women's prison periodical, *Do What?*

Ella made her way down to the association area, rubbed shoulders with the mad, the butch, the pregnant, the young, the old, the mainly black, the always angry other women. She stood in line for the telephone, drinking in the smell of chips, tobacco and sweat. She tried not to make eye contact with the others. Tonya and Big Michelle were a lifetime ago now – sent to another facility in another part of the country. Ella was a battered, broken satellite lost in the vacuum of deep space.

Buzzing chatter hushed suddenly. The queue moved aside to let somebody through. A big-busted woman in her fifties who looked like she'd had her hair cut with a knife and fork emerged and pushed in front of Ella. Welsh Mavis. Ella knew the woman was on remand for murder but still …

'Hey, I'm next,' Ella said.

Welsh Mavis looked at her with heavily medicated eyes. 'Get fucked, bitch.'

Ella sized up the Thai tattoos that curled out from under the cuffs of Mavis' voluminous tracksuit top. Exotic, toxic, they inked their way down her forearms to her hands, fringed by *LOVE* and *HATE* on her red, scabbed knuckles. A clichéd fighter's hands. Ella touched her already bruised eye, fell silent and backed up several feet.

Eventually she reached the phone and dialled Letitia. It was the first time she had managed to get through to her since she had been incarcerated.

'Yeah?'

'It's me. Don't put the phone down.'

Silence.

'Listen, I don't want to know why you've not been to visit me in four fucking weeks or tried to help me get the hell out of here but I wanna hear from you why they wouldn't grant bail. My solicitor said they reckoned I was a flight risk.'

'Yeah, well.' Letitia chewed gum noisily down the phone. 'You know how it is.'

Desmond Dekker serenaded in the background. Ella knew something was up. Letitia only played Desmond Dekker when she had a man on the scene.

'How can I be a flight risk if you vouched for my accommodation? You didn't vouch for me, did you?'

Chewing. Rhythmical clicking of molars on tasteless gum.

'Letitia!'

'Listen, Ella. I got a new live-in boyfriend since you was arrested.'

'What?'

'You was out all the time with Danny and that. I got lonely. So when you got nicked, Leroy moved in for a bit.'

Ella felt hot lava roil around her stomach. A volcano of *why didn't I see this coming?* About to erupt.

224

'You're letting your own child rot on remand. I did all this to save your arse but you couldn't wait to see the back of me. Just so you could install brand new loverboy? Jesus, Letitia. When I get out of here, I am never, and I repeat, *never* going to speak to you again. Do you get me?'

Ella smashed the receiver repeatedly onto its hook until two screws gripped her hard by her shoulders and dragged her away.

It was a long time until unlocking at 7.45am. As Ella lay scrunched up like an unwanted foetus in her hard, narrow bed, she listened to the other inmates jeering, joking and thumping on their doors as they were banged up for the night. For the foreseeable future, she was trapped in this nightmare where the wailing of desperate women, seeking ice-cold solace in self-harm, always cut through the few peals of last-resort laughter.

A further two months had passed before Ella had a breakthrough. It was a Tuesday morning when finally she was told she had a visitor. She had not looked for him or expected him after such a long time.

'Gordon!'

The Gargoyle stood before her, pale and weak. His suit seemed too large for him. His face was sunken. He held out his hands to Ella.

'Lovey. I'm so sorry. I've been in hospital. My ticker. I had to have a triple bypass. They screwed up, didn't they?'

Ella felt tears flow freely down her face, onto her neck and the collar of the tracksuit. She tried to speak but the words wouldn't come. Her body shook with emotion as the despair started to work its way free.

'How can I ever apologise? Listen,' he said, putting an arm around her. 'It's over now. They're making me take retirement. I shouldn't be here but the prison psychologist got in touch with me. You see, the arresting officers never told me what happened.

I didn't even know where you'd been sent. But I'm making it right now. I've sorted it all.'

Ella looked at his bloodshot eyes and whisky drinker's nose. It looked too big for his face now. This kindly man had finally come to rescue her; had come to unlock the door to her new life. *Three months fucking late but still …*

'Don't make me go back to *her*,' was all she could manage.

Wracking sobs of overwhelming relief. Ella was still crying when the screws handed her back her clothes in a black plastic box with her photograph and name stuck to the lid. It was the same pair of jeans, T-shirt and cardigan she had worn briefly in Amsterdam.

Months later, when the case finally came to court, giving evidence against Tonya and Big Michelle was hard but Ella did it. At no point did she have to come face to face with them. She recorded her testimony in private, silently berating herself for giving up their skins in return for her own. Within the safe confines of her thoughts, she said goodbye to those flint-faced calamity queens and apologised for the betrayal.

Danny and Jez had been picked up by the Dutch police. Ella wondered if they had suspected her involvement. Been tipped off somehow.

'I wish I'd seen them get nicked. With my own eyes. Like with Tonya and Big Michelle.'

'Ella, let it go,' the Gargoyle said. 'You've got to stop worrying. They're over there. You're over here. We've recorded your testimony. It won't go off. It's finished.'

'We worked for a year to get enough evidence to bring them down.' Ella sat in the spartan safe house, cradling her heavy head in her hands. Wondering if she had left any loose threads to unravel. 'I risked everything.'

The Gargoyle patted her hand. 'Listen, lovey, you've got your place at university now. Just get on with your new life. Make it count. As for Danny and Jez, they'll go down. They'll get a good long stretch, no danger.'

Ella smiled wistfully as she thought of the university offer letter she had received through the post only two days earlier. It was typed on heavy, quality paper, bearing the lions and fleurs-de-lys of the St John's College crest.

Yes, Ella Williams-May, we thought you conducted yourself impeccably at interview, despite your frenzied rearranging of the pens on the desk in the office into parallel lines. Your school has stood by you and speaks highly of you. Yes, you may come and join us in a privileged world where people hold their cutlery properly, know which spoon to use for sorbet and where the furniture is not bolted to the floor. We are endlessly impressed by your unwavering self-discipline in the face of adversity and your moral fortitude. In short, Ella Williams-May, we know the score and we like it.

It was a letter Ella would frame and hang somewhere special.

Ensconced in the safe house on her own, she had studied hard for her mock A levels using the books that her school had sent into prison. She knew she would get four A* grades when exam time approached. It was in the bag. But there was still one question left to be answered.

'What's my new name going to be then?' she asked the Gargoyle.

The Gargoyle frowned. He dipped a rich tea biscuit into a cup of coffee and held it to his mouth.

'What do you want to be called?'

Ella let her eyes wander over the stack of second-hand and library books on the otherwise empty bookshelf of the safe house. Her gaze fell first onto a dog-eared copy of George Orwell's *Animal Farm.* Then it fell onto an obscure tome she had found in a used bookshop. It was *Redefining the Bonds of Commonwealth, 1939–1948.* The author was Dr Francine McKenzie.

'Georgina McKenzie,' Ella said.

The Gargoyle nodded. The end of his limp biscuit fell into his coffee with a plop.

'Georgina McKenzie it is, then.'

Ella grinned and massaged her scalp with happy fingers. 'Call me, George.'

CHAPTER 24

Amsterdam, 25 January

From: Sally.Wright@cam.ac.uk 09.02
To: George_McKenzie@hotmail.com
Subject: Disciplinary Action

Morning, George

I have had a written complaint from Dr Fennemans about your behaviour. You told me that you were barred from class but now it seems you are ditching his one-to-one supervisions. I have also had several anonymous complaints about your pro-terror article in the online periodical, *The Moment*. Your mother is also still driving me crazy with repeated phone calls demanding that you return home immediately and meet with her face to face. She refuses to tell me what the urgent matter is.

Given the news about the third faculty student being found dead, I **insist** you come back to Cambridge for a break. If you want to avoid disciplinary action, you and I had better talk. College will pay your airfare and give you a room for a week. I have booked you a flight from Schiphol to

Stansted for Monday lunchtime. I will text flight number and times later. Be on it.

Sally

Dr Sally Wright, Senior Tutor
St John's College, Cambridge Tel ... 01223 775 6574
Dept. of Criminology Tel ... 01223 773 8023

George read the email and grunted at the laptop screen.

'Bollocks to Fennemans,' she said.

Sipping her hot coffee, she thought about the enforced trip home. She missed Cambridge. In truth, it felt like a lifetime since she had been back. She knew that recently her smooth exterior had begun to flake and crumble. Perhaps homesickness played a part in that. But she was in the middle of something in Amsterdam and she wanted to see it through.

She delved into a packet of savoury crackers and ate carefully, trying to avoid dropping crumbs beneath her modest dining table or her keyboard. What the hell did Letitia want? The question that she had put off asking for long enough rolled around inside her like a bagatelle ball of bad blood and unease. It was time to face the music. She emailed Sally back that she would indeed come to Cambridge and she agreed to meet Letitia the Dragon in a public place for ten minutes, and ten minutes only.

Her phone rang. It was van den Bergen.

'What?' she asked brusquely.

'Hello, Cagney. I'm fine, thanks for asking.'

'You never usually worry about making nice.'

Van den Bergen sighed heavily on the other end of the phone. 'Come over. I want to talk to you.' He hung up.

Another person insisting I give them face-time. What the hell have I done? And that bastard Karelse still hasn't phoned.

Ad leaned against the orange Formica worktop in his mother's kitchen in Groningen. Fingered the plain steel handle on one of the pistachio-painted cabinets. Looked inside, gripped as he was by an unexpected hankering for a beer. No beer. Just baking products. Mostly out of date. Everything in the house was a relic from the 1970s and early eighties. Frozen in time. Petrified with age.

'Sit down, dolly. I've made your favourite apple tart,' his mother said, squeezing a steaming flan dish between oven-gloved hands.

'I'll pour the coffee,' he said, remembering to smile at the tart and nod to show his appreciation.

Ad looked at his mother. Her top half was obscured by a pink spotted apron. Her wide bottom was wrapped in an unflattering yellow nylon skirt, which was undoubtedly home made. Mum liked to make clothes. Hadn't she made him wear those horrible brown polyester trousers as a kid that were always too short in the leg? Hand-knitted jumpers with snowflakes that made him look like the retarded son of a Friesian farmer. Homespun, church hall, bring and buy thrift. Now her swollen, varicose-veined legs looked red and sore through the support stockings. She was getting old.

'Shall I get the plates?' he asked.

'There's a good boy.'

Ad felt pangs of nostalgia. He had not really paid attention to his mother in a long time. His life at university in the big city had quickly started to unfold before him like the road to Xanadu. He travelled along that road blinkered and intoxicated; a twenty-first century Marco Polo marvelling at Kubla Khan's riches. Nowadays, coming home seemed like a disappointing dream.

And his parents would never accept George.

'Mum, I've got something to tell you,' he said, pouring strong coffee into espresso cups from a small cafetiere.

Sitting in the interview room, facing an exhausted-looking van den Bergen, George rocked back on the hind legs of her uncomfortable chair.

'Well?' she said. 'Have you arrested Biedermeier? I presume that's why I'm here.'

Van den Bergen leaned forward. Under the harsh, institutional strip lighting, his normally lived-in-looking, still-handsome face looked flinty and enigmatic.

'George. Klaus is dead.'

George blinked repeatedly, looked questioningly at van den Bergen. 'What? Did he commit—'

'He was murdered. Blown up by a Second World War hand grenade.'

She wondered how she felt about that. Was she happy? Sad? Relieved? She decided she felt nothing. She just felt dead inside. Maybe disappointed. 'Are you sure?'

Van den Bergen produced a folder. 'I don't want to show you these but I know you won't believe me if I don't.' He placed photographs from a crime scene on the table with care. One by one.

George gulped. 'Christ,' was all she could manage. She looked away. Anywhere but at those photos.

Van den Bergen gathered the photos up. 'Sorry,' he said.

George looked at her dry hands, mentally sorting though the information as it came to her; analysing the shifting consequences. 'Where did it—'

'The police went to find him at the house where your little armchair-vigilante friend Mr Karelse had been staying.'

George noted the openly scathing tone that van den Bergen used when he referred to Ad. She held her breath for almost a minute while she absorbed the information. Then she spoke her thoughts aloud.

'Another faculty student, dispatched with fire or brimstone. There's somebody linking all of the victims. Someone in

Amsterdam who mixes on a daily basis with us all. Somebody with a thing for explosives. An arsonist. Back-bedroom bomb maker but not a stereotypical terrorist on a divine mission.'

Van den Bergen ran his finger and thumb along the edge of his unfashionable silk tie.

'It was your idea for Adrianus to go gallivanting off to Heidelberg, wasn't it?' van den Bergen asked, studying her from beneath those angular dark eyebrows. 'You really are like a dog with a bone, aren't you? How do you feel now? Do you feel stupid?'

George felt suddenly like she was being emotionally backed into a corner. Put under a spotlight. But in truth, she did feel idiotic. She had been cheated by Klaus. Everything had pointed to him, and George had been wrong. She, who prized her insight into people's characters and behaviour so highly. She, who was usually the skilled manipulator, infiltrator, interrogator. She felt the urge to hit back at van den Bergen, lash out at him as he perched on his lofty moral ground.

'Hey, you roped me into this investigation, *Inspector*. You asked me for help, not the other way round.'

'I asked you to write an article and keep an eye out for suspicious goings on among students, especially Muslims. Not to steer a multiple murder investigation down the wrong path.'

George silently conceded van den Bergen was right. She swallowed a defensive, pointed retort. It scratched and threatened to choke her on the way down.

'Listen. You need to find unsolved cases where somebody has been beaten or burned,' she said. 'And as it happens, my neighbour mentioned a Thai prostitute who was badly burned by a customer not so long ago. What about that?'

Van den Bergen perched on the edge of the scuffed table. She heard his hip click. He pushed two painkillers from a blister pack that he pulled out of his trouser pocket. Downed them with a swig from his oily-looking coffee. Clutched at his stomach and scowled. 'I remember that,' he said. 'That was nothing like this. He was a drunken john who didn't get what he wanted. For a start, she's not a man or a student. The attacker didn't kill her. You're barking up the wrong tree. Go home and lock your door, George. Stay out of mischief, young lady.'

George stood up abruptly, knocking her chair to the floor. 'Fine. I'm going to Cambridge anyway. I need a break.'

To her surprise, van den Bergen moved around to her side of the table, righted her chair and encased her shoulder in his large hand.

'You're something else, do you know that? Look, if it's any consolation to you, I thought you really were on the money with Biedermeier. So don't be hard on yourself. But cut the private investigator crap, okay? Just enjoy being a kid and keep safe.'

His face softened into a smile which revealed genuine affection. George touched his hand and left without saying anything more.

Fennemans slammed his front door. He slipped his keys into his coat pocket, juggling awkwardly with his briefcase, an umbrella and the post that the postman had just shoved into his hands.

On top of what looked like an electricity bill and a reminder to pay a parking fine he had picked up en route to his mother's, he spied a letter from the university.

'Odd,' he said. 'I'm not expecting anything.'

Tearing open the envelope, he straightened out the letter. It was from the Executive Board but had not been signed by Saskia.

Gripped by blind panic, he picked out the words, 'replacing Professor Saskia Meyer while she is on an extended sabbatical' and 'Miss Georgina McKenzie has lodged a formal complaint of harassment and bullying, corroborated by other students'.

'Shit!' Fennemans shouted.

He crumpled the letter in his sweaty fist and hit himself in the forehead.

'I'm going to kill that bitch.'

When she returned to the Cracked Pot Coffee Shop, George ate a sandwich of stale bread, tomato ketchup and crisps while she waited until Katja had finished with a client. She knocked on Katja's door. She was standing by the window, squeezing antibacterial gel onto her hands.

'Hello, darling,' she said with a freshly lipsticked smile. 'Is everything okay?'

George leaned against the door frame and peered at the glowing red light. 'I've been thinking,' she said. 'Can you get me an address for the Thai girl who was burned? What was her name again?'

'Saeng? I don't know, honey. Maybe if I ask some of the other girls when I get a spare minute. Why?'

'I wanted to pay her a visit.'

Katja's eyes widened. She raised an overplucked eyebrow at George. 'I don't think she'd want to speak to you, darling. She's probably gone to London by now, anyway.'

'If you could get me the address …' George forced her face into the most earnest shape in her repertoire but could see from the way Katja's smile faded that she would not willingly oblige. George sensed she had overstepped an invisible boundary.

'I wouldn't put money on it, darling,' Katja said. She struggled to tighten the ties at the side of her white Lycra bikini bottoms with impractical, talon-like nail extensions that reminded George of Letitia.

George was about to leave when she was struck by a thought. She fingered the peeling paint on the door's deep architrave and then fixed her attention on the roll of kitchen wipes by Katja's narrow bed.

'Those Middle Eastern girls …'

'Yes. The ones from Taliban land that come and go.'

'Do you know if they've ever been attacked by a customer? Have any disappeared that you know of?'

Katja shook her head and stepped into black patent stiletto heels.

'Like I said, darling, they have a chaperone. You could try asking Indonesian Tom but if I were you I'd keep yourself to yourself.'

'What do you mean?'

Katja smiled and adjusted her buoyant breasts inside their tiny triangular hammocks. 'You live with us but you're not one of us. Don't go looking for trouble.'

Ignoring Katja with great enthusiasm, George Googled rehabilitation clinics for burns victims. She came up with the Free University Medical Centre in De Boelenlaan, and placed a call to the hospital, putting on a distinctly dubious Thai accent; pretending to be Saeng Pradchaphet's long lost sister. On six separate occasions, George was told in no uncertain terms that Saeng had been long discharged and the hospital would never give out information about patients' subsequent whereabouts, particularly not over the telephone. On the seventh attempt, George was put through to a receptionist who had a young voice and seemed inexperienced and uncertain of herself. She gave George the address of sheltered accommodation run by a charitable organisation that provided outreach to prostitutes, including those who were victims of human trafficking from Eastern Europe, Asia and Africa.

George felt the rollercoaster, powered by her modest triumph, pick her up out of the trough that Klaus, van den Bergen and Ad had left her in. It pulled her along its arc up towards the summit, where she felt sure on reaching it, she would see exactly how the land lay before her.

She printed out the photographs Ad had taken in the Heidelberg heavy metal pub and put them in her bag. Then, she celebrated with a cigarette before donning her coat and boots.

Fennemans concealed his Swiss Army knife in his overcoat pocket. Lectures could wait. Any residual desire he felt for Little Miss McKenzie had been numbed by the public left hook of her formal complaint.

There she was! Fennemans shook with adrenalin as he watched her pull the glass door to the coffee shop open and put on her hood. She had a cigarette dangling out of her mouth. She looked agitated and unkempt. He would give her agitated all right!

Inside his pocket, with practised dexterity, he readied the blade. Took a few steps towards her. In a busy area like this, nobody was paying attention to anything but the girls in the windows.

Then he felt a hand on his shoulder.

'Not so fast, Doctor. I want a word with you.'

Fennemans looked round. He felt his face collapse as though he had been struck by a palsy of horror.

George sat down on a high-backed chair, facing Saeng. The lounge of the charity-furnished sheltered accommodation had all the elegance of an institutional old people's home. It smelled of over-cooked cabbage and burnt coffee. The sill of the enormous picture window was crammed with overgrown pot plants, making what should have been a bright room dark.

She forced herself to look at Saeng as though there was nothing unusual about her appearance. But everything about her was unusual. George judged her to be late twenties. A diminutive woman, she wore velour blue jogging bottoms and a tight white T-shirt that showed she had a body to die for. But the skin on the lower half of her face looked like partially melted cheese. Where skin grafts had not quite worked, red welts had been left as though somebody had thrown a bottle of cherry syrup onto her mouth, jaw and neck. Mercifully, the upper half of Saeng's face, her eyes and curtain of shining black hair were unaffected. George could see that she had been stunning.

George spoke in Dutch. 'Shall we talk in English or Dutch?'

237

'English. I speak little Dutch only.'

'Fine.'

George sipped from the mug of green tea that Saeng's carer had given her. Saeng watched.

'Thanks for agreeing to see me,' she said.

'If you friend of Katja and Inneke, I speak to you.' Saeng spoke broken English with a heavy speech impediment, as though her tongue no longer hit the roof of her mouth. 'But maybe I don't tell you thing. What you want to know?'

George cleared her throat and smoothed an invisible wrinkle in her jeans. How could she succeed where the police had failed? She felt certain Saeng would be offended but she resolved to question her anyway.

'Have you heard about the bombs in Amsterdam and Utrecht?'

Saeng nodded abruptly. 'Student.'

'One of the victims was beaten and then set on fire in a dustbin,' George said, trying to illustrate fire with waggling fingers.

She looked for a reaction in Saeng's eyes but saw nothing beyond her black irises. Saeng merely sipped her tea through her damaged, too tight mouth and stared at her.

'You had a client that beat you and then set fire to you. I know you didn't—'

'Why you think I talk you about this?' Saeng's heavy voice was laced with tart acrimony. 'Who you? What you want know about me?'

Saeng rose from her chair. George sensed that she was about to walk out. She hastily pulled the photographs from her bag. 'Please. He's killed five that the police know of. Please just look at these photos and tell me if you recognise anyone in them.'

Saeng glanced over at the large prints. George could see her curiosity was piqued. She needed to push her, get her to see that George was somebody she could confide in.

'I'm not the police. I'm just a frightened woman. I could be next. Please look.'

Saeng sat back down and studied the prints, one after another. George noted that her hands were also scarred from her attack. She wondered if the burns were still painful.

Suddenly, Saeng took a sharp intake of breath. The photograph in her hand started to shake.

'Do you recognise anyone?' George asked.

Saeng stared blankly at George. Her hands stopped shaking. Instant composure. It was as though she had abruptly let down impenetrable shutters, keeping George out. She shook her head.

But George knew she was lying. 'I can tell you've spotted someone,' she said. She moved in closer to Saeng and pointed to the man she too had a feeling she recognised. It was the disfigured man. The dealer. 'Is it him?'

Saeng shook her head violently and thrust the photographs back at George.

'Nobody there.'

Frustration started to pick at George's calm veneer. 'Look, did this guy threaten you? Is that it?'

Saeng stood once again. The photographs cascaded from her lap onto the grey linoleum floor. 'You leave now. You ask too many question.'

George clasped her hands together in supplication. 'People are dying, Saeng. I need you to tell the police if you recognise this man as your attacker. They can stop him. They can protect you.'

No reaction. Hard, staring eyes.

'Why are you so afraid?'

A tear slowly emerged from Saeng's left eye, followed by a copycat from the right. She perched on the arm of the chair and looked up at the ceiling. 'You not understand. I have hard life. You come from England, right?'

George nodded.

'Easy for you. My family live on river in Bangkok. Very poor. I work as prostitute in Patpong from fourteen. Right? Then I get mixed up in Chinese-run brothel and go-go bar. They sell me to

German brothel. Say, I go to Europe, earn more money. They pay my family. But I get to Germany and get no money. I live in small room in club with other girls. We prostitute for farang and massage but also must clean club.'

George offered Saeng a clean tissue. She took it with a stiff smile and dabbed at her moist eyes.

'Go on,' George said.

'So I run away and get to Amsterdam. Better life in Holland and I meet other Thai girls in red light area. Meet Indonesian Tom and get window. I work for myself. So it's okay long time, right? Then this guy,' she pointed at the disfigured dealer in the photograph, 'he come to my window and want extra. When I tell him no, he burn me. He say if I tell anyone, he come back and kill me. He say he know where my family in Bangkok. He know people in Thailand and all over. So, I tell police nothing. Maybe now I get to London and work in cousin restaurant.'

George absorbed Saeng's story slowly, as though digesting a heavy meal. *A man who deals drugs and has international contacts. Germany. Thailand. The Netherlands. Somebody familiar to me. Have I seen him around the Cracked Pot? I must have done. Wait a minute.* George felt a cold sweat break out on her forehead. This was the man that was limping into the sex show the day she had been followed. *This is my fucking stalker.*

'You okay?' Saeng asked her.

George looked at her, eyes narrowed, cogs in her mind whirring in overdrive.

CHAPTER 25

Later

Van den Bergen was digging over his vegetable patch when George appeared unannounced and uninvited at Sloterdijkermeer. At first, he did not notice her. With his spade, he levered out a stubborn dandelion tap root intact. He breathed in the smell of damp soil, fingering his trophy with some satisfaction.

It was the methanol stink of George's cigarette that alerted him to her presence. He looked up and smiled. When he saw her thunderous expression, his smile faltered.

'Detective Cagney. What's wrong?'

George pulled a photograph out of her bag. She poked at the disfigured face of a man sitting in the shadows. He recognised it as one of the photos that interfering, have-a-go-hero Karelse had taken in Heidelberg.

'You said there was no connection between the Thai prostitute, Saeng Pradchaphet, and these murders,' George said.

'Yes.' He wondered why she, of all people, had to be so prickly when he'd had a morning from hell that had already made him feel like he was permanently sitting on a cactus chair.

'You're wrong,' Irritation rippled through her voice. 'I've just been to see Saeng.'

Van den Bergen stood abruptly. He scowled at George, briefly

241

supplanting her beautiful face in his mind's eye with that of Elvis. 'What did I tell you about going home and locking your door?' He wiped muddy hands on the bib of his dungarees. 'You don't listen, do you?'

'No.'

She became George again. Not his subordinate. But still, a protégée of sorts.

'It's time you listened to me,' she said, pointing at him with her glowing cigarette. 'Now, Saeng recognised this man. Ad says he's a dealer that all the neo-Nazi thugs in this Heidelberg bar seemed to know. So, he had a connection to Joachim and Klaus.'

Van den Bergen shuffled over to George in his giant wellington boots and grabbed the grainy photo of the scarred man from her. He buried deep his shame at having failed to pursue the line of enquiry himself.

'How the hell could she tell from this?' he scoffed.

'I could see from her body language she recognised him straight away. And she was petrified. The guy threatened her and her family back home. Said he knew people in Thailand.'

Van den Bergen searched for the right words. How should he deal with this girl, showing him up for being all the things he detested – lacking in thoroughness, dismissive, stubborn?

'Hmm. She wouldn't tell the police anything.'

'Suppose I've got the magic touch, then,' George said, winking. 'Have you got any of that coffee in your flask? I'm really thirsty.'

'No.' Van den Bergen scratched his thatch of white hair and grimaced as a burp of indigestion forced its way up and out. She was being gracious about the whole thing. He allowed his scowl to soften. 'So, you think we're looking for a German drug dealer?'

He caught George studying his face. He had got rid of the goatee but hadn't shaved for a couple of days. He touched his jaw self-consciously, wondering what she thought about the stubble that popped out of his skin like steel and iron filings. Did she think it … attractive? Or did he repel her?

'This guy flits between Amsterdam and Germany,' she said. 'He knows the students in my faculty enough to select victims from among us. Perhaps Klaus and Joachim led him to Amsterdam but later pissed him off. How long ago was Saeng attacked? It was November last year, wasn't it?'

Van den Bergen nodded. 'Klaus and Joachim had been in Amsterdam for a couple of months.' He leaned on his spade, which he had thrust into the fertile earth. Then he strode over to his summerhouse, erected two fold-up chairs and took out his flask.

'I thought you didn't have any coffee,' George said.

Van den Bergen seated himself gingerly on the flimsy chair and treated her to a wry grin. 'I didn't think you deserved to share it. You're very disobedient.' He knew he was flirting with her now. It seemed entirely the wrong thing to do under the circumstances and yet, here he was, babbling on like an idiot. And blushing! Perhaps the ibuprofen and small beer that he had found hidden behind his rose fertiliser were a poor lunchtime combination.

He handed her two cups and poured them out a drink each.

George took her cup and warmed her fingers around it. She downed the contents in three gulps.

'Your coffee tastes like shit, Inspector.'

Van den Bergen shot her a sideways glance and smirked. 'Has anybody ever told you, George, you're a real charmer?'

George patted her hair, set her cup on the mosaic patio and stretched out her arms. 'Listen! There's something else. I've had a stalker these past few weeks.'

Van den Bergen's flagrant, burning desire to flirt with a girl half his age was immediately snuffed out. He watched George's expression change from mischievous to troubled, as though some shadow had passed across the sun. She looked suddenly vulnerable.

In an uncharacteristically shaky voice, she told him how she had found matches and a semen stain in her room. She relayed her sense of being followed and then explained how she had discovered Peeping Tom equipment on the other side of the canal, facing directly into her room.

'It took speaking to Saeng for me to realise that I saw this disfigured guy limping into a sex show after I'd been to the flower market. Now I come to think of it, his face looks like he's been burned or wounded beyond recognition in an explosion or something.'

'Why the hell didn't you report it?' van den Bergen demanded.

George crossed her arms. 'Like I said, I thought it was some one night stand gone wrong. I didn't want to bother you. I didn't think it was relevant until Klaus entered the picture, and by the time I was ready to say something, you call and tell me he's dead.'

He tutted and shook his head. 'Silly girl.'

Then, silence for a while, which George didn't interrupt. He needed to think. What kind of a man had burns like that?

'Maybe this guy's ex-military,' he said. 'There are a lot of men coming back from active service in Afghanistan who have terrible bomb-blast and shrapnel injuries. I'll get my people to look for German or Dutch soldiers with criminal records who have gone AWOL or been discharged.'

George then told him about a mystery foreign-sounding middle man who was shepherding the Middle Eastern girls through Amsterdam from a comfortable distance.

'My housemates think the girls are muling drugs to the UK,' she said. 'Here we have a drug dealer. Now you're saying maybe this guy might have been injured in Afghanistan. I have a theory …'

Van den Bergen wiped out his empty coffee cup with a tissue and screwed the lid back on the flask. His synapses were crackling and flashing with anticipation. 'You think our murderer is possibly ex-military, involved in a big international vice ring? Well, that's not unfeasible. And we break rings like that once every few years.

Maybe once a decade, even. Career cases for the vice boys. And this guy has Afghan or even Taliban connections for drugs and girls? Okay. That's where a lot of the heroin is coming from.'

'Got any murdered prostitutes or young girls of Middle Eastern origins?' George asked, sipping a second cup of coffee despite her protestations that it was shocking. 'Any unsolved drug murders in Germany or the Netherlands as a whole? They could all be worth looking at. This guy struck before with Saeng.'

Van den Bergen unexpectedly found himself putting his hand on her forearm. It was time to say something. Drop the facade. 'How does an academic goody-two-shoes know so much about international vice, Georgina McKenzie?'

George looked directly into his eyes. He could see, as her pupils dilated, that she had stumbled on the truth.

'You know about me,' she said.

Van den Bergen allowed the chuckle of the resigned and world-weary to stagger from his lips. 'I was the junior inspector in charge of the Dutch end of your drugs bust, George,' he said pointedly. 'Or should I call you Ella? You didn't suit the nun's habit at all!'

George concealed a childish, embarrassed grin beneath a shaking hand. She lit a cigarette. Dragged hard on it.

Van den Bergen didn't want to belittle her or make her feel uncomfortable. He resolved not to mention the Rotterdam Silencer and her accidental connection to him again. But he did feel a degree of satisfaction that now they had only truth between them.

He stood up. He removed his boots and beat the mud from the soles against the side of his summerhouse. 'But I tell you what, before you fly off,' he said, 'let's get our forensics team to take a look around your bedsit. See if they can lift any prints. And while we're at it, I'll get a warrant to look in the store room that faces into your place.'

'Hey, Georgina, everything all right here?' Jan asked, peering at her through smudged glasses.

George could see her landlord was nervous as he toyed with the buttons on his waistcoat.

'I'm okay, Jan. I'll fill you in later.' The last thing George wanted was Jan clucking around her room, winding the police up, spouting half-baked hippy politics and pretending to be the laid-back, cool uncle she neither had nor needed.

Jan cocked his head to the side and hooked a chunk of fuse-wire hair behind his ear. 'You look like you're going to be sick,' he said. 'You come down and get me if these guys are giving you hassle.'

George gave a half-hearted wave as a mountain of a forensics man made to shut the door in Jan's perplexed face. But a question popped into her head like a giant cartoon question mark. She wedged her foot between the man and the door just before it closed.

'Do us a favour, Jan,' she said.

'Anything.'

'Ask Katja or Inneke if they know the names of the English guys who do fake ID for some of the girls. If I'm out, get them to text me.'

The forensics man mountain had his way. He slammed the door shut on grumbling Jan.

George found the intrusion of the three forensic crime scene investigators almost intolerable. Every surface was covered in grey dust, highlighting the plethora of fingerprints that George had hitherto not been aware of. She stood with arms folded, mouth curled downwards into a scowl, wishing she could take a hot, damp cloth and some cream cleanser to the mess they had created.

Using what looked like women's blusher brushes, they were dusting every surface. At least the men wore plastic overshoes. It was a small consolation.

Van den Bergen emerged from her kitchenette, just as she was

246

examining her phone display for the twelfth time to check in vain for a text or voicemail from Ad. The dungarees had given way to his usual dark trousers and a beige raincoat, worn over another ageing blue shirt. In his latex gloved hands, he carried out a clear plastic bag containing the cook's matches. The only thing that hinted at him having been at his allotment not forty minutes earlier was the honest dirt beneath his fingernails.

'Nothing so far?' van den Bergen asked the fingerprinting team in a gruff voice.

One of the men, a barrel-chested, short man with a ruddy face, nodded. 'Over here, boss,' he said, pointing to a photograph in an Ikea pine frame.

The photo was of George and Ad outside the impressive arched portico of the Rijksmuseum. Ad's arm around George's shoulder. Both smiling. Before their first, abortive kiss.

'See these prints?' the barrel-chested man said.

George followed van den Bergen over to the photo. She peered at the grey dusty pattern of the fingerprint. Instead of it being the usual elliptical maze of tiny lines, the print was completely blank in the middle. Only around the outside were there traces of a pattern.

'Our perpetrator has no prints left on the pads of his fingers,' van den Bergen said.

'Burned off,' George suggested, looking at the barrel-chested detective for corroboration.

He nodded. 'Looks that way.'

George looked at the photograph again. 'Why is he so interested in me?'

She felt van den Bergen's eyes boring into the side of her head. 'He could have been watching every student on your course, George,' he said. 'We're going to have to pay a visit to everybody's accommodation.'

Van den Bergen's phone rang out with a deafening blast of music from some ghastly grunge band that made George jump.

'Yes,' he barked into the receiver. 'Oh.' He turned to George. 'You'd better come with me.'

His voice had a deadpan, cold tone to it that made the hairs on George's arms stand on end.

Wordlessly, they marched over to the sex shop on the other side of the canal. She clambered up the tenants' steep stairs behind van den Bergen, who took them two at a time. They passed the first floor, where, like Katja and Inneke, two prostitutes occupied rented rooms with red lights in the picture windows that faced on to the canal. The girls stood in see-through chiffon robes in their doorway, chatting amiably in heavy Eastern European accents with one of van den Bergen's detectives.

She continued up to the top floor, where finally they reached the store room that contained the boxes stacked against the back wall. The door stood open. She followed van den Bergen inside, who ducked to avoid banging his head on the low threshold.

The floorboards were bare and dusty. A female detective not much older than George was leafing through the boxes' contents, which appeared to be dog-eared leather-bound books. Perhaps antiquated library stock. George couldn't see clearly enough to make out any titles on the spines.

'Over here, boss,' said a dark-haired detective whom George remembered was called Elvis. At least, that's what van den Bergen called him. He was wearing a black leather biker's jacket today. He still looked a prat.

George followed Elvis' pointing finger to a patch of wall next to the window, out of the line of sight from her room. Then, her world abruptly came to a standstill. Blood froze in her veins. Breath seized up in her lungs. Even her heart forgot to beat.

Tacked to the wall were eight-by-ten-inch photographs of every man on her course, clearly taken from a distance on the university campus using a long-range lens. Ratan's, Joachim's, Remko's and Klaus' faces had been crossed out with thick black felt-tip pen. The photographs of six other course-mates, whose names she was not familiar with, were untouched.

There was a high-resolution photograph of Ad. In it, he was standing at her window with George's ear and part of her hair visible on the edge of the frame. Judging by the angle and height, it had clearly been taken by the photographic equipment she had spotted in the window of the store room. Ad was smiling into the unseasonably warm mid-autumn morning sunshine, with his eyes shut. He had brought her fresh croissants for a late breakfast. She remembered they had been looking out over the rooftops together, talking about him coming to stay with her in Cambridge. At no point had she suspected that a serial killer had been capturing those tender moments; spying on their blossoming friendship from a vantage point just a few metres away. Now Ad's sun-kissed face was ringed with bright red felt-tip pen. Perhaps what was equally disconcerting about this collage, though, was the fact that all of the photographs of the male course-mates were arranged in a ring around photos of one woman. Pulling on her underwear in the morning. Staring down onto the street in the afternoon sun. Dancing on her own at night, dragging on a cigarette. The only woman that featured on the wall. Her.

George felt the blood drain from her face with a prickle. Dizziness threatened to topple her. *Breathe. Remember to breathe.*

Her gaze drifted along the wall to a series of news clippings – coverage of the bombings similar to the ones stuck onto the back of Klaus' wardrobe. Next to those were pasted technical diagrams, giving step-by-step instructions on how to make a simple but high-powered suicide bomb, using a mobile phone as a remote detonator.

'Where is young Karelse?' van den Bergen asked, putting a supportive hand on her shoulder blade.

George shook her head in silence. Her eyes wandered to the window and the view of her bedroom.

'Phone him,' van den Bergen said.

She pulled out her phone and dialled his number. The phone was about to go to voicemail yet again when he picked up. George felt relief cut through the crisp, cold dread, flooding her with warmth.

'You okay?' she asked.

'Of course I'm okay,' he said. There was no trace of animosity or awkwardness in his voice. It was as though he had never stormed out of her room. As though he hadn't been avoiding taking her calls.

'Where are you?'

'Look, I'm in Groningen. I got here just an hour ago. I'm at Mum and Dad's. Hang on.' There was a rustling sound and a pause. 'That's better,' he said. 'I had to get out of earshot of Mum. I'm going to break it off with Astrid later. I'm sorry about—'

Van den Bergen interrupted her deliberations and his apologies by grabbing the phone out of George's hand.

'Listen, Karelse. Stay in Groningen. Stay with your family and don't go anywhere until the local police have put a patrol car outside your house. No heroics. They don't bloody suit you anyway. Do I make myself clear?'

Van den Bergen cut Ad off and gave abrupt orders for the police protection to be arranged for his parents' Groningen address immediately. George felt tears caused by a peculiar mixture of relief, panic and wistful emotion stab at the backs of her eyes. She had a sudden impulse to hug the inspector; to thank him for the practical help and protection he was offering to Ad, though it was concealed behind a veil of misanthropic bluster. She resisted.

Van den Bergen squatted to examine the bomb-making guidelines on the wall.

'I wish you would switch that darned thing off when you're at home,' Ad's mother said. She put down her fork, reached over her plate of apple tart and patted his hand. 'Who was that? You look twitchy and pale.'

Ad was just about to answer her when she overruled her own question.

'Now, go on, love. You were going to tell me something. Are you going to propose to Astrid? Is that it?' She clasped her hands to her apron-clad chest. 'That's it, isn't it? Oh, my boy. At last! My baby's getting married.'

'No. That's not it at all.' He had been about to tell her about how he had fallen in love with George. But that he was going to break it off with Astrid first. How he thought it was only fair after four years. Shit. He was such a wimp. Perhaps telling her about the police was preferable.

'There's going to be a squad car outside for a bit,' he said. 'Because of the murders in Amsterdam.'

His mother stopped chewing. She smoothed the edges of the oak kitchen table with fat-knuckled hands that showed the beginnings of arthritis.

'You what? Have you been in trouble?'

'No, Mum. The police are worried I might be a target.'

'But the dead men were terrorists.'

'No they weren't, Mum. They were men on my course. Like me.'

'One was a Negro, wasn't he? And a Jew. You're not a black or a Jew.'

The rosy, baking day nostalgia he had momentarily felt for his mother faded at once to cold, hard grey.

'I don't like it when you speak like that, Mum. It's not nice. Really.'

His mother pointed her fork at him and paused. She narrowed her eyes. Brown like his but devoid of tenderness. Pursed her lips, which took on a thin, mean appearance. 'Astrid's told me you've been hanging around with foreigners. Think you're clever, don't you, son? Mr Arty Farty Gad About Town.'

'Look, Mum. I'm an educated man and I don't like—'

'I don't care what you like, Adrianus. You just leave your worldly, high-falutin' rubbish at the door, young man, because this family has traditional Calvinist values and we're not as impressed with your airs and graces as you think.'

'Mum, this is about a killer. The police think I may be in danger!'

'What do you make of this room?' van den Bergen asked George.

George looked around at the old boxes, the naked bulb and the sinister collage.

'There's nothing else in here that says it's his main workspace. He killed Klaus on the hoof but he has to have taken the others somewhere before dispatching them. He needs peace and space to strap explosives to somebody's chest.'

She breathed in the essence of this predator. She shivered with distaste. 'He needs equipment and somewhere easily accessible with parking. This place is too far from ground level.'

'Good,' van den Bergen said. He thumbed through one of the old leather-bound books and turned to the female detective. 'Have we found a contact name in the university for the person renting this space?'

The female detective stood up, eyed George warily and checked her phone. 'Email just in, boss. It's registered to a Dr Vim Fennemans.'

He hummed 'Crazy in Love' by Beyoncé to himself as he drove the van up the motorway. The driving conditions were good. The asphalt sped smooth and flat beneath his tyres. He felt back on top of things. It was going to be a great day. Without swerving, he checked his crowbar was safely stowed under the passenger seat and that his gloves were in the glove box, where they belonged. Yes. All present and correct.

It was indeed going to be a great day.

'I'm going out,' Ad said, scraping his chair against the terracotta tiles of the floor.

He felt old resentments begin to resurface. Little Ad, living in Jolanda and Matthijs' shadow. The apples of his parents' eyes. Apples that didn't fall far from the tree. He had always just felt like windfall rolling down a different path. Astrid had made him temporarily palatable to them, but it was clear that leaving her for George would drive a permanent wedge between him and his parents. He no longer cared, though. George had woken him from his slumberous half-life and he wasn't ready to slip back into an emotional torpor.

His mother forked a large piece of apple tart into her mouth. 'Where are you going?'

'I'm going to meet Astrid.'

She breathed out hard through her nose. 'Okay. Look, I'm sorry, dolly. I didn't mean to ... Just leave your dirty washing at the bottom of the stairs. I'll do it while you're out.'

Ad patted the phone in his pocket and nodded.

'Don't get killed,' she shouted after him through her mouthful.

Ad walked through Villabuurt West towards the Quintuslaan bus stop, just missing the police patrol car that pulled up outside his parental home. The middle-class lanes were lined on both sides with almost identical sloping-roofed, chalet-style houses, brick built in the seventies in an exciting shade of drab brightened only by flashes of plain, white weatherboard cladding. Dull and characterless. Just like Mum and Dad. He cursed under his breath.

'I hate this soulless shithole. I hate them. I'm never going back.'

Hands stuck resolutely in his reefer jacket pockets, he walked briskly past the Saabs, Audis and BMWs of the newcomers with money. Families with young children. Aspirational and professional. Not like Mum and Dad.

He planned what he would say to Astrid. He would take her into town. Find somewhere public, like a café that was open on

253

a Sunday. Not for dinner. That would send the wrong message.

Should he make small talk first? Pretend like there was nothing wrong? But you couldn't drop something like that gently into the conversation. 'Oh, and by the way, I'm in love with another woman and we half had sex.' No. That would not do. How about the old line, 'It's not you, it's me'? Except it *was* her. Ad chewed the inside of his cheek. There was no easy way to dump a long-term girl-friend. He would just have to play it by ear.

When a white Renault Espace van slowly pulled onto Elsschotlaan, Ad was so engrossed in his plans that he was unaware of its presence. Its diesel engine went unheard. Its long wheel-based bulk went unseen.

The houses stood further apart here, near the cut-through to the bus stop. Even if it had not been almost deserted for a Sunday afternoon, evergreen trees grew dark and dense, meaning Ad's progress towards the bus stop could not be seen by the occupants in the surrounding houses.

'Oh, God,' Ad said to the overcast sky. 'Let me find the right words to say.' He kicked a stone into the street. 'I wish George was here.'

The van pulled alongside Ad and came to a standstill. He merely glanced at the driver, not really registering his appearance. Astrid and his mother had taken up residence in his mind's eye and together they blocked out all other peripheral visual informa-tion or salient thought, including van den Bergen's warning to stay put. Consequently, he was taken by surprise when heavy, lopsided footsteps quickened behind him. Ad just had time to look round before a man yanked his arms up behind him with one hand and silently placed a cloth over his nose and mouth. Two things dawned on him at that moment.

The first was that his assailant was the drug dealer from Heidelberg with the disfigured face and the limp. Up close, his dark eyes were too small. His nose was misshapen. His skin was shiny, lumpy in parts and too tight over the jaw. He wore what appeared to be a dark blond toupee. His grip was fiercely strong for a man of reasonably small stature.

The second thing that dawned on Ad was that the cloth that the man held over his face smelled strange. It had been soaked in something. Ad remembered the chemical smell from biology in school. Ether. But oddly, it wasn't knocking him out. He just felt slightly woozy.

Ad was so taken aback by this attack that his survival instincts had taken over, banishing any fear completely. He swung around drunkenly and thumped his attacker squarely on the side of his jaw. Blood from his knuckles left a four-point imprint on the man's face.

The man gasped, as though winded, but said nothing. In response, he merely reached inside his zip-up hoody and pulled a crowbar out from the waistband of his jeans. Before Ad could even shout for help, the man brought the crowbar down hard on his head. Broken glasses on the pavement and the ground rushing up at Ad were the last things he remembered about Elsschotlaan.

CHAPTER 26

Cambridge, 26 January

The black cab bounced into town. George sat bolt upright, watching as Parker's Piece shot by on her right. Downing College waved hello on her left. Then, the warm stone of Emmanuel. She got out there and walked through the pedestrianised centre, down Sidney Street, past Sydney Sussex College, squatting like a grand old man behind its walls. Past Sainsbury's. Down through the narrow Bridge Street to St John's. And there it stood before her, like an old, beautiful creature lying on its back, stretching its glowing, pale stone legs into the blue sky. St John's College Chapel. She didn't bother going to the Porters' Lodge. She slipped through the gate at the side and made her way straight to Sally's room, via the 1930s quad at the back of the Chapel.

Dr Sally Wright's room was on the first floor of the early seventeenth century Second Court. She looked out through large oriel windows over bright green, perfectly square lawns broken up by a grid of cobblestone pathways travelling at right angles to one another. From her room near the north-east corner was visible the famous Shrewsbury Tower with its brown Tudor brick turrets and sandstone edging. George's senses were overwhelmed both by the feeling of being back in that place and also by its sheer beauty. It was a million miles away from the squalor she

256

had always known on her South East London estate. She had never quite got over the fact that this visual, historical banquet was now her alma mater. She was a Johnian. She belonged here. Nothing short of amazing.

George tentatively knocked on the heavy wooden door.

'Yes,' came Sally's throaty smoker's voice from inside.

With some trepidation, George pushed open the door.

'So, these are from the unsolved cases of the two dead prostitutes?' van den Bergen asked.

Marianne de Koninck laid a series of photographs on the desk and spread them out so that they were facing van den Bergen.

Van den Bergen unfolded his reading glasses and put them on with all the flourish of a precise middle-aged man. He observed that her hands looked strong. You needed to have strong arms and hands to work with the dead. Realising he was becoming distracted, he looked down at the photographs and grimaced reflexively.

'Two years old now,' she said. 'It's funny you should have asked me to pull these records. Only the other night I was thinking that there's almost certainly a link between these women and Remko Visser.'

In one photograph lay the corpse of a young woman of about seventeen. In the patches of skin where she was not badly burned, her dark olive colouring hinted at Middle Eastern or North African origins. The burns had left the upper layer of skin blistered, white and peeling, revealing livid flesh beneath.

'This girl was a Jane Doe, wasn't she?' the pathologist asked.

Van den Bergen stared down at the photo, rifling through his memories.

'A patrol car discovered her lying in a doorway in the red light district but I didn't work on the case. I'd only just transferred back to homicide cases from a spell concentrating on narcotics. I seem to remember she died on the way to hospital.'

Two vertical frown lines between the pathologist's eyes deepened. 'Seventy percent burns. Poor girl. I performed the post mortem on her. The burns are the work of a blow torch. The skin around her genitals had not been torched though. She had been very sexually active about twelve hours prior to death. We swabbed her and found semen samples and pubic hair from several different men.'

'Unusual for working girls from the red light district not to insist on condoms,' van den Bergen said. 'Very unusual.'

'My guess is she was struck on the head with a blunt instrument first. Then torched. Her index finger had been cut off.' De Koninck tapped the photograph of the girl's mutilated hand with a Biro.

'Beaten first, like Remko Visser, who was also missing a finger and Joachim Guttentag,' van den Bergen said. 'I think I've found my missing link.'

'Ah, good. There you are,' Dr Sally Wright said, peering over red, 1950s-style winged glasses at George.

Sally was sitting with her thermal-sock-clad feet up on a chaise longue, red pen in hand, reading through what looked like an undergraduate essay. She was clad head to toe in an off-beat ochre ensemble, the kind only an academic would be seen dead in, George mused. Around her neck hung oversized chunky beads the same colour grey as her short, bobbed hair.

After they had air-kissed on both cheeks and shared the stiff half-embrace that middle-class people liked to do, Sally pushed up her paperwork and made George sit down.

'Tea? I've got an urn. It's so damned cold here. We had snow last week. Only a smattering but still ...' Sally pottered around with china cups on a large tea tray. She fought with a giant catering urn until the urn gave in and scalded her with boiled water. 'Terrific bastard!'

George smirked. She loved the way it sounded when Sally swore.

'Earl Grey do?' Sally asked, fumbling with a box of tea bags.

'Great. Dutch tea is shite. All you can get hold of is Lipton's. Gnat's piss.'

'Poor poor girl.' Sally shook her head and carried a rattling cup and saucer towards George. She held it out in front of her as though it contained plutonium. 'Here. Thaw you out.'

They exchanged pleasantries and ate biscuits for thirty minutes. In the back of George's mind, she was trying to assess when the hammer would fall. It fell at thirty-two minutes in.

'Now, George. Your serial killer ...'

George folded her arms. She had expected to be grilled first about Fennemans. This was a surprise. How much did Sally know?

'I've been following the gruesome progress on the internet,' she said. 'This isn't the work of a terrorist, you know. This is the work of somebody trying to look like a terrorist. Trying and failing.'

'That's what I thought,' George said. 'A fictitious cleric leading a fictitious Islamist terror cell.'

Sally pulled at her blunt fringe in thought. 'So, you have two murders rigged to look like suicide bombings. By the time of the third murder, the real killer has lost interest in trying to make it all look like a grand act of terrorism. His third murder is a much sloppier, straightforward burning, you see. He left the body in a public place in a bin. The fourth murder is just an open air attack. The police have really been given the run-around trying to track this man down.'

'Yes. They have. At least, I think so. From what I've heard on the grapevine. You know.' George looked down at the rug beneath her feet, keen not to make eye contact with her insightful senior tutor.

Sally pulled her thermal socks up, taut over her knees. 'Right, so the killer is targeting boys he sees every day. He's obsessed by fire. You know, most arsonists don't get caught because of the lack of evidence left behind and most set fire to buildings just to

259

make fraudulent insurance claims. The ones who are straightforward pyromaniacs are usually mentally ill. This guy is without doubt a sadist and a sociopath; thinks he's doing a public service, ridding the world of these students. He has a normal job on campus; in your faculty where nobody thinks twice about him. He's familiar with everyone on your course; familiar enough with their movements to abduct the boys successfully before murdering them. But first, he loathes them from a distance. He watches.'

'What about the other victim?' van den Bergen asked.

'Well, this is interesting,' the pathologist said. 'Similarly, a young girl. There were copious amounts of uncut heroin in her stomach, shreds of plastic and one small plastic bag, intact, containing the drug. She had been cut open with something like a meat cleaver, post mortem. My opinion is that somebody must have made her swallow bags of heroin ready to export, killed her and then cut her open to retrieve the drugs. They burst most of the bags with the blade they used. She too was missing an index finger. She had dirt trapped under her toenails that we traced to the Helmand region of Afghanistan.'

Van den Bergen gave a low whistle. 'My informant, Georgina, told me there were girls coming into Amsterdam from Taliban-ruled territories. She was right. I read that Helmand is one of the most notorious culprits for opium growing. Nobody there gives a hoot. Not NATO, certainly not the US and they could do something about it. No, they're too busy recruiting local warlords to help them collect anti-terrorist intelligence. The Russians want to spray the crops but nobody else is interested.'

'You seem to know a lot about it,' the pathologist said.

Van den Bergen gave a hollow laugh. 'I've done most of my time working homicide but I spent five painful years chasing after the sons of bitches that bring hard drugs into the country. Plus, I've got a very good, young teacher in Georgina. She's quite a girl. Gave me a reading list on the politics of it, would you believe it?'

The pathologist's cheeks coloured. Van den Bergen wondered if the mention of little Detective Cagney had made her think about her own fresh-faced squeeze. Wasn't he a flatmate of that boy, Karelse, with his delicate stomach and his long, useless fingers that had never seen a day's work?

Van den Bergen was sure George could do far better than Karelse.

He observed the Dutchman as he lay beneath the strip light on the slab, out cold. The blow to his head had left a large cut which had bled heavily during the long journey south. It had forced him to put a compress on the lesion, tape it and then seal what he could with plastic wound spray. It would hold for now but he suspected he had fractured the Dutchman's skull. There was a certain satisfaction in knowing he had smashed up his perfect, unblemished dome.

He had already given the Dutchman a shot, but his waking up at this stage would be an inconvenience. Now he wheeled the drip stand over and hung a bag of the liquid sedative onto the hook at the top. Then he connected up a bag of saline and a bag of universal type O blood to keep the Dutchman going until he had decided where he would dispatch him. He inserted a catheter into the Dutchman's penis – amazing the things you could learn by sitting in on the odd medical lecture and by scouring the internet. It wouldn't do to have piss all over the slab. Next, he inserted a cannula into the Dutchman's arm with expertise, connected all the tubing and watched with fascination as the life-giving and consciousness-stealing liquids started to drip through slowly. That should keep the Dutchman out of mischief. He would give him just enough sedative and then stop, timing it perfectly so that he would start to come round just as the phone rang. Just before the explosion. Then he would know fear and his punishment would be perfect.

Fennemans sat stiffly against the cold radiator in his basement. He strained against the duct tape that had been plastered across his mouth and bound around his hands. But nobody would hear him and nobody would find him. Not in time. Of that, he was certain. After all, who would actively seek out Vim Fennemans, apart from Senior Inspector van den Bergen?

He watched the pigtailed young girl as she bled slowly to death beside him on his thin camp-bed mattress; the rank, dark smile cut into her neck sneering at him. With regret, he realised that this too would be his fate: to die slowly in a freezing, damp basement. He wasn't even able to reach the fruit he had put out for his contraband houseguest.

Perhaps worst of all though, Fennemans mused wryly, was the fact that his own prints were now all over the knife that had cut the girl's throat. He had clutched at it under extreme duress, but the police, if they eventually came, would never believe him. Whichever way he looked at it, he was, for once, the one that had been well and truly fucked.

'Is the killer an academic?' George asked, wondering if there could be any connection with Fennemans. In her heart of hearts, she hoped so. Fennemans' name was on the store-room rental paperwork, after all. It was almost enjoyable to believe that her academic tormentor was capable of being even an accessory to murder.

Sally pushed her glasses up her nose and toyed with her beads. 'No. These killings are too unsophisticated to be the work of an educated killer. Bombing. Burning. Blowing up with a Second World War grenade. That's blunt-minded, straightforward aggression. It pretends finesse but ultimately lacks it. And you say that two victims were ethnic minority and two were right-wing Germans?'

'Yes. Neo-Nazi sympathisers.'

'Well, I think your killer has an identity crisis. Low self-esteem.

Negative associations with minorities *and* fascism. An inherent dislike of any foreigners, maybe. Very strange, to tell the truth. But he works alone, I'm sure of it. The cardboard indicates that his victims are being transported in large boxes.'

'I thought so,' George said, feeling proud that she'd had that very same lightbulb moment so many weeks ago. 'So, he must have transport and the sort of equipment that removal men have access to,' she added.

George reached out to the small side table that held the plate full of biscuits. As she stuffed her fourth down, she chewed over whether to tell Sally the full story of her involvement and the latest developments.

'Partial decomp?' van den Bergen asked, forcing himself to look down at the photograph of the second girl.

The pathologist nodded. 'Yes, this one's death pre-dates the other girl by a month. We were lucky to find the dirt. She must have worn sandals, hence the particles under her toenails. Her entry to the country would have been very recent, I'm guessing, because if she'd settled somewhere and showered, the dirt would be gone. Illegal, obviously. No records for either of the girls, as I understand it.'

'Drugs mules, buying their way West with a spot of sexual slavery.'

'I'm certain this girl had the same bludgeon and blow torch treatment. There was no evidence of this one having participated in sexual intercourse but then the body had started to corrupt.'

'How was she found?'

'Shallow grave in Oosterpark. Wrapped in a tarpaulin. It was summer.'

'But the other one was—'

'Found alive in a doorway.'

Van den Bergen stretched his arms up in the air. His back cracked. It felt looser after that. 'He got sloppy with the second.'

The pathologist sipped from a plastic cup of water and studied the photograph of Remko through narrowed, green eyes.

Van den Bergen leaned forward. 'May I?' he asked.

She held it out so that he too could examine it. Hardened though he was to scenes of violent death, van den Bergen felt pangs of anguish as he looked again at the carbonised, folded shape in the bin that was the final bleak representation of all that Remko had been.

'He just knocked this one out and threw him away,' van den Bergen said.

'We found traces of sedative in Ratan Patil's and Joachim Guttentag's blood. Unfortunately, seeing as only one intact body part was retrieved for each man, we can't read the entire story. There was no sedative in Remko Visser's or Klaus Biedermeier's blood.'

Van den Bergen crossed his long legs and banged his knee on the underside of the desk. It made a nasty cracking noise. He was sure he had a spot of water on the knee. Too much kneeling when he potted up his dahlias.

'He kept the bodies of the bombers somewhere before he delivered them to the target of his choice,' he thought aloud. 'He wanted to keep them alive before the bombs were detonated. He stalked the other two successfully but tried different techniques on them. I'm no psychologist,' van den Bergen said, running his hand through his stiff white hair, 'but I'd say he's experimenting. Maybe. Trying to find the most enjoyable way of dispatching these wretched souls. Different ways of playing God.'

When he returned to the station, Elvis swaggered towards him, grinning.

'Why are you looking so pleased with yourself?' van den Bergen said.

'There are no ex-military men, discharged with burns, that measure up to the photo of our guy. Our photofit specialist

264

compared all the facial proportions in the squaddies' head-shots against our man,' Elvis said.

'Did you check Germany, the Netherlands and Belgium like I asked?'

'Yep. Nothing.'

'Oh? So? That's not good news.'

Elvis brandished a copy of an email under van den Bergen's nose. 'But our guy *has* been to Marienhospital in Stuttgart for burns treatment. They're trialling some new bandage technique there called Suprathel or some shit. Like artificial skin. So, our guy goes in with severe second-degree burns, some third-degree burns all on his face, neck, upper body. Won't say how he got them. But they're happy to treat him as part of the trial.'

Van den Bergen's heartbeat broke into a canter like a spooked horse. The tic in his right eye started up. The telltale signs of being on a hot trail. A perk of the job.

'Name?'

'Second name is German. First name sounds American. Oh, shit. Hang on, boss. That was sent in a subsequent email. I didn't print out the full exchange. I'll just go and get it …'

Van den Bergen wondered if Elvis could feel his eyes burning into the back of his head as he shuffled off in the direction of his computer.

Elvis stared intently at his screen for a moment, clicked for an irritatingly long time with his mouse and then looked up.

'Brandon Köhler. That's it,' Elvis shouted.

'We got an address?'

'Yes, boss. A Heidelberg address.'

'Get Dieter Mann on the phone immediately. We need to move fast.'

CHAPTER 27

Later

'Look. I've got something to tell you,' George said, staring out of the window to the opposite side of the quad. She could trust Sally. She was sure of it. *To hell with it.* 'I've been helping with the investigation all along.' There. She had said it.

Ten minutes later, she and Sally were sitting and studying the same grainy photograph, taken by Ad, that Saeng had peered at only the day before.

Sally shook her head. 'You lied to me.' The bitterness was audible in her voice. She fixed George with a hard, penetrating stare. 'You're not supposed to be doing anything that could compromise your new identity. And yet here you are, gadding around Europe, chasing neo-Nazis by proxy and finding yourself the focus of a murderous psychopath. For God's sake, George, do you know how much it costs the government to assign someone like you a new identity?' Her arms moved through the air with drama.

George felt like a scolded little girl. 'I'm sorry. I wasn't to know this crackpot would get a fetish for me.'

Sally tutted and rolled her eyes. 'George, practically every man you come into contact with ends up with a fetish for you. Well, listen, at least you're safe now. You'll stay here until the Dutch police have caught this guy. I'm not letting you leave the country. With a bit of luck, they'll catch him this week and only then can you go back with an easy mind.

'In the meantime, I've arranged for you to meet your mother in the Copper Kettle café opposite King's at three pm. I want to see you back here by four thirty pm at the latest. You'll need to get changed into something smart. You'll be sitting at high table with me for dinner. There's a gown in your room.'

Letitia, George thought as she marched grimly down Trinity Street. *What the hell has she got to say that's so urgent, she's breaking a three-year silence?*

He had thought about leaving this Dutchman … this little prick she called Ad … until last. After all, he already had a girlfriend. Technically, he should have been no competition at all. But then he had observed the first buds of a clandestine romance fattening. They were falling for one another. He had watched Ad's frequent visits to her room from the discreet hidey hole that Fennemans had so kindly furnished him with in return for a free weekend with the girls.

He didn't want *her* to fall in love with this Dutchman. It made sense after Klaus to take this one out of the picture before it was too late.

Poor Klaus.

As he measured Ad for a box, he thought about the little Graf. They had been almost friends. Klaus had even been inside his room in the faculty. Shared a pot of coffee and a couple of lines of coke. It was almost tragic that he had felt compelled to dispatch such a good payer, but Klaus had to go. First Joachim came knocking for services rendered. Next thing, everyone knows about the girls, when they should be tucked up, nice and anonymous in the brothels until their paperwork was ready.

He had always wondered about using a grenade in the past and, as he had anticipated, it had made an outstanding mess.

Almost a work of modern art. Problem was, the fire was underwhelming. On reflection, he'd only do it again if he was, say, producing some quality snuff porn. Yes, that could make an interesting film. That would make some serious cash. And it would do his reputation no end of good.

And now he had this little dipshit on his slab. He poked Ad in the face. *She* thought he was good looking, did she? Maybe she liked him because he was educated? Sensitive. Well, this myopic bastard wasn't the only one who was clever and sensitive. He could be that too. He was an international business man of repute, wasn't he? Educated at the University of the Street, graduating with a starred first.

Even Fennemans respected him. Said he was a cunning linguist and purveyor of fine exotic substances and women. Wasted in the faculty in a domestic capacity. But of course, Fennemans was just another randy old pervert with a penchant for young girls and recreational drugs. Fennemans just thought he was a small-time university pusher with some connects in the red light district. He didn't know about his other work. This plan to make *her* notice. The smart pads in towns where he operated. Or his house in the country furnished with the finest antiques. His library full of books. His workshop, here in the garage.

Anyway, never mind Fennemans. If he died from dehydration and hypothermia, fine. If the cops found him, he'd also take the rap for Janette Polman or whatever she was called. It was nothing more than Fennemans deserved for stealing pigtails.

He took a tourniquet and tied it tight around Ad's index finger until the end of the finger turned white. Then he padded to the kitchen and pulled his sharpened meat cleaver from the magnetic knife rack on the wall.

George felt lightheaded and sick as she walked along Trinity Street in the direction of King's College. It was a cold day but the sun had come out. Mullioned windows looked down onto the cobbled street from both sides. Gargoyles peered at her from above, welcoming her back, promising her protection from the Devil.

She passed Heffers bookshop on her left. Remembered silent mornings, spent thumbing the spines of knowledge on its shelves, luxuriating in the smell of brand new paper, feeling the thick carpet beneath her feet before parting with cash she couldn't really afford to part with for books she would absorb in a feat of intellectual osmosis.

Happy memories, dampened by thoughts of Letitia.

Further on, hands dug deep inside her coat pockets, she passed Gonville and Caius on the right – a grey, stately queen, beckoning her forward to King's Street where the Church of St Mary's, like a plain older sister, looked upon the glamorous young upstart of the Senate House – neo-classical white with its perfect lawn. It spoke of graduation days full of gowned twenty-one year olds, clutching their certificates, elated and at the same time burdened by anti-climax as they began their real adult lives amongst the overdressed chintz of proud, grinning relatives on sweaty summer mornings.

And there was King's College Chapel. The jewel in Cambridge's crown, stretching its spires like slender arms up to the skies. Henry VIII's most beautiful mistress, now admired by throngs of American and Japanese tourists who gathered in clumps outside its white stone to take photographs that never failed to be perfect – but for the unphotogenic idiots sitting on the low perimeter wall.

But George couldn't appreciate her homecoming now. Opposite King's was The Copper Kettle and on the other side of its welcoming windows, perched on a hard, wooden chair, uncomfortably the only person visible from outside, sat Letitia. George knew her hands would shake, even before she pushed open the door. She clenched and unclenched her fists until they got the message that no shaking was permissible. Letitia must not know that she was perturbed.

Why the hell have I agreed to this? I must be mad.

The door tinkled. George ignored Letitia and walked to the servery.

'Pot of tea for one, please,' she told the ginger-haired skinny girl behind the counter. Her voice was almost calm, almost devoid of telltale waver. *Good. Let Letitia sweat just a little longer.*

She carried her tray over to the laminate little table behind which Letitia sat with folded arms. George took in every detail. She had not really aged in three years. Her hair was thickened with extensions. She was heavily made up with rose-pink lips and glitter eyes. She was wearing a tight-fitting sequinned top in black with an appliqué orange lily on the front beneath a faux-fur coat that looked like silver fox. Ghetto glamour. TK Maxx at Christmas time. Apart from being a good stone heavier, which showed around the jowls and her fat neck, Letitia looked good. Clearly, the old cow had lost no sleep. *Do I feel any pangs of nostalgia? Should I want to hug or kiss her? Did she leave me languishing in prison for three months? Fuck that bitch.*

'Hello Letitia,' George said, feeling pleased by the steadiness of her voice.

'It's Gloria now,' Letitia said, flashing bright red talons that made George think of Katja. 'Them police didn't offer *me* no new identity. I had to fucking change my name by deed poll and move to frigging Kent, innit?'

George poured a dash of milk into her cup and poured her strong tea. The tea started to leak down the side of the stainless steel teapot. The lid was warped. Spattering everywhere. Spitting burning blotches onto her lap. *Don't wince. Just pretend that didn't hurt. Be cool.* She looked at her cup and noticed with distaste that there was a mouth mark on the porcelain. Changing her cup would have to wait. She spat onto a napkin and wiped the cup.

'What do you want, *Gloria*?' George said, meeting her mother's loveless eyes.

Letitia took a lipsticky bite from her doughnut. Chewed in

silence. Wiped her fingers on a napkin. 'I come to warn you, didn't I?'

He returned to the garage. Angled Ad's hand so that the index finger was easy to strike. Raised the blade in the air and brought it down hard, clean and fast on the finger. The blood was minimal. He held the finger up, smiled at his handiwork and walked back to the kitchen. He opened the freezer door and put it into the test-tube rack with the others. He had quite a collection now.

Back in the garage, despite the spray-on plaster, this Ad's head wound had made a bloody mess on the polished concrete floor. That wouldn't do. He'd need to clean that.

He moved aside a large, red plastic jerry can of petrol to reach for the bucket and scrubbing brush. He shouldn't keep petrol stored in the garage really. He knew it was a fire hazard to him personally and he'd learned his lesson about not treating the fire with respect after that time he'd ended up in Stuttgart, covered in bandages for weeks on end.

But he'd needed the can. He'd done the Jew with petrol and a match, old style, after all. It was good that he'd done it and he felt justified because the Jew had stared at his face in the cafeteria and said something patronising to one of his friends about him being a 'poor disabled guy'. That sort of disrespect could never be tolerated, especially from a Jew. The fire was beautiful. He had controlled everything perfectly.

But it didn't have the same impact as the bombings. Nothing had quite topped that. The bombings were a logistical pain in some ways, especially now there seemed to be police patrolling every public building in Europe since Bushuis and Utrecht. Where exactly could you do another if everywhere of interest or note was being watched? But if he could overcome these complications, it would be worth it. And this Ad, he deserved it. He had kissed her. Hadn't he fucked her?

The man looked at Ad's naked body. He had his finger. But

maybe he should take an additional trophy. Another appendage. He thought about his bolt croppers.

'Don't say I didn't make nothing up to you. I'm telling you this 'cos I know I did wrong,' Letitia said, looking over George's shoulder at an old couple at the next table.

'Is that an apology?'

'Word on the estate is, Jez was looking for you. Offering good money to anyone with information.'

George studied Letitia's face and saw fear hiding behind the makeup. 'Jez? What do you mean? He's banged up.'

'Where did you get that idea? He ain't banged up.'

George froze. All sound was drowned out by the intense rushing of blood in her ears. 'Thomson, the old cop, told me. They were nicked in Holland at the same time I got nabbed getting off the ferry.'

'Well, he's been feeding you duff information.'

George remembered how the Gargoyle had been so ill. It was not inconceivable that, in the same way her informant paperwork had been a shambles because of his heart attack, the facts behind Danny and Jez's arrest had somehow been tangled up and misconstrued.

'What about Danny?'

'Nah. He ain't banged up neither. Only you was banged up, tough girl. And them slags. Word is, Jez and Danny both been laying low, building an empire.'

Danny and Jez were at still large. This was not a good development. And her ex-lover had not sought her out. How did she feel about that? Rejected? Disappointed? No. Relieved. Danny was like Filip. He should never have happened. But Jez. That psycho. That was a much more worrying prospect.

'What do you mean, building an empire?'

'Same old shit, I expect. They still got lads working for them on the estate, so Leroy's sister Shanice says. No one I know's seen them in person for a good long while, like, but word is definitely that Jez himself was looking for you.'

'How long ago was this?'

'A year maybe. Yeah. Then I start hearing he *knows* your whereabouts.'

George's thudding heart was deafening. 'And when was that?'

'Wait. Let me think. Yeah. Six months.'

George slammed her thick, pot cup onto her saucer, making it rattle. An elderly man in a pork-pie hat looked askance at her. She smiled at him apologetically and turned back to Letitia.

'Six months? You knew this and didn't think to get in touch sooner?' she said in a low voice through gritted teeth.

Letitia looked blankly out towards King's Chapel and shrugged. 'I been trying to get in touch the last month but you was blanking me. What can I do if my only daughter don't wanna know her mum? Filtering everything through that Doctor Whatshername. That's proper shameful shit, Ella.'

George forced her brain to rattle through the myriad calculations. Six months. Could Jez have traced her to Cambridge? Who would have let the cat out of that bag? Letitia maybe?

'Did Jez get to you?' she said, bending over the table in the most confrontational way she could.

Letitia sucked her teeth and sneered. 'No way. I been in fucking Ashford. Middle of nowhere, man. I only heard this when I was visiting Leroy's Shanice.'

'Leroy this. Leroy that. Who the hell is Leroy?'

'My fella.' Bristling with self-satisfaction when she said this.

'Oh, yes. I remember. The one you chose over your falsely imprisoned daughter.'

George felt a sourdough lump of resentment start to bubble up inside her. But for now, she had to mentally throw a cloth over it. It could wait.

'You're talking very fancy these days. You sound like the Queen. Forgetting who you are.'

George said nothing. Stared ahead. Remained an indolent statue. She had more important things to consider. How had Jez tracked her down? Six months. Hang on. That was when she had first moved over to Amsterdam. The Netherlands. He had found her in The Netherlands. It was the last place she had seen him before her fateful return trip on the *Hollandica*. When the thought struck her, it was as though a broken clock had started to tick again. Jez had never left mainland Europe.

And if Jez, Danny's favourite arson-obsessed handyman, never left mainland Europe, is it not inconceivable that Jez is my little serial-killing stalker?

She flicked hastily through her archived memories; travelled all the way back to her conversation with Jez in the South London park on a cold, moonlit night. That night that he had asked her out. What had he said about fire as the moonlight had reflected on his black, unfathomable eyes?

'It's beautiful and deadly both, Ella. Giver of heat and light and death. And now, I'm the Firestarter. It's the language of anger. It's the language of love. Bringer of endings and new beginnings.'

Jez the Firestarter, twisting Firestarter. How could she have forgotten?

Panic and adrenalin surged through George's body. Suddenly, she felt like the entire café was spinning around her like a carousel, while she remained still at the centre. All there was, was her and Letitia, trapped on a ride that they couldn't get off.

He decided against removing the Dutchman's penis, instead whistling happily while he calculated how much plastic explosive to put in. And when should he do it? Decisions, decisions …

As he walked over to his shelves, he caught sight of something shiny poking out of Ad's jacket pocket. He retrieved it. It was Ad's mobile phone. Oh. Interesting. A chance to see inside this loser's world. He would quite like to send her a text from this phone. That would be a nice touch.

Curious to see the extent of her relationship with this Ad, he flicked through the many texts that were stacked in his inbox. Lots from the girlfriend.

Here was the latest one from *her*. Kisses at the end. She'd taken a flight somewhere and would be away for a week. But where? Damn. This messed up his plans. He couldn't keep this Ad on a drip for a full week until she returned. There was no point dispatching him unless she was around to see it either. No, he had to find out where she was. Needed to see when she was coming back. Or if she wasn't too far away, it might be quite nice to pick her up and bring her back.

'So, what you doing here, then?' Letitia asked, gesticulating at the charm of the safe, privileged world outside.

George held her hand up, fighting to catch her breath. Her head nodded in time with her thunderous pulse. 'Wait. Let me think.'

The room opposite with the camera. The limping man who had followed her from the flower market. Scarred. By burns of course. No fingerprints. Someone who knew Klaus and Joachim. Still supplying drugs. Still the crazy fucked-up grandson of a right-wing, blackshirt Millwall supporter. Speaking Arabic, a Taliban go-between, spouting English Defence League bullshit. Except now, of course, he was operating in Europe, so it was the National Democratic Party of Germany or whatever other bunch of subnormal morons with persecution complexes he had allied himself to. Someone who had at least seen Ratan, Remko … all of them every day. And Ad. Ad.

George switched on her phone. She had one message. It was from Katja.

Brit who does passports called Danny.

Shorter breathing now. Brain whirring round like a supersonic fan. Overheating. Danny doing dodgy passports. Jez in charge

275

now. How did that happen? But Jez was always brighter. Or maybe he's just the one taking the risks for Danny. But still working. Ad. Ad now.

She punched Ad's name into her phone and waited for him to pick up. Three, four, five seconds. Nothing. Six, ten, straight to voicemail. She didn't have his mother's number in Groningen.

'No, no, no.'

'So, I was thinking of going on holiday with Leroy,' Letitia said, clearly unaware of the maelstrom of panic and fear that whirled relentlessly around George.

'Shush, for God's sake.'

Van den Bergen's name. In the phone now. Ringing. Answering. Thank God.

'Yes?'

'It's George. Listen, I can't get hold of Ad. I know who the killer is. His name is Jeremy Saddiq. I know him. He was one of Danny's crew. The gang I ran with before. He's dealing in Amsterdam and Germany. He's an arsonist.'

'Georgina, slow down,' van den Bergen barked down the phone. 'There's a patrol car stationed outside Karelse's house. And Jeremy Saddiq is not the name we've got. We know who our killer is. He's a German called Brandon Köhler. We traced him through Stuttgart hospital burns unit. He lives in Heidelberg on the Neckarstaden. German police are storming his apartment now. It's okay. We're one hundred percent certain he's the right man.'

George worked her way through the tangled meaning of van den Bergen's words. It didn't make sense. She was sure about Jez. Jez, the Firestarter. But Danny was knee-deep in falsified ID. Brandon Köhler. Click.

'It's a false identity,' she shrieked down the phone. 'Brandon Köhler. Sounds like mashed-up Dutch for flaming and German for hot coals. Come on! Think about it.'

'Let's just see—'

'Look, Dr Wright thinks our guy works at the faculty in a

domestic capacity. He has transport. Look at the list of non-academic staff. See if you can find a Jeremy or a Jez or this Brandon on the roll. Please.'

Silence the other end of the phone. Then: 'Look, George, apparently the German police have just gained entry to the killer's apartment. I'll see what they've found and I'll call you back.'

Predictably, van den Bergen rang off without saying goodbye.

CHAPTER 28

Amsterdam, 27 January

The Baden-Württemberg State Police had raided the Heidelberg address in the late afternoon of the previous day, around 4pm Central European Time. One of the officers carried a buttonhole camera, enabling live footage of the break-in to be streamed to a Kripo detective's laptop, which, in turn, was emailed within minutes as a video file to van den Bergen in Amsterdam.

Ten hours later, van den Bergen leaned back in his ergonomically incorrect typing chair, put two painkillers on his tongue, took a swig of his cold coffee and wiped his reading glasses on the tails of his shirt.

'Damn this bastard,' he told the computer screen. 'Flaming Hot Coals? He's making utter fools out of the Dutch and German police and there's nothing I can do about it.'

Jabbing a long finger awkwardly onto his mouse button, he let the high-resolution footage spring forward yet again.

He had been expecting a house that allowed space and privacy. Instead, the address had taken the German police to a Neckarstaden apartment on the second floor of a building which looked like it had been put up in the sixties. The staircase leading up was some way inside, set back from the street. The battering ram had to work hard for its money against the plethora of locks. The alarm had the sort of sophistication one would find in a high-class jewellers or a small bank. Then … masculine elegance.

Le Corbusier sofa. Stylish mid-twentieth-century furniture, otherwise. Was that a Persian rug? An Isfahan, judging by its intricate pattern and bright colours. Yes, van den Bergen had let his ex-wife keep theirs along with his daughter.

Further into the large, open-plan living room, which the officers, clutching at guns, reported was clear, were bookshelves full of medical textbooks, chemistry books, poetry books, philosophy tomes. Was this really the drug-dealing serial killer they were looking for? And if George was right, and it was the pyromaniac thug she had been allied to as an informant, could he actually read and understand those books?

'Self-taught? Or just self-aggrandisement?' van den Bergen asked the screen.

The rest of the apartment had the same feel to it. Interior designer chic. There were scant but corruptible contents in the fridge that the camera-wearing officer pointed out. A lettuce, still fresh. Cheese and milk, both used but not mottled with mould or curdled into lumps.

'Of course. You were in the heavy metal pub when Karelse was playing the Last Action Heidelberg Hero, weren't you?' Van den Bergen chewed thoughtfully on the end of a Biro and then tapped his nose with the damp pen. 'But how do we know Brandon Köhler and the killer are one and the same?'

Van den Bergen scrutinised the artwork on the walls of the apartment: a canvas depicting fire on one wall. Possibly Grace Turnbull. On another wall, the Great Fire of London, where people rowed for their lives in overcrowded boats on the River Thames to escape the inferno behind them. Finally, as if van den Bergen needed any more visual corroboration, over the leather sofa, there hung a large traditional Chinese painting of a red dragon, floating in a rough sea, coiled around a beautiful woman who looked perfectly at ease.

'A fire breather. A symbol of nobility, power, ambition … are these all qualities you see in yourself, Mr Flaming Hot Coals? Jesus. What kind of a delusional monster have I come up against this time?' van den Bergen said. He sighed heavily, feeling the twinge in his hip; a memento left long after the Rotterdam Silencer's bullet had been removed.

George sat on the dais in hall, next to Sally Wright, feeling uncomfortable in her L.K.Bennett dress and black, billowing undergraduate gown. A council estate crow in a debutante's frock, crumpled and a little too tight around the waist. She thought fleetingly of Letitia's fat neck and the rolls of flesh around her middle. Instinctively, she grabbed at her own stomach beneath the table. *Snap out of it.*

Pheasant on the menu too. Jez and Danny were on her trail and here she was, sawing away at too-tough pheasant and industrially tasteless gravy.

Sally Wright leaned in, disturbing George's sour introspection.

'How did it go with your mother?' she asked.

George bit into her stringy pheasant thoughtfully, ground it between her molars, swallowed, took a sip of pinot grigio and said, 'My cover has been blown.'

Sally looked at her and stopped chewing the potato she had just daintily put into her pruned mouth.

'Oh?'

'And she wanted to borrow money. No surprises there.'

Sally Wright set her cutlery down carefully on her plate. 'Scroll back to the bit where you say your cover has been blown.'

George felt a deep blush proclaim her embarrassment loudly. Under the potential scrutiny of over a hundred of her fellow students and within earshot of the Master of St John's, George was forced to give a brisk synopsis of all Letitia had said.

George could still see fear in Sally's hooded eyes, behind the lenses of her glasses.

280

'First you tell me you're up to your neck in the investigation of these serial killings. Next you say the psychopath and gang leader that you infiltrated as a supergrass are on your trail? My God. It's like a terrible story in a tabloid newspaper. How the hell did that happen?' Sally said. 'You are deep deep in the mire, young lady. I take this as a personal betrayal of trust between you and me.'

George rubbed the grosgrain ribbon trim on her dress. One, two, three with the left hand. One, two, three with the right. She loathed the feeling of being chastised by someone she respected and consciously sought the approval of. What could she say in her own defence? Nothing. It wasn't really her fault. Arrange the cutlery. Position the cruet set as it should be. She opened and closed her mouth, wanting to apologise but the words were lodged in her throat.

Finally she managed, 'I don't know how it happened. I was discreet.'

Sally looked at her from over the top of her glasses. Accusatory eyes. 'If this serial killer is your former squeeze's muscle,' Sally said, 'the Dutch and German police are going to be unwittingly stomping all over a drugs and vice case that CID has been trying to put together for years; which you were only the start of. Years of surveillance wasted. And you've exposed yourself as well, which will probably mean you will need assigning a new identity. Again.'

New identity? George felt the food sitting like a stone in her stomach. 'I can't do this again. I don't want to change from who I am now,' she said, polishing her dessertspoon on her napkin. She needed to make Sally understand and hopefully forgive. 'Do you realise how it feels to live a lie? To live as someone with a manufactured past and no contact with the world she knows. It's like … like trying to wear in an unforgiving shoe. It was hard but I've managed to become George McKenzie. Respectable orphan, left behind by tax-paying folk who died in a car crash.

Come on, Sally! I haven't got the energy to become another person and I'm not giving this up.'

She looked up at the vaulted, intricately beamed ceiling of the ancient hall, atmospherically lit by chandeliers and casting splendid shadows. She could not see the colours in the tall, ecclesiastical leaded windows, as darkness had fallen outside, but she remembered what they looked like in the day. The musky, beeswax aroma of the parquet floors and wood panelling. The dusty gilt-edged portraits of old Masters and Fellows.

A poor girl who earned her own slice of rich man's heaven. I ain't giving that back. No way. And Ad, of course. Her first chance of love. How could she throw that into the Herengracht and watch it sink?

Sally frowned. 'You make it sound like starting fresh was a chore. You told me you were delighted to leave your old life behind.' She picked at the pheasant carcass with her knife and fork and ushered some stringy dark meat into her mouth. 'Wasn't that why you agreed to work with the police in the first place? So you could begin again from scratch? Bury your skeletons, you said.'

George thought about the intimacy she had shared with her skeletons, Danny and Tonya. They ruined people's lives with boundless enthusiasm. But, when all was said and done, the three of them had been bonded by sex and the irrefutable knowledge that they had all been failed by their parents. Theirs were drunks and drug addicts. Hers was just plain selfish and manipulative. And now, the hateful mother that she had once loved as a small child was Gloria, born-again housewife to Leroy, consigned to a brick built box in Ashford. Danny was God knows where, probably selling fake passports in Amsterdam and Tonya was, she was fairly certain, still banged up in women's prison – both, no doubt, with Ella Williams-May's betrayal scratched indelibly on their hearts. Those bridges would never be unburned. Thankfully.

'Yes,' George said. 'My life was terrible. That's why I'm desperate to hang onto this one. George lives the life of Reilly. Ella Williams-May is dead. Long live the McKenzie.'

Sally drank from her glass of red wine and breathed out heavily through her nose. 'One thing's for certain,' she said. 'You are not going back while the killer's over there on the prowl.'

George immediately thought of Ad. Felt for her handbag at her feet which contained her phone. Wondered if he'd texted yet. 'I can't stay in England. There's people I care about … They're in danger.'

Hooking her hair behind her ear, Sally stared in silence at George. Was she making her stew in her own juices? Or just reflecting on what she was about to say? George didn't have Sally down as the cruel type.

Finally, she sniffed and said, 'If you try to go back, I will have the police incarcerate you. I *know* you wouldn't like that, now would you?'

George stared at Sally open-mouthed. For the first time, it made sense that this middle-aged woman who rolled her eyes back into her head, showing only disconcerting whites when she was deep in thought or explaining something complicated to a student, this deep-voiced woman who seemed at times scatter-brained and odd should be the senior tutor of one of Cambridge's wealthiest colleges.

'Sally!'

Sally put her veined hand on top of George's arm. Her index finger was nicotine-stained brown. Her palm was surprisingly warm but clammy. 'Georgina, I am responsible for you. I care about you. The college cares about you. Nobody but you, your mother and I knows you're in Cambridge. While you're here, you're safe.'

He saw her from the street below. Her blood-red hair was curled like corkscrews and backcombed into a big frizz. She had the high Baltic cheekbones typical of an Eastern European. Her

283

pneumatic breasts strained against a tiny bikini that would be easy to get off with one tug of the ties at the back. Research had its bonuses. It had been a while since he had been with a female over the age of fifteen but this one was pert and he was in the mood.

'What's your name?' he asked, after they had negotiated a fee.

She licked lips that were the same bright red as a fire engine. In the hellish glow of the red light, up close, she looked seedy and past it.

'Katja, darling.'

She didn't even wince when she looked at his face, though. A real pro.

When she had yanked the drab, brown curtain across the window and switched off the red light, he grabbed her around the middle.

'I've thought about coming to you for a while,' he said. 'I've seen the girl upstairs too. Is she expensive? I'd pay more for you and her. Together. Now.'

'She's no whore, darling and she's not here anyway.'

'Oh? Where has she gone?'

Drumming his pen against his front teeth, van den Bergen thought about what George had said. He should check the non-academic staff attached to Fennemans' faculty.

'Elvis!' he shouted. 'I've got a spot of urgent research for you.'

Elvis swaggered over, leather jacket slung over his shoulder. 'I was just going out to get something for dinner, boss. Want a kebab?'

Van den Bergen hadn't eaten for twelve hours. His appetite for anything but resolution was dead.

'I want you to run a name check on the Social and Behavioural Sciences faculty's staff roll,' he told Elvis. 'See who we've interviewed so far. See who's still down to be questioned. Anyone called Jeremy Saddiq. Jez. Abdul Youssuf. Al Badaar. Brandon

Köhler or any combination of those names. Look for office staff or domestic in particular.'

Elvis had grabbed a notepad from his jacket breast pocket and was scribbling away furiously with a furrowed brow.

Van den Bergen noticed that he had snatched up his chewed Biro. 'Get your own pen,' he said, holding his hand out.

Elvis looked at the wet, heavily masticated pen, wrinkled his nose and nodded. 'Sorry, boss.'

'Oh, and fine work with the Marienhospital match, Elv ... er ... Dirk.' He cleared his throat; felt suddenly righteous in his heart that he had said something pleasant to somebody that day.

'Dirk? Seriously? You going to start using my real name?'

'Don't push it.'

Now van den Bergen needed to get away to think. It was too late to go out to Sloterdijkermeer, so he had to content himself with twenty minutes' peace and quiet in the disabled toilet on the top floor, scratching at the grout in between the tiles with his fingernail until his eye had calmed down or he had a stroke of blinding inspiration.

Seventeen minutes into his retreat, he heard footsteps and a knock on the door made him jump.

'Boss,' shouted Elvis. He sounded high-pitched. 'Are you in there?'

Van den Bergen looked up at the strip light overhead and sighed heavily. 'What is it that's so exciting it couldn't wait for nature?' He emerged from his cubicle reluctantly.

'I think I've found your man, boss. Brandon Saddiq. British passport. Tax-paying janitor of the Social and Behavioural Sciences faculty on Roeterseiland. A disabled man, interviewed originally by Dr Vim Fennemans and employed by the university on a one-year renewable contract. Clean criminal record under that name, but *Jeremy* Saddiq is wanted by British Intelligence in connection with a vice and drugs ring that has its roots in Afghanistan's Taliban, no less. He's on Interpol and Europol's wanted lists along with his number two, Daniel Spencer.'

Van den Bergen washed his hands in stupefied silence as he mentally, piece by piece, slotted the jigsaw together and saw a picture of a disturbed London back-street gangster, usurping his own king and then burning and pillaging his way around Europe like a marauding Viking until one day he spots the turncoat, former girlfriend of his sidekick, right under his very nose. Perhaps with his change in fortunes, what he once coveted as the underling, he now saw as rightfully his.

'George was right. And her Firestarter is top dog now.' He splashed his face with water and spoke to his own reflection in the water-splattered mirror. 'But cocky, using his real surname. Too cocky. Got you, you little scrotum!'

'Boss?' Elvis said, interrupting van den Bergen's monologue. 'Are you coming?'

'Yes.' Van den Bergen straightened up and bent sideways to loosen his locked hip. 'We need Mr Saddiq's home address.'

It was almost one in the morning now but van den Bergen was buoyed by adrenalin. He felt alive. The net was coming down on this monster's head. He knew it.

The sight of George's neighbour, Katja, instantly recognisable as a prostitute with her big red hair, heavy night-time makeup and her tight fitting denim jacket and hotpants, jerked him out of his euphoria. She was sitting in a chair by his desk, dimpled, false tanned long legs crossed. The clothes said seductive. The body language said, 'Shut up and take me seriously.'

'You're George's neighbour, right?' van den Bergen asked. 'Want a coffee?'

Katja stuck out her hand, which he duly shook. Businesslike. Manly, in fact, despite the flashing pink nail extensions and hand-cream soft skin.

'I've not come here for a hot drink, darling,' she said.

He studied her face. Under scrutiny, she was late thirties. Polish or Latvian maybe. A ballbreaker with Botox.

'What can I do for you then, Miss …?'

'Just Katja. Look, I've had a punter. I didn't like him.'

'Would you like to report an assault?'

'I can handle myself good, believe me. No, the thing that gave me the creeps was that he was asking about the people in the house. Before we'd even agreed a price, he asked about Jan. Okay, no big deal. Jan runs the coffee shop, so the public see him all day long. Then Inneke. Well, maybe he's interested in visiting her some time. That's fine. But then he starts asking about George. Wanted to know where she was. Really grilling me, you know?'

Katja locked eyes with van den Bergen. Van den Bergen shook his head slowly and groaned aloud as he wiped his face in his shovel-like hands. 'Did you tell him where?'

Katja chewed on her bottom lip and looked at her stiletto shoes.

'I'm *so* sorry. I just didn't think. But I remembered you guys had been dusting her place for prints, and hell, there's a killer on the loose.'

'What did this man look like?' Van den Bergen asked, wondering, just wondering if his hunch would be ghoulishly correct.

CHAPTER 29

28 January

'Well?' van den Bergen asked.

Elvis approached, looking uncharacteristically grim faced, although that could have been down to fatigue and unflattering strip lighting, under which even Marianne de Koninck looked rough.

'Sorry, boss. No address for Saddiq. Only a PO box contact on the university's books and the bank account he uses for salary payment. And another thing. Adrianus Karelse's mother has reported him missing.'

'But there's a patrol car outside his damn house!' van den Bergen bellowed.

Elvis shrugged.

Van den Bergen thumped his desk. Was he doomed to keep hitting dead ends? George wasn't answering her phone and the killer had actively sought out her whereabouts. Karelse was gone. *For Christ's sake!* He looked at the clock as the seconds ticked by ominously, feeling that time was something he didn't have enough of.

Drained and dizzy, now. Silently, he prayed that George was still safe.

'How do you fancy heading up the team for a bit?' he asked Elvis.

'What do you mean, boss?'

'I'll be back by dinner time at the latest.'

George woke stiff and dry-mouthed on her friend Caroline's sofa. Only the need for a cigarette and a feeling of general unease had driven her out of King's Cellars, where they had danced until the early hours. Now, she got up and wandered into the unfamiliar kitchenette. Nauseated by the smell of stale kebab wrappings, she washed her hands with boiling hot water and a pan scourer full of washing-up liquid. She hastily opened the kitchen window to allow fresh air in.

Outside was an empty courtyard. George stared blankly at the drab scene until she heard Caroline's phone buzz in the adjacent bedroom. Then, she remembered she'd had three missed calls from van den Bergen. Her phone had died on her before just as she was poised to call him back.

'Got to get my charger, man. What does that old bugger want?'

Leaving a note on her sleeping friend's desk by the window, she put on her shoes, gathered her coat and hastened down paths, thick with early morning frost, to her guest room in the 1960s boxy annex, Cripps.

Her walk took her over the Bridge of Sighs. She allowed herself a moment to take in the crisp, heavenly view of willows, horse chestnuts and beeches that would soon be in leaf along the backs of the River Cam. The earliest cherries had already started to bloom, oblivious to and showing no signs of intimidation by the chill Siberian winds that blow through that flat land unhindered.

At 6am, there was nobody around but the odd porter, a member of college domestic staff wheeling a trolley or small gaggles of early rising rowers, making their way to the boat house. But she still felt uneasy. She felt eyes on her.

When the plane landed at Stansted, van den Bergen hastily unbuckled and switched on his phone. He was immediately greeted by a text from Elvis, saying Kamphuis was going to book him a one-way ticket to a euthanasia clinic when he returned. There was still no sign of Karelse.

Was it possible that Karelse was still alive? The whole of van den Bergen's department was searching desperately for him. Van den Bergen berated himself silently for thinking that while the killer was occupied with him, at least there was a strong possibility that George would still be safe.

George was careful to wedge a chair under the door handle once she had shut the door. The room that Sally had allocated to her was kitted out in utilitarian non-style; intended to double both as student accommodation and as a room for conference guests. It was clean. She was also pleased to note that it had a tiny en suite shower room as well as tea and coffee making facilities. George immediately gobbled down the two complimentary shortbread biscuits as a makeshift breakfast. The coffee sachet spilled everywhere as she emptied it into the cup.

It felt good to strip off her stale clothes and laddered tights. She took her charger out of her weekend bag and plugged in her phone. Immediately, there were two pings, showing she had new phone messages or texts in addition to the missed calls from van den Bergen. She booted up her laptop and put the kettle on. *Phone, then shower, then email.*

The first text was from van den Bergen. Cryptic as ever, all it said was:

`Call me a.s.a.p.`

The second text was from Ad. George smiled as she opened it.

`I love you. I'm finally coming to get you.`

290

She grinned at the message. 'He loves me,' she said to her reflection in the en suite mirror. Her lips stretched wide over her teeth. She almost felt happy enough to weep. But then she realised there was something about the wording that seemed at odds with Ad's usual style. He was not one for gushing confessions. He was a careful man. Though she didn't doubt he was privately passionate, he chose his words with thought and spoke about his emotions sparingly. The proclamation of love via text did not ring true, neither did use of the word 'finally'.

'Oh stop being so cynical!' she told her reflection. Then she allowed herself another grin. 'He must have jacked in the Milkmaid. He must be coming to England!' She clapped her hands.

When she tried to call Ad, his phone went straight to voicemail. Maybe he was flying. Yes, that was it. He would call when he landed.

The kettle clicked. She poured boiling water into her coffee cup, being careful not to spill any on her naked body. She was flushed warm with happiness. She started to sing about how, like Aretha Franklin, Ad made her feel like a natural woman.

Though his reflection in the chrome of the kettle was clear, she was too distracted by thoughts of Ad to notice the disfigured man, standing perfectly still by the curtain.

'St John's College, please,' van den Bergen told a cab driver at Cambridge station.

He had been travelling for four hours. It was just past 8am. George was still not answering his calls.

The cab driver dropped him in a narrow side street.

'That's St John's through there, mate,' he said, pointing to a grand stone building behind high railings. 'You wanna go to Porters' Lodge on the right, see? Big medieval-looking place with a wooden door.'

Van den Bergen struggled to understand the man's accent but nodded. Who the hell knew what a Porters' Lodge was?

He ran to the college entrance as the cab driver had indicated, narrowly missing being mown down by several students on bicycles.

'I am looking for Georgina McKenzie,' he told the balding, middle-aged man behind the polished wood counter.

He showed his police identification card. The man took the card and fished around in the top pocket of his black suit jacket for a pair of spectacles.

'Let's see who we've got here,' he said, eyeing van den Bergen and then studying the ID card with almost melodramatic disinterest.

Van den Bergen drummed his fingers impatiently on the counter. 'This is a matter of great urgency, connected to a criminal case in the Netherlands.' Why would this pot-bellied idiot not just let him through?

'Here, Alf. Look at this,' the man said to another, older, balding man who wore a sweater beneath his black jacket. 'What do you think of this then? Dutch police. Wants to speak to an undergrad who's visiting Dr Wright.'

The first man seemed to defer to Alf. Pretty soon, not one, but three identically dressed men were studying van den Bergen's identity card. Van den Bergen realised that these were porters. He was surprised that they seemed to have the elevated status of official gatekeepers, rather than being men who simply carry heavy luggage around, like train station porters.

'Fancy that, eh?' the third porter said.

Alf took the card from the first porter and gave it back to van den Bergen. 'Leave a note,' he said, pointing to row upon row of pigeonholes behind him. 'She'll get it later.' Alf's teeth were tea-stained. He looked the sort of old-fashioned man who set a lot of store by knowing the extent of his own authority and obeying orders only from his superior.

Van den Bergen felt his eye start to tic. He wanted to grab Alf and his suited collaborators by the scruffs of their necks and see if they felt more co-operative with their jowly faces ground into the counter. Instead, he took a deep breath and smoothed down his raincoat.

'This is a police matter. It's urgent that I speak to Ms McKenzie. She may be in grave danger.' He gave the men his sternest look that he normally reserved for instilling the fear of God into low-life perpetrators.

The first porter he had spoken to turned his back on van den Bergen, picked up a ledger and started to leaf through its pages. He said nothing. The third proceeded to ignore him as soon as a man with wild grey eyebrows, clutching a battered leather briefcase, entered the Lodge. The porter addressed this man deferentially as Doctor Somethingorother and talked about a Fellows' Drawing Room, so van den Bergen assumed this was an academic affiliated to the college. Perhaps a little light manip-ulation was his only way of gaining entry to this seemingly closed world.

'Excuse me,' van den Bergen said to the academic. 'I am a friend of Dr Sally Wright. I need to speak urgently with an exchange student who is a guest of hers at the moment, but these fine gentlemen won't let me into the college.'

The academic looked suspiciously up at van den Bergen through tortoiseshell-rimmed designer glasses. He smoothed one of the leather elbow patches on his tweed jacket defen-sively.

'A friend of the senior tutor? What kind of friend?'

Van den Bergen brandished his ID card for the second time. 'An inspector of the Dutch police kind of friend. I'm hunting a serial killer who might be on your premises.'

The academic studied the identification and seemed to blanch. 'Amsterdam?'

Van den Bergen nodded.

'I've read about a serial killer there. The same one as in the papers?'

Van den Bergen nodded stoically, wanting to push the man aside and barge through unhindered to whatever lay beyond. He felt like he was dealing with suspicious, stalling pensioners from Breda.

The academic's eyebrows bunched together. He turned to Alf. 'Call the police, Alf,' he said.

'Are you going to let me through?' van den Bergen asked.

Alf leaned forward, supporting his upper body on the counter with folded arms, as though protecting his turf. 'This is St John's College, sir. We've got hundreds of students and Fellows living behind this Lodge. You could be anybody. We get all sorts of crackpots trying to get inside but you're not *British* police and you're not a member of college. Sightseeing's restricted to just a couple of courtyards. You're too early for that an' all.'

Van den Bergen had never come across such obstinacy before. He felt tightness across his chest as though somebody had strapped him up with elastic baggage ties.

'Do you want to be responsible for the death of a student and the escape of an internationally wanted criminal?' he asked the self-satisfied-looking porter.

'Look, this chap seems to be genuine,' the academic suddenly said. 'Kindly accompany him to the student's guest room. But do call the police in the meantime. We can't have mad men wandering round, threatening our students, can we, Inspector?'

Begrudgingly, Alf shoved a guest book under van den Bergen's nose.

'Sign in,' he said, tapping his finger on an empty line.

Then he nodded to van den Bergen and, jangling an enormous set of keys, indicated that he should follow.

George hopped into the shower, which was deliciously hot and refreshing, despite the hard water which refused to foam up no matter how much soap she used. Steam billowed all around her, obscuring the mirror. She dried off with the fluffy, oversized towel, leaned over the sink to brush her teeth and failed to see the disfigured man as he stood behind her not three feet away. When she wiped the mirror with her hand, there was nothing but her own reflection staring back at her.

'Oh, my days. You look like a wreck, girl. You need some early nights and a new liver.'

She was careful to apply plenty of moisturiser and deodorant, in case Ad came to find her. She wanted to be fresh and fragrant for the big seduction. She felt hot anticipation between her legs and had to take a deep breath to calm herself down.

'Emails. Focus.'

She sat on the bed and checked her Hotmail account. Unusually there was an email from van den Bergen.

'Jesus. He's persistent. What does he want?'

From: Paul van den Bergen 02.10
To: George_McKenzie@hotmail.com
Subject: Karelse has disappeared

Karelse is missing. Brandon Köhler is Jeremy Saddiq. Have tracked him to university. He has been sniffing around your neighbour, Katja, asking about you. Be extra vigilant.

Paul

George frowned at the screen. Van den Bergen had still been trying to get in touch with her at two in the morning.

He must be agitated. Ad's missing.

'Well, of course he's missing!' she proclaimed after some thought. 'He's on the road, coming to see me, me, little me.' It did occur to George at that moment that, although she was likely to flout a police curfew, Ad was not. She opted to ignore the nagging little doubt.

George was just about to call van den Bergen when she altered the angle of her laptop screen to deflect the early morning sunlight. What was this smudge on her screen? She tried to wipe it away. When the pale shape remained, her senses sharpened, and then she realised. She was staring at a reflection of a scarred face. Everything seemed to stop. Breath. Sound. Light. The world froze; a split-second calm prelude to that horrifying moment.

'Hello, Ella,' Jez said.

They set off at a snail's pace through a warren of courtyards and medieval gateways, each one revealing something more beautiful, antiquated and foreign to van den Bergen.

'We don't get no serial killers here,' Alf said to him. The porter chuckled and poked at his comb-over hair.

Van den Bergen remained silent, ensuring his face was still set in his favourite grim-reaper expression. This place was too big. This walk was taking too long for his liking. Irritation had a vice-like grip around his chest.

George did not look behind. She lurched across the bed and made for the door. But Jez was too quick. She felt herself snatched up in strong arms like small bush meat being felled by a leopard. Thrown on the bed. Pinned to the mattress. She screamed out, but a hot hand covered her mouth. He was on top of her now.

She looked into his face. He was completely unrecognisable. Horrifying. Melted skin just about covered his flesh and bones like a bad paper towel wrapping around a barbecued chicken drumstick. He was wearing a dark blond wig. No black hair. No dark eyebrows any more. Only his eyes were recognisable. Black, piercing, wild. Utterly frightening. George could see the absence of remorse in them.

'I've dreamed of this moment for four years,' he hissed in her ear. 'Just me and you. Alone together.'

He pinned her down with the length of his body, rummaged

in a pocket. Deftly silenced her screams with hard, unyielding duct tape.

George tried to kick out, to punch him, but he was so incredibly strong. Unnaturally strong, as though he had boosted his average frame with steroids. In a blur of practised movement, he flipped her over like a rag doll and taped her wrists together behind her back. She felt him caress her hips, the naked cheeks of her backside. He groaned.

'Oh, you're beautiful.' His speech sounded laboured and impaired like Saeng's had.

George felt him press against her, excited. She whimpered, face down in the pillow. 'You were a very bad girl to lie to me and Danny all that time. I found out, you know. I know you testified against us. I was looking for you. But I never stopped loving you, Ella. And now I'm the boss, not Danny. I'm not like I was. I changed. I'm an educated man now. Well read, just like you.'

She could feel his breath against her cheek. Smelled powdery airline coffee and cheese buns. There was still the cloth of his trousers between them. He rubbed himself against her rhythmically. Started to explore her with insistent fingers. She wanted to stab him in the head.

'You got caught right in my little web in Amsterdam,' he said. 'Out of the blue, along you came, like a beautiful, stupid fly and got yourself all tangled up.'

George squeezed her eyes shut. Prayed she would pass out and be spared this agony. His touch made her flesh crawl. She thought of her dead, mutilated friends and Saeng's sad, once beautiful face.

Without warning, Jez flipped her onto her back so that she could see him. She was certain he was going to rape her. Could she knee him in the balls?

She breathed fast and hard through her nose. Her arms stung with the agonising pain of being pinioned behind her at an awkward angle, with both his and her own weight on top of them.

Without warning, George tried to buck him off with her hips but he was too heavy. Clenching her stomach muscles, she brought the upper half of her body up fast and nutted Jez squarely in the nose. Blood spattered down over his too-tight mouth. But he seemed unfazed. He merely pushed her back down onto the bed. Wiped his bloody nose on his hand and his bloody hand on the bed.

'I'm going to make you happier than Danny did because I'm a better man. I want you to want me.'

He prised her legs apart under his weight. Started to kiss the insides of her thighs.

Oh, my God. I don't want that face down there. George thought quickly. He was vulnerable. She could do some damage with her cyclist's legs. Hadn't Jan told her that she could crush a man between those thighs? Yes. It was worth a shot.

She clamped her strong thighs against the sides of his head and squeezed with every last ounce of strength she had. He started to shake as her flesh suffocated and her muscle constricted his airways.

He's really dying. Is he? No. He was digging his nails into her delicate skin. Biting her inner thigh. Agony. He gained the upper hand once again and levered her legs apart.

'Bitch!' He was panting hard, gasping for breath. Clearly enjoying her challenges.

George shook her head from side to side like a rabid dog.

'You're gonna love this. All the girls do, and I've got plenty of girls now. You can be my best girl.'

George tried to shriek, begged God, if he was listening, to allow a neighbouring student to hear her cries for help. She forced herself to look at his nightmarish face and gave him the most venomous stare she could muster. Tears of hot defiance started to seep out of the corners of her eyes. Shook her head again. Enough to make the bed shake this time.

Jez frowned. 'No? Are you telling me no?' His ruined face

twisted into a mask of pure hatred and aggression. He thumped her once on the side of her head. Twice. Started to grin as she tried to scream.

Three times. Four times. She was out cold.

CHAPTER 30

Somewhere in the Netherlands

Ad's eyes opened. His head throbbed. His whole body screamed with stiffness. Pain. There was a strip light above him. It wasn't switched on. He was in semi-darkness. Had he been asleep? This wasn't his room.

He felt nauseous. He started to vomit but couldn't move his head. For a second, he was paralysed by fear that the vomit would catch in the back of his throat and choke him. With great effort, he turned his befuddled, slow head to the side. The sick made a splattering noise as it hit solid ground beneath him.

The sound forced his stodgy brain to make sense of things. He was raised up on something. What was he lying on? A stone slab of some sort. It felt unforgiving under his almost numb body. Numb but for the agony in his head and his hand.

Then he spotted a large, fat needle protruding from beneath the skin in the crook of his right arm. There was a tube coming out it. His eyes followed the tube up to a connector from which several other tubes flowed, leading to bags of clear fluid hooked on a stand. One bag was empty. Another was almost empty. Instinctively, Ad pulled the needle out of his arm. It was a struggle. His left hand felt sluggish and just beyond his control. But he did it. He knew enough about needles to put pressure on the hole with his clumsy fingers. But where was the index finger on his right hand? He pulled his hand up towards his face and stared in open-mouthed horror at the tourniquet that was wrapped tightly around the bloody dark red stump. He tried to scream but could only whimper.

'Her room's just up here.'

Van den Bergen's heart thudded. He scanned the white concrete blocks of the modern courtyard.

The ageing porter knocked on an anonymous-looking door. Van den Bergen towered over him, praying George would open it. He wasn't a religious man but he had decided long ago that praying when the odds were stacked against him couldn't do any harm.

No response.

'Open the door,' van den Bergen said.

Alf looked at him with scorn clear in his eyes.

'Please,' he added.

Jangling of keys. Fumbling with the lock. *Come on, for Christ's sake, you bumbling prick!*

The door was flung wide. Van den Bergen pushed Alf aside and entered the small room.

'Oh, my Lord!' Alf said, clasping his hand to his mouth.

What van den Bergen saw made his stomach contract with fear.

'Do not enter the room,' he barked at the porter.

A dress on a hanger was hung up on the side of a wardrobe. The mirror in the bathroom beyond was still partially steamed up, as though somebody had showered recently. He checked the bathroom. Empty. Back in the bedroom, a bag had been unpacked carefully onto the desk. But a mirror on top of the modest dressing table was cracked. A stool was upturned. A lamp lay smashed on the floor beside the bed.

On the floor were clumps of something brown and shiny. What

were they? One of the clumps stuck to a pen that he fished out of his breast pocket. Screwed-up, discarded strapping tape. He scanned the carpet. He found five small shreds of cardboard.

Van den Bergen immediately recognised the fall-out from packaging up a large object.

But the bed … The bed was what really caught his eye. The bed was a mess.

'Blood,' van den Bergen said simply as he touched the small, dark patch towards the bottom of the duvet. It was viscous between his fingers. Not enough to be somebody's life's blood. There was a spatter pattern at a peculiar angle and a bloody handprint that looked like a man's, judging by its size. Had George been standing on the bed and then been injured? Had she injured her attacker? Van den Bergen could only guess. Blood on the pillow too.

'Have you got a walkie talkie?' he asked wide-eyed, uncomprehending Alf. 'Chase your police. Tell them to get a forensics team down here immediately. And trained police dogs. This is a crime scene.'

His eyes scanned the rest of the bed and settled on a smear of thick, white liquid. He leaned down and sniffed it. He looked bitterly at George's dress, hanging limp and crumpled on the wardrobe. He felt the duvet with the back of his hand. It was still warm.

'Stay here,' he told the shaking porter. 'Don't cross that threshold. Don't let anybody in until the police arrive.'

Van den Bergen stepped outside the room. Not five metres away he saw a small drop of blood on the ground. Further down the walkway, he knelt to the ground, tracing his finger along narrow, parallel tyre marks. He looked around. Students walked with purpose, chattering and laughing in the early morning cold. But there were no cycles. These were not the markings of bike or tricycle tyres. Too close together to be a wheelchair.

Then he realised what had made the tyre marks. Brandon

302

Saddiq. Janitor. Less like a Cambridge University porter and more like a train station porter. A man who carried things around using a trolley. A man who wheeled heavy boxes to public places, unremarkably, noticed by nobody. Cardboard boxes.

'My God. He's going to blow her up!'

Breathing ragged now. Trying to focus on his surroundings. It was difficult for Ad without his glasses. Power tools on the walls. Gardening implements hanging from hooks. The smell of petrol. *I think I'm in a garage. Where the hell am I? What happened? Why am I naked?*

Slowly, Ad tried to reconstruct what he had been doing before he had woken up in this strange place. Astrid. The walk to the bus stop. A vague recollection of a man with a scarred face. There it ended. No more memories. *Got to get to a phone. Where's my phone?*

Ad swung his legs over the side of the slab he had been lying on and fell to the floor. Jelly limbs did not want to obey his brain. Slowly, he pulled the warm urine-filled catheter out of the end of his sore urethra. It stung hot. He started to crawl along the floor using only his left hand, squinting through the blinding pain in his head, trying to find a door. On a low shelf within a steel shelving unit, he noticed a blow torch and a pair of boots that seemed familiar to Ad. They were distinctive. Doc Marten, red, eight hole boots. But his brain felt like it was caked in mud. The stink of petrol overwhelmed every thought. He couldn't place the boots.

Pushing through the door, Ad saw that he was in a house. The floors were polished planks, covered by expensive rugs. The furniture, fuzzy until he got up close, was antique. A chair with heavily carved legs. A spindle-legged table with a potted fern on top. He was in a hallway with blurry stairs just a few metres away. If he could crawl to the stairs, he could sit himself up, get his bearings.

303

But where in the world was he? He had been in somebody's garage. Where was the car that belonged there? Car.

Click.

They were putting a patrol car outside his parents' house. All at once, Ad remembered van den Bergen's voice.

'No heroics. They don't bloody suit you anyway. Do I make myself clear?'

Click.

He was in the killer's house, now. He had been abducted. Those boots next to the blow torch. He recognised those boots. He had last seen them on Remko's feet. Jesus.

Ad wanted to scream but knew he must not under any circumstances make noise. The killer had to be close by. And yet, he must have made quite a lot of noise scrabbling around, trying to get out of the garage. Was the killer watching him silently from a vantage point? Ad squinted up the stairs but saw only a landing, brightly lit by the sunlight coming through a small square window. He peered past the wooden newel post of the banister. He could see right through to the blurred shapes that indicated an orderly living room. Empty. Silent. Nobody was watching from there.

His heartbeat was sluggish. He felt like he was going to vomit again or pass out. *No. You can't pass out. This bastard is going to kill you. You've got to get out. Get to a phone. Call the police. Then find George. Make sure she's safe.*

The front door was five metres away. *Stand up. Come on. You've got to try.*

On trembling legs, Ad stood, swaying, fighting nausea; grappling with intense, pounding pain. He gingerly raised his fingers to the back of his head and felt stickiness. Dark red fingertips. Further down, the skin on his neck was rough with dried blood. *I've got a head injury. I've vomited. I've got to get to a hospital.*

He stumbled to the door, tried the handle with shaking hands.

Locked. Damn, damn, damn! How could he be so close to freedom and find the way was barred? Could he shout for help? There had to be another door. He could try that … if the house was empty.

Steeling himself, he went back into the garage. He tried the garage up-and-over door. Locked. He switched on the light, which flickered into over-bright life, making him wince. *Arm yourself.* He found a claw hammer, stained and clutching what appeared to be a human molar stuck between the claws. *Oh, God. That's disgusting.* He plucked the tooth out with the fingers of his left hand and set it carefully on the shelf next to Remko's boots. Then he realised he needed clothing. Looking around, feeling his way, he came across his own clothes in a neat pile on a musty old chair. His shirt and jacket were still slightly damp with blood but his jeans were acceptable. He put them on, falling twice. But no shoes. What size was Remko? *I can't believe I'm doing this.* Remko's boots were a little large but they would do. Ad fumbled with the laces, handicapped by his missing finger. He just needed a coat now.

Stumbling from room to room, peering at fuzzy shapes and colours, Ad realised that the house was indeed empty. No phones anywhere. He would check the back door. If the worse came to the worst, he would somehow smash a window and climb through it.

Hammer held high in his left hand, he entered the kitchen. He didn't know much about kitchens, but even without his glasses, he recognised that it was state of the art. Sleek, shiny, lots of steel appliances. It smelled of kitchen cleaning solution. Disinfectant.

He spied an American-style fridge freezer wedged into a purpose-built nook. Realising he was desperately thirsty, he put the hammer down and opened one of the large doors. Expecting milk or juice, he blinked hard as his eyes and brain worked together to make sense of what he was looking at. He had opened the freezer. Arranged in test-tube holders, rammed in next to frozen chips and pizza, were human fingers. Ad moved in close to be sure. He stared blankly at the fingers, still blinking hard, as though blinking would help him formulate sensible thoughts about what he saw. He looked at the stump on his hand. He looked at the fingers. It didn't compute. He closed the door and backed away from the fridge freezer, breathing quickly through flared nostrils.

Ad cocked his head and listened. No traffic. No city noises. Only birds and the distant rhythmic rumble of a vehicle – possibly a tractor. Was he in the country? He peered through a window. Saw a blur of green, stretching to a flat horizon. Above it hung grey skies. His suspicions were confirmed. *I'm in the middle of nowhere.*

He tried the back door. Locked.

As he galvanised himself to smash the glass with the hammer, he heard a vehicle out front. Thrumming engine. Pulling up. Footsteps. Ad lumbered to the front of the house and peered through the bevelled glass. He could make out a blue smudge that could have been a small blue van. A man was approaching the house. *It's the killer. He's come back. Christ, I've got to get out of here.*

Ad couldn't think fast enough. Where could he go? Upstairs? Back into the garage.

Knocking at the door.

It's not the killer. It's someone else. A delivery man, maybe. He can help. Shall I shout?

'Help!' Ad's voice was croaky. 'Help me!'

A face peered through the glass. Then there was a key in the lock. The door opened abruptly inwards, knocking Ad to the ground.

Ad's hope of escape had begun to solidify. The moment the visitor had put a key in the lock, he felt that hope crumble.

'Who the fuck are you?' the man said in English. He peered down at Ad with a questioning face.

'Is there an address on it?'

'How should I know? All I did was report the obstruction.'

'Aren't you the head porter, sir? What if it's a delivery for a college member?'

'Look, officer, it's in Trinity *Street*, not Trinity *College*. I can't be responsible for boxes left on a public highway, can I? It's a security risk. Shouldn't you be calling the SAS or something? Al Qaeda and all that.'

George became aware of the conversation at the same time as the throbbing in her jaw and a desperate ache in her hips and knees. She was freezing cold. Her hands were tied behind her. She was kneeling in a box, judging by the exchange between the two men. Left by Jez. Which could mean only one thing.

Panic overwhelmed her. In her head, she screamed, 'Get me out of here!' but with tape over her mouth, she managed only muffled protest. Her instincts told her to rock from side to side to alert the two men to her predicament. But she looked down and in the dim light of her cardboard confinement, she could make out small packages strapped around her person.

Is this what it had come to? She was a human bomb. A madman's revenge on the world.

George started to weep. Carefully, though, because she was sure if she moved she would somehow trigger the explosives. She attempted more muffled screams but the two men were now busy arguing. They didn't seem to hear her.

'I need you to calm down, sir. I'm not trying to verbally abuse you.'

'Bloody right, you're not. I'm taking down your number.'

Beyond the bickering men, she could hear the whirr and click of bicycles changing gear, footsteps and excited gossiping girls nearby. They didn't know about her. They didn't know it was all about to end.

Resigned now.

George thought of her mother. Oddly. Unexpectedly. If only she had said something to her in the Copper Kettle about how she had loved her as a child. How she wished dearly they could claw back that innocent time; that bond. Letitia in her fun fur. So close and yet so far.

And Ad. George knew, now she was going to die, that she loved him more than anything else. He had penetrated the defensive wall that she had so carefully built. But she would not be able to tell him. She just prayed that he would get away, go to ground, be safe.

Suddenly, she was aware that she was clothed. *How did that happen? Didn't he rape me?*

George knew she should be preparing herself for the end, but instead found she was checking various areas of her body for signs of intrusion. She felt normal in those intimate places. Only her inner thigh stung from his toxic bite. *Bastard.*

It was at this point that George's temper unexpectedly took her fear hostage. How dare Jez violate her? How dare he track her down to her safe place and take everything from her? Her future. The safety of these passersby.

She started to rock back and forth. She reasoned he had jostled her around to get her there in the first place. It was her only chance.

Suddenly, screams around her. Police car sirens. Heavy, thunderous footsteps.

'Get back. This is a terror alert. Clear the area.'

More screaming. The sound of dogs barking. Sniffing near her. Snuffling.

Then: 'Get out of the way, you idiots!' A Dutch voice. An older man's authoritative voice.

Frenzied growling.

'Get that fucking dog off me. If you don't all want to die, move it.'

Tearing at the cardboard by her left ear. A shaft of light blinded her abruptly. George blinked. Above her was van den Bergen's flushed face, framed by strong fingers that were busy peeling back the thick, corrugated walls of her musty prison.

There was a tiny, lucid part of George that wanted to tell him to run; to scream that she was wired up and ready to blow. But even if she hadn't been silenced by the tape across her mouth, when tears of relief and regret came hard, she was barely able to form coherent thoughts, let alone speak.

Van den Bergen squinted at the tangle of wires, duct tape and packages on chest. She could see he was calculating something. Weighing it all up.

George felt sweat pouring from her armpits, down her back and the sides of her head.

'Step away from the box, sir,' came a man's voice through a loudhailer. 'Step away or we'll shoot.'

'I'm Dutch police,' van den Bergen shouted. Agitated. He held up his ID. '*I* called *you*. Has your bomb disposal operative arrived?'

'No. ETA is forty minutes.'

'Forty minutes?' George heard van den Bergen swearing to himself in Dutch. 'Stay back,' he shouted. 'I've had military training in explosives.'

Has he? Has he really?

Van den Bergen lunged inside the box with those shovel-like hands and tugged one wire free. He ripped the tape from George's mouth. She let out the scream that she had been bottling up. She knew it was futile but she did it nonetheless.

'Help me!' She knew tears were streaming down her face. She wanted to be a strong woman. A heroine. But she conceded that, right now, she needed to be rescued. Just this once.

Van den Bergen nodded at her. 'It's going to be okay, George.'

More fumbling at her chest, despite the rifles cocked in the direction of his head and the tinny voice that screeched through the loudhailer, imploring him to step away from the box.

Then the mobile phone strapped to George's sternum rang.

CHAPTER 31

Later

Close up, Ad saw that the man was just a little older than he was. Powerfully built. Shaven head. Tattoos on skin darker than Ad's. But pop star looks. Plucked eyebrows. Designer casual clothes. A vain man. He seemed out of place in a scarred serial killer's house.

The man pulled out a gun. Ad knew nothing about guns but this was a large dull metal pistol affair and did not look like a toy. Ad stared into the nose of the weapon and tried to swallow down spit he simply didn't have.

'Drop the hammer, arsehole,' the man said.

Ad dropped the hammer, regretting he had not risen to the occasion when he'd had the chance.

'Do you owe me money?'

Ad shook his head.

'What happened to your head?' The man pointed to Ad's bloody scalp.

'Serial killer,' was all he could manage. 'Please help me.'

The man frowned. 'Why are you here? Where's Jez?'

If the man was asking questions, perhaps Ad had a shot at escaping. He forced himself to speak. To appeal to whatever charitable spirit this man might have. 'Let me go. Please. He's going to kill me. He's coming back. There's fingers in the freezer.'

'Fingers? Fish fingers? What the fuck are you talking about?'

Ad held up his bloody stump. 'Human fingers.'

The man shrugged. 'Are you or aren't you a dealer?'

'No. I'm a student. The man who lives here is the Bushuis bomber. He's killed my friends.'

The man frowned again, stooped down and helped Ad to his feet.

'Please let me go,' Ad said.

'Hang on, mate,' the man said, raising his free hand but still pointing the gun at him with the other. 'I've got to think about this.' He screwed up his over-groomed face as though thinking were an effort.

'Look in the freezer if you don't believe me. He's a psycho.'

'Oh, I know he's a psycho,' the man said. 'But Jez ain't no serial killer. I don't think, anyway.'

'You're wrong.'

'Am I? How do I know you don't owe me money? You could be feeding me a pile of bullshit. You got any ID?'

Ad shook his pounding head and immediately regretted it. He steadied himself on the hall table. His eyes were drawn to a small, black lozenge-shaped object sitting on the tabletop next to his good hand.

The man snatched the thing up. Ad squinted until he understood what it was. Something he had not noticed before, even though he had been frantically searching for it. His phone.

'What's this then? This ain't Jez's. It's yours, yeah?' He switched the phone on and a picture of George appeared as the wallpaper.

Open-mouthed. Flabbergasted.

'Ella?' The man stared at George's photo. His skin paled. The muscles in his neck and jaw tightened. He glowered at Ad. Poked the gun into his chest. 'What the fuck are you doing with my bird's picture on your phone?'

Ad shook his head desperately so that the room spun. The

311

metal of the gun was cold and hard on his skin. 'No. She's George. *My* girl.'

The man held up the phone for Ad to see. 'She English?'

Ad nodded.

'That ain't no George, mate. That's Ella Williams-May. She's *my* bird. I thought she was doing time for me.'

'Time?'

'Prison. For drugs.'

'But she can't be.'

'Well, she wasn't. Turned out she was a grass.'

'A what?'

'An informant. So, I told that old slag, her mother—'

'George's parents died in a car crash.'

The man snorted with derision. 'That what she told you?'

Ad looked at the man and wondered briefly if he was still asleep on the slab.

'Who are you?' he asked the man. Hell, if the gun was poking into his chest, he had nothing to lose.

The man cocked the safety off the gun. 'Danny. That mean anything to you, Dutch boy?'

Ad shook his head.

The two men stared at each other in awkward silence.

When Danny's face buckled with hatred, Ad's heart quailed.

'You cheeky bastard. Nobody fucks my bird.'

Ad's last thought before the bullet from Danny's gun punched its way into his body was that he had been played for a fool by everyone.

George looked at van den Bergen. The laughter lines around his eyes and his mouth were furrowed deep but devoid of all humour. He was wearing his reading glasses. *Funny what you notice.*

She peered down at the buzzing, chiming phone. *I'm going to die right now. Say something.*

'I'm sorry,' she told him.

312

Van den Bergen's mouth opened. The phone continued to ring. Nothing happened.

He reached into the box and yanked the phone from George's chest. She shrieked, more from the shock of what he had dared to do than anything else.

'I've disarmed it,' he said, sounding shocked. 'Or maybe it was wrongly assembled.'

George gently took the ringing phone from him and answered it. Jez's eerie, laboured voice spoke to her.

'Have I got your attention now?' he asked. She could hear amusement in his voice.

The phone shook in her hand. Her brain searched frantically for the right words to say. She wanted to convey the depth of her loathing. She wanted to make him feel small. 'You've failed,' she said. 'I'm still alive.'

'You thought I was really going to blow you up like the others.' He said it like a statement.

There was a pause. She realised. Jez had not set out to kill her. He just wanted to subjugate her using terror; make her docile and listless and his.

She switched off his voice; hurled the phone to the ground so hard that the casing came apart. The battery and sim card scattered. George looked down at the packages that formed a ring around her middle.

'Get them off me!' she cried. 'Get me out of here!' She could hear her voice was quaking with emotion. She wanted to control it. Control this ludicrous situation. Get Jez.

Van den Bergen tore the packets from her chest and offered them to an armed policewoman standing two metres away now. 'Take these,' he snarled. 'The response of your explosives experts has not been rapid. Bunch of fucking amateurs.'

But George was not interested in the delicate handling of Jez's possibly real, possibly fake handiwork. She was already looking around at the bookshop, at the café, at the bank. Where was that creep? Her heart slugged against her ribcage. Red mist had descended. She no longer feared for her own safety.

'He's here somewhere,' she said. 'He's watching.'

It didn't matter that she was only wearing a short nightdress. Whose fucking nightdress was it anyway? Not hers, that was for sure. It had Disney's Tinkerbell on the front. It was a crime against adult bed attire.

She zoned out from van den Bergen, who was now engaged in an indignant argument with the barrel of a rifle and its black-clad, Kevlar-vested owner.

Pacing down the street with bare feet, she looked into every shop window. The place was deserted; an elegant Marie Celeste now that the early morning crowds had been evacuated right down to Caius College. She scanned the expectant faces behind the blue and white police cordon. Animated chatter ricocheted off the stone buildings on either side as they spotted her.

'Oi! Come back here!' a young policeman bellowed at her. He shouted into his radio that a barefoot woman was padding along the empty street. He started to give chase but fell back as advice crackled back to him.

She retreated towards Trinity Street, careful to cling to doorways and avoid the sharp-eyed scrutiny of the police gathered by the main gate. Where was Jez? Not in the empty shops. Not in the deserted cafés.

Rounding the corner, she looked up. And there she saw him, perched behind the parapet of Trinity College's Great Gate. He had eyes for everything. Clearly on the lookout for her. He momentarily stared down at van den Bergen, who stood with his hands in the air, surrounded by five armed British police, while the rest of the boys in blue scurried like startled rats, trying to work out what to do with the abandoned box and dismantled bomb.

Jez had not noticed her yet.

George skulked along the college's outer wall. Darted into the Porters' Lodge. Unseen. Everybody seemed to have been evacuated. Where were they? She entered the Great Court expecting to see a muster point for the students and staff but saw not a soul there. She had no idea how to get up to the roof of the great gate but she knew there must be a staircase. There was a flagpole behind the castellated facade after all. Porters somehow got up there to raise a flag when necessary.

Instinct told her where to go. She climbed a steep, winding staircase. At the breathless summit, she found a door she felt certain would lead outside. *I've got you now, you son of a bitch.*

She tried the handle. It opened. There he was, crouched low. Watching. Not anticipating that the hunted had become the huntress.

'Bastard!' she shouted as she lunged at him.

She knocked him to the ground, punching him repeatedly on the side of the head until her own knuckles felt like they had shattered. His toupee flew off to reveal a hairless scalp, scarred and wrinkled like skin that had been in water too long. When her blows seemed not to hurt him, she realised that he must have no feeling in his face at all. Was he medicated?

She kneed him in the groin. Then, at least, he had the decency to buckle up, groaning.

'Why? Why did you do this?' she cried.

But Jez glared at her through those deadly black eyes. She could see bloodlust rising within him. Wished to God van den Bergen and the police below knew they were up there.

He overpowered her easily for the second time that morning. George was forced up against the low stone barrier that stood between a blistering view of Trinity College's courtyards and rooftops and her own certain death by broken back on the cobbles below. But she was on the wrong side of the parapet for the police in Trinity Street to see.

She screamed as Jez tipped her further and further backwards over the periphery of the abandoned Great Court. Fighting back, now, scratching and kicking whatever she could.

Unexpectedly, he pulled her close to him. Away from the edge.

'I took everything I wanted,' he hissed in her ear. 'The fire gave me the power. I took everything Danny had. I earned it. I'm the better man. But there was one thing I still wanted and that was you.'

She spat in his ruined face, plastering him in ill-intentioned mucus. She wished it had been acid but he probably wouldn't even have felt its sting. 'Why did you kill all those students? All my classmates. What had they ever done to you?'

He slapped her hard. 'Spitting's not very ladylike, is it? But then, you've never been a lady. Just a lovely dirty whore.' He wiped the spit away and stood back for a moment, as if in contemplation. 'Your classmates were just college-boy wankers, buzzing round you like bees round a bloody honey pot. An Indian. A Jew. Two over-privileged arseholes. No loss there.'

'You're evil!' George said. 'Demented! Have you been stalking me all year? Did you follow—'

'I was already there. Working at the faculty for Fennemans. A nice little cover for my European business enterprises. There was me and Danny, thinking you was doing time for us. Then you showed up. What were the chances of that? Little Miss Erasmus, walking straight back into my arms. That's fate, that is.'

George rubbed at her stinging cheek. She righted herself and started to edge away from him. Adrenalin pulsed through her body, but she had no plan.

'Those boys didn't deserve to die,' she said.

He seemed not to hear her. Looked wistfully beyond her to the rooftops. 'You rejected me all those years ago. You were the only woman I really wanted. I needed you to see the power I can wield. The power of life and death. I'm a craftsman, Ella. A king. I knew you'd eventually beg me to make you mine.'

His arrogance and utter absence of remorse dumbfounded George momentarily.

'Beg?' she said, blinking hard. 'You think I'd beg to be with you?'

Jez grinned. He sidled up to her and stroked her breast. She pushed him away, sneering into his mouldering face.

'Get your filthy hands off me. You make me sick.'

'I've got your loverboy in my workshop,' he said.

George felt the blood drain out of her legs. Felt her knees give way.

'What do you mean?'

'I told you I sent you a text from his phone, didn't I?'

```
I love you. I'm finally coming to get you.
```

George knew now why the words had not rung true. She felt faint at the realisation. Jez wasn't bluffing.

'How do you think I did that, Ella? If you play nice, I might let him go when I get back. If you don't, and this ends badly, I'll get the chainsaw and blow torch on him.'

She felt bile rising in her throat. There was no time to ponder whether she could buy Ad his freedom. She needed to gain the upper hand physically.

'You sick, lying bastard,' she said.

Running at Jez hard, George barrelled into him with such force, he crashed into the low wall. But the momentum was too great. He rolled over the parapet, his body dangling Trinity Street side, against the edge of the Great Gate. He clung on with his shiny, burned hands.

George reached out to him, baffled that she had done what she had done. Unsure what to do. If he died, Ad would die.

'Give me your hand,' she said. 'If you tell me where Ad is, I'll pull you up. I'll go with you. I promise.'

Below, she spied at least six armed police training their weapons on him with deadly focus. Van den Bergen looked at her, open-mouthed. Imploring eyes.

'Come on, Jez. It doesn't have to be like this. I know you've had it tough. I can help. Just give me an address.'

'Tell me you love me.' He looked at her, his black irises intense but still lacking warmth.

She evaded his gaze. Looked blankly at some flaked skin on his shoulder. 'Give me your hand.'

'You want to find lover boy? Try Vim Fennemans.'

'Give me your hand, Jez!'

'No.'

Her eyes met his. He let go. Fell too many metres to the ground. He landed awkwardly, leg bent at the wrong angle to his body. Eerily silent but not dead. George would never forget how he stared up at her, smiling like a hyena that had simply missed out on one easy meal.

Tears came again then, as George thought of Ad.

CHAPTER 32

30,000ft above the North Sea, 29 January

'What if we're too late?' George asked van den Bergen.

'Cross that bridge if we come to it.' He patted her hand. His smile was uncertain. She was sure it belied real concern. 'I've got my best disciple heading up the hunt. He's an irritating sod but a brilliant detective.'

George nodded. She stared out of the small oval window of the plane, tracing her finger along the beautiful web of frost that had woven itself on the outside. The sky was a perfect delft blue where it met the upper atmosphere. Up there in the aircraft, with the hum of the engines and the occasional whine of adjusting wing flaps as they descended, she could almost detach herself mentally from what had happened. Forget Jez had ever existed. Banish from her memory his menacing, silent grin as the paramedics had put him into a neck brace. Leave behind the indignity of having to be examined in Addenbrooke's Hospital where doctors took swabs from her body for his fluids. Shelve the notion that every minute she had spent protesting her innocence to the British police was a minute closer to Ad's death.

'I can't stop thinking about him,' she said. 'Tied up in some godforsaken place. He's going to die, isn't he?'

'For Christ's sake, George,' van den Bergen said, encasing her wrist in his long fingers. 'Drink a gin and tonic and calm down. Leave it to the police. We'll find him.'

'I can't drink. I'm on painkillers for this bloody fractured cheekbone. Bastard packs one hell of a punch.' She touched her cheek tentatively and winced as pain pierced through the prescription-strength codeine.

'You were lucky he peaked too early to rape you,' van den Bergen said.

George squeezed her eyes shut, trying desperately to dispel the memory of an aroused Jez; full of savage hatred. Then she thought of Ratan, Joachim, Remko, Klaus ... Ad. Enduring a far worse fate. 'This is all my fault. I inflicted the Firestarter on my friends.'

'You mean, you caught the Firestarter! Look, kiddo, none of this is your fault. If that psychopath hadn't targeted you and your classmates, he would have found others. He's killed before. Many times. When we find his place, and we will,' he inclined his body towards her, peered at her over his reading glasses as if to persuade her that he knew best, 'I'm hoping we'll find evidence that will link him beyond doubt to some missing persons cases and homicides that have been unsolved for the last four years. If he's torturing people in a house or lock-up somewhere, there must be victims' DNA everywhere.'

The sign to fasten seatbelts illuminated. The captain announced that they would land at Amsterdam's Schiphol airport shortly. The North Sea rushed up at them, seemingly never ending. Suddenly, mercifully, dry land appeared. The aeroplane screamed its way overhead towards the welcoming lights of the runway.

She was back.

She watched van den Bergen switch his phone on as they unclicked their seatbelts. Hope surged inside her. He had an abrupt exchange with Elvis. His mouth was a grim line.

'Anything on Ad?' she asked.

320

Van den Bergen shook his head. 'Not yet. They've searched Fennemans' place and found nothing.'

Fennemans felt the energy slowly drain from him, like the battery of an old car that had been parked overnight with its lights still on. He had already unavoidably urinated in his trousers three times and soiled himself once. Even though he had passed into the realm of not fighting death but just waiting for it, he still considered it denigrating in the extreme that an academic, epicurean man of his standing should have been left to rot like some overdosed junkie in a back alley.

There was no point in trying to free himself from the radiator pipe. Even for those few hours where he had had stamina enough to struggle, his business associate's bondage was accomplished and unyielding. All he had succeeded in doing was saturating his feet in the pool of his little pigtailed houseguest's life-blood. Within twenty minutes, a vengeful Jack Frost had started to bite relentlessly through his wet socks.

Everything below the waist was numb now. His mouth was painfully dry. His thoughts were sluggish. But even in this transitional state, hovering between a fast life and slow death, he could smell the girl. Had it really been three days since it happened? Her body was corrupting. Despite the winter chill, flies seemed to come from nowhere, buzzing around the thickening blood.

Before his business associate had left, the bastard's final quip had been, 'Play with fire, Vim. What happens when you play with fire?'

Trapped in his duct-tape prison, enveloped by the freezing damp and the desperation, Fennemans conceded that he had been badly burned.

'I'm telling you, boss,' Elvis shouted above the growl of the Mercedes' engine and the ironic guttural buzz of 'Love' by the

Smashing Pumpkins on the stereo, 'there's nothing there. We turned the place over. No sign of Fennemans. He never showed up at lectures on the twenty-sixth and he hasn't been seen since. Not a trace of Karelse. And we've checked everywhere Karelse might hang out. All his university friends. The lot.'

Van den Bergen felt a twinge in his armpit and half registered a thought about lymphoma. He would have to get that checked out. 'Got plans for the house?' he asked.

'Yes, boss.'

Elvis started to unfold a large sheet of paper containing the blueprints for Fennemans' 1980s-built townhouse. Van den Bergen snatched them off him and started to open them fully on top of his steering wheel.

'Boss! Let me do it. You're going to crash the car,' Elvis said, covering his eyes.

Van den Bergen was coasting on autopilot, strong caffeine drinks and multi-vitamins. He resented Elvis' vote of no confidence in his driving ability.

'I've never crashed a car in my life. Shut up and give me plenty of warning if you spot a red light.'

Keeping less of an eye on the road than he knew he should, van den Bergen quickly absorbed the layout of Fennemans' house. Three bedrooms and a bathroom on the third floor. Small loft space above. Living room and dining area on the middle floor. Large open-plan kitchen, utility room, WC and a small garage at ground level.

A truck's horn honked aggressively as van den Bergen swerved out of his lane. He flung the plans back at Elvis, wracking his brains for where a Pandora's box might be concealed in such a house.

'Have you checked the loft space?'

'Of course!'

'Is there a party wall with the neighbours going straight up to the roof, or is the loft space open?'

322

'Closed. Party walls on both sides.'

He gnawed at the inside of his cheek with powerful molars. His eye twitched furiously. He would have to wait until they got inside the property and do what he always did: follow his gut instincts.

Pulling up opposite the house, van den Bergen eyed the neat, grey-brick exterior. The windows were clean. Fussy Austrian blinds hinted at a man who had let his mother furnish the place for him – or else he had the ghastly, froufrou taste of a meno-pausal woman trapped in the '80s.

Inside, it was dated but orderly.

'Where do you want to—'

Van den Bergen held his hand up. 'Be quiet, Elvis. Your voice sounds like nails scraping on a damned blackboard.'

In silence, van den Bergen clambered into the dusty box-filled loft. Nothing. He worked his way down through the chintzy house, through the country-style kitchen and right back to the front door.

'That English serial-killing bastard has played us like a fiddle. There's nothing here,' van den Bergen said, squeezing the bridge of his nose. He thumped the wall.

'I did tell you,' Elvis said.

Van den Bergen stared at the staircase that led back up to the living room. He was strangely reminded of the first *Harry Potter* film, which Tamara had dragged him to see at the cinema on one of 'his' weekends. Harry Potter had lived in the cupboard under the stairs.

'Did the dogs check that?' van den Bergen said, pointing to the small triangular hidey hole.

Elvis nodded. But van den Bergen was still drawn to the cupboard. He yanked open the door. It was carpeted inside. It contained a solitary overcoat on a hanger, hooked onto a peg, and a shoe rack containing two pairs of men's size 42 shoes. The shoes were designer, fashionable and completely at odds with the decor in the house. There was an ironing board stacked against the tallest wall.

'See, I told you, boss,' Elvis said, toying with the lapel of his leather jacket. 'It's just a little cloakroom.'

Van den Bergen tried to block out the sound of Elvis' voice; the way he was snorting heavily down his nose. Was he doing that just to irritate him?

'Blow your fucking nose, Elvis.'

'I've got hayfever.'

'It's too early for hayfever.'

'You'd be surprised. The blossom's starting to come out.'

Carpet. *Who the hell puts carpet in a tiny cloakroom?* And if Fennemans already had a utility room, why was the ironing board in there? It seemed to van den Bergen almost as if the space had been staged to look like a cloakroom.

'Are you coming?' Elvis asked, hovering by the front door with his hand on the lock.

Van den Bergen looked at the carpet. He sniffed hard, trying to work out what the funky smell was in there. Was it the shoes? He picked up the shoes.

'Jesus! Fennemans' feet are rotting away. Smells of old Gouda.'

He tossed the shoes into the hallway.

'Come here, Elvis! What can you smell?' His instincts were on overdrive. 'I mean, apart from Fennemans' shoes.'

'My nose is blocked,' Elvis said. 'But it certainly didn't smell the other day. The dogs would have picked it up.'

Van den Bergen systematically removed everything from the cupboard. Even at a glance, he could see that the carpet had neither been shoved under the skirting board with the blade of a carpet fitter's tool nor fastened to the floor with carpet gripper rods.

'I think this has been glued down onto something,' van den Bergen said.

With cracking knees, he knelt down, committing himself to

this thorough examination. He groped along the carpet's edge, just beneath where the ironing board had stood. He felt unsanded wood. Then, he felt the thing he had been looking for. It was cold and hard and round. Unmistakeably a handle.

'My God, what happened to your face?' Jan asked, as George trudged up the stairs to her room. He stood at the bottom of the stairs with an open mouth and wide eyes behind glasses. 'Did you fall off the side of a mountain?'

She felt his concern radiate towards her, but could only manage to look at him blankly through eyes she knew were bloodshot and puffy from crying.

'There aren't any mountains in Cambridge. I don't want to talk about it right now,' she said. 'Maybe later.' She gave him a weak smile. If his hair hadn't been quite so greasy, she would probably have given him a wordless hug.

Her room was neat but for a fine layer of dust that had settled over everything during the last three days. This time, the dust could wait. There were no signs of intrusion that she could see. In any case, Jez was in Addenbrooke's Hospital under heavy police guard. No chair under the doorknob, now. No checking behind furniture. George did not have the energy. All the self-absorbed anxiety from before had gone. It had given way to something far nastier – a black hole of worry for somebody else.

She threw her bag onto the floor, switched on her television and sat heavily on the chaise longue where she and Ad initiated their failed attempt at making love.

Flicking through the channels impatiently, she looked for a news programme. The dinner-time news would not be on NPO 1 for another twenty minutes. She pulled her laptop out of her bag and booted up. Checked the Dutch news sites and the BBC. There was nothing about Ad's disappearance on there. Nothing new about the serial killer or the terror alert in Cambridge. Her heart sank further than she had thought possible.

She fixed herself a cup of tea without milk, wondering if the gut-wrenching feeling of grief would ever leave her. Her body told her that it wanted to sleep but her brain shouted that Ad had perhaps an hour or two to live and nobody had found him yet. The worst thing about falling asleep, she knew from experience, was that she would forget about how disastrous and heartbreaking her life was. When she woke up, the whole damn mess would bludgeon her over the head again and again, as if she were realising the enormity of what had come to pass for the first time.

The little girl in George thought briefly about calling Letitia. *Cold comfort there. What on God's earth are you thinking?*

On the hour, the news began. She stuffed damp, bendy crisps into her mouth and watched the anchorwoman speaking. A smiling, bland Barbie, coiffed to within an inch of her life and wearing too much makeup. She prattled on and on about remarkable schoolchildren meeting the Queen in Hilversum and other inane matters.

'Get on with it, bitch.'

Then George's broken heart was freshly torn asunder when Ad's picture flashed up on screen.

Has anybody seen this man? Adrianus Karelse. Aged twenty. Medium build. One hundred and eighty centimetres tall. Dark hair and eyes. Last seen making his way to a bus stop in Groningen. Rumours that an English serial killer operating in the Amsterdam area and responsible for the Bushuis and Utrecht bombings, dubbed 'the Firestarter' by British police, has been caught in the UK. Victim is still missing. Call this hotline with information.

A tearful plea from Ad's parents, speaking into a long microphone at a police press conference. Flashing lightbulbs. The Milkmaid, of all people, red-faced and weeping black mascara onto a white tablecloth for the cameras.

'What use is that, you cow? You're not going to find him by

blubbing and snotting everywhere on TV!' George shouted, hurling her remote control at the TV set. She made a mental note to cry less.

George's remote control broke in two when it hit the thin carpet. The batteries rolled under the 1930s battered cabinet that held the bulbous TV set. Grumbling, she forced herself to trudge over and retrieve them.

'Where have they gone? Why do I screw everything up? Even the remote!'

Tapping the floor, being careful not to brush the underside of the cabinet with her bruised fighter's knuckles, her fingertips came across a piece of paper. She pulled it out. Frowned. There had not been a piece of paper under there before she had gone away. She knew this because she had pulled the cabinet out to vacuum underneath, of course. She unfolded it. The childish handwriting was familiar. The spelling was appalling.

Van den Bergen took his service pistol out of his holster. With his left hand, he pulled the iron handle of the trap door up quickly. Immediately, he was hit by a dreadful stench.

Beckoning Elvis to follow him down the stairs, he crept into the murk, following his nose, straining to hear the sound of an attacker above the thud of his heart. Behind him, Elvis hit the light switch.

'Fennemans!' van den Bergen said, feeling like his heart would rupture with the simultaneous thrill and horror of the discovery.

Fennemans' eyes were screwed up against the sudden light. But when he opened them and met van den Bergen's icy, appraising stare, he made a muffled sound behind the duct tape that sounded very much like a groan.

'Hello, Dr Vim. You look indisposed,' van den Bergen said, gesturing to Elvis that he should radio for backup and forensics immediately. 'And who is this poor unfortunate young lady chained to the radiator? Why, Elvis, I do declare it's an underaged, probably illegal prostitute with her throat cut. Fancy that. And look! A murder weapon.'

Van den Bergen donned a pair of latex gloves. Carefully, he picked his way across the human waste and detritus of death to where Fennemans lay. He grabbed the academic gingerly by his collar.

'Where's Ad Karelse, you perverted fucker?'

Fennemans squeezed his eyes shut and shook his head.

Dear Ella,

Whats' upp? Youre boyfriend iz @ Jezes house. I feel bad knowing he iz there. I ain't like Jez. For wot its' worth, I still luv u. But u was wrong 2 grass us up.

Jezes house is The Farmhouse, 2 Achterveldlaan, Nieuw Naardendrecht. Its' south of Amsterdam.

Don't come looking 4 me n I won't come looking 4 u.

Luv Danny xxx

Pulse racing, breath short now. George felt lightheaded as she dialled van den Bergen's number. No answer. *Fuck*. Taxi then. Running down the street without a coat, flagging one down. Arriving at the station only to be told that van den Bergen was at a crime scene. Screaming at the uniform on reception until he was radioed. Hooking up with him on the way. Squad cars following them, as he floored his Mercedes. Sirens wailing and lights flashing all the way out to the countryside. Counting the minutes as the flat fields sped by. Ambulance and fire service already there, as they arrived outside a traditional Dutch barn-style farmhouse. In the middle of nowhere. Guns drawn.

'Get that door broken down now!' van den Bergen yelled, pistol in hand, just in case.

A ram battered against the door as George quaked, whipped by the freezing wind and wordless dread outside the remote farmhouse. *Is he alive? Please God let him be alive.*

The door wouldn't open.

'He's behind the door. He's on the floor, boss.'

Van den Bergen blanched visibly. Tears uncontrollably coming now, as George imagined Ad dead. Grey and lifeless on the floor. A bubble in his bloodstream. Firemen breaking in through the garage. Paramedics and police all jostling to secure the house, to get Ad out.

George tore at her hair in anguished silence. Found herself crossing her fingers like a child.

'He's been shot,' came the cry. 'And there's head trauma.'

An ambulance gurney was taken inside. The front door was still shut. George could bear it no longer. She ran inside, pushing her way through a blur of people. She slid on the polished wooden floor of a grand entrance hall and there he was. Foot in a puddle of blood. Wearing only jeans. Out cold but still the colour of someone who breathed. Just.

George reached out to touch his face as two paramedics lifted him onto the gurney.

'Ad,' she shouted, wanting desperately to reach him inside his sleep.

She found herself being grabbed from behind by van den Bergen. His strong arms lifted her out of the way like a doll.

'Let them take care of him.' His normally gruff voice was soft and comforting. His grip was unyielding as iron.

As the gurney rattled past her on its supermarket trolley wheels, pushed in concerned haste by the paramedics, Ad opened his eyes. He looked straight at George. She saw recognition flicker in his pale, blood-streaked face. She held her hand out, anticipating he would reach for her, perhaps even manage a smile. But he clamped his eyes shut again.

She turned to van den Bergen, looking up at him questioningly.

'Try not to worry,' he said, squeezing her shoulders, 'I'm sure it will all pan out fine.'

But George trusted her gut instinct, and the irritable butterflies in her stomach told her everything might not pan out fine. At all.

CHAPTER 33

Amsterdam, 2 February

The croissants George had bought from a boulangerie in Nieuwezijds Voorburgwal were still warm in their greasy paper bag. She peered through the glass in the hospital door and winced at the limited view she had of Ad. His head was bandaged. His foot was in plaster, raised off the bed by a pulley system. He was wearing his second-best pair of glasses and a pair of blue and red striped pyjamas. Sipping water from a glass. Where were the peonies she had delivered to him via van den Bergen the previous evening?

As she was about to push the door and walk in, all romantic, patisserie gestures and declarations of amour, she caught sight of a frumpy, overweight middle-aged woman. She was reading through several get well soon cards on Ad's nightstand. Sitting in a chair in a corner of the room, looking bored, was a middle-aged man. The woman had a Gallic, olive complexion and dark hair. The man had the same features as Ad but they seemed weighted down; made heavy by a disappointing provincial life. They had to be his parents.

George combed her fingers through her curls. Could she do this? Could she make nice with these people, whom Ad had not even bothered to damn with faint praise? Yes. She could do it.

331

She had to. They had both been to hell and back so that they could be together, hadn't they?

George put her hand against the door and took a deep breath. But then an apparition in candy-pink jeans and a prissy white sweater wafted past the window at close range. Blonde bouncing hair in a ponytail. Pink cheeks. Imitation pearls. Homespun, homecoming queen. It was the Milkmaid.

'Oh, hang on a minute. This wasn't mentioned in the small print,' George said. She looked despairingly at the hapless Ad, who had just been annexed by the Milkmaid: sitting on his bed, all concerned smiles and taking his hand into hers like a benevolent dictator.

Hastily, George backed away from the window. She chewed furiously on her bottom lip. Started to rearrange some health information posters on a corridor pin board so that they hung properly perpendicular to the ceiling. Cancer awareness. Detect the early signs of dementia. Just say no to drugs. Stop smoking. *But I want to be there for him.*

Astrid. Still on the scene, putting her territorial paws all over *her* man.

George started to shake. She fled down the shiny-floored corridor, past grey-faced people with flattened, greasy bed-head, wearing pyjamas, as they were being pushed to the café in wheelchairs by glum relatives. She forced her way through too-slow-to-open automatic doors. The aseptic, institutional walls started to close in on her. Bewildering signs hanging from the walls and ceiling, shouting that it was this way to the oncology department, that way to the radiology department. Way out, dead ahead. The air conditioning sounded too loud in her ears, too hot on her skin.

'Chocolate. I need chocolate,' she said.

She sought out the cafeteria, where she was surrounded by squalling babies and foul-smelling old people and drunks. Chewing on her chocolate bar with salty tears streaming down

332

her face, she realised that she was suffering from delayed shock. Post traumatic stress disorder or whatever it was the shrinks called it. Hadn't they spoken about it in group therapy and at her psych-assessments in prison?

A foul tsunami of memories suddenly threatened to drown her. She allowed each and every gruesome twist and turn a moment in the spotlight of her mind.

She gave this display of vulnerability a full fifteen minutes but fifteen minutes only.

She sobbed aloud, without inhibition. People gawped. Mothers pulled toddlers away from her. She chewed her way through three chocolate bars and a bag of crisps. Then she pulled herself together as she had always done. Downed a hot latte. Went back up to Ad's side room before visiting time ended.

As she approached, she passed Ad's parents and Astrid in the corridor. She held her head high. Finally, she would get Ad to herself. There was a whiff of recognition from the Milkmaid as she looked a little too long at George and frowned. But the only time the Milkmaid had seen George was now a long while ago, and George had looked different back in the autumn. She had been wearing her makeup and hairpiece. She hadn't had a swollen face or puffy eyes.

Deep breath now and into Ad's room. All smiles on her part.

Ad had been sitting, propped in bed, surrounded by his family when he had first seen George peeking into his room. The morphine stripped him of any visceral excitement or anger or passion, but his brain registered that he didn't want the cuckoo in the nest coming to visit. Her peonies were in the bin, put there by a vengeful, mistrusting Astrid. He had not tried to stop her.

Here she was again. Danny's girl. The liar. The betrayer. Ella Williams-May was persistent, if nothing else. When she walked in, he was overcome by weariness. He suppressed any urge to smile.

She, on the other hand, was all smiles. 'Hey, stranger,' she said. 'I've been trying to get to see you since last night. You're in demand.'

George made her way to his bedside and kissed him tenderly on the nose, below his bandages.

'How are you feeling?' she asked.

Although he didn't really want to engage in conversation with her, he answered in what was more of a reflex action. Looking down at his bandaged hand, scratching the morphine itch on his arm, he sighed.

'Terrible. Okay. Alive, at least,' he said. 'Better than expected. You?'

There was something suddenly tentative and wary about the way she sat. Upright. Stiff. Hesitant.

'Not bad,' she said. A gush of emotion brought forth what could only be crocodile tears. 'Oh, Ad, I'm *so* relieved we found you. I couldn't stop thinking about you. I'm so so sorry.' Then, abruptly, she stemmed the tide. 'Did you hear what happened in Cambridge? They've caught him.'

Ad breathed out heavily through pursed lips and snatched a look at her before turning to the television that flickered in silence in a corner of the room. 'Yes. I heard. He was going to blow you up.'

'It was fake. Can you believe it? He just wanted to blackmail me.'

The bitterness effervesced inside him; an antidote to his anaesthesia. 'And how did you come to know him, George?' he said pointedly. 'How did you come to know a drug-pushing people-trafficker from London?'

Now he turned to look her directly in the eye. He made his face hard like granite, with the downturned mouth of disappointment, not dissimilar from his father's.

George's eyes darted around the room, seemingly searching for something neutral to land on.

'It's complicated. Look, I don't know where to begin.'

'You can begin by telling me the truth.'

She stared at him; probing behind the protective Perspex veneer of his glasses. Was she wondering how he knew? Van den Bergen had clearly not yet told the full story of Ad's frank exchange with Danny Boy.

'Ad, I don't—'

'Why don't you start with Danny? Tell me about Danny, *Ella*.' He made sure his voice dripped thickly with sarcasm.

George grabbed Ad's hand, but he pulled it away; put it out of her reach beneath his blanket. She looked at his neck, spiky with days' worth of black stubble. Her eyes would not meet his now.

'Look at me! Tell me about Danny,' he demanded.

Her voice was small and thin. 'He was the one who told me where you were,' she said. 'He broke into my room and left a note with the killer's address on it. Said he saw you. He felt bad about what Jez had done.'

Ad looked up at the ceiling, willing himself to keep the hurt inside. But he was beyond that now. 'Danny Boy didn't seem so charitable when he blew a hole in my foot.'

George looked at Ad askance. '*He* shot you? I thought—'

Ad folded his arms. 'What were his words again before he pulled the trigger? They were charming. Oh, yes. "Cheeky bastard. No one fucks my bird."'

Tears appeared at the corners of her eyes. 'I'm not his bird. I'm *your* bird.'

'You're not "my bird".' He did the inverted commas with the fingers of his left hand. His resentment was tart and tangible and he wanted it that way now. 'You're a convict and a liar. For Christ's sake, George, I love you but you lied to me! I fell in love with a lie.'

George's chin dimpled up.

'I had no choice.' Suddenly, her voice was low and calm. She enunciated every word correctly. It was like somebody had flipped a switch. 'I was an informant in a big drugs case. I was given a new identity and signed the Official Secrets Act. I couldn't tell you. Don't you see?'

He stared at her, watching her lips move, hearing sound, but struggling to piece together the sense in the outlandish things she was saying.

Her back stiffened. 'And I'm *not* a convict,' she said. 'I was mistakenly put on remand for months because my CID contact had a heart attack the same day I was supposed to get busted and taken into protective custody. It was a cock-up.'

Now she was pointing at him. The vulnerability had gone. Ad sensed a subtle shift in power from himself, the injured victim, to her.

'Don't punish me for things you don't understand nothing about.' In place of declarations of relief and love, in place of the deadpan delivery of cold, hard fact, here was an outpouring of concrete-jungle attitude. All her skeletons were now tumbling out of her hand-fashioned, flimsy closet.

Ad felt his face succumb to the vice-like grip of a pained expression.

'But how could you be with that man?' he asked. 'With him? He's a thug and a drug dealer. He plucks his eyebrows!'

George stood up. Impatient, fists balled. He was shocked.

'I met you in September,' she shouted. 'I've known you for less than a year. I will not seek your approval for the things I've done in the past which are of no concern to you, in the same way that I do not give a monkey's flying arsehole about you poking the Aryan Milkmaid since you were sixteen.'

He was confused. Drowning in contrition. Ad knew he was not a natural candidate for flint-faced, steel-hand-in-a-velvet-glove crap. 'George, sit back down. Please.'

Backing away. Backing towards the door. He knew her well enough to see she was building the bricks back up one by one.

The wall grew quickly in height around her, shutting him out.

'You saw Jez,' she said. 'He's a monster. You should know why it was important I tried to bring him down. That psycho tortured me and my mother for years before any of this. Back in London. Back in a life you wouldn't begin to comprehend.'

She approached a table holding neat, overspill rows of get well soon cards from Ad's family and college friends. With one swipe from her arm, she knocked them to the ground. She walked out of the hospital room without a backwards glance.

'Come back!' Ad shouted.

'Fuck you!' she yelled as she marched down the corridor.

He had never thought she would say that to him.

'What the hell did you think you were doing?' Kamphuis yelled.

The door to Kamphuis' office was shut, but van den Bergen knew Elvis and Marie would be listening outside in the open-plan space, straining to catch the inevitable bellowed threats from Kamphuis. That kind of schadenfreude was a perk of their job.

Kamphuis thumped the desk. 'How often do I have to say it? You're an embarrassment to the department!'

Van den Bergen sat comfortably, with his right leg folded over his left knee, in the deliberately low seat opposite Kamphuis. It had been a week good enough to make him smile.

'Oh, now, Olaf, I think you're exaggerating. You'd never have let me go to England if I had asked. We both know that. Not at such short notice and not on a hunch.'

'I might have.'

'Really?' He leaned in towards Kamphuis, feeling like today, he wanted to step right over the line. Just for fun. 'You furnish your office with original works of art. You take home a better salary than anyone else at your level but you query the cost of a new set of tyres on a patrol car or overtime payments for a surveillance team. Don't make me laugh. Look, I've won you a truck-load of kudos for your department.' He ruffled his white

337

hair and started to bounce his shoe up and down for good measure. 'Just be grateful.'

Today van den Bergen had worn basketball boots into the office because not only was he feeling like a younger man with a spring in his step, he also knew Kamphuis detested the sight of middle-aged men in youthful clothing or footwear.

'Grateful? Arrogant son of a bitch! You think this is all down to you and you alone?' Kamphuis narrowed his eyes at van den Bergen and toyed with his naked lady statue.

'Well, you were the one that doggedly wanted to pursue the Islamist terror cell angle to keep the top brass and the media happy. If I hadn't hooked up with Georgina and kept an open mind, we might never have found our man. But you're right. It isn't just down to me. My team, Dirk and Marie, were excellent ...'

'You're no team player, Paul. You wouldn't know that kind of caring, sharing crap if it came up and punched you on the nose.'

'...*as* was Marianne de Koninck and her forensics people *and* Dieter Mann, my colleague in Heidelberg. It's been a triumph of *teamwork* between disciplines and countries. All pulling together. Despite weak management above me.'

Yes, van den Bergen was enjoying himself. He had a meeting with lovely Marianne later on. They were going to discuss eighteen severed fingers, eleven missing persons' cases and six unsolved dead Jane and John Does over a working lunch.

That afternoon, while forensics were still combing Saddiq's country home for the flotsam and jetsam of death that would tie him to the victims, Elvis and Marie would continue to examine the computer hard drives that had been found in the house.

At three o'clock, he had scheduled a conference call with his old narcotics boss, his opposite number in vice, some bigwigs in Scotland Yard and someone high up in the German Federal Intelligence Service to discuss links between the Firestarter case and the trafficking of illegal, underage prostitutes and Class A drugs from Afghanistan via Germany, then Amsterdam to the UK. Daniel Spencer was at the top of his 'to do' list.

'Do you know what, Olaf?' van den Bergen asked. 'I think I might be asked to head up this new multi-national, drugs and people-trafficking task-force. Don't you?'

Kamphuis snorted.

'And perhaps I'll accept.'

'You don't have it in you,' Kamphuis said.

'Ooh, I don't know,' van den Bergen said. 'I think they're looking to recruit someone on the strength of good police work and nothing more. No arse-kissing at fancy fundraising dinners. No back room politics with brandy and cigars.'

'I want a formal apology for your insubordination,' Kamphuis said, pointing and spitting slightly.

Van den Bergen levered himself out of the child-sized chair, straightened out his six-foot-five frame, clicked his hip back into place noisily and smiled at Kamphuis.

'Go fuck yourself, Olaf.'

He had always wanted to say that.

George read the email from Sally three times as she chewed at a peanut butter sandwich made with stale bread.

'Damn you, Sally,' she finally said to the laptop screen.

She looked around her room with an ache in her heart. Unexpectedly, what had seemed such a beautiful, seedy, hidden gem had now become a fallible prison. Danny and Jez had both defiled her sacred space with their sinister acts of trespass and subtle intimidation. Matches and notes. There wasn't much difference, was there?

No, Sally was right. She was no longer safe in Jan's attic. She had to go.

George stood and walked over to the photograph of her and Ad outside the Rijksmuseum; an optimistic time, heartbreakingly in the past now and buried beneath a mountain of hurt.

'How do I break the news to Jan and the girls?' she asked the smiling, two-dimensional Ad. 'And what about me and you?'

In the hospital lift, George agonised over what she would say to Ad. Twelve hours later now. Had she given him long enough to think? Did he want a stake in her future?

The lift doors opened. George nervously tapped her cigarette packet in her coat pocket. She walked along the corridor to Ad's room and was surprised to see him fully dressed in jeans and a cable-knit sweater, although still wearing a cast on his foot with a bandage over his head and hand. His mother was fussing around him, packing his things into a small suitcase.

George was already inside the room. There was no walking away now.

Ad looked at her, at first with a glimmer of naked glee, which he quickly masked with a thin-lipped nod.

His mother spun around. She eyed George with undisguised disgust before pointedly turning back to the suitcase.

'I'm just going to get something from the car,' she said to Ad. 'I'll be back in a few minutes. I'll leave you with your … classmate.'

They were alone.

'Look, about before,' Ad began.

George approached him and put her finger on his lips, gently. 'It's okay. We can just start fresh.'

Ad picked up his reefer jacket from the day chair next to his bed. He held it like a barrier between them. 'No, George. We can't just start fresh.'

'What do you mean?'

'I mean, you and me. I can't do it.'

The moments of intimacy they had shared flashed quickly by in George's mind. The meals he had cooked for her. The long afternoons they had spent together, talking, laughing, putting the world to rights. The kisses and the unspent passion they had

340

snatched in the midst of all that horror. The case that they had both risked so much to help solve.

'How could you walk away from all we have?' she asked, feeling tears spill onto her cheeks.

'What have we got? Nothing!' he said, pushing her hand away. 'Whatever we had was built on a lie.'

George realised then that she had brought a kingdom of empty promises crashing down at his feet. She allowed regretful tears to flow easily. Watched how Ad's eyes became glassy with emotion.

'Come on, Ad,' she said. 'This is ridiculous. We've got something special. Anyway, what will you do? You're going to see me every day at lectures. Are you going to ignore me? Are you going to jettison our friendship?'

'I'm dropping out for the rest of the year. I need to get well, you know? I'm going home to Groningen.'

'No,' George mouthed.

Ad pushed his tear-splashed glasses up his nose and started to pull his jacket on, as if he wasn't crying; as if this conversation wasn't taking place. 'You should go now,' he said, turning his back on her; starting to shut his case with his left hand.

His rejection felt like a stinging slap. *This isn't how it was meant to turn out!* George could feel her dignity and hope slipping away. After all she had been through, she had somehow turned into the bad guy. It wasn't fair. *Walk away, before he breaks your heart.*

Her heart overruled her brain.

'I love you!' she said.

Her declaration was met with deafening silence.

CHAPTER 34

Dominican Republic, 27 February

Danny was woken by the discreet buzz of his BlackBerry. It journeyed across the mahogany nightstand, buoyed by its persistent vibrations, telling him to answer. Danny was quickly alert. Saw from the glowing display that it was Rodriguez. He picked up.

'I've got the perfect guy for you,' Rodriguez said, wrapping his Columbian tongue clumsily around the English words. 'He's willing to travel. We can meet later.'

Danny glanced at the young Dominican girl who lay sleeping between the 400 count Egyptian cotton sheets. He didn't want to have this conversation in front of her. In fact, if Rodriguez's guy didn't have what he needed, there was no point even in meeting.

'Does he speak Arabic?'

There was a pause and a quick exchange in Spanish at the other end of the line.

'No.'

'Then he's not the guy for me. And, Rodriguez ...'

'Yes?'

'Don't chat this shit on the fucking phone with me, man.'

He hung up, swung his legs out of the emperor-sized bed. Admired his six pack in the mirror. *Looking good.* He pulled on some Calvin Klein shorts and strapped on his diamond-studded, custom-made Breitling Avenger watch before the girl got any wise ideas about pocketing it.

He had enjoyed his four easy years. From his comfortable position in the wings, he had directed a grand production according to his own vision. Too bad he was going to have to step up again onto centre stage now Jez was gone.

He padded barefoot on the grey marble floor to the balcony and looked out over the Caribbean Sea. Below him, pristine white colonial-style villas peeped through the foliage of the tropical gardens. The fiery orange blossom of a flamboyán tree clashed with the strappy green fronds of coconut palms, the wide leaves of banana trees and giant fans of traveller palms. Danny didn't know the names of any of that shit but it was nice to look at and the lazily rippling green sea beyond was Bacardi Island beautiful, like in James Bond films and that.

He liked to come to this place to hook up with the South Americans. Sometimes even some boys from New York. It was convenient and luxurious. But with the overweight, middle-class European families basting themselves with SPF30 on the beach, it was not too obviously gangster-glamour as to attract unwanted attention.

Later, after breakfast with this girl – what was her name again? Pilar or some Spanish shit – he would meet the Mohican by the pool and see if he had what it took to oversee what Jez had been doing in Germany. Danny doubted the man had any of Jez's style or knack for moving around unnoticed but it was worth a go. It was only a small slice of his pie.

He eased himself into the rattan armchair on the balcony, stretched out his tattooed, tanned legs, put his feet up on the glass-topped table and lit a cigarette. This paradise was a long way from the grey concrete of South London. His mum, the drunken old slag, was proud. And he was pleased with himself that he'd managed to put her and his gran in a well smart bungalow with electric gates in Surrey's most expensive village, even though they moaned that they couldn't get to the shops no more.

But he had paid a high price to get this far.

Danny was not one for deep thoughts or reflection of any kind. He was a doer. A man with a plan. But today, he caught himself thinking stuff. Watching the pelicans diving for fish in the sea, he mulled over how he had lost all of those who had started out with him. Jez, Tonya, Big Michelle.

Her. Ella. Bitch. She was to blame.

He flicked his ash angrily onto the terracotta tiles. Tonya and Big Michelle were out now but they were too hot to have anything to do with, business-wise. Tonya looked like shit since she'd been inside anyway, so he didn't even fancy fucking her on the odd occasion that he went back to the estate. She was rough, poor cow.

And Ella was to blame. So much to love. So much to hate.

What were the odds of her being on that Dutch loser's phone? He'd told Jez to put feelers out to find the bitch. He hadn't realised Jez was stalking her; popping off all the guys around her like some fucked-up Jeffrey Dahmer bullshit.

'Jez, Jez, Jez, you twisted, stupid dickhead. You screwed up the whole game with your perverted Firestarter crap. All them books you read to be like her didn't do you no good, did they?'

When he'd seen that squinting, poor fucking Dutch boy stumbling through the house and he'd got mad and shot the bastard, he felt bad. So, he slipped her that note and at the time, he really did feel all wrong and dirty that he had got wrapped up in Jez's psycho mess. Part of him didn't want to hurt her. But now he realised his business empire was vulnerable because of what *she* knew and some pain in the arse, dog-with-a-bone old detective she'd got pally with. She'd nearly taken everything from him once. Now he couldn't afford to let her do that again.

Inhaling deeply from the hot end of his cigarette, he

contemplated his next move. Those two would have to go. *Her* and the cop. But he'd have to find the right man for the job first. Someone skilled and discreet. It wouldn't be that hard. Danny was a patient man.

CHAPTER 35

Groningen, 13 March

'Does it hurt, darling?' Astrid asked Ad, as he pulled one of the socks she had brought him over the cast on his foot. She flapped around him, trying to pull the woollen toes straight.

The pain shot up his calf to his groin. Ad winced. 'Jesus, Astrid. Leave it!' He wanted to swipe her away like an irritating bluebottle; be left alone to watch MTV in peace. She just wouldn't leave, no matter how heavy a hint he dropped. But swiping women wasn't something he would ever do. So, he sat and took it. Constant fussing. Poking the healed stitches in his scalp. Remarking how the hair had grown back almost perfectly. He looked like his old self again.

He didn't *feel* like his old self.

He'd left his old self in George's bedsit weeks and weeks ago. The day he had come back from Heidelberg. A lifetime away, now.

'But your tootsies. They'll get cold,' she said, smiling with pearly white teeth, a flush of exasperation in her perfect peach cheeks.

'They're fine. Just let it heal. Let me heal. Okay?' He couldn't abide that faux-crestfallen look on her face. A rebuked child in a woman's body. Subtly controlling him through acts of acceptance-seeking kindness.

And here came Mommie Dearest. Gliding out of the kitchen with another hot casserole dish full of some tasteless baked crud which she would waft in front of him. Mum knows best. Wink wink. Mum's taking good care of her boy now. Her little boy who can't be left on his own for five minutes. Passed from the maternal tit to Astrid to suckle for life on watery, fat-free milk.

'Hungry, son?'

'Oh, that looks lovely, Mum. But only a bit for me.' *Christ, I've got to get into town and go for an Indonesian on my own. Even a kebab would do. Oh, no. It's witlof. Endive, choking, gagging snot.*

'Nonsense. Astrid, you're staying for lunch, aren't you?'

Astrid nodded. Bright shining blue eyes like aquamarines. Always the poor man's sapphires or diamonds.

'Oh, you bet, Griet.' Perky voice. Bouncing ponytail.

That 1950s, sanitised American sitcom persona had been endearing when she was sweet sixteen and Ad was a horny virgin but at twenty, every time she spoke, it was like biting into too much sickly white chocolate. Overfacingly sweet for a palate that had matured.

'My boss has given me another week's compassionate leave. I only nipped in to get these socks for Ad with my staff discount.'

Ad's mother, half way to the kitchen to serve up the endives, leaned backwards and beamed at Astrid. 'So thoughtful.' She looked pointedly at Ad. 'What a catch you have there, dolly. Just think how much better off you are here, at home with us. Not in grotty old Amsterdam with all those hoity toity so and sos and foreigners.'

'Oh, what a waste of time that was,' Astrid said. She turned to Ad. 'Honestly, darling, you've got everything you could possibly want for right here in Groningen.'

His mother beamed. 'Yes! Daddy's going to see if he can get Ad a job in admin in Energy Valley.'

Staring blankly at the television that had been turned low, Ad wondered how George was doing; what George was doing. Was she plagued by the same nightmares as him? Did she see that monster's face? She couldn't have known about the fingers in the freezer or that he had worn dead Remko's boots, but he was sure she had her own nightmares to wrestle with.

How could he have been so stupid? He had turned away from her. He only had an inkling of what had happened to her in Cambridge. Scant details, barked at him by that sour, surly, well-meaning old bastard, van den Bergen, who was now putting her up in his spare room.

George had brought him pink flowers.

How could she have kept her past so well hidden from him?

'My parents died in a car crash.'

It seemed like a cliché now but why hadn't he seen through it then? He tried to imagine her, a common criminal, the drug-pushing child of a single mother who didn't care a damn. Locked up in some ghastly women's prison. Peering up at the sky through bars. That was not the George he had fallen for. His vision of her as an intellectual goddess of ivory tower refinement and slick, capital city culture was now sullied and poisoned by cheap back-street sex with a man called Danny, who sold coke and trafficked underage whores.

The lies were huge.

Ad's head was a mess. His heart was in ruins.

And now all he had left was Astrid and his mother's cold comfort, a plate full of endives and sausage and the gut-rotting feeling that leaving Amsterdam and George were the two biggest mistakes he would ever make in his life.

Had he left it too late? Could he do the right thing?

'Astrid,' he called. 'Have you got a minute? There's something I need to tell you.'

What a shame he was not allowed to set fire to his cell. It would have been such an entertaining distraction in an otherwise dull day. But Jez wasn't really complaining. He was due a visitor.

As he was pushed by the screw in his wheelchair through the heavy barred security gates, under the vaulted Victorian ceilings of his new home, he thought about how brilliant it was that now he too got to live in a place of great beauty. Just like that fancy, historical Cambridge College that Ella belonged to. They were so alike. But then, he had always known that.

As he entered the room where the hospital psychologist normally conducted the group therapy sessions, he saw a middle-aged woman with an ugly haircut and bad jewellery. She wore red winged glasses, like some old bird from the 1950s.

'Who are you?' he asked.

The woman sat in silence and seemed to be consigning the contours of his face to memory.

'I'm Dr Sally Wright. I'm a criminologist. Tell me, how are you enjoying Broadmoor, Jeremy?' she asked. Her voice was throaty and rasping like a man's.

He threw himself forward, out of his chair and across the table that separated them, so that he was closer to her. He didn't like her cocksure confidence. She should be quaking with fear in his presence.

The screw pounced and pinned him back in his seat. 'Behave, Jez. You promised you'd be good for me.'

Jez nodded.

Dr Shit Haircut and Shit Glasses pursed her wrinkly old hag lips and asked again, 'Tell me how you're enjoying Broadmoor.' He could see her teeth were stained brown with nicotine.

He sniffed. 'My neighbours are the Yorkshire Ripper and the Stockwell Strangler. Man! Even Ronnie Kray lived here. These are hallowed fucking halls. How do you think I'm enjoying it? I'm an A-list celebrity. I'm with my own kind. What? You going to write a fucking book about me?'

'Yes, Jeremy. As long as we've got you on English soil, I think I probably will.'

His scarred mouth stretched into a wide grin. It felt like the perfect ending to a long, long chapter.

Fennemans had spent several days wondering how to fashion a noose for himself out of the bedsheet he had been given. It was good to have something to preoccupy his mind; a little project that would distract him from the pain and humiliation of having his reputation systematically decimated by the legal system and the tabloids. Dr Vim Fennemans: a lynchpin within a vice ring that peddled barely pubescent prostitutes and hard drugs to Amsterdam's students, amongst others. Verified as a user and abuser himself. Held responsible for a murder he hadn't committed.

What a pity that even Saskia had not come to his rescue this time.

Now, he stared down at the makeshift shiv that he had fashioned from a razor blade, embedded into the head of a toothbrush. Considered the jade-green veins running beneath his translucent, pale skin. Surely its sting would be preferable to the living hell of being an inmate with a doctorate, branded as a paedophile.

George had no idea from which carriage Ad would emerge. The train spewed its late-night passengers forth – mainly drunken Ajax Amsterdam football fans coming home from a match against Groningen, singing at the tops of their voices; still clinging to long-empty beer cans. She searched beyond the sea of unfamiliar faces, willing the violent butterflies in her stomach to calm. Where was he?

Van den Bergen had passed Ad's message on but had given no indication as to what this unexpected rendezvous was … after all this time.

As the crowds dispersed, she still couldn't see him. Her heart started to sink slowly.

Then, she spotted him. Sitting on a bench; two crutches

propped against his knee with his phone in his good hand. Forlorn.

Their eyes met. His smile was uncertain, hopeful. He struggled to his feet.

She started to run towards him. She ran through the wall of mistrust she had built back up. She ran through her fear of rejection. She pushed her past and her nightmares onto the tracks.

'I wasn't sure you'd come,' he said.

'I would always come,' she said, allowing her final defences crumple and give way to tears.

'I'm so sorry it took me so long.'

'It doesn't mat—'

'I love you, George.'

Those words were the feast she had spent her life praying for at the starving man's table. 'I have always loved you.'

And in the middle of an empty platform in Amsterdam Central Station, George kissed Ad, hungrily, finally aware that the empty longing inside her had finally gone.

Amsterdam, 10 May

Outside in the wooded area below Ad and George's new studio flat, cherry blossom trees of the same variety as the one in Letitia's old back garden bloomed. Prunus kanzan. Ablaze with candyfloss pink flowers only. Now these were hers to look at and enjoy.

Ad propped himself on his elbow. Pushed her hair carefully off her forehead. He leaned in towards her and kissed her with passion and conviction.

She looked up at the ceiling. Rainbows of colour played on the plaster, as the sun shone through the large window and bounced off a bevelled cheval mirror in the far corner. Everything that had at first seemed so wrong, so broken, had turned out just right.

Rolling onto her side, hooking her right leg over his naked frame, she put her ear to his sternum. There she lay, listening to his heart beating strong and steady.

'You know, just before I moved out of the Cracked Pot, I sat in the coffee shop with Jan,' she said. 'He was so cut up that I was leaving. Probably because he'd be down on the rent, knowing him. But we sat and shared a smoke and he did me a tarot reading.'

'Go on,' Ad said.

'I pulled out death. Can you believe it? And I realised it wasn't about murder or loss. It meant sometimes you have to let go of something if you're going to start over.'

'It's okay to let the past die,' Ad said, holding her close.

They finally managed a breakfast of burnt toast just after midday. George drank her now cold coffee and cocked her head sideways, studying her soul mate as he lounged on the second-hand Ikea sofa that van den Bergen had given them as a moving-in gift.

On Ad's stereo one of her soul CDs played. Curtis Mayfield sang that she wouldn't slip, despite the wet road that may lie ahead; encouraging her to just move on up and she would find peace.

George looked wistfully out at the cherry blossom trees as their petals were blown away on a sudden gust of wind. And she smiled.

Acknowledgements

Novels are not developed in a petri-dish, and I'm glad they're not. Writing is perhaps the most fun I could ever have with my clothes on. But it's arduous graft too. In fact, the path to publication can be so fraught with travails and disappointment, at times, that this author would not have travelled far down it without the help of the following people:

I owe an enormous debt of gratitude to my family for their love, unflagging moral support and encouragement, so thanks to Christian, Natalie and Adam, always.

For his loyalty, patience and friendship, I would like to thank my partner-in-crime – special agent, Caspian Dennis. Had he not championed my writing so valiantly, *The Girl Who Wouldn't Die* would still be just another file on my laptop.

Thanks are due, of course, to my editor, Katy Loftus and the team at Maze/HarperCollins for their energy and professionalism in publishing and marketing the series, enabling me to push George and van den Bergen out into the big, wide world, where they belong.

Two people whose help was invaluable during the research phase for this novel are Sebastian Tredinnick and my bez, Louise Owen. What they don't know about Heidelberg ain't worth knowing. Cheers, guys!

Huge thanks are due to these fine people:

To fellow writers, Steph Williams and Wendy Storer for listening to my almost constant fretting, griping and melodramatic nonsense. They kept telling me I *could* do this, so I did. To Ann Giles, aka Bookwitch, who persuaded me I have something to offer the crime genre. And to poet, Martin de Mello for his sage-like pronouncements on the other bits of my life.

The idea for *The Girl Who Wouldn't Die* took shape during a dinner I had with author, Melvin Burgess, where I realised I could draw inspiration from my own youthful experiences and turn them into the sort of thriller I'd always aspired to write. Ta, Melvin!

Author, Anthony McGowan persuaded me to keep going with the manuscript, even in the face of a difficult birth, so thanks, Tony. The literary stretch marks and knackered pelvic floor have been worth it.

Font of publishing wisdom and excellent mate, Shannon Cullen has spurred me on every step of the way. She told me that I had a voice that people would want to read and steered me in the direction of the Abner Stein Literary Agency, which led me to the esteemed Mr. Dennis. Her encouragement has been vital in my getting to this point. Thanks, Shannon.

Finally, thanks to the charismatic and strong women I met through Commonword/ Cultureword in Manchester. George is for you, ladies! I hope I've done her justice.

Enjoyed *The Girl Who* series? Get your hands on the fifth gripping thriller in the George McKenzie series.

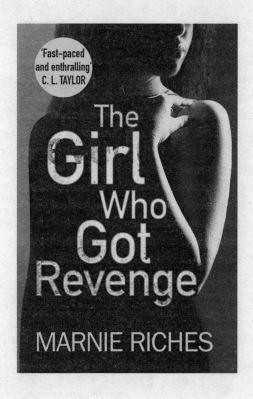

Find out how it all began in *Born Bad,* the first in the gritty Manchester crime series

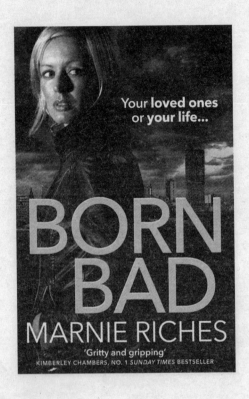

'A leading light in Mancunian noir' *Guardian*

How far would you go to protect your empire?

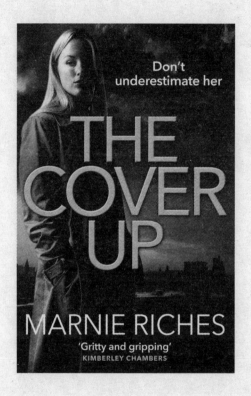

A heart-stopping read with a gritty edge, perfect
for fans of Martina Cole and Kimberley Chambers.